a bos

CROSS THE LINE

USA TODAY bestselling author
julie johnson

Subscribe to Julie's newsletter: http://eepurl.com/bnWtHH

This one's for the girls who laugh a little too loud
and fall a bit too fast.

The ones who believe in soul mates
and second chances.

Who break their own rules
and chase their own destinies.

Never stop.

"I WONDER HOW MANY PEOPLE I'VE LOOKED AT ALL MY LIFE
AND NEVER SEEN."

JOHN STEINBECK, THE WINTER OF OUR DISCONTENT

PROLOGUE

I WASN'T LOOKING FOR TROUBLE.
HE FOUND ME ANYWAY.

Phoebe West, reflecting on her love life.

THE FIRST TIME I ever met Nathaniel Knox, I was crying my eyes out.

(In retrospect, I see this as a fitting prelude to our relationship.)

Sitting on the grass in the back yard of our estate on Nantucket, I was too focused on the dead bird lying under our maple tree to even notice the new boy next door hopping over our fence from his yard to ours. It wasn't until he'd settled in the grass beside me and asked why I was crying that I lifted teary eyes to the most stunning face I'd ever seen in my five years on planet earth.

He was older, that was certain — at least eight, maybe nine. Tall, like my brother Parker, but there was something sad about his dark eyes. I was too distraught by my gruesome discovery — and, even back then, too captivated by a single glance at him — to work up any sense of stranger-danger.

"The bird," I'd hiccupped, turning back to the tree and pointing with a shaking finger. "It's... it's...."

"Dead." The boy nodded and leaned closer, eyes flashing with annoyance as he took in my tears. "So? It's just a stupid pigeon."

"It's n-n-n-not a pigeon," I managed to squeak out between hiccups. "It's a t-t-t-turtle d-d-dove."

"Sorry," he said, voice a bit softer. He rubbed the back of his neck, looking nervous and uncomfortable. "I didn't mean to upset you, or whatever."

I took a deep breath and stared at him, tears still dripping down my cheeks.

"Tell me about the pigeon." He sighed. "Sorry. The *turtle dove*."

"That's the boy husband bird." I pointed at the dead dove. "The girl wife bird is up there in the tree." My finger lifted straight up to the branches overhead. "They lived in a nest together. They sang every morning and every night. I could hear them from my window, right there." I swung my arm around to point at my bedroom window, halfway up the lawn. His gaze followed my finger, then returned to my face. I hiccupped again. "They were m-m-married. But now the husband bird is dead."

"Are you stupid?" His face contorted into a scowl. "Birds don't get married."

"My m-m-mom says turtle doves mate for life." I wiped my

running nose on my sleeve. "She says they're just like humans. And now..." My eyes watered again.

"Now what?" he asked, curious despite his best efforts to act otherwise.

"Now there won't be any singing."

"You *are* stupid," he said decidedly. "There's still one dove left. That one will sing."

I shook my head. "The wife bird won't sing anymore. Because her heart is broken. Mom says she might even d-d-die."

Something strange moved at the back of his eyes. It looked almost like fear.

"You can't die from a broken heart, can you?" I asked, wiping my nose again.

"Well..." His scowl reappeared. "I don't know for sure. My parents definitely aren't in love anymore, but they haven't died or anything. *Yet.*"

"How do you know they aren't in love?" I asked.

His scowl deepened. "They fight all the time. That's why we moved here. My mom said she wanted a divorce if my dad didn't buy her a bigger house and stop sleeping with something called Cheyenne." His eyes narrowed in thought. "I don't know what a Cheyenne is, but my mom was real upset about it."

"What's a divorce?"

He sighed. "How old are you?"

"Five. How old are you?"

His chest puffed out a little. "Nine."

"My brother Parker's nine. He's at soccer right now, though." I tilted my head to get a better look at him. "What's your name?"

"Nathaniel Xavier Knox. You can call me Nate."

"I'm Phoebe," I said, ducking my head. "You can call me Phoebe."

"Have you lived here a long time?"

"Only, like, my whole entire life."

"I think I'm gonna like it." He stared at the water. "It's near the beach."

"Yeah." I nodded. "Sometimes there are jelly fish and seals and stuff. It's cool."

We were silent for a while.

"We should bury him," I said, staring at the dove again. "The husband bird deserves a funeral. Maybe it'll cheer the wife bird up."

"How do you even know that one's the boy and the other one's the girl?"

My bottom lip started trembling again. When he spotted it, he sighed.

"All right, don't be a cry baby. Let me go get a shovel."

And so, the strange dark-eyed boy-next-door went back over the fence and returned ten minutes later with a gardening shovel. Together, we dug a hole — well, mostly I watched *him* dig a hole while I stared forlornly at the dove — and then he used a stick to push the bird into the tiny grave. It took barely any time to cover his soft, winged body over with a mound of dirt.

"We should say something." I stared from the mound at the base of the maple tree to the boy with dirt under his fingernails sitting beside me. "They always say stuff at funerals."

"It's a bird funeral," he pointed out. "You can't say normal human stuff. That's stupid."

My lip trembled again.

"You're not gonna cry, are you?"

"No," I said in a choked voice.

He paused. "I'll say something."

My eyes were wide on his face as he cleared his throat, closed his eyes, and grabbed my hand. I stared at his fingers — large, grimy, and tangled with mine — and felt comforted for the first time since I discovered the bird an hour before.

His voice was steady and serious as he started speaking.

"I believe I can fly," he intoned somberly. "I believe I can touch the sky."

My eyes locked on his face. *Whoa.* He was like a real priest.

"I think about it every night and day," he continued in that even voice. "Spread my wings and fly away."

He was like... a *poet.*

He cleared his throat again. "I believe I can fly."

"I believe I can fly," I echoed, in awe of his originality.

(Looking back I can't believe, even at five, I didn't recognize R. Kelly lyrics when I heard them.)

His eyes opened and met mine. We both looked up at the same time when, a second later, a bird chirped in the tree overhead. Not a song — just a single, solitary chirp.

"Think that was the wife bird?" I asked hopefully.

He shrugged.

"Maybe the funeral cheered her up," I said, brightening. "She chirped. Maybe that means a broken heart can't kill you."

"Maybe," he muttered. "But, just in case, you'll never catch *me* falling in love." He looked horrified by the mere idea.

"Me neither," I agreed immediately.

He scrambled to his feet, brushed off his hands on his jeans, and stared down at me.

"See you around, little bird."

His lips twisted in a smile as he grabbed his shovel, crossed the lawn, and hopped back over the fence... landing firmly in the flesh of my heart as soon as his sneakers hit the grass.

CHAPTER 1

SOME PEOPLE BRAG ABOUT ONE NIGHT STANDS.
WHATEVER. I'VE GOT TWO NIGHT STANDS.
EITHER SIDE OF MY BED.

Phoebe West, upon hearing her best friend lost her v-card after prom.

MY NAME IS Phoebe West and I've been kidnapped.

I think. Maybe.

It's kind of a long story.

See, it wasn't supposed to happen this way.

For the record, it *never* would've happened this way if my life were a movie. (Preferably a rom-com of some sort with a kickass soundtrack and a happy ending, starring a fabulously-styled version of myself opposite Michiel Huisman. Or Liam Hemsworth. Or Henry Cavill. I could go on, but I won't.)

Point is, I had a plan. A pretty good one — or so I thought until yesterday, before it all went to hell faster than you can say *Phoebe-you're-a-nutcase* in Pig-Latin.

Sigh.

This calamity began, as they usually do, because of a boy.

No, not a boy.

A *man*.

A smoking hot, sexy as sin, *older* man who just so happens to be my big brother Parker's best friend — and has been since they were, like, ten and still thought girls were weird and covered in cooties.

Oh, how I wish *that* phase had lasted.

It would've saved me the torture of watching my undying preteen crush work his way through half the girls at the private prep school he and my brother attended. He would've worked his way through the other half, too, but he and Parker had a strict rule against going after each other's girls. (Part of their man-code or whatever.) For that, at least, I could be grateful.

Or, so I thought.

Because a few years later — by which point my binder-doodling, call-and-hang-up, harmless little crush had blossomed into full-on love (or *lust* depending on the day) — I realized that same man-code which forbade boys from ever stealing each other's girlfriends also extended to other things.

Specifically, to little sisters.

More specifically, to *me*.

There I was — *BAM!* — smack dab in the fine print of their bro bible:

RULE #1:

No dating ex-girlfriends, current girlfriends, or potential future girlfriends.

RULE #2:

Absolutely no touching, fucking, or corrupting little sisters.

RULE #3:

Pizza without meat on it doesn't count as a meal.

I PROBABLY SHOULD'VE BEEN FLATTERED that I ranked above pizza when it came to male priorities, but all I could feel was heartbreak that I, Phoebe West, would never be able to call Nathaniel "Nate" Knox my own.

Never feel the weight of his eyes moving over my face with heart-stopping heat.

Never know the touch of his hands, big and rough, gliding across my skin, as I'd envisioned since I was barely old enough to understand my desire for such things.

The closest I'd ever get was a brotherly pat on the back and that same cool, narrow-eyed stare he used on everyone. The cocky, condescending, infuriatingly attractive one that made a tiny crease appear in the space between his eyes and clearly said, *Yes, I'm measuring your worth* and *No, you don't live up.*

Even his blatant indifference wasn't enough to deter me. Because, well, here's the thing.

I love him.

I always have.

Falling for Nate wasn't something I was ever really conscious of doing. It was just something I *knew,* in the pit of my stomach, in the marrow of my bones, in every dark, secret corner at the back of my mind. Ingrained so deep I wouldn't know how to begin to overcome it — like my hatred of chocolate in breakfast foods and my love of Old-Fashioneds with top-shelf bourbon.

It's set in stone.

Unchangeable, no matter how hard I wish I could let him go.

I can't help it. From that very first day I met him, it was like my body had been programmed to fall head over heels... and my mind had absolutely no say in the matter.

So, you can imagine how frustrating it was when, after years of patiently waiting — for my boobs to come in, for my wardrobe to sort itself out after that weird retro-Punk phase I went through, and, most especially, for Nate to come home from his first semester of college and notice that I'd grown up — he didn't even blink an eye at my high school freshman field hockey skirt and newly minted set of knockers.

In fact, if anything, he pulled away more, until I'd been demoted from *honorary little sister* to *invisible girl who lives with Parker*. That first winter break, he barely spoke to me at all unless it was to say something banal like "excuse me" as his body brushed past mine with new carefulness on the way to the fridge, or "is Parker home" when I'd hear the doorbell chime and race downstairs as fast as my legs could carry me, determined to be the one to greet him.

At first, I hated how much those tiny, bland niceties meant to me — how one thoughtless word from him could make or break my entire day. Each "hey Phoebe" and "tell Parker I called" was a bone thrown to a desperate dog, who'd live on any scrap of attention that came her way so long as it came from *his* hand. It made me feel weak. Pathetic. Invisible.

But afterwards, when Nate dropped out of Harvard — and, for all intents and purposes, out of my life — I missed his strained small talk, his tossed scraps. Oh, how I wished he'd come back from wherever he'd gone and look through me while saying "pass the pepper" at dinner. Because, as sad as it was to admit, having Asshole Nate around was better than no Nate at all.

His father, an influential Boston defense attorney with big plans for his only son, was pissed beyond belief when his sole heir joined the special forces and disappeared without so much as a discussion.

Parker, his best friend since elementary school, wasn't thrilled to lose his partner in crime, but he vowed to be supportive if it meant making Nate happy.

And me? Well, there've been several stages of my post-Knox life.... starting with pure, undiluted misery.

The slightly melodramatic *wherefore-hast-thou-forsaken-me-o-beloved-one* phase was essentially an eighteen-month period during which I consumed a lot of chocolate chip cookie dough ice cream and listened to Damien Rice songs on repeat until my eye sockets physically refused to produce any more tears.

Then, when I turned sixteen and was finally done feeling sorry for myself, the numbing sorrow of missing him wore off and I realized how freaking pissed I was at him for abandoning me.

This may've been because my pride was a bit wounded that Nate hadn't even bothered to come back and *notice* my months of moping, which was pretty inconsiderate, since it was all over him. Even later, when I learned he was halfway around the world training for a tactical team so lethal they didn't even have a name, the firestorm of rage-fueled, unrequited love continued to scorch my insides.

My angry phase lasted longer.

Approximately six years, to be exact, until both high school and college were fading in my rearview and I was a twenty-two year old woman with a pitiful amount of experience with the

male sex, all because my stupid, stubborn heart refused to relinquish hope that someday, my soulmate would wake up and smell
the freaking pheromones.

But eventually, as I moved to the city and settled into new
patterns in my Back Bay brownstone, as my "real life" started and
— alarmingly — began to slip by without anyone to share it
with.... I was forced to accept the fact that my reckless, hopeless
(and occasionally dirty) dreams of Nate would never be fulfilled.

With that realization, I transitioned from anger into the indifferent phase, where I've been dwelling unhappily for nearly a
year, now.

The main rules of indifference are:

Don't think about Nate.

Don't talk about Nate.

*And never, ever, talk to Nate at the few family gatherings
where our paths cross.*

It's kind of like my own personal Fight Club, except less
violent and way more pathetic since I'm the only member.

Before you judge me for giving up on the man I've loved for
almost my entire lifetime, you have to understand something — a
girl can only handle so much rejection. And, over the years, I've
had more than my fair share of it.

First, there was the time in fourth grade when I stole Nate's
cellphone and spent an entire afternoon — practically an eternity, at age nine — locked in my walk-in closet, scrolling through
his text inbox and sending eloquent "Dnt txt me! I h8 U!"
messages to every girl in his contact list. (I know, I know. Not my
proudest — or smartest — moment. But, in my defense, no one
told me he'd be able to see them in his SENT folder as soon as he
miraculously found his missing phone on the kitchen counter
later that night. *Oops.*)

And I can't forget the incident in sixth grade — well before
my boobs came in, mind you — when Parker threw a huge pool

party for his sweet sixteen and, jealous of the *totally* mature tenth-grade girls wandering around with what, at the time, seemed like Victoria's Secret model bodies in comparison to my mosquito bites, I went into the bathroom and stuffed the cups of my bikini with enough tissues to keep Kleenex in business for at least the next decade.

A mistake — the repercussions of which I didn't even fully realize until one of Parker's bitchy girlfriends pushed me into the pool, the impact dislodging my stuffing like confetti from a canon. The two minutes I spent floating in the water, makeshift boobies drifting around me like white, translucent jellyfish as I listened to the older girls giggle, were bad enough; the fact that it was *Nate* who reached in, pulled me out, and wrapped a towel around my shaking shoulders was worse. Mainly because, as soon as my feet hit dry land, the tissue began fusing to my limbs, clumping on my skin like some grade-school paper maché project gone terribly awry.

Somehow, when I'd imagined Nate seeing my boobs for the first time, I hadn't reeked of chlorine and they hadn't been made of paper.

Oh well. You win some, you lose some.

(I seem to lose most, actually.)

And yet, even the pool party wasn't as abominable as the time in eighth grade, when I asked him to be my date to the Sadie Hawkins dance. He didn't even bother letting me down easy. He just grinned, ruffled my hair like I was an adorable-but-idiotic golden retriever, and walked away, laughing as though the suggestion was the funniest thing he'd ever heard. His rejection stung, don't get me wrong, but it was the aftermath that really kicked me in the shins. Without Nate as a date, I had no option other than to ask my friend Lila's older brother, Duncan, to go with me. He was cute in a clean-cut, average kind of way — not dark or dangerous-looking, like other boys-who-shall-not-be-named, but handsome enough to get my fourteen-year-old heart pumping.

Duncan was a charmer when he picked me up in his father's Porsche, smiling as he slipped a corsage on my wrist, driving with one arm thrown across the back of my seat. Just when I was beginning to think things might not turn out so bad... he downed six shots of whiskey in the school parking lot, which left him so incapacitated he couldn't even slow-dance with me *once* during the hour I spent leaning against the wall of the Starry-Night-themed reception hall, watching him gyrate questionably against several unsuspecting girls in taffeta.

When I called Parker to come get me, he — somewhat grudgingly — showed up... with Nate in tow, because apparently the universe thought I hadn't suffered enough humiliation for one night. Crammed in the backseat next to a moaning Duncan, I listened to Parker and Nate talk about the "hot chicks" they'd had to bail on to pick me up, and prayed to disappear. When Duncan puked in my purse halfway home, I knew my perfect night at the middle-school dance was finally complete.

Ah, memories.

I could go on, but I'm sure you get the picture. When it comes to Nate, my life has been one long string of humiliation and horrifyingly bad luck. Before he disappeared, taking my heart with him, I tried *everything* to get his attention.

Okay, not *everything*. I stopped short of stripping to my skin and climbing into his bed naked because *hello*, I still have some pride left. (Not much, but enough to know that ambushing him in my birthday suit and demanding that he finally remove my pesky virginity — only to be rejected and dismissed with the same detachment he'd use to send an overcooked steak back to the kitchen — is a blow from which my self-esteem would never recover.)

But I've tried everything *else*.

Heated glances. Cold shoulders.

Sidelong-looks. Full-frontal stares.

Ignoring him. Adoring him.

And you know what?

Not a damn bit of it worked.

It doesn't matter what I do — Nate still treats me with the same aloof disinterest he always has, since the day I hit puberty.

In a few days, I'll be twenty-four, which means I've been in love with Nate for more than a decade. And not once in all that time has he shown me so much as a flicker of reciprocal interest. Hell, he doesn't even check out my boobs — which are now very real, thank you very much — if I walk around in a bikini when he comes to visit Parker in Nantucket. And it's not like there's nothing to look at — I'm a generous C-cup, for god's sake. (Frankly, I think the universe realized it owed me, after the pool-stuffing incident, and bequeathed me with a really stellar set of ta-tas to even the score.)

But, it was with a heavy heart and some seriously neglected lady parts that, two months ago, I decided to toss in the towel for good. I'm not usually a quitter, but it seemed there was no choice other than to lock my heart away in an impenetrable steel box inside my chest and move on — to new men, who actually noticed I was alive and worthy of love. Or, at the very least, a little below-the-belt action. After all, a girl can only wait so long.

So, I did something seemingly harmless.

I accepted a date to a stuffy dinner gala with a wealthy, eligible bachelor named Brett from one of Boston's most prominent families. With dark hair and ice blue eyes, he looked a tad like Ian Somerhalder, which was about his only redeeming quality because most of the time, he gave off seriously creepy vibes. Not that it mattered — I wasn't interested in him. I just thought, after years listening to Lila barrage me with advice about *The Top 10 Successful Ways to Make a Man Jealous* and *12*

Irrefutable Strategies to Forget That Rat Bastard, I should finally give it a go. One last-ditch attempt to catch Nate's attention, before my ovaries dried up from lack of use. I figured it couldn't hurt, right?

I just never in my wildest dreams imagined it would actually *work...*

CHAPTER 2

WAIT, *THAT'S* WHAT THAT SONG IS ABOUT?

Phoebe West, after listening a little closer to the lyrics of Madonna's "Like A Prayer."

TWO MONTHS EARLIER...

I SET my clutch purse down on the counter with a heavy sigh.

It's been a weird night, to say the least.

That's not much of a surprise, though. Blind dates are probably always weird, even when they aren't at boring business galas full of somnolent speeches and really gross arugula salads, with only a semi-lecherous date to keep you company.

Not that I'd know. My dating experience is limited to

watching ten-year-old reruns of *FRIENDS* on Netflix, while Boo — the only man in my life with whom I don't share DNA — snores gently by my side. (Don't get too excited. Boo is a pure white mini Pomeranian with so much sass, he could intimidate a Great Dane.)

He doesn't even lift his head from the gray sectional cushion where he's sprawled when I cross through the low-lit kitchen into the adjacent living room. The space is dark, but I easily make out the outline of his tiny furry chest, rising and falling with each snore. There's a puddle of doggie drool forming on the $300 chenille throw beneath his slackened jowls, growing larger with each rattling exhale.

For such a small dog, he makes quite the racket.

I brush the bangs out of my hazel eyes and run fingers through my dark brown hair, hoping it might soothe my headache as I plant one high-heeled foot on the edge of the coffee table and begin to undo the straps of my Louboutin.

I seriously can't believe I wasted shoes this hot on a night this lame. Not to mention this dress. The long, flowing white Vera Wang, with its paper-thin straps and subtle embroidery, was made for a night with Prince Charming. It's practically a crime that I wasted it on *my* dud of a date — Brett spent the vast majority of our evening distracted, more preoccupied with family drama than wooing me. Adding insult to injury, he didn't even bother to kiss me goodnight when he dropped me at my front door.

Lame.

As soon as the skyscraper-high heels are off, I sink my feet into the plush carpet and hum in contentment as feeling tingles back into my pinched toes. I know beauty is pain and all that jazz, but you'd think spending upwards of two grand on a pair of pumps would ensure, as a minimum requirement, that you don't feel like a victim of Chinese foot-binding by the end of the night.

Speaking of Chinese...

I know for a fact there's a carton of takeout lurking somewhere at the back of my fridge.

Immediately, I turn and head for the kitchen, fully intending to gorge myself on days-old lo mein, despite the fact that it's past midnight and my yoga instructor would sincerely disapprove. (Whatever. *She* wasn't the one forced to choke down that wholly unsatisfying dinner of salad, steamed broccoli, and organic free-range chicken.)

I'm halfway across the living room, face pinched in concentration as I try to estimate the approximate shelf life of crab rangoon, when my eyes catch up to my brain and I register the sight before me. All thoughts of midnight snackage fly from my head. My stomach, only seconds ago rumbling with hunger and anticipation, clenches hard and turns to stone as my feet slam to a standstill.

For a minute, I just stand there in total silence, staring at the man silhouetted in the archway of my kitchen, his muscular frame backlit by the low light and his face in full shadow.

A man I don't recognize.

A man I most definitely did *not* invite into my home.

Holy frack, this isn't good.

My frantic gaze sweeps the intruder in disbelief as he takes a step closer to me.

It's then that I scream. *Loudly.* A real, honest-to-god, banshee-like wail.

I mean, I didn't even know my voice could hit an octave that high. I'd be impressed with myself, if I weren't nearly peeing my pants in unabashed, girly terror.

The scream shatters the midnight quiet, instantly waking Boo from his slumber. Not to be left out, he promptly begins barking his little head off, leaping from the couch to stand guard at my feet, as though he, in all his five pound glory — at least a pound of which is pure fur — has the intimidation tactics of a Pit Bull, rather than a Pomeranian.

His whole body lifts into the air with the force of each bark.

Yip-jump, yip-jump, yip-jump.

Very intimidating to the man about to rob, rape, or kill me, I'm *sure.*

I'm still screaming — and quickly backpedaling away because, *hello,* there's a strange man in my house — when I register that he's *big.*

Not just tall, but muscular. Even in the dark I can see the outline of his shoulders, the triangular slope of his torso narrowing to a V at his hips. For a split second, I wonder if his face is equally well proportioned.

Good lord.

I've started questioning the hotness of home invaders. I really need to get laid.

A low curse vibrates from the man's mouth, but I barely hear it over the sound of my own screams as I back away. When I see him take another step toward me, my indiscernible babbles of panic turn into words.

"Stay away! Don't come any closer!"

Hands held out in front of me, heart in my throat, I try not to freak out as he takes yet another stride in my direction.

"Take whatever you want, just don't hurt— *Eeeek!*"

My words are cut off as my feet catch on my discarded high heels, knocking me off balance. I feel myself start to trip backwards, head over feet, and I know I'm going to crack my head on the coffee table on my way down, which is probably going to dent the oak and *definitely* going to knock me unconscious. Or trigger some kind of cerebral hemorrhage, from which I'll bleed out and die. Alone, with only Boo to witness my passing into the afterlife, as this man steals my valuables to sell on Boston's black market.

Death by table.

God, I hope Parker doesn't include that in my obituary.

Time seems to slide into slow motion as I fall through the air, arms windmilling, helpless to stop my descent. My eyes slam closed as my face contorts into a wince, already anticipating the pain of impact. Any second now, my skull will crack against that table and my fragile life will flicker and die faster than a candle in the wind.

Hey, maybe Sir Elton will write a song about me...

Great. I'm going to die, and my last thought is of a sassy gay man. If that isn't a testament to the pathetic nature of my love life, I'm not sure what is.

I'm so preoccupied with my impending doom, it takes me a minute to realize I'm still alive.

The impact I was so sure would steal my breath simply... never came.

In fact, even my descent has halted.

I'm hovering mid air, locked in what feels like a set of steel bands.

Except they aren't steel bands.

They're *arms*.

Really freaking muscular arms.

Arms that, if I weren't a click away from death, I'd have to admit feel really good wrapped around me.

My eyes are still pressed closed, but I hear the distinct sound of a low, pissed-off male voice muttering close to my ear.

"Fucking Christ, are you trying to give me a heart attack?"

Recognition jolts into me harder than a punch to the gut. Every muscle in my body freezes like liquid nitrogen has been shot through my veins. My heart actually stutters inside my chest, its equilibrium totally and completely thrown off by the proximity of this man who, abruptly, I know is not an intruder.

I'd know that voice anywhere.

I've heard it in countless replayed memories, in hundreds of unspoken fantasies, in endless unfulfilled dreams.

Nathaniel Jackass Knox.

(His middle name is actually Xavier. Whatever.)

Nate.

The man who's been steadfastly ignoring my existence for the past ten years as he traveled around the world doing dangerous things for even more dangerous people. The man I only very recently decided I was completely, certifiably, one hundred percent *over* being obsessed with.

Last I heard, he was in the Middle East, doing some kind of private security gig for a Saudi prince.

And now, he's *here.*

In my brownstone.

Holding me in his arms.

Saving me from certain death-by-coffee-table.

Holy frack.

———

MY LIDS SNAP open and take in the face mere centimeters from mine.

Sharp, angular cheekbones.

Broad, chiseled jawline.

Alert, assessing eyes.

His dark beauty steals what little breath is left in my lungs as I stare up at him, reveling in the fact that, after all these years, I'm *finally* in his arms — my soft girlie parts pressed firmly against the hard plane of his body, the scent of his skin invading my senses. He smells like leather and smoke and the sharp, coppery tang of metal. Or blood.

Maybe that's just my imagination.

He's still muttering under his breath though, in all honesty, it's hard to hear him over Boo's ceaseless barking.

"...falling over her own feet." He shakes his head, as if deeply pained. "...off herself on a goddamned coffee table...those damn *come-fuck-me* heels..."

My spine stiffens as his hushed words register. "What did you just say?"

His eyes lock on mine, infuriating me all the more when I see how empty of emotion they are. Just two dark pools, staring back at me.

"Are you trying to kill yourself?" His arms tighten reflexively as the words slip out, revealing his anger — a small breach in that impeccable control he usually exhibits around me. I'd normally be stunned at any show of emotion, but right now I'm too pissed to do anything but narrow my eyes at him and glare. Which is hard because, well... did I mention that his face is about three inches from mine, and I can feel every contour of his muscular body hard against my front?

"Those fucking heels are a deathtrap." His voice is low, vibrating with sheer intensity, but that's nothing new. Nate always sounds like he's got one finger in an electrical socket— his every atom charged with tense, elemental energy that buzzes off his skin. His arms tighten around me again, as though he's having a difficult time bottling up his anger. "Don't know why you insist on parading around in them."

I blink. Hard. "*Excuse me?!*"

His dark eyes flash with something I can't name. "Think you heard me. Shoes like that do one thing — they *break*. Hearts or ankles, well, that depends on the woman." His eyes flicker over my face and I get the sense whatever he sees, he finds lacking. "Guessing you're the ankles variety, West."

For a moment my mouth gapes, torn between shock that Nate has even *noticed* my penchant for designer footwear, and rage that he thinks, after years of barely meeting my eyes during the few mandatory social situations that have forced us together since we both became adults, I'd give a flying frack about his opinion on my fashion choices.

Boo is still running in circles around us, trying to get in on the action. Silently, I give him full permission to bite Nate's calves.

It'd serve the Louboutin-hating jackass right.

My eyes narrow further. "I'm a grown woman! I'll wear whatever goddamn shoes I want!"

"You used to wear flats," he grunts out, his gaze still locked on mine. "Yeah, they were always covered in glitter and sparkly polka dots and shit, but at least you could run in them if you had to."

I blink, shocked once again.

He remembers the shoes I wore in middle school?

Entirely too stunned to process *that* little tidbit of information, I instead search for the deep well of hurt and rage I've been harboring for the past decade. If I let it fill me up like acid bubbling from the depths of my soul, maybe it'll incinerate the butterflies that have begun to swarm in my stomach. Maybe, if I'm burning with anger, I won't notice how good it feels to be in his arms, my lips inches from his, those dark eyes finally focused on me with every ounce of his attention.

How many times have I dreamed of his hands on the bare skin at my back, of his nose so close it practically bumps mine with each muttered word?

Even after he joined the military and got all scary and damaged and distant, I still wanted him to hold me like this, so I could see the demons in his eyes up close... and so maybe, just maybe, he'd see *me* in return for once.

I just didn't think, when it finally happened, we'd be talking about shoes.

"I'm not sixteen anymore!" I snap, trying on my iciest tone, which is kind of hard since I'm feeling so breathless. "And if you hadn't shown up in the dark like some kind of creepy home invader, I wouldn't be running around in the first place! I'd be gorging myself on leftover lo mein right now, instead of nearly tripping over my heels, dying young, and not living long enough to read the next *Game of Thrones* book, assuming George ever finishes writing it. I've been waiting *four years* to learn what happens to Jon Snow. You almost took that from me!"

I swear, I think his lips twitch at that — just the tiniest tug at the left side of his mouth — but his expression flattens so fast I decide it must've been my imagination.

Boo's barks have subsided into yips of displeasure, interspersed with the occasional growl. Finding no success from his spot on the ground, the tiny Pomeranian leaps up onto the sofa. I won't be surprised if he launches himself at Nate — aerial assault seems the next logical step.

"Still don't know why you need to wear those things." Nate's words are tight as his eyes flicker down to the heels scattered on the carpet. "Five inches off the ground, teetering around like the fucking Tower of Pisa."

Well!

"Because I had a hot date, if you must know!" I taunt, hoping to piss him off.... Until his eyes flash with something seriously dark and I decide that's probably a bad idea. "But mostly, because I like them!" I hurry on, trying to maintain my bravado. "And I so do not *teeter*. I've been told I could strut the runway with the pros."

His stare narrows as he glares back at me. The cold fury burning in his eyes is hands-down the most emotion he's shown around me in the past decade. Maybe ever. "By who? Guys trying to get in your pants?"

Well, actually by Lila in eleventh grade before junior prom, but...

My mouth flattens into a frown. My arms, which I've only just noticed are wound around him like a starfish clinging for life, tighten as my hands clench into angry fists at his back. My body has reached peak rage levels.

Unfortunately, my brain is still a mushy, hormonal mess due to the fact that Nate is touching me, so I don't have time to formulate a snappy retort. I just stare at him, mouth gaping, as he continues insulting me.

"Hate to break it to you, West, but you're 5'3" — never gonna be a runway model." He gives me a hard, humorless smile. "Thought you were smart enough to know a guy will say just about anything to get you into bed."

An outraged sound flies from my lips.

God, he's a jackass.

God, I barely care.

If he asked, I'd pull this dress up over my head and jump him, right here on my brand new Anthropologie rug.

No! Bad Phoebe. You've moved on, remember?

His eyes flash again, as though he can read my thoughts. I swallow roughly.

"Are you *trying* to be an ass?" I hiss.

"Are you *trying* to be stupid?" He hisses right back. "You show up looking like that for a date, you're giving a guy certain expectations. The wrong kind of expectations."

Oh, no. He did *not* just say that.

My brain catches up to my body, anger overtaking my every neuron and synapse in one swift instant.

"Who I date is none of your business!" I bite out coldly. "Never has been, never will be."

His eyes flash again and his jaw tightens as a muscle jumps in his cheek, but he says nothing.

Typical.

If this were any other guy, I'd say he was jealous. But this is *Nate* we're talking about. The very idea is ludicrous.

We stare at each other in stony silence, still pressed together, our chests heaving in sync with the strength of our breaths, our hearts pounding in perfect rhythm. Anger sparks in the narrow slice of space between our faces, so hot and visceral, it practically bends the particles like ultra-heated air on asphalt. For a second, I think I see something else in his eyes, but it's buried so deep it's easy to dismiss it as nothing but a trick of light.

One more mirage on a desert road.

"Did you come here to talk about shoes, Nate?" My words are breathy — I tell myself from anger, not desire. "Or did Parker con you into checking in on me while he's off gallivanting through Europe with his parade of bimbos?"

At the sound of my brother's name, Nate seems to snap back to his normal self — eyes blanking, expression shuttering until his face is an emotionless mask. In a flash, I'm out of his arms and back on my own two feet, toes sinking into the plush carpet. I don't see him move, but when my eyes locate him again, he's across the room once more, leaning in the archway of the kitchen, his face cast in shadow.

"No. That's not why I came." His tone is empty, indifferent — back to the hyper-controlled Nate I recognize. "I'm discrete — if Parker needed me to check in on you, you'd never know I was here."

Cocky, much?

Rolling my eyes, I smooth my hands over my dress and shake the too-long bangs out of my face. I straighten to full height — which, granted, isn't that tall — but with my hands planted on my hips and my spine stiffer than a steel rod, I feel a little more in control.

"Yeah, yeah, yeah. You're a super badass mercenary. I get it."

My voice is ultra sarcastic. "Care to share with the class something we don't already know?"

He bristles. It's not so much something I see, since he's still standing in the shadows, but something I feel — a change in the atmosphere around us, as waves of anger begin to ripple out from his spot in the archway. Something I said clearly struck a nerve. Before I can begin to guess what, he steps closer. The expression on his face makes my mouth go dry.

Holy frack.

I've never seen him look so intense. In fact, I've never seen *anyone* look so intense. I can almost see the electricity moving under his skin, waves of energy surging through him like a storm. There should be a 10,000-volt hazard sign engraved on his chest:

DANGER! SEVERE INJURY OR DEATH *WILL* OCCUR!

A warning to those who might be foolish enough to take a man this lethal into their arms.

He's a live wire on the side of the road — dark, immobile, and seemingly harmless until you step too close and sparks fly out with one fatal snap, killing you where you stand.

He's brutal. Barbaric.

He's the most beautiful thing I've ever seen.

CHAPTER 3

LET'S JUST SAY, I SLEEP DIAGONALLY
ACROSS MY MATTRESS. EVERY NIGHT.

Phoebe West, reflecting on her relationship status.

NATE STEPS TOWARD ME, his expression darkening like the thunderheads I watch roll across the ocean on summer nights from my balcony in Nantucket. When he speaks, his words are a lightning strike.

"Your date tonight."

Flash.

"Brett Croft."

Crack.

"You're not seeing him again."

Boom.

His declaration echoes for a moment in the darkness, leaving me paralyzed — as though I really have been struck by a bolt of electricity. Volts of confusion whisper through me as I search for words to counter his startling statement.

This — him being here — is about *Brett*?

Brett?!

As in, the snooze-worthy date I barely spoke to, tonight?

Boo barks again, angry at being ignored, and Nate and I yell at the same time.

"Quiet, Boo!"

With a resentful growl, the small dog falls grudgingly silent and settles on the couch pillows. His shiny, beady eyes never move from Nate and I'm sure, if I gave him the smallest of signals, he'd be only too happy to vault from the cushions, intent on destruction.

I don't blame him. I myself would like to bite Nate, right now. And not in the sensual, earlobe-nibbling way I typically dream of.

"What are you talking about?" I ask, my voice laced with genuine bewilderment. "Why would you give a rat's ass about Brett Croft?"

Nate takes a step toward me, gaze locked on my face. "He's dangerous."

I can't help but scoff. It's funny — the most dangerous man I've ever met, warning me away from someone like Brett.

His eyes narrow. "Something funny?"

"Brett's a bored billionaire with a gorgeous face and an ass that won't quit." I roll my eyes. "Delicious? Perhaps. Dangerous? Definitely not."

"For once in your fucking life, would you just listen?" he snaps, striding closer as his hands fist at his sides. "Brett Croft is involved in some fucked up shit. So, I don't give a damn if you think he's *delicious*." He spits out the word like it's toxic. "Stay the hell away from him."

"And if I don't?"

A perilous glint creeps into his eyes. Seeing it sends a chill racing down my spine.

"If you don't..." He steps closer, his voice dropping to a low rumble. "I'll find you and I'll drag you back here, kicking and screaming."

"You're absolutely outrageous!" I huff, crossing my arms over my chest. "I haven't seen or spoken to you in years — *years!* — and now you think you can just barge into my life and boss me around? Tell me what to wear and who to date? No. Nuh uh. Not happening."

He glances toward the ceiling, as though praying for composure, and when he looks back at me, his eyes are calmer. Marginally.

"West, I'm not fucking around. This guy is bad news. I'm working a case for a friend right now, and Brett's square in the middle of it, doing his best to cause a lot of drama for people I like. He's not a good guy. So, do me a fucking favor and for once in your life, do as you're told."

"Who?"

He stares at me. "Who, what?"

"*Who* is this mysterious friend of yours, that thinks Brett is such bad news?"

I watch the muscle tick in his cheek — one, two, three times — before he grunts out a name.

"Chase Croft."

"Brett's cousin?" I ask, incredulous.

Nate nods tightly.

"Oh." I can't help but be crestfallen.

Both Croft boys went to the same prep school as Parker and Nate, a few grades ahead of them. Though Parker has never been close to them, I know Nate sometimes handles Chase's private security, especially now that he's taken over Croft Industries as

CEO. In addition to being wealthier than Taylor Swift, Chase seems like a genuinely a good person, is charming as hell, and has an ass like a hot-cross bun — a trifecta which makes him unquestionably the most sought-after bachelor in all of New England's high-society.

Though, after tonight... his *bachelor* status seems like it might have an expiration date.

At the gala earlier, he had a really freaking awesome girl named Gemma on his arm, who he stared at with a reverence I usually reserve for filet mignon at Davio's. She was gorgeous, sure, but it was more than that — her quirky, offbeat personality and tendency to spout verbal diarrhea at a moment's notice made me like her instantly. And seeing Chase with a girl like Gemma made me like him even more.

...But the two of *them* definitely hadn't liked his cousin Brett.

The air was so frosty at our table during dinner, I was afraid the water was going to freeze over in my glass. Gemma even went so far as to warn me away from him, when we made a trip to the ladies room together.

Which means, as much as I hate to admit it, Nate is probably right about my date tonight.

It's not exactly a loss — I had no intention of ever seeing Brett again — but it does piss me off that, if I wanted to, Nate thinks he could tell me differently.

Ugh! That bossy, arrogant, son of a...

My eyes lift back to Nate's, and I see him watching me carefully. Whatever he reads on my face seems to satisfy him — a tiny bit of tension slips from his shoulders and his jaw stops ticking like a bomb set to explode. Still, he's glaring at me like I peed in his Cheerios, so I do the only thing I can: glare right back at him.

"You didn't have to come here, you know," I snip, crossing my arms over my chest.

He doesn't respond. *Rude.*

"You could've called."

Again, no response.

"You can't just go around breaking into people's houses."

"I didn't break in," he corrects lowly. "I have a key."

"What?" I screech. "How?"

I *never* gave him a key to my brownstone. The only other person on the planet with a key is Parker and he's in Europe. So if Nate has a key...

Ugh, I'm going to *kill* my big brother for assigning Nate to check on me like I'm still nine and need supervision.

"Give it back!" I take a step toward him, hand outstretched. "Parker never should've given it to you."

"No."

"Nate!"

"I didn't come here to argue with you about a goddamned key," he mutters, frustration bleeding into his tone.

"I know. You came here to boss me around, insert yourself into my love life — a place you most definitely do *not* belong — and reestablish yourself as an all-round jackass. *Congrats!*" I announce, making jazz-hands in the air between us. "You succeeded."

His eyes flash with something scary again and he goes so tense, all my bluster and brass evaporates in an instant. When he strides closer, so there's only a foot or so between us, my palms stop jazzing and go flat against his muscular chest.

I want to push him away.

I want to pull him closer.

I do neither.

He glares down into my eyes with a thunderous expression, and it takes all my strength not to give in to his intimidation and shy away like a scared little girl.

"Stay away from Brett Croft," he rumbles at me, deadly serious.

"Stay away from me!" I yell back, angrier than I've been in a long time. Partly at him, because he's the most domineering, overbearing man in the history of human existence, but mostly at myself, for being so affected by him despite that fact.

Yip! Yip! Yip! Boo chimes in from the couch.

Neither of us looks at the dog. We're too busy glaring at each other, our faces so close I can feel his breath on my lips. His eyes seem to burn into mine, intense and angry. It's almost painful to hold his stare, to resist the pull that — despite my best efforts — still exists between us. Thankfully, I've had a lot of practice looking at Nate with indifference on my face while my heart's aflame in my chest.

He's just never been standing so close before, looking back at me like he's on fire, too.

For a split second, his gaze darts down to my mouth, lingering there for no longer than a heartbeat before flashing back to meet mine. I can't help the surprised hiss of air that escapes my lips, as I try to keep myself under control.

He's never looked at me like *that* before.

My nerve endings are frazzled, divided — half enraged, half enamored, equally angry and aroused. I'm being torn in two with opposing needs.

To kiss him.

To kill him.

To claim him.

To curse him.

With Nate and me, it all comes down to need. To *lust* — that driving force, that infatuating, life-creating elixir that ties me up in knots of desire, of passion, of pain. Even before I had words to define my feelings for him, I was consumed by it.

Wanting. Craving. Longing.

I lust for his body on mine as much as I lust for my own

retribution, for my own selfish need to unhinge him like he's always unhinged me. That familiar, heady, heart-stopping yearning, born of half a lifetime of cumulative *need* stirs in my veins.... but it's not alone. No. Bloodlust — a darker, deeper, more dangerous desire, born of resentment and rejection — stirs there as well. It near tears me in half, the wanting. The needing. The lusting. The loathing.

The line between wanting him and hating him for never wanting *me* is so blurred, I can barely sort out my own feelings.

Still glaring down at me, he makes a sound at the back of his throat, almost a growl. Thoughts move in his eyes, but I can't for the life of me decipher them.

"Is that all you wanted?" I whisper, gaze locked on his. I have no idea what emotions are swimming in my eyes. "To talk about Brett?"

He doesn't move. I don't even think he's breathing. Boo has fallen eerily quiet, as though sensing the extreme tension between Nate and me as we stare at each other in the dark. It's so still, so silent, I can almost hear the locking of his jaw, how his teeth grind together as he searches for control.

I've never seen him like this — his eyes a little wild, his words a little reckless. Around me, he's never been anything except the epitome of restraint. Until now.

I wish I could say I didn't like it.

I lean closer, maybe a centimeter, but that tiny distance feels like a leap off a cliff into the unknown. Our eyes never break contact, our breaths don't slow. I wonder if his heart is beating as fast as mine.

"West..." His voice is low, warning.

My name is Phoebe, I want to say. *No amount of forced formality can cut these ties between us.*

I want to say it, but I don't. There are more pressing *wants* on my mind.

I want him to sate the storm that's been building since we were hardly more than kids.

I want his tongue in my mouth, my name on his lips, the look on my face when he comes into me burned into the back of his eyelids every time he closes them, just so he knows what it is to be owned entirely by another human being.

I want him to bury himself so deep beneath my skin he'll never find his way out, so he knows exactly how it feels to have someone so enmeshed in your soul, it's impossible to remove them without tearing yourself in two.

In this frozen instant, I'm honestly not sure if, given the chance, I'd slap his cheek or crush his mouth to mine, as I've wanted to for so long.

Let's find out, a crazy voice at the back of my mind whispers. *You know you want to.*

I sway forward, unable to deny his pull for another moment... and try not to scream in frustration when he instantly takes two steps back. The haze clears from his eyes so fast you'd think it was never there at all, and his face shutters in an aloof expression I recognize all too well.

"Yes," he says flatly, no longer looking at me. "That's all I wanted."

Shame, hot and hurtful, burns through me.

"Great," I snap. "Well, if we're finished here, I need to go schedule a prefrontal lobotomy to scrub this encounter from my memories, so..."

I turn on one heel.

"I mean it, West." I flinch to a stop at the steel in his tone. "Stay away from Croft."

My eyes flicker back to his, refusing to show any intimidation. "You gonna add the cliché '*or else*' to that statement, or...."

He doesn't say anything, but the skin around his eyes crinkles up the tiniest bit — anyone else, I'd say they were fighting a grin.

But it's Nate. He's probably picturing ways to chop up my body and dispose of the pieces where no one will ever find them.

I swallow hard.

"Oh, goodie. Another scintillating moment of silence," I mutter, rolling my eyes to prove how cool and collected I am. *Psh.* "You can see yourself out, *Nathaniel*."

I use his full name just to goad him, knowing he detests the formality of it. Spinning around, I grab Boo off the couch and storm from the room before he can say another word.

Before he can see the angry tears glossing over my eyes.

Jackass.

I am *so* fracking done with Nathaniel Knox and his mind games.

CHAPTER 4

HE PROBABLY ONLY DATES BAD GIRLS.

PERFECT.

I'M BAD AT PRETTY MUCH EVERYTHING.

Phoebe West, giving herself a pep talk.

OKAY, so, that's a lie.

I'm not done.

I can't be.

Where Nate is concerned, I don't think I'll ever be completely able to cut ties. Not unless I want to cut my heart from my chest, as well.

But I'm most certainly done dreaming about some kind of deluded happily-ever-after with him — a big white dress and him waiting at the end of the aisle, eyes tearing up with joy at just the sight of my beauty. A disheveled fixer-upper house we lovingly restore together, until each floorboard is imprinted with the strength of our relationship. A nursery painted a safe, gender-neutral yellow.

Phoebe, you lunatic, you are not the heroine of a Nicholas Sparks novel.

After I hear the faint click of my front door closing as Nate leaves, I let Boo out the back for one last pee break onto the tiny patch of grass my real estate agent called a "hidden city gem" just so he could charge me five grand over the initial asking price. Staring up at the stars while Boo makes a show of sniffing every square millimeter of the property in his quest for the perfect spot, I have half a mind to pull out my cellphone and dial Parker. The rage fraying my nerve endings needs an outlet — screaming at my big brother for giving Nate my brownstone key might just do the trick.

My cell screen glows blue-bright in the darkness as I click it on and look at the time.

Midnight. The witching hour.

Fitting, since I was just visited by a demon in black leather and combat boots.

It's barely dawn in Europe — Parker won't bother to answer, this early. My best friend, Lila, is no doubt out on the town at some fabulous party or another — chances of sober conversation at this time on a Friday night are nil. My father's away on yet another business trip — China or Japan, I think. He's gone so often, it's hard to keep his destinations straight.

I sigh deeply.

I've got a gorgeous house in Boston's most desirable neighborhood.

I've got more money in my trust fund than I'll ever know what to do with.

And I've got not one single person in my entire phone contact list that I can call, right now.

I wonder fleetingly if it *had* been an intruder tonight, instead of Nate, if I really had fallen, cracked open my head on a coffee table, and died of an improbable aneurism... how long would it take the people in my life to notice?

A day?

A week?

A month?

Could I just disappear one instant, like a star winking out of existence, without anyone close enough to realize I'd gone?

Poof! Phoebe West evaporates in a puff of stardust and smoke.

One less bright dot on the far-reaching edges of the universe. Already so far removed from everyone peering upward, it could take ages for anyone to recognize my absence.

I shiver in the damp April air, hugging my arms closer around me. It does nothing to warm the lonesome chill inside my chest.

Maybe I should call *him*. The devil incarnate.

Incar-Nate.

Dial him up — quite brave, though the safe separation of a phone line — and unleash all the sassy, intelligent retorts I thought of only after the door closed behind him, when they were of no use to me. Tell him he has no business butting into my life. That I don't care how sexy he is, or that he makes me feel more alive than anyone on earth has ever managed to, or that just his presence in my space is nearly enough to make me combust.

(Okay, not that last part.)

It doesn't matter — I couldn't call him, even if I wanted to. I don't have his number anymore.

Lila convinced me to delete it last spring, asserting it wasn't remotely healthy to stare at someone's name in your contact list, willing the phone to ring for years on end. She was probably right.

I climb the stairs, Boo at my heels, seeking the solace of my bed.

I don't find it.

Instead, I toss and turn for hours, thinking about him. About hate. About lust. About love.

God, the love I have — *had!* — for that man.

For years it burnt me up, broke me down. Images flash through my mind — I try to block them out, but the memories are too strong.

Nate, passing me a toothbrush after Parker put food coloring in my cereal and turned my teeth bright green.

Nate, knocking the schoolyard bully into the dirt after he called me a nasty name in second grade.

Nate, teaching me to ride a bike in our long, curving driveway, his arms strong and steady as he ran at my side.

Nate, patching my scraped palms and bleeding knees when I toppled onto asphalt.

Nate, making me burned mac 'n' cheese on the stove when Parker was at soccer practice and Dad was busy working.

Nate, hugging me close after he found me sobbing on the back lawn by the maple tree, a dead bird in my hands.

Nate, holding my hand so tight I thought my fingers would break as we watched my mother's casket lowered into the earth.

Goddammit! Now I'm crying like a loser at two in the morning, with only Boo to witness my humiliation.

I know there's about a snowball's chance in hell that I'm going to fall asleep at this point, so I climb out of bed and pad down the hall to the guest room. When I reach the closet I grab the case, flick open the clasps, and a second later, feel the utter relief of smooth wood beneath my hands.

My violin.

I don't care that it's late or that I'll be tired in the morning. I position it just so beneath my chin, rotating my shoulder until

I've found the playing posture I've been perfecting since I was five years old and my mother placed a string instrument in my tiny hands. The bow is light as air between my fingers as I lift it to slide across the strings. The mournful wail, melancholy and ethereal, vibrates through me from the tips of my fingers to the soles of my feet.

A mindless sense of peace settles over me as I find my rhythm, plucking out notes like my life depends on it.

I don't use music. I've played this piece by heart for years.

Lux Aeterna.

Not a classic. By no means Mozart or Beethoven.

But I'm not playing for crowds or accolades. I'm playing for myself.

The bow moves faster and faster, my fingers gliding over the strings with such intensity I can't think about anything except which note comes next. I play until Nate is pushed from my head, the melody of his touch replaced by crescendos and cadenzas. Until every word he spoke tonight — so intent, so electric — is forced from my memory.

The notes fly out, my fingers a blur of motion, and I close my eyes, wishing I could stop seeing him in my mind. The way he looked — all lithe grace and dark promise. And the way he looked at *me* — with anger, mostly, but those undeniable flashes of something foreign in his eyes couldn't have been entirely my imagination.

Conflict.

Pianissimo.

Restraint.

Mezzo piano.

Lust.

Forte.

I strike the last note, breathless and exhausted from my efforts. My hands shake as I place the instrument back in its case.

It's the best I've played in ages, and I couldn't care less. All I can think of is Nate. Of the fact that no amount of musical distraction can push him from my thoughts. And undeniably, of the lust in his eyes when they flickered down to my mouth for a fractured instant.

I saw it there, in the depths of his gaze, before he buried it away beneath layers of icy indifference. Just a flash, just a split second of clarity, but I saw it and I know what it meant.

On some level — and I'm not sure how deep that level is — he feels it, too. The magnetic pull between us.

Finally he feels it, too. Even if he can't admit it.

Part of me wants to spin in dizzy circles around the room, screaming to the heavens.

YES! NATE ISN'T TOTALLY UNAFFECTED BY ME! ALL HOPE IS NOT LOST! I MAY FINALLY ACHIEVE ORGASM AND AVOID DYING AN OLD, CELIBATE NUN!

The rest of me wants to climb back in bed, yank my Egyptian cotton sheets up over my face, and never come out.

NO! IT'S TOO LATE! HE WAITED TOO LONG! AFTER ALL THESE YEARS OF TORTURE, HE CAN'T JUST FLIP A SWITCH, THE BASTARD! NOT WHEN I'VE FINALLY DECIDED TO MOVE ON AND FORGET ABOUT HIM!

Sigh.

I walk slowly back to my room, feeling dazed and dejected. Boo is experiencing none of my split-personality disorder. He's snoozing soundly at the end of my bed, nestled in a mountain of throw pillows. When I grab him and cuddle him close to my chest, his eyes flicker open to shoot a resentful glare in my direction and he promptly squirms away with a toss of his tiny head.

Christ, even my dog doesn't want to sleep with me.

Maybe I should get a cat. Then my forever-alone status as a spinster will truly be complete.

I'd laugh if it weren't so goddamned sad.

———

"...SO, he basically broke into my house. Then he *yelled* at me. How messed up is that?"

Even two full weeks later, the memory of that night still burns through me like wildfire — singing my nerve endings, quickening my breath, sending my heart into a pounding, painful rhythm inside my chest.

Striving for composure, I take a sip of my drink — a sinfully sweet tequila-based concoction the bartender at *Lolita* whipped up for me — and eye my best friend, Delilah "Lila" Sinclair, across the table. Strawberry-blonde head bowed, plush bottom lip trapped between her mega-white teeth, she's totally concentrated on the cellphone in her hands. Not even attempting to listen to me.

"Apparently, he has Parker's key to my place." I forge on, pathetically determined to share my story with the girl who, as my best friend, is supposed to give a damn about this stuff. Or, you know, at the very least *pretend* to give a damn. "And he refused to give it back. Total jackass."

"Mmm," she murmurs distractedly. "Totally."

"Lila?"

"Yeah?" A secret smile plays on her lips as her fingers tap out another text message.

"Did you hear me?"

Her eyes dart up to mine for a fraction of a second. "Nate came. Has Parker's key. Total jackass." She rolls her eyes like *I'm* the one being inconsiderate. "I'm listening, Phoebe. Jeeze."

Before I've had time to respond, her eyes fall back to the screen and she's typing again.

I fight the urge to toss my drink at her.

Lila's been my best friend since... forever. I don't even

remember meeting her. I just know she's been there through it all — every bad hair day and broken heart, every embarrassing moment and important milestone. Twenty odd years, three graduations (four, if you count pre-school), countless petty fights, so many shared secrets it's a wonder we still have anything to talk about... and here we are. Still friends, after all this time. Even if she does drive me crazy on a regular basis. Like right now, when she's blatantly tuning out every word of the story she begged to hear only minutes ago.

I take another sip and try again. "Anyway, I told him to get the hell out of my house."

She doesn't respond. I watch her fingers move again.

Tap, tap, tap.

Frustration stirs to life in my veins. "And then..." I drop my voice to a low, sultry whisper and lean across the table. "I pulled my dress up over my head, told him I was a virgin, and asked him to *teach me* like Lexi did to Sloan back in the good old *Grey's Anatomy* days, before Shonda went completely off the rails and killed all my favorite characters."

"Mmm."

My voice goes so breathy it could make a porn star blush. "So, he threw me down on the floor and ravaged me within an inch of my life."

"Mhm." *Tap, tap, tap.* "That's nice, Phoebe."

"Now, I'm pregnant with his love child. If it's a girl, I'm thinking we'll name her Lila." I tilt my head in contemplation. "Or something truly embarrassing, like *Chrysanthemum.* Or *Lemon.* Or maybe *Butterfly.* A healthy amount of humiliation is good for a kid growing up in this Everyone-Gets-A-Trophy generation, don't you think?"

She finally looks up at me, features twisting in confusion. "Wait, *what?*"

"Never mind." I pop open my clutch, grab a few bills, and lay them down on the tabletop. "I'm tired, Lila. Think I'm going to call it a night."

"But we just got here!" Her voice is petulant and her big brown eyes are glossy, pleading. I recognize it instantly — her famous puppy-dog look. It's broken the resolve of more men than I could ever count. "Don't go. I want to hear about Knox."

"No, you don't." I shake my head. "You want to text whatever new piece of man candy has caught your attention this week. And that's fine. But I would rather eat a full serving of my own hair than sit here like an idiot, talking to myself while you do it."

"Okay, okay! I'm sorry. Look — phone's going away." She shoves her cell in her purse, a tiny flicker of regret flashing over her features as she zips it closed, and lifts her eyes to mine. "See? All gone."

I stare at her fingers, which have begun to tap an anxious beat against the tabletop. "Are you having cellular separation anxiety?"

"It'll pass." She swallows a sip of her margarita. "So, Knox finally showed up, huh?"

Lila always calls him Knox. In fact, pretty much everyone on the planet calls him Knox. Except me. To me, he's always been Nate. Always will be.

I nod. "Yes, but not for any of the reasons I wanted him to. For instance, to declare his undying love for me. Or to dust that really hard-to-reach area above my stove. Oh! Or to move my fridge, so I could clean behind it." I narrow my eyes. "Come to think of it, I don't need a relationship at all. I just need a tall man to occasionally lift large objects and help with housework."

"Men don't help with housework. Men *say* they'll help with housework in exchange for sex, but then the stairs end up half-vacuumed and there's hand soap in the dishwasher and all the windows have paper towel streaks, and you end up having to do it all yourself anyway. Then, after giving him the sex he did *not* earn, you get to spend the rest of your married lives listening to him throw *that one day he vacuumed* in your face every time you accuse him of not pulling his weight."

My eyebrows lift in amused speculation. Lila's never been in a relationship in her life.

"Um…" She shrugs, slightly embarrassed by her rant. "That's what my sisters say, anyway."

"Right." I fight a laugh. "Well, Nate didn't do any of my housework. Nor did he show up outside my door like that guy in *Love Actually* with a sign that says, 'To me, you are perfect.' Nor did he apologize or even *pretend* to be civil as he barked orders after ten years of selective mutism."

"I'm guessing he didn't pop your cherry, either," Lila announces loudly, drawing glances from several men at the surrounding tables.

"Could you say that any louder? I don't think the bartender on the lower level heard you. *Oh!* Maybe I could find you a bull-horn so you can broadcast it to the entire bar…"

She rolls her eyes. "It's nothing to be embarrassed about. And if it's really such an issue, there are plenty of men who'd be more than happy to take care of that little problem for you."

"You mean Steve, the guy who watches Boo and waters my plants when I go away for the weekend?" My nose wrinkles. "He smells like tea tree oil and I think he still lives with his mom."

I grimace at the thought and take a large sip of my drink.

"No." She leans in, eyes alight with mischievous thoughts. "I mean Duncan."

I nearly snort alcohol through my nose. "Your brother?" I choke, trying to catch a breath.

"Maybe." A coy smile twists Lila's lips. "He's asked about you, the last few times we've done lunch. And now that he's moved back from California…"

"I haven't seen him since he puked in my purse after the Sadie Hawkins dance."

Her eyes narrow defensively. "Well, he's grown up. He runs his own company — some kind of social media startup. He's very successful."

I force myself not to scoff. Every rich kid with a trust fund has a startup, these days, just for the thrill of calling themselves CEO. Whether they actually do any work in that position... *Debatable.*

"That's great," I say, hoping the words don't sound as lackluster as they feel coming out of my mouth.

"You could do a lot worse, Phoebe. Duncan is wealthy, nice, good-looking, and — unlike that other asshole you've set your heart on — he's *interested*. If you give him a chance, I know you two will hit it off."

I try not to twitch. Lila has always harbored a cliché fantasy that one day her best friend and her brother will get married, and we'll all live happily ever after in adjacent mansions on Nantucket with a brood of children.

Let's just say... it's a dream I've never shared.

In fact... let's *also* say I'd rather wear perfume scented like the Boston Bruin's hockey locker room for a straight week than go out on another date with Duncan.

"Maybe," I murmur noncommittally.

"Wow, Phee, that was *so* enthusiastic."

"Sorry. It's just—"

"Knox." She sighs deeply. "I know."

"Believe me, I wish it *weren't* Nate. I wish it were anyone *but* Nate. But he's like..."

"An STD." Lila nods sagely.

"What?"

"Irritating. Indisputably linked to your lady parts. Can go

years without making an appearance. And ultimately... incurable."

"Wow. That was beautiful, Lila."

"I try." She grins. "So, let me see if I've got this straight." She begins ticking off points on her fingertips as she speaks. "You finally take my advice and go out with another man. Then, like clockwork, Knox shows up at your house. He tells you not to see said man anymore in that scary, intense way of his. And then you kick his butt to the curb. Right?"

I nod.

"If I wasn't such a good friend, this is the part where I'd scream *I TOLD YOU SO* at the top of my lungs."

CHAPTER 5

ONE OF THESE DAYS, I'M GOING TO BURN THAT
FUCKING FIELD HOCKEY SKIRT.

*Nathaniel Knox, upon returning home from college and
finding his best friend's sister all grown up.*

I BLINK IN CONFUSION. "What are you talking about?"

"Do I really have to spell it out for you?"

"Apparently."

"God, it's like dealing with an Amish girl on her Rumspringa.
Starting from square fucking one." Lila shakes her head and pins
me with a steely look. "Phoebe. Honey. He was *jealous.*"

I snort. "No, he wasn't."

"He *was.*" She sighs, deeply exasperated. "Why else would

he have shown up *that night*? As in, the first night you've ever heeded my sage advice and gone out with a hot guy?"

"*Trust* me," I choke out. "Nate didn't come over because of some kind of long-buried romantic feelings. Parker probably asked him to check in on me."

"Oh, my poor, sweet, dim-witted little virgin." Lila shakes her head. "Have I taught you *nothing*?"

"I don't follow." My eyes narrow. "And I may be dim-witted, but you've blown a goddamned fuse."

"He. Was. *Jealous!*" She casts her eyes heavenward. "You're worse than Amish. Swear to god, I'm living an Anne of Green Fucking Gables episode. *Anne's First Crush.*"

"Hey!"

"Phee, get with the program. He wants your bod."

"Did you just say *he wants your bod*?"

Her mouth opens, closes, and opens again. A hint of a blush colors her cheeks. "Maybe."

"Wasn't that the slogan of those horrible '90s commercials for men's body mist? You know, the kind that smells like testosterone mixed with lighter fluid?"

"BOD spray." Lila nods. "Or, as I like to call it, *Eau de Jersey Shore.*"

"Eau de Seventh Grade Boy," I counter.

She giggles. "Eau de Small Penis."

We both dissolve into laughter. I'm wiping tears from the corner of my eye when Lila's hands clap together abruptly, startling me. My gaze flies back to hers and I find she's staring at me, all humor forgotten.

"Hey! Focus! No more tangents." She leans forward. "We were talking about Knox and your deluded belief that he came over out of some kind of brotherly duty."

"It's not deluded; it's the truth. He came because he thought I was in danger with Brett. Which, it turns out, I was. Have you seen the news? He's kind of a minor-league sociopath."

A few days after Nate's surprise visit, I logged onto the web and was immediately assaulted by news stories about my gala date.

BRETT CROFT ARRESTED IN CONNECTION TO KIDNAPPING

CHARGES BROUGHT AGAINST BILLIONAIRE CROFT HEIR

FAMILY FUED: CROFT COUSIN'S SECRET VENDETTA

Apparently, no matter how much money you have, it's still not enough to bury kidnapping and attempted murder charges. Let's just say, I was more than relieved that I hadn't called Brett for a second date.

"But he looks like Ian Somerhalder," Lila protests. "How can someone so hot be so evil? It's against the laws of nature."

"Lila, I don't care how hot he is. Brett Croft is bad news. He was arrested, like, two days after our first date for basically trying to kill his cousin's girlfriend, Gemma — who is really freaking nice, by the way. The story's been in every single newspaper. Which you'd know if you ever bothered to read one."

"First of all, I follow the news. Sometimes. When forced." She fights a smile. "And, secondly, you should be excited. Brush with death, and all. It's like you had dinner with Jeffrey Dahmer and walked away without becoming one of the entrees. You deserve some kind of medal." Her eyes narrow. "Or at the very least, several sessions with a renowned therapist."

"Thanks, Lila." I roll my eyes. "That's *so* helpful."

She cocks her head to one side. "Just because he orchestrated a kidnapping and tried to ruin his cousin's life doesn't necessarily mean he's a sociopath. Maybe he's just... emotionally damaged and in need of a good woman to straighten him out."

"Now who's the dim-witted one? Are you really falling for the damaged bad-boy trope?"

"You know I have a weakness for pretty boys with secret pain."

"Lila!"

"Shhh." She sips her margarita and examines me like a lab specimen. "This is the part where I dispense more sage wisdom."

"Honestly, I think I've had my fill."

"Too bad." She rubs her hands together. "You ready?"

"No."

"Okay, here it comes." She shuts her eyes and pulls in a deep breath, like she's about to execute a particularly difficult yoga position. Before I can flee, her eyes snap back open and she turns the full force of her stare on me. Her voice is intent, her glossy brown eyes pin me to the spot.

"You want Nathaniel Knox. You've wanted him for as long as I can remember. True or false?"

I don't answer.

"True or false?"

"You're really going to make me say it?"

Her eyes narrow.

"Fine," I mumble noncommittally. "True. Whatever."

"That's what I thought." She smiles. "You've spent the better part of your life either gaga in love with the guy or out-of-your-gourd pissed at him for not loving you back. You can't get over him. You don't *want* to get over him. You won't even *try* to get over him. Frankly, it's a little pathetic."

"That's not true," I protest. "I want to get over him."

Lila's face contorts in a skeptical look. "Uh huh."

"Lila, I'm serious. I don't want to keep living like this — stuck in limbo, wanting a man who'll never love me back. Frankly, I hate him for doing this to me for so long, for reducing me to this weak little girl every time he's around. He walks back into my life and suddenly I'm fourteen again, gawky and awkward and unsure." I swallow. "I don't want to be that person. I'm *not* that person."

"I know you aren't, hon." Lila's face is suddenly concerned. "Why didn't you tell me you've been feeling like this?"

I shrug. "It makes me feel weak. *He* makes me feel weak. Why would I want to talk about that? Love is supposed to lift you up, not tear you back to your humiliating, orthodontic middle school years." I take a large sip. "I hate him. Officially."

She sighs. "Phoebe, I hate to break this to you, but hating someone and being over them are not the same thing."

Damn. I knew she was going to say that.

"You either spend all your time thinking about how much you love him, or all your time mulling over how much you hate him. Either way, he takes up all your mental energy. That's not healthy, hon. When you're over someone, you don't think about them. *Period*. Like my first boyfriend, Eric Sanders, who turned out to be gay and broke my heart in seventh grade. I don't think about him at all. And my second boyfriend, Bill Nelson—"

"Lila! Please get to the point."

"Fine, *jeeze*, I didn't realize I was out for drinks with Grumpy Cat," she mutters. "My point is... It's time you either stop obsessing over him altogether and move the hell on with your life... or stop waiting around for him to wake the fuck up and realize he wants you too."

Images of sodden boob-stuffing and puke-filled purses flash through my mind.

"Because trying to get his attention has gone *so* well for me, in the past."

"Oh, come on. You haven't really tried anything for *years*. You've been too pissed off and he's been god knows where, doing that freaky Blackwater shit he's so good at." She swirls her margarita glass. "He moved back here permanently over a year ago and you've seen him, what? *Once* in all that time?"

"Twice."

"Whatever." She rolls her eyes. "Frankly, this whole pining-from-afar, *I-hate-your-guts-but-I'd-like-to-ride-your-face* thing you've got going is *not* working for you."

"That was... visual."

"Bottom line: what if Brett *had* gone psycho and killed you? What if you'd died without laying everything on the line, without looking Knox in the eyes and just saying, flat out, *I want you, I've always wanted you. Please do naughty things to me, ASAP.*"

My eyebrows lift.

"Okay, maybe not those exact words." She sighs. "But seriously, honey — something's gotta give. And, in this case... it's you. Either give *in* to your passion or give *up* on him altogether. But don't keep doing this to yourself. You deserve someone who's capable of loving you back. And, if I'm being totally honest... I don't think Knox will ever be that guy for you. He's too damaged, too dark. The look in his eyes..." She shudders. "It gives me the heebie-jeebies."

"The *heebie-jeebies*? What are you, five years old?"

She continues, unfazed. "Looking at him is like staring down a well. Nothing on the surface, but a hell of a lot of scary shit hiding underneath."

I know what she means — I've always thought of Nate's eyes as a black hole.

Dark, bottomless, and likely to swallow you up if you lean too close.

"I thought you had a thing for pretty boys with secret pain," I say teasingly, trying to make her laugh.

"He's not pretty — he's *haunted*." Her eyes find mine, deadly serious. "And his pain isn't secret, honey. It's brimming over."

I swallow hard, unable to contradict her words.

"Phee, be honest with me for a second. Do you really think a man like that — a man who's never loved a goddamn thing in his life except maybe the sound of gunfire and the spilling of his enemies' blood — is capable of a functional relationship? Of being a husband? A father?" Lila shakes her head. "I'm sorry, honey, I just don't see it. The only things Knox will ever be able to give you are the greatest orgasms of your life... and a big, fat crack through the middle of your heart when he walks away. You deserve more than that. More than *him*. And I love you too much to sit by the sidelines and watch him destroy you."

I stare at her, heart pounding painfully in my chest. Lila's never been Nate's biggest fan, but she's not usually so vocal about her dislike. She means well, but that doesn't make it less painful to hear.

Sad as it is to admit, I don't have an answer to her questions. I don't know if Nate could ever give me more than physical gratification. For as long as I've known him, he's never been in a relationship. Never expressed any interest in one. I don't know if normal things like marriage, or houses with white picket fences, or squirmy babies with chubby little fingers, will ever be a factor in his future.

"I just want you to be happy, Phee." Lila grabs my hand and squeezes. "And I don't think that's ever going to happen until you move on from that intense bastard. Even if you don't want to."

"I do want to." I clear my throat lightly. "I'm done being this pathetic girl obsessed with a man she can never have. I do want to move on. I do want a normal life with someone who can love me back. I'm over him. Or... I *want* to be over him. So bad. I just..." My voice wavers and I take a deep breath to steady it. "I don't know how. How do you stop wanting someone you've dreamed of for most of your life? He's a habit I don't know how to break."

"Are you sure you're ready to give up on him?"

"Yes," I lie, wishing the words felt as convincing in my mind as they did leaving my mouth. "I'm done waiting for Nathaniel Knox to love me back. It's time I focused on loving myself, instead."

TWO ROUNDS LATER, we've cooked up a plan to help me get over Nate. And by *we* I mostly mean Lila.

"I don't think this is a good idea," I say for the tenth time, my words a bit slurred.

"You agreed!" Lila protests. "You can't back out now."

It's true — I had agreed. But what seemed like a good idea forty minutes ago feels a touch too real, now that I've agreed to it. Lila had sounded so convincing...

I replay our conversation in my mind as we wait for the bill.

She leans across the table and speaks in a hushed voice. "I'll tell you from experience, dating a million other dudes to forget about him isn't going to work, not after all this time... he's embedded too deeply to be pushed out of your heart with only the force of another man's penis."

"Ew!"

"There *is* a way to get over him." Her head tilts as she stares at me, a contemplative expression on her face. "But you won't like it."

"How do you know?"

She gives me the look — the one that says *honey, I've known you most of your life. I know you better than you know yourself.*

I sigh deeply. "Just tell me."

"Are you sure?"

"Lila."

"Fine! But don't bite my head off." She tries — and fails — to hide a smile. "You won't get over him until you've taken him for a spin."

"What do you mean?"

She glances up at the ceiling, as if seeking guidance. "God, it's like talking to Rory Gilmore, season *one*. Except she had more sense when it came to boys."

"Lila."

Meeting my eyes again, she grins. "Sometimes, the best way to get over someone emotionally is to get under them." She pauses a beat. "Physically."

"Nakedly?" I squeak.

She laughs. "All I'm saying is... give that bike a ride around the block *once* and you'll realize it's not all that special. There are plenty of other bikes in the shop with cushier seats, and better bells and whistles. Some of them have seven speeds and when those gears click into place.... *Damn*, it's the best ride of your life, if you know what I mean."

I stare at her blankly. "I have absolutely no idea what you mean."

"Sex, Phoebe. I'm talking about *sex*."

My mouth drops open. "You think if I *sleep with him*, it'll be easier to forget about him?"

"That's exactly what I just said."

"Actually, you gave me a very convoluted metaphor about bicycles and—"

"Phoebe!" She cuts me off. "Just trust me. Guys like Knox... it's all about the allure. The initial attraction. Once that wears off... you'll realize it was nothing but infatuation. *Lust*, not love."

"That makes no sense."

"Well, you've tried everything else — including pretending he didn't exist for ten years — and none of it has ever worked.

You're still as bonkers for him as you were that time in seventh grade when you walked in on him buck naked in the pool house with his hands—"

"AH!" I cut her off. "You swore you'd never mention that! And I am *not* bonkers for him. I hate him, remember?"

She snorts. "*Riiiight.*"

"Lila."

"I don't know why you're giving me such a hard time. Of the two people at this table, I'm the only one with real, actual relationship experience."

"One night stands with half the male population of Boston is certainly *experience*. But I don't think it qualifies as *relationship* experience."

"Do you want my advice, or not?"

"Not really."

"Fine." She pushes back her chair in preparation to stand. "Good luck getting over Knox on your own!"

"Wait!" I say instantly.

She freezes, a smug smile on her face, and settles back into her seat. "That's what I thought."

"So." My voice is grudging. "You suggest...what, exactly?"

She gives me a look. "Seduce him. Screw his brains out. And then walk away without any questions or regrets, finally free to move on with someone who deserves you." She leans in. "Make *him* suffer over *you* for once."

"That simple, huh?" I ask skeptically.

"That simple."

I consider her words for a moment. "Even if you're right, I wouldn't really know where to start. When it comes to seduction..." I search for the right words. "I'm sort of..."

"Virginal?"

I glare at her.

"Hey, don't shoot the messenger." She holds up her hands in surrender. "And your Virgin Mary status doesn't really matter. That's why you have me. I'm basically an expert at catching men. Keeping them, on the other hand..." Her grin twists into a grimace and a tiny pang of sadness flashes through her eyes. She quickly buries it. "Just think about it, okay?"

I fall silent, mind reeling with possibilities, heart racing inside my chest.

Could I really do it? Go after Nate? Seduce him, sleep with him, and then walk away, like an addict who promises to quit after just one last drink, *that* final drink, *the one they need before they can finally get clean?*

He won't give me forever... but maybe he'll give me one night, just enough to sate my desire and allow me to move on, scot-free, with someone new. And, as an added bonus, in the process, maybe I'll make him taste regret when *he* has to watch *me* walk away for once.

It's actually kind of a perfect plan.

I'll get my night of passion. Then, I'll get my life back, unencumbered by longing from someone who's never felt the same.

I just hope it doesn't cost me my heart, in the process.

Lila might think it's just infatuation — primal, surface-level attraction — that will go away once I've banked the flames burning inside me. But I know the truth — what I feel for Nate is a hell of a lot more. A hell of a lot *deeper*. And once I get a taste of him...once I cross that line... I worry I'll be more addicted than ever. A junkie, strung out on heartbreak.

Lila's words taunt me.

You've tried everything else — including pretending he didn't exist for ten years — and none of it has ever worked...

At this point, she's right... I don't have any other options.

"So?" Lila's voice snaps me back into the present. "Which is it? Giving up or giving in?"

I swallow hard. "Do I have to decide now?"

"You've had nearly twenty-four years to think about it. Now's as good a time as any, don't you agree?"

I clench my fists so hard I'm surprised my nails don't break the skin of my palms.

"Tick, tock." Lila stares at me. "Life is slipping away as we speak. The sooner you decide, the sooner you can seduce him, the sooner your real life can start with someone new."

"Fine," I whisper, voice shaking. "I'm in."

Lila cups one hand over her ear and leans across the table. "Sorry, what was that?"

"I'm in," I repeat, a fraction louder.

"Again?"

"Crap on rye," I grit out. "I'm *in*! I'm so *in* it makes me want to die."

"So, you'll listen to me? Let me be your seduction guru? Your sex coach? Your erotic instructor?" She grins. "You'll follow my flawless plan to trap, tag, and tap the elusive Nathaniel Knox?"

"He's not an animal, you sociopath." I stare at her. "Maybe you and Brett Croft would be perfect for each other, after all."

"Oh, shut up." Her voice is laced with excitement — she's practically *giddy* — and I wonder, not for the first time, if Lila likes living on the edge a bit *too* much. "Step One in our plan of attack — you have to do it again."

"Date a sociopath?"

"No, idiot. You have to make Knox jealous." Her eyes gleam. "And, thankfully, driving men crazy is one of my specialties. When I'm done with you, he'll be eating out of the palm of your hand."

I nearly choke on my sip of tequila. "You do realize this is *Nate* we're talking about?"

"Honey." Her grin widens. "The wildest stallions are the most fun to break."

"Sociopath," I mutter, taking another gulp of my drink.

Lila claps again. "Ohh, this is going to be so much fun!"

Fun is one word for it.

Personally, I think *terrifying, mortifying,* and *nauseating* fit the scenario better.

CHAPTER 6

I ONLY CUT CARBS WHEN I'M USING A PIZZA CUTTER.

Phoebe West, considering the Atkins diet.

"HELLO?"

"I told Chase this was going to happen. Told him! But did he listen? Noooo." A familiar female voice bursts over the line, far too peppy for this time of morning. "*Open your own gallery,* he said. *It will be fun,* he said." She snorts. "Well, *it'll be a freaking disaster* is what *I* said, but does he listen? Nope. Why listen to Gemma? She's only ever right... Oh, yeah! That would be *all the time.*"

"Gemma?" I ask, rubbing bleary eyes and feeling like my head might explode.

"No, it's Danny DeVito." I can practically hear her rolling her eyes. "Yes, it's Gemma. Keep up, will you?"

I sit up in bed, phone pressed to my ear, and glance at Boo with my eyebrows raised.

Don't look at me. You know I like my beauty rest, he conveys, flashing a row of pointy white teeth as his mouth widens in an adorable doggie yawn. His head cocks to the side as he pins me with a pleading look. *Though, now that we're awake... time for walkies?*

I shake my head at the dog and try to focus.

"Gemma, did we have plans?" I murmur, voice still scratchy with sleep.

"What do you think of calla lilies?" she asks, totally ignoring me. "Too macabre? Do they scream funeral parlor?"

"Um... lilies are nice?"

"You're right," she continues. "Too macabre. Thanks, Phee."

I blink slowly. "I have no idea what's happening right now."

"You and me both, girl. See you tonight!"

She clicks off without another word.

"Bye," I murmur to no one.

What the frack?

I stare at the disconnected phone in my hand for a few moments, totally stupefied, then collapse back against my pillows with a huff. My eyes slide closed. *Maybe I can fall back asleep for a few more minutes...*

The thought has barely left my mind when I feel Boo's weight settle in the middle of my chest. A second later, something warm and wet darts out and licks the length of my cheek.

"Not the face, Boo!" I grumble.

He ignores me.

FEET STUFFED INTO SLIPPERS, silk bathrobe wrapped tightly around my body, I fight off shivers as I wait for Boo to do his business. Which, I know from experience, could take anywhere between three minutes and seventy years. I take a big swig of my coffee, hoping it'll ward off the chill while kickstarting my brain into gear.

Gemma's wake-up call came far too early. I consider redialing her, just to grumble about the indecency of ringing someone at six on a Saturday morning, but I know she won't answer. Her gallery, *Karma*, opens tonight, and I'm sure she'll be running around like a fangirl at Comic Con all day, trying to get everything done before time runs out. Then again, even if the opening wasn't tonight, she probably wouldn't answer. I've never met someone so unreliable with a cellphone in my entire life.

In the few short weeks since we met, I've witnessed her slaughter four different iPhones. One fell in front of a taxi as we crossed Comm Ave on our way back from brunch. Another slipped from her grip and plunged straight down a sewer grate on Newbury as she flipped off a rude cabbie. I think she flushed the third one down the toilet at the penthouse loft she shares with her mega-hot boyfriend, Chase. And I have no idea what she did with the fourth one, though I'm sure it came to a colorful end, like its brothers before it.

It's become a cycle, of sorts — she'll violently massacre one phone; Chase will quietly replace it with a new one. And so it goes.

Totally symbiotic.

This would be weird, if it were anyone else. But it's *Gemma*. The girl flies through life like a kite without a string, driving everyone around her crazy — including Chase. (Who, I might add, is nothing like his cousin — in either looks or personality. Brett Croft is dark, Chase Croft is light. Like Loki and Thor. Or, if we're sticking with the Somerhalder theory... in vampire-speak, if Brett is Damon Salvatore, Chase is Carlisle Cullen. Just, you know, hotter and not at all sparkly.)

Shit, did I just make a Twilight reference?

I will spontaneously combust in shame in three... two... one...

Gemma and I became fast friends after we met at the gala last month. I made a point to visit her in the hospital after her brush with death (it's a long story) and as soon as she was released, she called and asked me to brunch — which was basically three hours of drinking mimosas and dishing over Croft family drama. I'm not entirely sure why she decided to insert herself into my life — she already has a group of seriously kick-ass friends — but she seems hell-bent on getting to know me.

I'm hell-bent on letting her.

Gemma is a hoot to be around. Witnessing the sheer chaos of her life is better than HBO. Hell, give me a bag of popcorn (extra butter) and a large Diet Coke, and I could binge-watch for days.

On our third girl-date, she got me drunk on Old Fashioneds at Top of the Hub (the panoramic bar on the top level of the Prudential Center, where the only thing steeper than the views are the cocktail prices) and I spilled *everything*. My love for Knox. His indifference. The night he stopped by my place. Lila's plans to help me get over him. My fears that the closest I'll ever get to a man seeing me naked is that one time Boo jumped into the shower with me.

Sigh.

She was sympathetic and, like Lila, determined to fix things. Though, I have a feeling Gemma is more interested in playing matchmaker than helping me move on. In fact, she's a tad *too* excited by the idea of me and Nate dating, as evidenced by the way her eyes lit up as she squealed, *Ohmigod! You and Knox? Together?! That is the cutest freaking thing I've ever heard! And once, I heard a baby panda sneeze at the zoo!*

I tried to get her on board with the plan to *love-him-and-*

CROSS THE LINE 67

leave-him — fornicate-and-forget? (I'm still working on the lingo) — but whenever I bring it up, she just nods with a dreamy look in her eyes, likely planning the color schemes of Nate and my wedding. Somehow my love life, which was nonexistent until about a month ago when he showed up at my house, has been snatched from my grip and placed into the control of two crazy women. Between Lila's grand plans pulling me one direction and Gemma's Yenta-schemes pushing me in another....

I'm totally fucked. And probably liable to get torn in half.

"Come on, Boo, be a man. Make a decision," I call into the crisp spring morning. "You'll never catch a bitch if your willie freezes off out here."

His head swings around and I swear, he narrows his eyes at me. Sometimes, I'm almost positive he understands English.

"Don't glare at me like that," I mutter. "I'm just looking out for your welfare."

Finally, he picks a spot and unleashes a seemingly impossible amount of pee for such a small creature. No wonder he's so sassy — he's literally full of piss and vinegar.

Back inside, I suck down another mug of java and check my phone. It doesn't surprise me to see three waiting text messages.

Lila: *Are you awake? We need to strategize for the gallery opening tonight.*

Lila: *A little birdy told me Knox will definitely be there. Time to put Phase 1 into effect! Tactical plans include a sexy dress and killer heels.*

Lila: *Are you awake now?*

I roll my eyes.

After I agreed to let Lila commandeer my sex life (a plan she immediately christened S.H.A.G. — Seduction Help and Guidance) and assist me in getting over Nate for good (now known to all parties involved as S.P.A.N.K. — Severing Phoebe's Attachment to Nathaniel Knox) she's been making plans. Semi-terrifying plans, all of which are intended to aid me in my quest to seduce him. The only problem is... he isn't exactly cooperating. A month has passed and, to Lila's mounting frustration, no progress has been made. If anything, I think we're backsliding.

For instance, three weeks ago, she spent hours dolling me up for my first visit to Gemma and Chase's penthouse, totally convinced that Knox would be there, as he often does private security for Croft Industries.

He wasn't.

The only people at the loft were Gemma and her friend Shelby — dressed in pajamas, drinking wine like Napa Valley had just announced it was going through a dry spell, and shoving popcorn into their mouths as *How to Lose a Guy in 10 Days* played on the flat screen. It was safe to say they looked at me strangely when I showed up in a sparkly Roberto Cavalli mini skirt and my new black Prada pumps. Sure, everyone knows I'm a clotheshorse... but that was pushing it. Even for me.

The following week, Lila set me up on a truly awful blind date with a man named Kirk, who she vaguely introduced as a "friend of a friend." Since I'm pretty much her only friend, and I sure as hell didn't set *myself* up with a man who called to mind *Star Trek* for more reasons than just his name (really, the mustard yellow sweater was a poor choice) she wasn't fooling anyone.

I don't care if your intentions are pure, Lila — stop setting me up with creepy dudes you meet on the internet.

If her plan was to make Nate jealous, Kirk was *not* a good choice. Yes, he was handsome — but the man was dull as a box of sidewalk chalk. I've had more fulfilling conversations with Suki, the three-year-old toddler whose family lives in the brownstone next to mine. When the night came to a close, I begged off with a fake headache and walked home alone.

To no one's surprise, Nate was *not* waiting for me in my darkened living room, vibrating with intensity and warning me to stay away from Captain Kirk.

When her set-up failed, Lila resorted to her tried-and-true high school tactics, back in the days when we'd stake out her crush-of-the-week in my SUV, hunched low in our seats to avoid detection. I'm not sure why she thought this would be successful — it hadn't worked on the star quarterback six years ago, and it's not the kind of plan that improves with age. Still, she staged a drive-by at Knox Investigations, the low-slung black building in the Seaport district where Nate runs his private investigations business. I've never been inside and, to my knowledge, neither has Lila.... But that didn't stop her from riding past it *three times* before I realized what was happening and was able to wrestle the wheel from her grip.

Clearly she's getting desperate, since none of her normal schemes are working.

But tonight.... Oh, tonight is the game changer. For the first time since I — foolishly — agreed to follow her lead, she knows with one hundred percent certainty where Nate will be.

See, tonight's guest list is sprinkled with Boston's elite, all eager to drop an obscene amount of money on pieces of modern art —one more canvas for their vast collections. It'll be a star-studded affair, full of venomous socialites, scheming business-men, and pretentious French finger-food that, for all the allure of foie gras, can't hold a candle to pigs-in-blankets.

My natural habitat.

Anyway, the result of all these wealthy patrons gathered in one place means one thing: paparazzi.

Lots of it.

Between the crowd of reporters staked outside and the hundred or so attendees wandering around inside... Chase won't be taking any chances with Gemma's safety. And there's only one person he'd trust to run point when it comes to protecting the love of his life.

I'll give you a hint — rhymes with *hate*.

He'll definitely be there and, in Lila's mind, that amounts to one thing — her plans finally being set into motion.

Hence the series of increasingly urgent text messages on my phone. As I watch, my cell lights up with a new one.

LILA: ANSWER ME! Otherwise I'm coming over, kidnapping Boo, and holding him for ransom. You know I will.

GOD, all this scheming is messing with her head — she's becoming downright maniacal. I don't doubt her threats, though, so I tap out a response, a vindictive grin twisting my lips as my fingers move over the screen. After the torturous Captain Kirk incident... I can't stop myself from returning the favor when such a prime opportunity presents itself.

PHOEBE: Actually, I'm not feeling well... I don't think I'm going tonight.

MY PHONE RINGS IMMEDIATELY.

I laugh as I connect the call and lift it to my ear. Before I can get out a single word, Lila starts yelling.

"WHAT DO YOU MEAN, YOU AREN'T GOING?! This is the plan, you ungrateful cow! You're not backing out. I won't let you. Not after everything I've done for you! Not after all my hard work and advice and outfit planning and eyebrow shaping and *years* of straightening the back of your hair whenever you can't reach that fuzzy layer that hides underneath! No. Phoebe Evangeline West, you are going to that fucking gallery opening looking like the finest piece of ass Knox has ever seen, even if I have to *drag you there myself!* DO I MAKE MYSELF CLEAR?!"

Wow, she didn't even pause to take a breath.

"Lila—"

"I SAID *DO I MAKE MYSELF CLEAR?*"

"You're acting like a crazy person."

"You're the crazy one if you think I'll let you get cold feet!"

"My feet are actually quite warm, I'm wearing those sheep-skin L.L. Bean slippers Parker bought me for Christmas last year—"

"That's it! I'm coming over there and kicking your ass."

"Jesus Christ," I mutter. "I'm going to the opening! It was a joke! Please relax. No need to kick my ass."

Stony silence blasts across the line.

"Lila?" I suppress a laugh. "Still alive?"

"That was *not* funny."

"I don't know, I thought it was pretty amusing."

"I can still come over there and kick your ass."

I stop laughing instantly. Lila does Krav Maga. For *fun.* She could totally kick my ass.

"Sorry," I mutter, like a five-year-old forced to apologize for kicking her sister under the table at dinner.

"Apology accepted," she says breezily, threats of bodily harm already forgotten. "I have a dry-bar appointment at *Blo* tonight, so I can't help you get ready. Can I trust you to wear something scandalously hot without me there to run inter-ference?"

"Firstly, my closet is bigger than yours. Secondly, I've spent twenty-four years dressing myself. I think I can manage one night without you."

"Mhmm." She murmurs, as though she doesn't quite agree. "See you there. Seven. Don't be late!"

She clicks off.

"Bye," I say to dead air, for the second time in as many hours.

My life is so fucked.

CHAPTER 7

T‌RUE FRIENDS DON'T JUDGE ONE ANOTHER.
    T‌HEY JUDGE OTHER PEOPLE.
    T‌OGETHER.

Phoebe West, ruminating on friendship.

BY THE TIME seven rolls around, nervous butterflies have taken up residence in my gut. I watch Boston drift by through tinted glass in the back seat of the town car I hired for the night and try to ignore the damned winged demons flinging themselves at my stomach lining on five-second intervals. The sun has nearly set — its dying rays turn the Charles River into a copper mirror as we drive over the bridge to Cambridge. Shifting in my seat in a vain attempt to get comfortable, my eyes absently track the movement of Harvard crew teams, their oars moving in perfect tandem, their sleek boats gliding across the gleaming surface like water bugs on a lake.

The hands on my lap are so tightly clenched, my freshly manicured nails cut crescent-moons into my palms. I can feel the fine boning of my dress pressed tight against my ribs. For a split second, I think that thin fabric might be all that's holding my quick-beating heart inside my chest.

I don't know why I'm so nervous.

Okay, that's a lie.

I know exactly why I'm nervous.

Nate.

Just the thought of seeing him sends a thrill shooting through my nerve endings, makes every fine hair on my body stand up straight, evaporates every ounce of saliva from my mouth. I'm not even near him yet, but if I close my eyes I can almost feel his presence. That dark gaze. That gritty tone. The sinuous way he moves, like a panther gliding through shadow. All coiled power and restrained strength — held in total check, but unleashed at a moment's notice.

He's always moved like that, I suppose, but for the last few years I've…. Well, not *forgotten*. You can't forget a thing like that, not entirely. But, through Herculean effort, I've managed to push thoughts of sleek muscle and lithe strides to the back of my mind.

Seeing him again last month, though…

It was a stark reminder of his allure, of the pull I feel whenever I'm around him. Just one glance, one touch, one fractured instant with his chest pressed against mine and our eyes locked, and all those forbidden feelings shot straight back to the surface.

Maybe that's why he's been stalking my dreams, every night since. My eyes press closed as I replay some of the (seriously NSFW) images my subconscious mind has conjured into existence during the past few weeks — the ones that make me wake suddenly, sheets twisted around my legs, heart racing inside my chest, hair mussed against my pillow, sweaty hands gripping hot blankets. Wishing I could hold onto something that would hold me back.

I shiver against the leather seat and tell myself it's from the chilly AC vent blowing air on me.

Just dreams, Phoebe. I'm sure, in real life, sex with Nate isn't remotely as...

Athletic?

Orgasmic?

Bendy?

I'm startled out of my reverie when we pull up to the funky, brick waterfront building Gemma's chosen as the space for her gallery. Warm light spills out of the large bay windows over-looking the Charles. As usual, I've chosen to be fashionably late — which will make Lila about as happy as a middle-school girl with braces on picture day — and can see there are already plenty of people milling around on the second floor sampling appetizers, making small talk, and pretending to study the art on the walls. A gleaming silver sign caps the doublewide doorway, stamped with a single word in clean, lowercase font.

karma

The place looks somehow elegant and edgy at the same time, tastefully decorated in an industrial-chic style. I can't wait to get inside and congratulate Gemma on how well it turned out.

She initially wanted a small, intimate opening — a few close friends, some crackers, maybe a bottle of champagne or four. But any successful gallery needs the rubber-stamp approval of Boston's blue bloods... especially one like Karma, which is basically a non-profit in disguise.

Tricking people into giving back through the brokering of ostentatiously expensive art!

That's what Gemma says, anyway.

Every penny made on sales will be funneled into public

school art programs across the city. Thus, true to the gallery name, every purchase is an instant karma point — stocking classrooms with paintbrushes, supplying the salary for much-needed art teachers, changing the lives of kids who've never held so much as a colored pencil.

Apparently, Gemma came up with the idea while she was "lying around like a log in the hospital" — again, her words, not mine. That wasn't even two months ago. I'm not quite sure how she's managed to throw together the most exclusive event on Boston's social calendar in such a short time. (Chase probably had something to do with it — that man has a way of making things happen.)

With practiced trepidation, I eye the dozen or so reporters staked out on either side of the black carpet that's been rolled from the doors to the curb. Velvet ropes are all that hold their questions and camera flashes at bay. I watch as a middle-aged couple steps from a town car a few ahead of ours in the queue, posing for a picture with fake smiles plastered on their lips. They wait a few seconds until the shutters click down, then move into the building, instantly replaced by another carpet arrival.

Snooze.

I've been to enough of these events over the years that the cameras and the questions don't faze me much anymore. It used to be overwhelming — now, it's mostly just annoying. I'll glide by them, face set in a politely detached expression, and pause with my hip dropped and my legs positioned *just* so, ensuring the picture of me that appears on Page 6 tomorrow is flattering. And it *will* appear, no matter how much I wish it wouldn't. In this town, being Milo West's only daughter holds a certain amount of cachet.

Smile. Pose. Say "Oscar de la Renta" when they ask the inevitable, inexcusably sexist question about my attire.

Easy.

It wasn't always. I still remember the first time they shouted, "Miss West, who are you wearing tonight?" as I moved along a red carpet, squinting against the strobes and trying not to sweat into my Chanel couture. It was the year my father took Parker and me to the TIME 100 gala as his plus one — the year Milo West made the list as the 10th most influential man in the world, when he perfected streaming technology that made all prior fiber optic carriers look like dachshunds at a greyhound race. The year we went from run-of-the-mill rich to *oh-my-fucking-god-that's-a-lot-of-zeros* rich.

I was eight; Parker was twelve. He held my arm and moved way slower than he would've liked, just so I wouldn't trip over the low heels I hadn't quite figured out how to walk in yet. Without him to steady me, I'd have fallen flat on my face and disgraced the family.

As soon as we got back to the hotel that night he teased me about my bobbling gate, but he never said a word as he held me up on that damn carpet. Even though his own hands were shaking, he never let me waver. Silent, steady, strong. Always the good man in a storm, the one constant I could count on.

Trademark Parker.

God, I miss him. It's been months, since I've seen him. He's always loved to travel, but it seems his trips are getting longer and longer as we get older. Three weeks then three months then six months then a year. Galapagos, Croatia, Canary Islands, French Riviera. I worry one of these times he'll hop on the WestTech jet with a backpack, fly off into the sunset, and never come back.

The thought makes my throat constrict and my chest ache, so I push it away. Just in time, too — we've reached the front of the queue. I slip on my game face, steady my shoulders, and force myself not to blink when the chauffeur pulls open my door and offers me a hand into the explosion of camera flashes.

Miss West!

Phoebe!

Look this way!

Who are you wearing?

Is that Versace?

No date tonight, Miss West?

God, they're so predictable. I resist the urge to roll my eyes — lest I want to land in TMZ's next "CELEBRITY NIGHT-MARES!" segment, like that unfortunate time a paparazzo caught me stuffing an obscenely large sausage-and-pepper sandwich into my face at that food truck on Boylston.

BREAKING NEWS: Phoebe West likes sausage in and around her mouth.

My smile doesn't waver, my steps don't falter. I glide past them like a mother-fucking starling in my blue-black silk, coasting on wind currents of false confidence and past experience. Head up, chest out, soft hands, demure laugh.

Easy, easy, easy.

I might not need him to hold me up in high heels, anymore, but I can't help wishing Parker was by my side as I make my way toward the building, fighting my watering, light-exposed eyes every step of the way and praying to god my smile isn't as cold in the pictures as it feels in this moment, frozen on my lips.

"YOU'RE LATE."

"Yep."

"You promised you'd be on time."

"Yep."

"You know I'd kick your ass if you weren't wearing couture."

"Yep."

Lila sighs. "You're impossible."

I hide my smile behind the rim of my glass and take a sip of

Dom Pérignon. A *small* sip. Champagne has a tendency to go straight to my head — I blame the bubbles.

"It wasn't entirely my fault," I murmur, swallowing delicately. "The vultures outside wanted pictures."

"Must be tough, being a celebrity." Lila shakes her head in faux sympathy. "How magnanimous of you to grace us, the little people, with your presence for the evening."

"Shove it up your ass, Lila."

"Oh, shush. You know I'm joking." She tilts her head. "Only about the fame shit. Not about you being inexcusably late."

"Thirty minutes is not inexcusable — it's fashionable."

"Not when there are people waiting on you!" She huffs. "And don't even start that *better late than never* crap. It's not a real excuse. Perpetually tardy people just bandy that about as a defense for never having their shit together."

"I'm not bandying anything about. I've never *bandied* in my life."

She cocks her head at me again, a dubious expression on her face.

I sigh. "Please, just relax. I'm here now." I stop a passing waiter, grab a flute off his tray with a wink of thanks, and shove it into Lila's grasp. "Have some champagne. Better yet, go bother your date."

"How do you know I brought a date?"

I shoot her a look. "When have you ever *not* brought a date to one of these things?"

She has the grace to blush. "Plenty of times."

Now I'm the one looking dubious.

"Fine. Not *plenty* of times." Her voice is defensive. "But I'm sure there's been a time. At least *one*."

"Not *this* time, though."

She says nothing.

"So, what's his name?"

A slow smile twists her lips. "Padraic."

"*Padraic?*" I snort. "Where'd you dig him up? The Emerald Isle? The Burren? *Tara?*"

She narrows her eyes at me. "He just joined my Krav Maga class. He asked me out. As it happens, I needed a date to this shindig, so I invited him to come. Don't get me wrong, track pants and a bare chest in a sweaty gym hold a certain appeal... but a suit and tie, on the other hand..." She whistles under her breath. "*Damn.*"

I arch one eyebrow. "So, you've been spending a lot of time rolling around with him both on and off the mats, I assume?"

Her mouth twitches in amusement. "You jealous?"

"Yep," I admit shamelessly, taking another sip.

Lila's grin widens. "Well, don't be. I have a surprise for you."

Anxiety grips my stomach like a fist, sending the butterflies still swarming there into a frenzy. Lila's surprises never go well.

Like the time she baked a "special" ingredient into a batch of brownies without telling me... which I consumed twenty minutes before field hockey tryouts, our junior year at prep school. And the time she bought me a DIY Brazilian bikini waxing kit as a birthday gift... which is still sitting, unused, at the back of my closet somewhere because, *hello*, if anyone's putting hot wax near my hoo-hah, it's going to be a trained professional.

Needless to say, news of her impending surprise is accompanied by a fair amount of dread.

"Please tell me you didn't buy tickets to Burning Man, Lila." I shudder. She's been threatening to drag us to Nevada's famed music festival in for *years*. "You know I can't handle that much bare old-man penis in one week. Especially in the middle of the desert, with no viable escape options."

"That's not your surprise." Her eyes dance with humor. "Plus, Burning Man isn't until September. You've got months to prepare."

"*What?!* Please tell me you didn't buy tickets."

"Focus!" She snaps a finger in front of my face. "We'll cross that bridge when we come to it."

"How can I focus with visions of ancient sausages dancing through my head like... like..."

"Sugarplums on Christmas Eve?" Lila laughs.

"I hate you."

"Noted." She doesn't bat an eye. "But your surprise tonight is a good one. I promise."

"Are there old-man penises involved?"

"Definitely not."

"Thank god."

"Just one perfect, well-proportioned, twenty-something penis."

I choke on my champagne.

Lila claps me on the back. "Breathe, tiger."

"What— Did you say—Penis—" I gulp to clear my airway. "*What?*"

"I may or may not have snagged you a date."

I stare at her, mouth gaping. She promised — *promised!* — she'd never force me into another set-up after the disaster that was Captain Kirk.

"I may or may not kill you," I hiss, advancing on her. "I would literally rather ride a camel bare-assed across Black Rock desert to Burning Man, get lost along the way, and have to drink my own *pee* than go on another date you've set up for me."

"Chill!" Her eyes dance again. "This is a good one. I didn't even find him on the internet."

"That's *so* comforting." My glare intensifies and my voice drops to a harsh whisper. "It's not Duncan, is it?"

"Would that be so bad?"

I fight the urge to throttle her.

"Jeeze, you're high-strung today." She rolls her eyes. "No, it's not Duncan. He's away on business."

"Thank god for small favors."

She shoots me a look. "You should be thanking *me*, not god. Very few friends would go to the trouble of setting you up — thankless task that it is. If I were a lesser woman, my feelings would be hurt."

"Okay, wait...." I throw out a finger and squint my eyes at her. "Attempting to give a fuck.... Still attempting to give a fuck... one more time...." My eyes snap fully open. "Nope, sorry. No fucks given."

"You're impossible."

"Seriously, Lila, I am *not* spending the night with some mouth-breathing cretin who thinks the use of dinner napkins is optional and monologues for several hours about his undying love for WWE fights."

"I prefer low-brow barbarian," a smooth male voice cuts in from my left. "Though, I *will* answer to mouth-breathing cretin, if necessary."

CHAPTER 8

Dɪᴅ ᴛʜᴇ ꜰɪʀsᴛ ᴄᴀᴛᴇʀᴘɪʟʟᴀʀ ᴛᴏ ᴇᴠᴇʀ ᴄʜᴀɴɢᴇ ɪɴᴛᴏ ᴀ ʙᴜᴛᴛᴇʀꜰʟʏ ᴊᴜsᴛ ᴛᴏᴛᴀʟʟʏ ꜰʀᴇᴀᴋ ᴛʜᴇ ʜᴇʟʟ ᴏᴜᴛ?

Phoebe West, pondering evolution.

MY GAZE FLIES in his direction. I feel my face reddening like a tomato on speed as I take in the man standing less than a foot away.

Coppery-gold hair, just a tad overgrown, falling over a set of greenish-blue eyes that are lasered-in on my face and, at the moment, twinkling with humor. A wry smile plays out on a set of seriously sexy, full lips — lips that my mortified brain is only now realizing, have produced words.

Words with an accent.

An *Irish* accent.

Holy frack. The sound alone makes my ovaries dance a double jig — two little sexual step-dancers, suddenly all too excited to meet my date who, I must admit, looks nothing like a mouth-breathing cretin. In fact, he looks like Jamie Frasier from *Outlander* — which, without the separation of a television screen, is nearly enough to make me stop breathing.

His eyebrows waggle in playful question, and I realize I've completely zoned out.

"Um," I squeak intelligently.

Lila's laughing — I can hear her cackling away on my right — but I don't move my eyes from the man invading my space.

He leans closer and I feel my mouth go dry. Other parts of my body are not quite so arid.

Like my sweaty palms. And the uncharted territory between my le—

"Sometimes," he whispers conspiratorially, cutting off a dangerous train of thought. "My dates even call me Cormack. Though, only when I monologue about wrestling. In my experience, girls *love* a lengthy discussion of muscle men in spandex."

He's teasing me.

My mind reels for an appropriately witty retort, but I can't seem to come up with anything. Not when he's staring at me with those *eyes*. Not quite green, not quite blue, altogether too focused on me. I search desperately for something — anything — to say, and finally settle on his name.

"Cormack," I echo, brilliant as ever.

His eyes glimmer with humor. Extending a hand into the space between us, he grins in what I can only describe as a devilish manner.

"And you must be Phoebe."

My stomach does a Celtic treble reel when he murmurs my name, his accent elongating the vowels.

Yeh must be Phey-bee.

Am I drooling? I think I might be drooling.

With as much composure as I can muster, I slide my hand into his. The skin of his palm is warm and slightly callused; his thumb strokes across my knuckles with feather-light sensuality — just once, but it's enough to send the butterflies into another tizzy. I take a deep breath and order myself to pull it together.

"Phoebe West," I confirm, craning my neck in an attempt at a flirty head tilt. It always seems to work for Lila. Judging by Cormack's raised eyebrows, I look more along the lines of a car-crash victim with whiplash.

Pretending not to hear the feminine snorts of amusement coming from my (former) best friend, I straighten my head to normal angles and suppress a mortified grimace.

My mortification quickly fades when Cormack lifts my hand to his lips and presses a soft kiss to the fragile skin there.

"It's a pleasure to make your acquaintance, Phoebe." A grin tugs at his lips. "Even if it's not a pleasure you share."

A pleasure to make your acquaintance...

Who talks like that?

Apparently sinfully attractive Irishmen with lips that were made for nibbling on—

Focus!

"I'm sorry. I didn't mean to be rude, before," I say, tugging my hand from his. He lets it go after a tiny hesitation, as though he doesn't quite want to break contact yet. I clear my throat. "I just wasn't expecting..."

I shrug, as though I can't find the words. I can find them, all right, I just don't want to say any of them out loud.

I wasn't expecting to get set-up with a man so hot he'd make a nun question her vows.

"Ahh, I see." He nods in understanding. "Your friend Lila told me you'd agreed to meet me. I didn't mean to catch you off guard."

"It's not you. Really. It's just..." I can feel Lila glaring at me with such hostility, you'd think I ate all the mint chip ice cream and left the empty carton in the freezer. I try not to squirm. "These things never go very well, in my experience."

His lips twist and he leans in so close, I smell his aftershave — crisp, clean, minty. "Do you have a lot of it, then?"

"What?"

"Experience," he whispers, chucking under his breath and staring at me like I'm vastly entertaining. Or, maybe like I'm a car accident — something so disastrous, he simply can't pull his eyes away.

"Um," I squeak again.

He laughs — rich, throaty, full-bodied — and the sound pools in my stomach like warm honey.

"I've no desire to ruin your night, Phoebe. I'll leave you to your friends." His lips twist again. "Though, I must say, I don't think I've ever been rejected by such a beautiful woman."

Damn, he's good. My mouth gapes.

"Goodbye," he adds softly. Keeping those intent eyes locked on mine, he bows his head before turning on a heel to leave.

My eyes fly from his retreating back to Lila, who's glaring daggers at me and gesturing wildly at Cormack.

Go after him, idiot! she screams mutely. Then, she mouths either, *I will flay you alive!* or *I'd like some good pie.* (Hard to say, for sure.)

Regardless, I did agree to follow her schemes to get over Nate — even if they lead me straight into hell. And a night with a sexy Irishman doesn't exactly sound like *torture*. So, I throw back my shoulders, brace myself, and call, "Cormack! Wait."

His grin is huge when he spins back around to face me.

I can do this, I tell myself as he crosses back to my side, gently takes my hand, and leads me toward the closest piece of art. *Just because I'm on a date with a man so good looking he actually induces a stutter... and Nate is here somewhere lurking in the shadows... and I've already begun to perspire in my* de la Renta... *and Lila will kill me if I mess this up... and it's the biggest night of Gemma's art career... and there are a thousand paparazzi parked outside, chomping at the bit for a scandal...*

Absolutely none *of that means something will go horribly wrong and make this the most mortifying night of my existence.*

Right?

God, I'm so totally fucked.

"WHAT IS IT SUPPOSED TO BE?"

"I think it's an eggplant." I squint my eyes at the canvas in question, not judging Cormack at all for his confusion. Modern art is always somewhat of a mystery — I think that's part of the appeal. The more confounding the piece, the higher the price. "Or... maybe it's a squash?"

Cormack chuckles. "I've never been exceedingly fond of vegetables."

Padraic remains silent, which isn't exactly a surprise. So far, the hulking redhead has said a grand total of one word — his name — in the twenty minutes we've been circulating the gallery space, trying to decode swirls of color in the frames on the walls.

"Come on, guys. It's definitely a penis," Lila chimes in, stepping up beside me. "You should buy it, Phee. It'd look great, hanging above your bed."

"I'm all stocked up on phallic artwork, to be honest."

She leans close, her lips practically grazing my ear, and drops her voice to a whisper. "I know you keep about a thousand bodice-ripping romance novels under your bed, but — lusty pirates aside — I don't know if I'd call those phallic *artwork*."

Thankfully, her voice is low enough that the men can't hear.

Ignoring her, I jab an elbow into her ribs as I turn to face Cormack, all smiles. "Let's go find Gemma. I have to congratulate her."

Lila's laughter chases us as we walk away. We're silent for a moment, weaving through the dense crowd, but he keeps a light touch on my lower back. Gentle, but possessive. It sends a guilty shiver through me, and I resist the desire to scan the corners of the room with my eyes. When I came in, there were two security guards stationed at the front doors, dressed in black from head to toe.

Neither of them were Nate.

Is he even here?

Is he watching from the shadows?

Does he see the stranger's hand on the small of my back?

Does he care?

I shiver again, for a different reason entirely.

"You've been friends a long time." Cormack's voice cuts through my mental ramblings and, for a second, I think he's read my mind.

"What?"

He glances at me, lips twisting in amusement. "You and Lila. You've been friends a long time."

Oh. *Lila.* Right.

"Since we were little," I confirm. "She's the closest thing to a sister I've ever had."

"Do you have any siblings?"

"Just one terribly annoying big brother," I say, fondness creeping into my tone. "You're lucky he's out of the country — he's an old hand at scaring away my dates."

The few that I've ever had, I add internally.

Cormack stops mid-stride and turns to glance down into my eyes. When he speaks, his voice is slow, thick, sweet — like melted chocolate. "I don't scare very easily, Phoebe."

Phey-bee.

Swoon.

I don't say anything — what exactly does a girl say to something like that? — so he just places his hand on my back and starts walking again.

Calling Cormack O'Dair *charming* is like calling a contestant on The Bachelor *dramatic.* The word falls pathetically short of reality.

With just one devilish grin, he could get a Royal Guardsman to blush redder than his uniform.

With only the sparkle in his blue-green eyes, he could talk the pants off a priest. (Is that sacrilegious? Oops.)

Point is, between his mega-bright smiles and quick-witted comments and, dear *god,* that accent... I'm feeling a shade out of my depth. Which is perhaps why I didn't immediately realize the wait staff have been supplying me with glass after glass of champagne since the moment my date arrived, or that I've been sipping them at an alarming pace, just so my mouth has something to do besides gawk or grunt unintelligibly in his direction.

The first glass works through my system like a pleasant anesthetic, loosening my joints and making my steps a little more languorous as I glide through the gallery on Cormack's arm.

By the second glass, I'm really *feeling* the art, in a way I probably — definitely — wouldn't be, without the aid of alcohol. 'Cause, I mean, it's not *just* a $6,000 painting of a white paper cup on canvas. You know? That cup — it's *empty.* Lying on its side. Which is deeply symbolic of...of... something. I think.

Don't snort bubbles out your nose. Don't snort bubbles out your nose. Don't snort bubbles out your nose.

Now, by glass number three, everything around me has adopted a kind of fuzzy, golden aura. Blurred at the edges. Mellow. Warm.

That handful of stale Cheez-its I ate earlier wasn't the most substantial dinner I've ever had...

Blessedly, Cormack hasn't seemed to notice that my brain is sloshing around inside my skull like a pickled egg. He's too busy charming the pants off everyone we talk to.

I can't decide if it's good or bad that I'm not wearing pants and, thus, cannot be charmed out of them.

(Probably bad.)

In any case, as we maneuver through the crowd looking for Gemma and Chase, we're stopped at least six times to chat with various family friends and some of my father's business partners. Several women ask — with a fair amount of shock in their tones — who my date is. I grit my teeth and pretend it doesn't bother me that they treat a deviation from my perpetual single-hood with such delighted dismay. The other women we come across are too busy sultrily eyeing Cormack behind their martini glasses to be bitchy. Their husbands aren't much better — they either ask after my father's whereabouts, let their gazes linger too long on my cleavage, or say nothing at all.

Cumulatively, I worry their antics will make my date run for the hills.

He doesn't. In fact, he's so good at working the crowd and moving us along through countless tedious encounters, I may have to consider bringing him along to every social event for the rest of my life. Hell, I may have to marry the guy for perks like these.

I don't need sex, love, or commitment. Just deflect the monotonous, socialite small talk away from me.

"Are you a magician?" I ask, when he somehow maneuvers us out of a conversation with Minerva Dupree, one of the most long-winded women I've ever had the displeasure of meeting, in under a minute. In that tiny sliver of time, she somehow managed to touch on everything from my brother's lack of interest in taking over WestTech to my spinsterhood to my father's decision to develop the Charlestown waterfront from a crime-riddled neighborhood into a stretch of luxury green-energy condos.

Minerva has a knack for locking you into hour-long lectures, if given the chance. But Cormack brushed her off like a piece of lint, shattering Lila's all-time escape record of five minutes at a Christmas party two years ago — and she had to spill eggnog all over herself to achieve that speedy exit.

"Nothing so exciting. I work in..." He pauses a beat, smiling to himself. "Let's call it... investments and trading." There's laughter in his voice, but I'm not in on the joke.

"Oh. That's nice," I say politely, thinking it sounds terribly boring.

"Though..." He leans closer. "I do have a magic trick or two up my sleeve."

My mouth gapes at the suggestion in his tone. *He can't possibly be talking about...*

His lips graze my ear. "Maybe I'll teach you a few of them, sometime."

Oh. Yep. He's definitely talking about sex.

I don't know whether to laugh or choke, so I simply swallow another gulp of champagne. Cormack's still leaning close, his mouth practically on my ear as he chuckles lowly, when my eyes cut through the crowd and find the one thing I've told myself over and over I haven't been searching for all night.

There's a man standing by the wall, practically blended into the shadows, his every muscle on high alert and his stare locked on me. His muscular body fills out a pair of dark slacks dangerously well. His biceps strain against the confines of his black button down; his tanned throat is on display with the top buttons of his shirt left undone.

My mouth feels suddenly dry.

Dark eyes meet mine, trapping me in an instant. I'm a deer in headlights, frozen, staring at him across a crowded sea of people. There must be fifty of them, standing in the space between us, but as seconds slip away with our gazes locked, every one of them simply falls away until we're the only two in the room.

Nate, Nate, Nate.

Every atom in my body starts to sing, totally entranced by his presence. There's something terrifying about a man who holds that much sway over you. A man who can just look at you — not even with kindness or love, but with a hard-set mouth and cold-burning eyes — and unravel you like a spool of useless thread.

One glance and I'm a goner.

I hear Cormack saying something at my ear but for the life of me, I can't make out his words. He's a candle throwing faint light... and Nate's the sun — eclipsing everything else, pulling me into his orbit.

I'm not breathing, as I look at him. I can't. Every ounce of control I have over my body is being used up with the effort of keeping my eyes steady on his face. His goddamned beautiful, haunted face. I wonder, if I ever got the chance to trace its harsh lines with my fingertips, to stroke that ever-clenched jaw with gentle hands... would it soften at all beneath my touch? Or would loving Nate be like touching stone?

You hate him. He's terrible. Stop looking at him.

Those dark eyes burn into mine and I think they'll never let go, never release me. That I'll age and wither and die right here, in this spot, because I can't look away. But then Cormack moves, his hand skimming my arm in a useless call for attention, and those consuming dark eyes shift. Breath whooshes back into my lungs as Nate stares at the man by my side. His eyes flash with something indecipherable, his jaw clenches, and then he's gone.

Slipping into the crowd like a ghost, until I've lost sight of him.

CHAPTER 9

I'M AN ADULT. JUST LAST WEEK,
I PURCHASED A VEGETABLE.
NOT ON PURPOSE, OF COURSE.

Phoebe West, on the meaning of adulthood.

"PHOEBE?"

I blink hard and turn to Cormack, wishing it didn't take such monumental effort to turn my back on the place Nate stood only seconds before.

"I'm sorry," I murmur, meeting my date's confused eyes and shrugging lightly. "Just spaced out for a second."

"Are you all right?"

"Yes." I try out a smile. It feels wobbly on my lips. "Too much champagne. All those bubbles go straight to my head."

Liar, liar, pants on fire.

Thankfully, Cormack doesn't seem to notice. Or, if he does, he's too much of a gentleman to contradict me.

"What were we talking about?" I ask, in dire need of a subject change.

"I was about to ask what you do for work." His smile is all easy charm.

"I'm a graphic designer." Pushing thoughts of Nate from my mind, I instantly feel steadier. "I manage the WestTech website and design promotional marketing materials— brochures, business cards, advertisements, social media campaigns. Stuff like that."

"And you enjoy it? Working so closely with your father?"

"I love it." I smile softly. "He's away a lot, so I don't see him that often. Which is okay — otherwise, we'd probably drive each other crazy."

The lie slips from my lips as easy as breathing. I've been saying it so long, I almost believe it myself.

Truth is, there's no such thing as seeing Milo West *too often* or working with him *too closely*. I took a job at WestTech not because it was the only option open to me — I had plenty of offers, when I graduated from MIT at the top of my class — but because I knew it was the only guarantee I'd have of ever crossing paths with the man who raised me.

Well... *raised* is a bit of a stretch.

Parker raised me. He was my big brother, but he did all the work — making sure my homework was done, that I'd eaten dinner, that no one at school was messing with me. He gave up being a kid the day our mom died, and stepped into the void she'd left behind.

My dad certainly wasn't going to.

Milo had more of a *consultant* role in my rearing. Sure, he'd get involved with whatever daily drama was boiling over in his children's lives — if he happened to be around that day. As a kid, the only sure way of seeing him was when Parker and I would beg our nanny to drive us to the WestTech tower, a soaring high-rise in the South End, where we were welcomed with the grudging patience of a man who loves his children... just not as much as his empire.

We didn't ask often. Eventually we stopped asking altogether.

"I'm sure he values your work very much." Cormack's voice shatters my reverie. "He's a lucky man, to have a daughter like you."

I smile up at him thinking, even if his words aren't remotely true, it's nice to hear them.

Before I can respond, a tinkling feminine laugh accosts my ears. A second later, a body slams into mine and arms wind around my frame.

"You're here!" Gemma squeals, grabbing me by the shoulders and peering into my face. Her grin is a mile wide. Her hair — the same shade as mine but longer — is twined up in a modern French twist, and she's wearing a killer boho-chic blue dress that matches the exact shade of her eyes. She's stunning.

"Wouldn't miss it." I grin back at her, feeling her exuberance infect me like an airborne contagion. "It's amazing, Gemma. Seri-ously, you've outdone yourself."

She waves away my words. "I barely did any of this. Have you met my friends? My boyfriend? Total control freaks, the lot of them. For some reason, they all seem to think everything I touch turns into a disaster."

This, from the girl who breaks approximately one iPhone per week.

I bury a grin. "I'm sure they just wanted to help."

She expels a gust of air. "It's a miracle they even let me pick the flowers."

"I see you ousted those *macabre* calla lilies in favor of peonies," I say with only a small amount of teasing in my voice, glancing around the gallery space where white, puffy blooms float in water crystal vases and saturate the air with sweet, fresh perfume.

"When in doubt, stick with the classics." Gemma smiles. "Chase knows they're my favorite. I think he buys them by the truckload."

I can confirm this — I've been to their penthouse. Practically every surface holds a vase full of the colorful blooms.

"Where is he?"

"Oh, off in a corner somewhere brooding, no doubt. He's not exactly a social butterfly in the best of times, and everyone here wants to talk to him about a partnership with Croft Industries." Her eyes go soft as she talks about him. "I wouldn't have been able to pull any of this together without him. None of these people would've shown up for just me."

I grab her hand and squeeze. "I would have."

Something warm flashes in her eyes. "I'm so happy you're here. Chase keeps making me *talk* to these snooty people, like I'm required to make nice just so they'll buy art. I've told him, like, a million times — it's a gallery, not a social hour. Does he listen? Nope. Overbearing caveman."

I hear a muffled chuckle from Cormack's direction. Gemma looks at him abruptly, seeming to notice him for the first time, then glances back at me with raised brows.

"Date?"

I nod.

Her happy expression crumbles and I know it's because of her dreams for my happily-ever-after with a certain someone. I don't have the heart to tell her that life isn't a fairy tale.

Not *my* life, anyway.

She quickly recovers, offering him a dazzling smile. "Well, hi there. I'm Gemma Summers. Phoebe's... friend."

Her beat of hesitation makes my heart skip a beat.

Aren't we friends?

I take another sip of champagne and try not to dwell.

"I'm Cormack." My date steps forward, hand outstretched. "You have a gorgeous gallery."

Gemma's eyebrows go up, up, up as she listens to his introduction. She shakes his hand politely, then leans close to me and whispers in my ear.

"Holy shit. That *accent?!*"

"I *know*," I whisper back.

We're both laughing as we pull apart. Cormack stares at us, amusement flickering across his face.

"You two wouldn't be joking at my expense now, would you?" he asks.

"Absolutely not," I deny immediately

"Oh, definitely," Gemma confirms at the same time.

We look at each other and dissolve into laughter again.

"Thanks for clearing that up," Cormack says, his voice wry.

When we've stopped giggling, Gemma grabs me in another tight embrace. "I suppose I have to go *mingle*." She says it like a dirty word. "But let's plan lunch sometime this week, okay?"

"Of course," I agree, hugging her back.

With a smile for me and a wink for Cormack, she's gone again, winding into the crowd and disappearing.

"Another childhood friend?" Cormack asks, stepping into the space she left behind.

"Actually, we just met about a month ago."

His eyebrows lift in surprise.

I can't blame him for being skeptical. Sometimes, I have to remind myself I barely know Gemma. There's just something about her that makes me feel totally at ease. Like I've known her forever, could tell her anything. I can't really explain it, so I just shrug lightly, wrap my arm through his, and lead us toward the canvas on our left, making sure my eyes never wander to the shadowy corners of the room.

Dark-eyed ghosts have a tendency to lurk there.

AN HOUR LATER, I'm several grand poorer and the proud owner of a gorgeous new pastel abstract by Sartre. Lila and Padraic have joined us again and, judging by the faint hickey blooming on Lila's neck, it's not hard to guess what they've been up to in our absence.

I'm on my fourth glass of champagne for the evening — at this point, mustering enough indignation to scold her about necking like a teenager in the back hallway of Gemma's black-tie event seems a daunting task. I watch Lila lean into Padraic's arm, watch his mouth twist into a knowing smirk as he whispers secret nothings into her ear and a giddy smile blooms on her lips, and feel a pang of sadness sweep through me.

I can't help wishing that at any point in my life, even for an instant, I'd felt that way. Happy and carefree and in love with nothing but the moment.

As handsome as the man standing beside me is, I know we'll never have that.

I'll never have it with anyone.

"Another champagne, Phoebe?" Cormack asks politely, as a waiter passes by. I notice he doesn't grab a glass for himself. In fact, he hasn't been drinking at all.

"I've had plenty." I rub at my temple. "I'm actually starting to get a headache. I'm going to step out on the back terrace, for a minute. Get some fresh air."

He looks at me with concern. "Want company?"

"No, I'm all right."

"We can leave," he offers, my own personal knight-in-tailored-Hugo-Boss-suit. "I'll take you wherever you'd like to go, just name the place."

God, he's nice. And charming. And good looking.

He's everything I could ever need in a man.

He's just not the one I want.

He's not...

Nate.

The mere thought of him is ruining the first good date I've had in... maybe ever. I hate that he has this hold over me. Blood-lust stirs inside me again, needing an outlet, but this time it's tinged with a sense of hopelessness.

If a man like Cormack can't make me forget Nate, I doubt any man on earth can.

I bite the inside of my cheek so I don't scream. Or cry.

"That's very sweet." I smile up at Cormack. "I'll be back in bit, okay?"

"Phoebe..." His gorgeous face wrinkles in worry, his hand grazes my lower back in a way that should have me doing victory cartwheels around the room. All I feel is tired. Empty. And frustrated that I can't stop wishing it were someone else's hand pulling me close, offering me comfort.

"Don't worry," I tell him, voice falsely bright. "I'll be back before you have time to miss me."

"Are you sure? I'd be happy to accompany—"

"No," I say too sharply. "I just need a minute," I add, my voice softer.

I'm not trying to be rude but I'm suddenly desperate to be out of this room, away from the lights and the noise. All the things I want to say — scream — to Nate have formed a lump in my throat so thick, I can barely breathe around it.

I feel abruptly very alone, in this crowd of people. Despite my date, despite Lila and Gemma and all the people who claim to adore the West family... I'm overcome by that feeling again. The one that whispers at the back of my mind that I could just evaporate into thin air without causing so much as a ripple in the party going on around me.

Poof! Gone.

I make sure to grab a fresh glass of champagne as I cut through the crowd and head for the French doors that lead to freedom.

THE TERRACE IS DESERTED. It's not quite summer in Boston and there's still a crisp chill on May nights, especially by the water. I lean against the railing, press my eyes closed, and pull a deep breath through my nose. Sometimes just the act of pulling oxygen into your lungs can feel like the hardest thing in the world.

"You shouldn't be out here alone."

The voice hits me like a wave, rolling over fragile limbs of sand, threatening to erode my very existence. Deep, gritty, and detached of all emotion.

Nate.

Abruptly, I'm covered in goosebumps that have absolutely nothing to do with the cold. I force my eyes to open, but don't turn to face him.

"West?" His voice is closer, lower.

I fight a shiver.

I hate him, I hate him, I hate him.

There's no heat to my internal chant — only resigned sadness.

"You hear me?" Closer still, and this time the iron in his tone is undeniable. He wants an answer.

I sigh and turn my head to look over one shoulder at him.

"I heard you," I echo softly, my eyes meeting his.

Something flashes across his face — *concern? surprise?* — when he catches sight of my expression and hears the exhaustion in my tone, but he doesn't comment. I watch his jaw tighten as his eyes roam my features.

He's devastatingly handsome, even in the dark.

It's pretty annoying.

"Go back inside," he commands, no kindness in his voice.

I'm too tired to fight with him and certainly too weak to keep looking at him without caving to the need to step into his chest and wrap my arms around him, so I just turn back to the water, lean deeper against the railing, and murmur, "Actually, I'm good right here."

I hear what I think is a curse and then he's there, right beside me, hovering so close I can feel the heat of his chest. Not touching me, but almost.

It takes physical effort to keep my body from leaning into his, to keep my eyes locked on the river — a spill of dark ink, now that the sun's set.

Love that dirty water, Bostonians everywhere chant at sports games and bar crawls, taking pride in the polluted Charles. Reveling in their adoration for something broken and toxic and wrong.

I know a little about that.

"West."

Am I crazy, or is his voice a fraction softer? A shade kinder?

I'm probably crazy. Or drunk.

Maybe both.

"It's cold as hell out here," he informs me unnecessarily. I know just how icy the air is between us, how many frozen degrees of separation divide his body from mine.

I nod and sip my champagne, lacking the energy to snap back at him, as I'd usually do in this scenario. There hasn't been a single conversation between us in the past ten years that wasn't laced with sarcasm and scorn.

First time for everything.

"Dammit, West." His words are harsh, but his voice is uncharacteristically rattled. Like he doesn't quite know how to handle me, when I'm not cursing at him. "Nothing's fucking easy with you."

"You've mentioned that before." My voice is so bland you'd think we were discussing cereal brands.

He's silent for a moment, before barking, "What the hell is the matter with you?"

I shrug, still not looking at him. "Nothing."

"Then why aren't you being a sarcastic pain in my ass and snapping at me for ordering you around?"

I turn my head to look at him — I can't help myself — and as soon as our gazes meet, I feel the breath seize in my lungs.

It's hard, so hard, to be indifferent with those dark eyes a half-foot away from mine.

Tension builds like a summer storm in the space between us — charged air currents zinging from my body to his.

His jaw starts to tick. "West—"

"Don't you ever get tired of it?" I ask, the words popping out before I can stop them. I'm not sure who's more surprised by my question.

His brow furrows. "Tired of you being a sarcastic pain in my ass?"

I try to grin but only half my mouth cooperates. I look away before he sees the flimsy smile, proof of my deep unease.

"No," I say, trying to keep my voice from cracking. "I don't think I'll ever get tired of that."

Indifferent, I tell myself. *You're indifferent to him. You've got a hot date inside who actually* likes *you. Why waste your time on someone who so clearly doesn't?*

My inner voice is about as convincing as an oceanfront condo salesman in Nebraska.

Silence drags on. After a second, I feel him step closer. It takes every ounce of energy I possess to remain still.

"Tired of what?" Nate mutters, sounding like he'd rather have bamboo shoots shoved under his fingernails than continue this conversation with me.

It's almost enough to draw out a real smile. Almost.

"All of it." I shrug and sip my champagne again. The glass is almost empty.

"Gonna have to elaborate on that one."

I finally look up at him and I swear he almost flinches when our eyes meet. I'm not sure what that says about the emotions in my eyes — I'm not sure I want to know.

"Don't you ever—" My voice cracks. I ignore it and start over. "Do you ever feel like you could just disappear and no one would even notice?"

He stares at me a beat — brow creasing, eyes active, mouth pressing into an even firmer line. My heart starts beating too fast. He's watching me so intently, it's like he's never seen me before. Like I've changed right before his eyes into a stranger.

I look away, because I can't look at him. Not with that mortifying question — a question that revealed so much more than I ever intended to — still lingering in the air between us.

The longer it's out there, the more exposed I feel. Like I've just reached into my chest, pulled out my beating, vulnerable heart, and handed it to him on a platter.

Worse still, he doesn't say anything. Not a single word. The silence stretches, grows, until it's a physical presence. Until it's so loud, my ears begin to ache with it, and suddenly, for no reason at all, I'm fighting tears.

I should've stuck with indifference.

Indifferent is always better than raw and afraid and lonely and broken.

Stupid, stupid, stupid.

Then, out of nowhere, a hand lands on the bare flesh of my arm. Every thought except *holy-frack-Nate-is-touching-me* disappears from my mind as lightning jolts through me, frying my circuit boards. I go completely still, barely breathing as my eyes move slowly from the hand curled around my arm — so unbearably gentle, like I'm made of glass — to his other fist, which is wrapped so tight around the deck railing, his veins pop like stark cords. It's a wonder the wood doesn't splinter under his hold.

As though he's so tense from just touching me, he needs a physical outlet.

As though the feeling of my skin under his palm is nearly enough to kill him.

I marvel at the tandem show of utter tenderness and brute force. At his ability to keep that pain contained within himself, never once tightening his grip on me. Such total control — I'd be intimidated, if I could feel anything at all, right now.

My entire system, every ounce of sensory input, is narrowed to a single point of contact. To five callused, masculine fingers, where they grip the fragile skin of my wrist.

My eyes trail up the muscled length of his arm to his broad chest, then to the tanned column of his throat where it peeks out the unbuttoned collar of his black dress shirt. Before I lose all my courage, I slide my gaze up over the planes of his face to meet his stare head-on.

He's not even looking at me.

His eyes are on his own hand, where it's curled reverently around my wrist. He's staring at it like he doesn't quite know what to make of it. Something stirs low in my abdomen, a pang of longing shooting through me like an electric charge.

"Nate..." I whisper, breathless.

His eyes snap to mine, but his hand doesn't move. "You drunk, West?"

"No," I say, even though it's kind of a lie.

"Five glasses of champagne say otherwise."

My mouth parts and my eyes narrow. "What, you've been spying on me?"

"Don't think watching the most boring date in history counts as spying. Even if you are wearing your fuck-me heels."

My brain actually stutters inside my skull, hearing the phrase *fuck me* come from Nate's mouth, watching those lips form such sensual, sinuous words. Words that should insult me, not turn me on.

"Excuse me?" I snap, mustering all the anger I can manage to cover my sudden lust. "For your information, Cormack is not boring. He's charming. And good-looking. And unlike *some people I know*, he doesn't feel the need to assert his manhood by brooding and glaring and grunting like a bull in heat."

"West—"

"Frankly, it's none of your fracking business who I date!"

"*Fracking?*"

"And furthermore," I barrel on, ignoring his amused question. "These are not fu... fu..." I swallow hard. "They are not *those* kind of heels."

His mouth tugs up at one side and the sight of it makes my heart skip a beat.

"Can't say the word *fuck*, West?" He sounds vastly entertained by the idea.

My cheeks heat.

Oh, I can, all right. I just worry that if I say fuck me *while you're standing so close, my body will disobey orders and wrap around you like a tree frog.*

"Just a word, West." He leans closer, practically inducing a heart attack. "No need to be afraid of it."

"I'm not afraid of anything, you condescending ass," I hiss, tugging my arm from his grip and praying I don't fall over. To my dismay, he lets me pull out of his hold. I miss his touch as soon as it's gone, cursing myself even as I curse him.

"I'm an ass, now? Thought I was a bull in heat," he mocks. "And I gotta say, charming as your elementary, barnyard-animal insults are... I've been called worse."

"Oh, *fuck* you, Nate. *Fuck* you, *fuck* off, go *fuck* yourself." I twist my face into the mimicry of a smile and make my voice sweet as pie. "How was that? Was my usage correct? My diction on point? Because, if we're quite finished here, I have to go do something more interesting. Like alphabetize my entire bookshelf by title, author, and genre. Maybe un-gunk the lint from my car speakers with a toothpick. Oh, or translate the entire works of Tolstoy into Pig-Latin."

He stares at me for a beat, those dark eyes glittering, that almost-smile playing on his lips. I'm breathing too hard and I tell myself it's from the anger coursing through my system. Not something else. Something stupid. Like attraction.

"There she is," he murmurs under his breath, those dark eyes locked on mine. His tone is hushed, amused — almost like he's talking to himself. About me, rather than *to* me.

"What the hell is that supposed to mean?" I snap, but my anger feels suddenly stretched thin.

There she is. There she is. There she is.

His words beat through my mind like a tribal drum beat.

He doesn't answer. His eyes are already shuttering away whatever emotion flashed there seconds ago. I glare at him, fully prepared to launch in again and ask why the hell he insists on antagonizing me at every opportunity, but before I can get out another word a voice cuts across the deck like a thunderclap, shattering the moment.

"Phoebe?"

Phey-bee.

"Crap on whole wheat," I mutter, taking an abrupt step back from Nate and turning to face Cormack, who's crossing the terrace with a look of concern on his face.

I think I hear Nate curse again, though I don't know what *he* could possibly be pissed off about, unless it's the fact that he can no longer taunt me with Cormack here to witness it.

"You were gone a long time. I thought I'd come check on you," Cormack tells me, though his eyes are locked on Nate. I can't help but notice his usual charming smile is nowhere to be found. When he reaches my side, his hand immediately finds the small of my back in that possessive way of his.

I fight the urge to stiffen at his touch, looking anywhere but at Nate.

"Just enjoying the fresh air," I say, forcing my voice to stay level. My eyes lift to Cormack's. "Thanks for checking."

He smiles faintly before his gaze shifts back to Nate, who's crossed his arms over his chest and adopted a seriously intimidating expression. It's one I've never seen before and I immediately dub it his Badass Mercenary look.

Tight mouth, scary eyes, pervasive silence.

So, basically his normal look... on steroids.

To my surprise, Cormack doesn't turn and run. His spine straightens as he meets Nate's hard stare, and he shoves a cordial hand into the space between them. Nate stares unmoving at the other man's hand and, eventually, Cormack drops it and shoves it back into his pants pocket.

"I'm Corma—"

"I know who you are." Nate's voice is arctic cold. Colder than I've ever heard it. "And I don't know what game you're playing here, O'Dair, but it ends now."

Cormack actually laughs — *laughs!* — like he isn't standing two feet from the most intimidating human on planet earth.

There's a strange gleam in my date's blue-green eyes that wasn't there earlier, and a smug smile playing out on those killer Irish lips.

I'm instantly set on edge.

Something's happening here. And, as much as I'd like to think the tension between them is because they're both madly in love with me — *HA!* — I'm pretty sure that's not the case. They clearly have a history.

Judging by the frost crystalizing the air between them, I'm guessing it's not a happy one.

At least a decade passes as the men face off, neither breaking the heavy silence. The tension builds until I can barely breathe around it.

"Maybe—" I start, but my words are immediately cut off.

"West, go inside." Nate never looks away from Cormack. "I'm going to have a chat with your..." He pauses intentionally, a hard smile curling at his mouth. "...*friend*."

"What?" I snap. "I'm not going anywhere."

"It's fine, Phoebe," Cormack says, glaring at Nate. "We have some things to talk about. I'll see you in a few minutes."

Dismissed like a little girl. By *both* of them.

Well!

"This is a joke, right?"

They both ignore me.

I plant my hands on my hips. "Seriously?"

Still, no response.

"You know, as a general rule, if you're going to act like total dicks, you should wear condoms over your heads." Their eyes snap simultaneously to look at me when the words leave my lips. I widen my eyes in an innocent expression and continue in a sweet tone. "It would help prevent the macho bullshit from leaving your mouths."

With that, I spin — not easy, on four-inch stiletto heels, let me tell you — and head for the doors. I don't stop to say goodbye to Gemma or Lila; I stomp straight for the exits and ask a startled valet to call my town car. The expression on my face must be seriously pissed, because he practically jumps out of his skin when he sees me coming. I'm too angry to care. (Much.)

Not even a minute later, I watch my car pull to the curb, blow past the paparazzi, and am settled in the backseat being whisked toward the city proper.

Screw Nate. Screw Cormack.

In fact, screw men altogether.

Celibacy isn't so bad. There are perks to dying alone.

For instance — never having to shave my legs ever again. Not worrying about rogue eyebrow hairs. Being able to watch seven consecutive hours of Netflix without anyone around to reprimand me for my poor life decisions. Never having to share my French fries when I order takeout. Being able to sleep diagonally across my queen-sized mattress.

See! *Perks.*

Totally worth a life of solitude and an endless sexual dry spell.

I sigh deeply and stare out the window. It doesn't matter what I try to tell myself — I'm still tormented by the knowledge that I'd trade any amount of single-girl benefits for just one night of sexy-benefits in Nate's arms.

CHAPTER 10

WHAT DID ONE OCEAN SAY TO THE OTHER OCEAN?
    NOTHING, THEY JUST WAVED.
    SEA WHAT I DID THERE?

Phoebe West, wondering if she should try her hand at standup comedy.

"BOOOOOOOOOOO." I tug at the leash. "Come on."

He's sniffing a tree so thoroughly, he looks like a kindergartener in possession of the coveted blue smelly-marker at the craft table. When I tug the leash again, his tiny head swivels my way, unmistakably peeved by my interruption. The glare he shoots at me is downright lethal.

"Dogs are supposed to bring warmth and joy," I inform him.

"Caesar Milan assured me I'd never have a more loyal, loving companion." I plant my hands on my hips and level him with a stare. "You, my grumpy fluff-ball, are supposed to adore me. Not flash vengeance in your tiny, beady eyes and drag my ass around the streets of Boston at midnight for Sniffapalooza."

He ignores me, per usual, trotting around to smell the other side of the tree and weaving through the wrought-iron fence until his leash is hopelessly tangled.

He totally did that on purpose.

"Don't make me play *Old Yeller* for you again," I mutter, sighing as I move to detangle it — a process which will take at least forty seconds, by which point he'll be ready to move on to another tree. Devious little bastard.

We walk Comm Ave toward the Public Garden, our usual late-night loop. Boo's white body practically glows in the dark, pristine fur catching the moonlight, proud profile clear even from ten feet behind him.

They say New York is the city that never sleeps. Boston, on the other hand, is the city that gets drunk in the middle of the day at a Patriots pre-game party and passes out by seven.

Sure, certain neighborhoods are lively until the wee hours — mainly the student-infested bars packed around Fenway Park — but Back Bay, with its tree-lined streets, clean-swept sidewalks, and population of young professionals and families, is quiet by city standards even at midday. By this time of night, it's practically deserted.

It seems emptier than usual, tonight — shops closed down, windows shuttered tight, hardly a soul out wandering the streets... besides a crazy woman talking to her Pomeranian, of course. At a cross street, a group of college girls stumble along, giggling and shushing each other as they try to sneak into one of the area's swankier bars. Down the block, a man and woman walk hand-in-hand, probably headed to the pond for a moonlit make-out session on one of the benches overlooking the swan boats.

Ah, romance.

I contemplate following them and ordering Boo to poop directly in front of their bench, thus ruining their ambiance, but I refrain. Just because *I'm* miserable and alone doesn't mean everyone else should be. I can rise above.

(I guess.)

By the time we've circled back to my brownstone, it's well past midnight, my stomach is rumbling — can't stress it enough, Cheez-Its are not an adequate dinner — and I'm no more in the mood to sleep than I was pre-walk. When I got home from Karma, I was so revved up, I spent an hour tossing and turning in my bed before I finally threw off the covers, pulled on the faded Harvard sweatshirt I stole from Parker ages ago, and grabbed Boo's leash from the peg by the front door.

I'm sure my cellphone has exploded with messages from Lila and Gemma... which is precisely why I powered it off as soon as I got home and haven't looked at it since.

I've no desire to be berated for skipping out on the gallery opening. Not tonight, at least.

Actually, I've no desire to do much of anything except microwave some edamame — my yoga instructor's "healthy alter-native suggestion" to delicious, buttery popcorn — plunk myself on the couch, flip on Netflix, and force Boo to snuggle with me for the next two to three years.

We finally reach my brownstone. My foot is on the bottom step as my mind scans through my to-be-watched queue, consid-ering movie options. I'm simultaneously tugging Boo away from the neighbor's flowerpots and fishing through my sweatshirt pocket for my front-door key, when a shadow detaches from the brick wall of my landing. Before I can blink, he's moved to the top step and is towering over me like a demon straight from the depths of hell.

The grim reaper.

On my stoop.

In the dark.

Ahh!

I remember some distant self-defense teacher telling me to use my keys as a weapon, so I reach frantically for them. When my fingers close over metal, I pull them from my sweatshirt pouch, preparing to jab.

Except... where do I jab, again?

Throat? Eyes? Testicles?

Somewhere in the back of my mind, Sandra Bullock is telling me to SING.

Solar plexus, instep, nose, groin.

Oh, who am I kidding? I'm barely coordinated enough to *walk* up my stairs, let alone conduct an FBI-inspired takedown on them.

Precious seconds slip away as I consider the best location to stab someone — not *fatally*, just enough to, like, get them off my stoop so I can go inside and watch *FRIENDS* in peace. The shadow descends another step.

Eeep!

I jerk involuntarily, panic overriding my system. My body swings backward and my hands flail out like a baby T-rex attempting a hug, the sudden move sending my keys flying. I watch forlornly as they arc through the air and land in a nearby bush, out of reach.

Boo, my demon-dog, is nowhere to be found, now that I need him. Apparently, protecting the life of his beloved owner falls below licking flattened sidewalk chewing gum on his list of priorities.

Typical.

"Frack!" I shriek. With no other weapons left in my arsenal — unless I want to shoot him in the eye with a hair elastic or beam a pink Ugg boot at his head — I drop into a ninja-like crouch on the bottom step and position my hands in front of me like fleshy blades.

"Okay listen, buddy, I don't know what you're doing on my steps, but you have about two seconds to vanish before the cops get here!" I yell, hoping my voice sounds menacing and not like I'm about to pee in my silk pajama shorts from Bloomingdales.

"West, are you off your meds?"

I freeze, heart pounding in my chest, hand-blades taught with tension.

No. Freaking. Way.

All the air whooshes out of me as Nate takes another step down, until he's standing on my level. He's so tall, he still towers inches over me — I resist the urge to ease onto a higher step, just to level the playing field. It doesn't escape my notice that his face is narrowed in anger.

At least, until his gaze flickers down to my hands. Taking in the sight of them, still extended ineffectually in the space between us, his mouth twitches and the skin around his eyes crinkles up, fine wrinkles feathering his temples.

You wouldn't think wrinkles would be hot but... *damn.* Seeing Nate almost-smile at me with those crinkly eyes... Let's just say it's a miracle I'm able to remain standing.

"You planning to karate-chop me to death?" he asks, voice thick with mirth.

Mirth!

My brain is having trouble processing a version of Nate who knows how to experience such an emotion.

"No," I mutter defensively, dropping my hands to my sides and curling them into fists. My mouth produces an incredulous puff of air, akin to an orca breaching. *Sexy.* "Of course not."

"Looked like you were."

"Well, I wasn't," I snap. I glance at my dog, who's given up sniffing the bushes in favor of Nate's shoes. "Boo, attack the evil man. *Attack!*" I order.

At the sound of his name, the Pomeranian glances at me with an utterly bored expression, then almost immediately resumes sniffing.

I sigh. "Some guard dog, you are."

Nate glances at Boo. "He seems like a real killer."

"We're working on it. For some reason, he only seems to have lethal tendencies when it comes to me. Oh! And his plushy duck toy. He has it out for that thing."

Nate chuckles.

The sound is so foreign, so achingly compelling, it melts through me like liquid gold. I haven't heard him laugh, *really* laugh, in years. Not since we were kids, before he left Harvard and went through the military training that left his eyes too cold and his words too guarded. Hearing it now, rusty from disuse as it rumbles from his throat, I fight the need to close my eyes and savor the timbre of it, like I do when I'm front-row at the Boston Pops listening to the orchestra crescendo.

He falls silent all too soon, eyes finding mine once more. They're no longer crinkly-warm as they scan from the dog at his feet to my hyper-short pajama bottoms to the baggy sweatshirt draping me to mid-thigh, taking in every detail with painstaking attention.

"You were out walking alone? At this time of night?"

"Um..." I gulp at the accusation in his words. "No."

He stills dangerously. "Someone with you, then?"

"Um..." I'm having trouble forming words. "Yes?"

He goes so tense, he's practically vibrating. "O'Dair?"

"What?" My mouth gapes.

"You meet up with O'Dair somewhere?" His voice drops

lower to mutter words I'm pretty sure I'm not intended to hear. I hear them anyway. *"Man has a fucking death wish."*

My heartbeat picks up speed. "Excuse me?"

"West—"

"I didn't meet up with Cormack. Why would you even think that?"

His jaw unclenches a bit. "You said you met up with someone."

"No, I said I wasn't walking alone."

"Then who the fuck were you walking with?"

"Um..." My voice gets small. "Boo?"

His mouth twitches as he stares at me, his expression flickering between frustration, anger, and amusement, like a slot machine spinning numbers. He settles on anger.

"You shouldn't be out alone at night, West." His eyes burn into mine. "Tell me you're at least carrying your pepper spray."

"Tell me you don't actually believe *I* own pepper spray." I snort. "Come on. Who do you think I am? Five minutes ago I was ready to karate chop you to death, for god's sake. You think if I had mace on hand, I would've been like *Oh, look! A creepy stranger on my steps! Yep, now seems like a good time to test my samurai skills. Let's do this. Crouching Tiger Hidden Phoebe."* I strike a ninja pose, hands slicing through the air between us in a faux-strike. *"Heeeeya!"*

His mouth tugs up against his will. "Are you a ninja or a samurai?"

I pause — hands dropping, head tilting. "Aren't they the same thing?"

He shakes his head, amused.

"Oh." I fight a blush. "Whatever. My lack of knowledge concerning ancient Asian warriors is not the main issue here."

"Really?"

"Really." I pin him with my best no-nonsense look. "Why are

you here on my stairs, scaring me half to death at one in the morning?" I glance down at my ninja hands then back at him, eyes wide with mock concern. "I could've killed you with these!" I waggle my fingers at him. "They're lethal when I unleash my qi."

His mouth twitches again.

You are not fourteen. You are a grown ass woman. Do not squeal or do cartwheels because the man deigned to smile at you.

"Seriously, Nate, I didn't send up the bat-signal, or anything." I shiver — more from the image of Nate dressed in a skin-tight Batman costume than the cold. "So... why are you here?"

"Let's talk inside." His eyes scan my body, taking in the goose-bumps on my bare legs. "You're freezing."

I sigh, but don't fight him. Truthfully, I am kind of chilly. And hungry. And horny.

Not that I'll be acting on those last two — not while he's around, anyway.

I climb the steps, rolling my eyes when I see Nate step over Boo with an uncomfortable grimace. Little dogs always have a way of making large men uneasy. As though if they're ever caught walking one or, god forbid, *cuddling* with one, it'll be an automatic deduction of masculinity points.

Hands searching my empty pockets, I pause at the door and groan. "Oh, frack."

Nate's eyebrows go up.

"My keys." I sigh. "They're in the bush."

Brows go higher.

"I kind of... threw them." I swallow and try not to blush.

"When you flailed like an epileptic fish on dry land?"

"Was that a *joke* that just came out of your mouth?" I ask, taken aback. "I didn't think you knew how to do that, anymore."

His eyes are steady on mine. "A lot you don't know about me, West."

Oh, I'm sure there is...

My heart is pounding so loud by this point I'm pretty sure they can hear it down the block. I try to swallow but find my throat is clogged by a bundle of nervous, sexual energy.

"Well, you surprised me, appearing out of nowhere like that." I cover hastily, making my voice haughty so he won't know I'm seriously considering the repercussions of dry humping his leg. "Which means it's *your* fault my keys are in the hydrangeas, and *you* are the one who's going to climb in there and find them."

"Or..." He steps closer, until our chests are nearly brushing, and I forget to breathe, forget to think, forget to do anything but stare as his face moves toward mine. Extending one arm behind my back, he comes to a stop before we actually touch, but his mouth is so close to my ear I can feel his breath on my neck when he whispers. "...I could just use *my* key."

The sound of a lock turning over and my door swinging inward snap me out of my momentary lust. I'm still standing there like a fool, attempting to process the fact that Nate just opened my door with "his key" when he steps around me and strolls inside. His gait is so casual as he strides through my foyer and disappears into my kitchen, you'd think he's stepped over my threshold every day for the past five years.

What. The. Frack.

"You coming, Miyagi?" he calls from somewhere inside.

I glance down at Boo, who's gazing up at me in expectation, clearly wanting to follow the strange man inside — the man who's likely looking through my private documents, hacking my hard drive, and cracking my safe as we speak.

"You do realize we're totally fucked, right?" I ask Boo in a serious voice.

Swear to god, he nods his doggy head in comprehension before giving up waiting for me to grow a set and trotting after Nate.

"Frack," I mutter, stepping inside with a groan and shutting the door at my back. If not for the sudden tension in Boo's leash, pulling me away from the entryway, I'd have happily stayed there all night rather than face whatever message of doom and gloom Nate's undoubtedly here to deliver.

CHAPTER 11

THERE'S A SPECIAL RING OF HELL FOR THE PEOPLE
WHO INVENTED PUSH-UP BRAS AND HIGH HEELS.

*Nathaniel Knox, watching a beautiful brunette glide out
of a town car in a blue-black dress.*

I FIND him in the kitchen — not rooting through my drawers for state secrets, but searching my fridge. As soon as I unhook Boo from his leash, he runs to his bed on the other side of the room and settles in like a king holding court. Nate's audible sigh brings my eyes back to him.

"What the hell is the matter with you, West?"

I hop up on the marble kitchen island, legs swinging, and contemplate his question. "Well, I've always wanted to be better at math. And sometimes, if I blow-dry my hair too much, I get really bad split ends. I'm an abominable public speaker. Oh! And I'm really terrible at remembering names."

After a few seconds, I realize I've been rambling and snap my lips together so I won't say anything else. Nate's staring at me with crinkly eyes again.

"You weren't talking about my flaws," I say dumbly.

"I was referring to the fact that you've got no food in this house," he says, voice choked like he's trying not to laugh. "But I'm glad you told me about the split ends. Sounds like a real trauma. Don't know how you managed to make it through all these years with something like that plaguing you."

I throw a dishtowel at his head. He dodges it easily.

"I don't know what you're talking about," I mutter, staring at the empty fridge to keep my eyes from undressing him. There's something about seeing Nate *playful* that practically undoes me. "There's leftover pizza in there. I think. And, uh, definitely a jar of maraschino cherries. Possibly a bottle of Sriracha. Plus, at least a half-bottle of wine."

He's silent.

"What? You could totally make a meal out of that." I shrug and dart a glance at him. "Haven't you ever heard of cherry-topped pizza with a Sriracha-wine glaze? It's all the rage in Europe."

"West, I've met stray dogs with more nutritious diets." His eyes flash down the length of my body, lingering on my bare legs. "Makes no fucking sense, you looking like that."

My heart stops. "What?"

He ignores me, shutting the fridge and moving to lean against the counter opposite me. His face flattens into a familiar mask as he folds his arms across his chest.

"We have to talk about O'Dair."

"Please tell me you're joking." I narrow my eyes at him when he remains silent. "Please tell me you're not seriously here to warn me away from another date."

His jaw starts to tick. "He hangs with a bad crowd. He's—"

"Wait! Let me guess... he's *dangerous!*" I gasp. "What a unique and original concept!"

"West, you have to understand, your family's wealth makes you a target—"

"No! No. Just because you think the only reason a man would be interested in me is to extort money or power doesn't mean I'm going to start believing it. *You* might not think I'm worth anything beyond my last name, but—" I slam my lips together so I won't do something stupid, like finish that sentence. Or cry.

Something flashes in his eyes — possibly surprise, more likely anger. "I never said that. Don't put words in my mouth."

"Well, you clearly believe it, or you wouldn't be here."

"Remember Brett Croft? Or have you forgotten so easily?" His fists clench at just the memory. "He nearly killed Gemma. Wouldn't have hesitated to kill you, too."

Some of the wind goes out of my sails. "Cormack is nothing like Brett."

"And you know this how, exactly? Woman's intuition?" His voice drips sarcasm. "Did you read his aura? Did he pinky swear he wasn't manipulating you?"

Okay, it's official. Playful Nate is much better than Asshole Nate.

The anger thrumming in my bloodstream makes me bolder than usual. "You know, if I didn't know better I'd swear you were jealous."

His eyes flash darkly and an incredulous sound erupts from his mouth. "I'm being serious here, West."

"So am I!"

His jaw ticks.

Watching him, something is abruptly clear. He doesn't want me — he'll never want me — but he doesn't want anyone else to have me, either. Like a Pit Bull with a bone it doesn't particularly like, but can't relinquish to another dog out of pride or some other deeply ingrained territorial bullshit.

"West, listen to me," he bites out, words icy. "Cormack O'Dair is—"

"Stop right there!" I snap, holding out my hands. "Whatever it is, I don't want to hear it."

"West—"

"Why do you suddenly care who I date?" I ask point-blank. "What changed? Because, up until about a month ago, you've pretty much pretended I don't exist."

He swallows hard — I watch his Adam's apple bob with the strength of it. When he speaks, his voice is carefully distant.

"It's *who* you're dating that I have a problem with."

"Ahh, right. Because everyone is trying to exploit me." I laugh but it's a humorless sound. "You know, I think I was happier when we didn't interact at all."

His eyes narrow. "I want you safe. I don't really give a shit if that makes you unhappy."

"Clearly, or you wouldn't be here."

He leans forward fractionally and I feel my heart clench. "I've got good instincts. They've kept me alive more times than I can count. So when they tell me O'Dair has another motive with you, I fucking listen to them."

"And that's different from woman's intuition *how*, exactly?"

He ignores me. "Something about him doesn't add up. I don't know what, yet, but I'm looking into him. It's only a matter of time before I find out what he's planning."

"Maybe he's just planning to take me on a freaking date!"

"West, listen close." He takes a step away from the counter

and closes some of the distance between us. "This is going to go down one of two ways—"

I gasp, throwing a hand over my heart in a parody of shock. "Let me guess — the *easy* way or the *hard* way?!"

"West—"

"My name is Phoebe. *Phee-bee.*" I sound it out slowly, as though I'm speaking to a child. "Two syllables. Rhymes with itself. Super easy to say. You should try it sometime."

"This isn't up for negotiation, West." He purposely ignores my suggestion, taking another stride toward me. "You're not seeing him again. And he's already been informed of that fact."

My blood runs cold. "What did you say to him?"

He stays silent.

"Ugh!" I screech. "You know what, *Knox?*" I watch him flinch when I seethe out his last name. Two can play this game. "I'm getting pretty tired of this. Of you — barging into my house, my life, my freaking *fridge*, and bossing me around like it's somehow your place."

"I'm trying to keep you safe." His words are flat, his jaw is ticking.

"Seems like you're trying to keep me celibate, actually," I snap, hopping off the counter in a graceful leap that rolls my ankle and nearly sends me sprawling on my face.

Excellent.

Blushing furiously, I right myself and try to ignore the fact that Nate went tense as soon as the word *celibate* slipped out. Turning my back on him entirely, I snap my fingers to call for Boo. When he trots to my side, I head for the stairs.

"Goodbye, *Knox.*" I don't look at him as the scathing words leave my mouth. "Let's do this again... oh, how about never."

A hand clamps over my arm, drawing me to a sudden halt. Every muscle in my body goes still when I feel the heat of Nate's body move closer, until he's practically pressed against my back. His voice is low, intent when it vibrates at my neck.

"I'd notice."

My mind swirls to a stop.

"What?" I whisper, confused.

There's a beat of silence before he speaks.

"Earlier, you said—" He clears his throat and his voice drops lower. "You wondered if anyone would notice if you disappeared." There's another heavy beat of silence. Not daring to shatter the moment, I hold my breath until it burns in my lungs. I get the sense he's doing the same.

"I'd notice," he says finally, voice softer than I've ever heard it.

Before I can respond, the hand disappears from my arm and his heat disappears from my back. I've barely turned around when I hear the front door creak open, followed by a terse order.

"Stay the fuck away from O'Dair."

Then, the door slams and he's gone.

Bones jellied, I sink down to the floor and stay there, back pressed against the kitchen island, legs curled to my chest, tears gathering in my eyes.

I hate him. Hate him! He's bossy and condescending and makes me feel like a discombobulated pre-teen girl. I hope he never comes back.

God, I'm unconvincing.

My internal rant is soon overtaken by another voice from the back of my mind — small but persistent as it replays two words over and over in a deep, rumbling growl.

I'd notice. I'd notice. I'd notice.

My breaths are shallow, my face is wet — it takes me a minute to realize I'm crying on my kitchen floor. Eventually, Boo wanders over and hops up in my lap, his tiny furry head nestling into the crook of my arm.

I must look even more pathetic than I feel, if my demon-dog is taking pity on me.

"CAN YOU SPRAIN YOUR VAGINA? Because I don't think mine will ever function normally again, after that last position we did."

Gemma's loud exclamation draws glances from several people in the surrounding booths. I shoot her a look and contemplate kicking her beneath the table. Lila chuckles so hard cupcake crumbs shoot from her mouth. Shelby just alternates glaring at the three of us in turn, likely wishing she had better taste in friends.

We're at *Crumble*, an adorable little cupcake shop Gemma dragged us to as soon as our Sunday morning yoga class was over.

We all need a sugar rush, after the trauma of exercising first thing in the morning. Especially Gemma, who's so uncoordinated she makes me look like a yogi in comparison. She spent most of the hour-long session lying flat on her mat, moaning in pain after her downward dog pose went horribly wrong, resulting in a face plant, two sprained wrists, and a pulled muscle in her thigh so bad, we practically had to carry her here.

Lila, on the other hand, spent the session hissing questions at me between poses, wanting to know every detail about Nate and Cormack's showdown last night.

I did my best to tune both of them out, mainly so I wouldn't lose my precarious balance during tree pose.

All the while Shelby, bonafide fitness guru, led the class from a mat at the front of the studio and shot eye-daggers at us for daring to interrupt her zen-like atmosphere. Honestly, I'm surprised she didn't kick us out after the first ten minutes. I'm even more surprised she let us drag her along for post-yoga cupcakes — Shelby is a twenty-seven year old Monsanto-hating vegan. She'll probably have a heart attack if she ever sees the processed snack foods in my pantry.

"God, my ass is sore. I think it's broken." Gemma moans lightly, face contorting in pleasure as she chomps into a double-chocolate cupcake.

"You can't break your ass." Shelby snorts. "And if you'd just get into a routine or maybe come to my class more than once every six months, it wouldn't hurt so bad every time."

"It takes me six months to *recover* from one of your classes," Gemma points out. "Otherwise, I'd totally be there."

"Right." Shelby rolls her eyes. "Sure you would."

"Hey, you can't be mad at me — Chrissy didn't even show up."

"Chrissy just had a baby," Shelby points out. "She's excused. For now."

"Babies get you out of exercising? Maybe I should get pregnant," Gemma murmurs thoughtlessly. When we all glance at her, she blushes bright red and her eyes go wide. "Kidding! Kidding. No babies. Nope. Not happening. Ever."

"Oh yeah? How's Chase feel about that?" I ask, amused.

"If it were up to him, I'd have been barefoot and pregnant the week we met."

"Oh, woe is you!" Lila rolls her eyes. "If a man that gorgeous wanted to give me his babies, you would *not* hear me complaining."

"Can we not talk about babies?" Shelby asks, grimacing. "Just thinking about the snot-nosed little rug-rats makes me nauseous. I'm really trying to hang onto my zen, here."

"I don't need babies. I just need some *sex*," I mutter darkly. "At this rate, I'm going to die a virgin."

They all glance at me.

"What?" I ask innocently. "It's true."

"Patience, grasshopper. My plan is working. Just like I knew it would," Lila says smugly. "Knox faced off with Cormack last night. It's a start."

"He also kind of... showed up at my place when I got home."

"What?!" Lila explodes, clearly angry at being kept in the dark.

"He did?" Gemma exclaims, so much excitement in her voice you'd think cupcakes were on a two-for-one sale.

I nod hesitantly.

"Spill," Shelby orders, tucking a strand of light brown hair behind her ear. "I need to live vicariously through someone whose love life doesn't resemble an episode of Mad Men."

Gemma's eyes get worried as she stares at her friend. "Things not going well with Paul?"

Paul is Shelby's husband. I've never met him, mostly 'cause he's never around. Apparently he's some kind of finance hotshot who spends too much time at work and too little time with his wife. A modern day Don Draper, if there ever was one.

"Same old." Shelby sighs. "But I don't want to talk about that." Her pretty brown eyes move to me. "Spill, Phoebe. We're not getting any younger."

I sigh deeply and tell them everything — about the confrontation between Cormack and Nate and the late-night visit that happened afterwards. I leave out the part about my night ending with me sobbing against my imported Moroccan floor tiles.

"So, in a nutshell... he stormed out yet again with no real explanation as to why I can't date Cormack... who seemed perfectly nice, by the way, until Nate showed up and ruined things." I peel the paper off my red velvet cupcake and swipe a finger through the decadent cream frosting. It melts on my tongue and I'm pretty sure I groan in pleasure. "Damn, that's good. Who needs men when there are cupcakes?"

"I don't know how you people eat those things," Shelby says, clearly revolted. "The amount of sugar alone..." She shudders.

"Um, because they're good?" Gemma rolls her eyes before turning her gaze to me. "And I'm sorry, Phee. I really am. But if Knox says there's something off about Cormack... I believe him."

"Wait just a goddamned minute!" Lila's glaring at me. "You're telling me Knox came to your house and you didn't jump his bones?!"

"Lila—"

"You didn't even *try* to jump his bones?!"

"Lila—"

"The plan was to seduce him." She shakes her head in disbelief. "Do you not remember the fundamental guidelines of Operation SPANK?"

"Spank?" Shelby asks.

"Severing Phoebe's Attachment to Nathaniel Knox," Gemma murmurs.

Shelby grins. "Best code name ever."

"Truth," Gemma agrees.

"Lila, it's not that simple." My voice is defensive. "What was I supposed to do, strip naked and launch myself at him like a heat-seeking missile?"

"Yes!" She practically yells. "That's exactly what you were supposed to do."

I sigh. "Well, I screwed up. Sue me."

"What the hell is going on with you, Phoebe?" Lila's eyes narrow. "Are you having second thoughts about the plan?"

"Of course not!" I swallow. "I'm *so* done with him."

Gemma snorts. Shelby hides a smile behind her water bottle. Lila outright laughs.

"Guys!" I whine. "You're supposed to be helping me, here."

"I can lead a horse to water, but..." Lila shrugs helplessly. "I can't screw his brains out for you."

"Maybe I don't have to screw his brains out. Maybe I can just keep dating Cormack until I fall in love with him and forget all about Nate. Fake it till you make it, right?" I straighten my shoulders, emboldened by the idea. "Honestly, I don't think my heart is so illogical it would keep pining for Nate when it could have someone like Cormack instead."

The three of them burst out laughing at the same time. Full-on hysterical cackles.

"Guys!"

"Sorry," Gemma gasps out, wiping tears. "Sorry. It's just—"

"The most naive thing I've ever heard," Shelby contributes between snorts.

"Naive?" Lila's holding her stomach, entire body shaking. "I was going to say batshit crazy."

I huff and cross my arms over my chest. "And you call yourselves my *friends*."

"Phoebe, honey, you can't keep dating Cormack." Gemma's blue eyes are twinkling with humor. "Partly because you're in love with another man, but also because if Knox says he's dangerous, I believe him."

"Why?"

"Well, he warned me away from Brett... and then I ended up in the hospital." Gemma takes a large bite of her double-chocolate cupcake. "So, I have a tendency to trust his judgment. He's not the type to exaggerate. Maybe there's more to Cormack than his charming disposition and killer accent."

"Maybe that's a good thing," Shelby murmurs.

"What?" Gemma and I ask in unison.

"Hear me out," Shelby says, eyes active with thoughts. "Knox only shows up when Phoebe's in danger — or when he *thinks* she's in danger. Right?"

"I guess," I mutter, taking another heavenly bite of my cupcake.

"So… why don't we just put you in a semi-life threatening situation — something minor, like a car accident or a fake kidnapping — after which he will swoop in, save your life, and carry you off into the sunset?"

"Life threatening!?" I squeak, alarmed.

"That's genius!" Lila yells at the same time.

"Are you out of your goddamned mind?" Gemma screeches.

"Chill!" Shelby holds out her hands defensively. "Jeeze, I was kidding. Mostly."

"I think our friend group has had enough life threatening scenarios to last a lifetime." Gemma glares at her friend. "Or do you not remember the car chase, kidnapping, and subsequent drowning just a few months ago?"

"For what it's worth, I think it's a great plan," Lila says, grinning at Shelby.

"Please, no hair-brained schemes." I grimace. "I would like to live to see my twenty-fourth birthday."

"That's only a few days away," Lila points out. "I think you'll make it."

"I didn't know it was your birthday! Are you having a party?" Gemma asks.

"No, I don't really celebrate." I shrug. "Usually I'll do something with my brother if he's around. Otherwise, it's just any other day."

"Where is Parker these days?" Lila asks. "Tahiti? Rome? Shanghai?"

"I think he might be climbing Kilimanjaro again? Honestly, I can't keep track anymore." I try not to sigh too deeply. "Needless to say, he won't be making it home this year."

"What about your dad?" Lila pesters.

Gemma seems to tense across the table, dropping her sky-blue eyes to her plate and tucking a flyaway curl behind one ear.

Weird.

I glance back at Lila. "He'll be in back-to-back business meet-ings for the foreseeable future. With the waterfront development breaking ground next week, he's busier than ever. I'll try calling him tonight. Remind him I'm alive, and all. Only daughter, requesting contact."

Gemma fidgets in her seat, clearly uncomfortable about something.

Shelby's eyes shift to look out the window, as though she's nervous.

I clear my throat to break the sudden silence. "Sorry, I didn't mean to make things weird. Things with my dad have always been—"

"We should throw you a party," Gemma announces, eyes lighting up. "It'll be great! We'll have it at Chase's penthouse, invite anyone you want. We could even do a theme! Golf Pros and Tennis Hoes – women being the pros, of course."

"Guys in Ties and Girls in Pearls," Shelby suggests.

"I always loved the Mathletes and Athletes combo in college," Lila adds, eyes sparkling.

"Oh! That's a good one." Gemma's nodding. "The penthouse can fit at least sixty people, maybe more. We could get a DJ and some lighting—"

"NO!" I exclaim, starting to panic. They all look at me, star-tled by my volume. "Sorry." I clear my throat and look at Gemma with guilty eyes. "It's really sweet of you to offer, Gem, but I'm really not into the whole birthday thing. I find them pretty depressing, to be honest."

"Oh," her expression falls.

"I'm sorry," I say, feeling like the ultimate party-pooper. "I'm just not a big party kind of girl. I've always been better with small groups or one-on-one interaction."

"Perfect! I'll send you a stripper-gram as a present," Shelby offers, grinning. "That definitely counts as one-on-one interaction, right?"

I snort. "A stripper and a virgin. Sounds like a porno waiting to happen."

"Oh, come on." Shelby laughs. "It'll cheer you up."

I roll my eyes and push away my empty plate. "Do me a favor and send it to Nate instead. Maybe it'll somehow dislodge the giant stick he's got up his ass."

"He'll come around," Gemma says gently, reaching out to squeeze my hand. "You'll see."

I sigh and hold my tongue.

I don't have the heart to tell her she's wrong. Me and Nate? Never gonna happen. Not even if Shelby has me hospitalized with a fake murder plot.

CHAPTER 12

ACCORDING TO CHEMISTS, ALCOHOL ACTUALLY *IS* A
SOLUTION.

*Phoebe West, defending her decision to stay in and drink
wine on Valentine's Day.*

AFTER SAYING goodbye to the girls, I catch a cab home from
Crumble and hop in the shower. My morning flew by in a blur of
stretching, cupcakes, and gossip — it's early afternoon already
and I've accomplished none of the things on my to-do list.

Great.

I take a quick shower and head into the small office off the
kitchen with my damp hair wrapped in a towel and my body
stuffed into my favorite yoga pants — the ones I never wear

CROSS THE LINE   135

outside the house because they have a hole in the right ass cheek, but can't quite convince myself to throw away.

As soon as my laptop powers on, I scroll through my inbox, deleting the zillion spam emails that have accumulated in the two days since I last logged in.

UNBEATABLE MALE ENHANCEMENT! GAIN FIVE INCHES!

Thanks, I'm all set.

I'll be the first to admit, working as a graphic designer is pretty sweet. I make my own hours, set my own pace when it comes to projects, and essentially get to be my own boss most of the time. There's never anyone breathing down my neck to make sure I've clocked in by eight every morning. I go to the WestTech offices *maybe* once a week.

There's a downside to all that freedom, though.

With no one watching to keep me on track every hour on the hour, I have a tendency to procrastinate. On rare occasions, I've even been known to forego work altogether in favor of an all-day *House of Cards* marathon.

I never said I was perfect. In fact, I've adamantly denied such accusations.

Anyway, it's all fun and games (and Netflix-binges) until I wind up with a veritable mountain of work. I'm currently juggling three different designs for WestTech's summer ad campaign, plus the website needs updating and a man from the art department wants my approval on our billboard overlooking the Mass Pike, which will advertise my father's new high-rise condo development.

The West Waterfront: Where Innovation Meets Luxury

No, I don't come up with the shitty campaign slogans — I just slap 'em on brochures and pick out the fonts.

The only thing that might get me through the stack of work

I've let pile up is if I handcuff myself to my desk and insert an IV of coffee directly into my bloodstream for the next week.

Cracking my neck like I'm preparing for battle, I click open Photoshop and dive in.

CHIRP, chirp, chirp.

"Ugh," I moan unintelligibly, sounding more zombie than human.

Chiiiiiirp. Chiiiiiirp. Chiiiiiirp.

"Kill me," I grumble.

Chiiiiiiiirp. Chiiiiiiiirp. Chiiiiiiiirp.

Something is ringing. Very insistently.

My bleary eyes blink open and I realize I've passed out on my keyboard. My cheek is wet from resting in a puddle of drool, my hair is a rat's nest of curls since I failed to brush it out after my shower, and my back is so sore I think I'll need traction. I'm completely disoriented, unsure whether I've been asleep minutes, hours, or days.

I finally locate my chirping cellphone beneath a stack of glossy photo paper.

"Hello?" I grunt, voice huskier than normal.

"Phoebe." The voice is warm and unmistakably male.

Phey-bee.

"Cormack?"

"Lila gave me your number. I hope it's okay to call." He pauses. "I didn't wake you, did I?"

"Of course not," I say, wiping congealed drool off my cheek with the back of my hand. *Cute.* It's really a wonder I don't have more men beating down my door. "I was just doing some work."

"For your father?"

My brows knit. "For WestTech."

"Ah." He clears his throat. "Well, if you're ready to take a break from work, I'd like nothing more than to take you to dinner."

"That's so sweet, Cormack, but I'm really—"

"I insist." Even while cutting me off, he maintains his über-polite tone. "It'll be my way of making up for last night. If I hadn't been such an oaf, you wouldn't have run off."

Nate will probably kill me if I go out with Cormack again. Show up here all brooding and angry...

Somehow, to my crazy brain, that sounds more like an incentive than a negative. I shake my head, hoping to clear the delusional thoughts.

"I really shouldn't—"

"Please, Phoebe? I feel like an ass. I never should've acted the way I did, getting into it with Knox."

"It seemed like you two have a history." My words are carefully nonchalant.

"We don't. Not really." He pauses. "I guess you could say we've... crossed paths, in the past."

"Oh." *That wasn't supremely vague, or anything.*

"I wasn't aware you knew him."

My lips twist. "I don't."

Not anymore.

"You're not close? He acted... territorial."

"I'd sooner hug a cactus than get close to Nathaniel Knox."

"Great." His voice is audibly relieved. "Then there's no reason you can't come out with me, tonight."

Damn, he's persistent.

"I actually have a lot of work to get through—"

"Lila gave me your address. I'll be there at seven." I can hear that dimpled grin in his voice. "And I won't take no for an answer."

"But—"

"See you in forty minutes, Phoebe."

What?!

"Did you say *forty—*"

He's already clicked off.

Crap on sourdough!

I jump out of my chair and sprint for the stairs, screeching in horror when I catch sight of my hair in the mirror across from my desk. Short of a miracle, there's no way I'll be buffed, polished, and ready for a date in forty — shit, make that thirty-nine — minutes.

Rushing through the archway, I cut through the kitchen so fast I almost miss the piece of paper taped to my refrigerator. Boo lifts his head from the plush doggie-bed where he's been snoozing when I slam to a stop, heart pounding in my chest.

My eyes move from the note to the countertop, where my house keys rest. My stomach clenches at the sight. I was in such a rush to get to yoga this morning, I didn't have a chance to search through the bushes to find them. And yet, there they sit.

Eyes narrowed on the note, I walk numbly to the fridge and lean close to read the blocky, masculine words scrawled on the paper.

Now you won't starve to death. Stay put until we talk.

He didn't bother signing it.

I reach out blindly and tug open the refrigerator doors. My heart starts to slam against my ribs when I see groceries on every shelf — more food than I think I've ever had at once. Fruits and vegetables and pre-made raviolis and a French bread and a big wedge of expensive cheese and my favorite kind of seltzer. Cranberry lime.

I don't have the mental capacity to wonder how he even *knew* it was my favorite, because my eyes are fixed on the bottom shelf, where a six pack of beer with a brand name I've never heard of sits unobtrusively.

Lagunitas India Pale Ale.

A man's beer. Definitely.

Nate's beer.

I stare at it for a long moment, wondering what it means that he left his beer here. Wondering *why* he bothered to do all this for me. And most importantly, whether he saw me sleeping in a puddle of my own drool with crazy, electrocuted hair and my holey yoga pants when he snuck in and stocked my fridge with groceries.

Fine, maybe *snuck* isn't the right verb. I was pretty much dead to the world — nothing short of an earthquake would've woken me. For all I know, he loaded in the groceries while blasting death metal so loud it shook the floors. My dreams of Henry Cavill would've continued undisturbed.

Whatever.

My eyes seem to be stuck on the sight of his beer sitting next to my seltzer. Never in my life have I been so entranced by the sight of a freaking beverage. I stand there for so long the fridge starts to beep at me, its automated alert system kicking on to tell me cool air is escaping.

The persistent beeps snap me out of my stupor. I shut the door in a daze, turning to lean against the stainless steel and hauling a shaky breath into my lungs. My eyes press closed. Maybe if I squeeze them hard enough, I'll erase what I've just seen from my memory.

Damn him.

Just when I think I really might be able to hate him, that he's terrible and bossy and no good... he goes and does something like this. Something that makes my heart ache so fiercely, it's all I can do not to curl into a ball on the floor and ride the waves until the ocean of longing recedes back behind safe banks of common sense and self-preservation.

Boo barks from somewhere at my feet and my eyes spring open, landing on the illuminated green numbers glowing from my microwave clock.

6:31

Crap on a corn biscuit with a side of fries.

Unless I want to look like Medusa on my date, thoughts of Nate are going to have to simmer on the back burner. I sprint from the kitchen and up the stairs as fast as my legs can carry me.

"DID I already tell you how beautiful you look?"

"Twice." I smile. "But that's really not the kind of compliment that gets old."

We're at a gorgeous little restaurant by the water, and I'm thanking my lucky stars my favorite little black dress was clean and wrinkle-free when I yanked it on at 6:57, because the decor here is fancy. Linen tablecloths, extensive wine list, candles burning low in crystal centerpieces. Cormack orders a bottle of white wine for the table and I bite my tongue to keep from telling him I prefer a pinot noir to its grigio counterpart.

What I'd really like is an Old Fashioned, but I don't tell him that either.

"So, tell me about your work," I say, realizing I know virtually nothing about the man sitting across from me other than that he's extremely handsome, once hailed from the Emerald Isle, and does, in fact, use dinner napkins properly.

Mouth breathing cretin, indeed.

"I could, but if I wanted to put you to sleep I'd have taken you to the symphony." He grins, dimples popping. "Let's talk about you. You're much more exciting."

"I like the symphony," I murmur, but he doesn't hear me — the sommelier's returned with our wine and Cormack is busy swirling, sniffing, and sipping.

"Perfection," he announces when he's swallowed. "Thank you."

The sommelier nods, fills our glasses, and disappears without a word. Cormack turns to me, glass raised.

"A toast." His eyes sparkle as they meet mine.

My eyebrows lift in tandem with my glass. "What are we toasting?"

"To new beginnings."

"New beginnings," I echo.

We clink glasses and drink, eyes locked. He's handsome, in the candlelight. Strong jaw, perfectly symmetrical features. And yet, not one single butterfly flutters in my stomach. My skin isn't on fire from just the weight of his eyes. My heart isn't having arrhythmias.

"Have you always lived in the city?" he asks after a beat of silence.

"I grew up on Nantucket, mainly, but my father sent me and my brother to boarding school in Rhode Island when we were old enough." I absently touch the gold pendant hanging around my neck. A gift from my father on my sixteenth birthday — a small, shining sun on a thin gold chain. Simple but beautiful. I remember the day he clasped it around my neck; he hugged me and whispered into my ear that it was a good omen to carry the sun by your heart.

I would've worn it even if it were bad luck.

It's one of the only gifts he's ever given me that wasn't picked out by a secretary or personal shopper. I rarely wear it out of the house, never wanting to risk losing it, but I was in such a rush tonight I didn't have time to swap it for one of my more elaborate pieces.

"At least you had your brother there with you."

"What?" My eyes lift back to Cormack.

"At boarding school."

"Oh." My cheeks heat. "Well, the boys' and girls' campuses are separate, actually. There were social hours and mixers, of course, but Parker's four years older than me. Our extracurricular activities rarely meshed."

"An all-girls school?" He grins wolfishly. "I'm sure you have some interesting stories."

"Believe me, it wasn't all naked pillow fights and painting each other's nails."

More like two hundred snotty, materialistic bitches who pray at the altar of gossip and sabotage. There's a reason Lila is the only one I've kept in touch with, after high school.

Cormack laughs and it isn't rusty at all. Like he does it often, freely.

It's a lovely sound — one that doesn't make my stomach clench or my breath catch.

I smile and pretend not to notice how empty that makes me feel.

To my surprise, the night passes easily. We drink crisp wine and eat delicious seafood and Cormack's charm keeps conversation light, putting a smile on my face and a warmth in my belly. There's no verbal sparring. We don't spit barbed comments back and forth. Our eyes never clash with so much intensity I think I might shatter.

It's all very normal. Exactly as a first date should be. As close to perfect as it gets.

I try to be happy about it.

After all, that's the goal, right? That's what we're all supposed to be striving for in this life.

Happiness.

But if this, here in this moment with him, is what happiness feels like... I'm afraid I don't like it half as much as my misery.

————————

WE WALK along the waterfront after dinner. Rowes Wharf glows in the distance, the trees on the promenade strung with white lights. Not many people are out walking — it's Sunday night, and chilly for May.

The wine in my system keeps me warm enough. When I came back from the bathroom after our entrees were finished, I found Cormack had refilled my glass to nearly the brim. I took a few small sips to be polite — it was a two hundred dollar bottle — but didn't come close to finishing it.

Still, I must've had more than I meant to, because the after-effects of the alcohol are hitting me. Hard. My gait is unsteady as I maneuver the cobblestones in my four-inch heels — jet-black Manolos with killer silver accents. On a normal day, I can walk a tightrope in these.

"Whoa, there!" Cormack's hand lands on my arm in a firm grip, steadying me when I bobble. "You all right?"

Actually, no. I'm not. My head is foggy and my toes are numb.

"I'm fine," I murmur, pressing two fingertips to my temple. "Maybe a bit too much wine."

Cormack laughs heartily. "We'll get you home soon enough."

I nod, distracted by the vibrations coming from my clutch purse. When I pull out my phone, an unknown number flashes across my screen.

"Who is it?" Cormack asks.

"I don't know."

"Let it go to voicemail." He bends to meet my eyes, all smiles.

"If it's important, they'll call back. The car's just up ahead, and I have a surprise for you. We should get going or we'll be late."

I grin weakly. "It could be my brother calling from overseas. Or Lila calling from jail," I joke. "You really never know."

"Lila's out with Padraic." His eyes flash with frustration for a brief second, but he covers the slip so quickly, I think I must've imagined it.

"That doesn't mean she hasn't been arrested." I try to smile but my lips are feeling numb.

"Of course." Cormack's jaw clenches in a surprising show of anger. "I'll wait here, give you some privacy."

"I'll just be a second." I stumble to a nearby bench over-looking the water, sliding my finger over the screen to accept the call. "Hello?"

"West, where the fuck are you?" a voice barks before the word has even left my mouth. "You're not home. *Again*. I thought I told you to stay put."

"Nate?" My breath huffs out — I see it steam the air in front of my face, but I don't feel at all cold. Strange. "Is that you?"

He pauses. "You don't have my number in your phone?"

"Lila deleted it last year." I sigh. "Told me it was time to let go."

Wherefore art thou, verbal filter? Why hast thou abandoned me?

There's another stony silence, longer this time. If I were sober, I'd worry what it meant.

"Are you drunk?" he asks abruptly, something strange and gravelly in his voice.

"What? No." I shake my head, perplexed when it takes my vision a moment to catch up to the movement. There's a three second delay between my eyes and my brain. "Ugh," I moan, feeling disoriented. "Okay, maybe I'm a little drunk. But I swear I only had a glass of wine..."

CROSS THE LINE   145

"West." Suddenly, there's steel in Nate's tone. And, if I'm not mistaken, concern. "I'm coming to get you. Tell me where you are."

"You can't come. I'm on a date."

"Fuck. You're out with him, aren't you?"

"I shouldn't be on the phone." My words have begun to run together. Everything is lagging, smearing around the edges. "It's impolite."

"I don't give a fuck about polite, West. Listen to me, he's not who he says he is—"

I snort. "And *you* are?"

"He's dangerous!" Nate snaps. I hear the sound of an engine turning over through the phone. "Run. Get away from him. Right now."

"Cormack isn't dangerous," I say, giggling. I don't know why I'm giggling — I'm not a giggler. But I can't seem to stop the hysterical noises as they bubble up from my throat.

There's a small part of my brain — a part I can't seem to access — that's screaming at me to listen to Nate. The rest of my mind feels empty, dark. Like a switch has been flipped off, my neurons blinking out like a light.

"Tell me where you are. Please, just— fuck, West!"

I must be drunk because I'm surely imagining things. That's not *panic* in Nate's voice. He's a super badass mercenary. He doesn't feel panic.

I sense movement in my peripheral. My head turns and, after a second, my eyes catch up. Cormack is standing there, frowning at me. His green-blue eyes are flat. When he speaks, that charming Irish accent I love so much has disappeared entirely, replaced by the flat, rough tones of a native Bostonian.

"Give me the fucking phone."

Gimme tha fahkin' phone.

"What?" I breathe.

Nate's shouting something through the speaker, but I can't make out his words. I'm frozen as Cormack reaches for me, one hand closing over my arm in a tight hold, the other pulling the cell from my weakened fingers.

I try to move, but my limbs aren't cooperating. Try to fight, but I have no strength. Try to scream, but I have no voice.

There's only darkness, spreading like a cancer through my mind, reducing my vision until the blurs of color fade to black.

The last thing I remember before Cormack tosses my phone into the ocean and everything slides out of focus is the sound of Nate's voice, tinny and distant, barking one word through the speaker.

"Phoebe!"

CHAPTER 13

WHEN I COME TO, I'm in a windowless room I don't recognize. There's a musty, dank smell like mold or mildew, and I get the sense I'm underground though I don't know for sure. Goosebumps cover my exposed arms and legs – between the fright in my veins and frigid air in my lungs, all my hairs are standing on end.

It's so dark in the room there's barely any difference when I peel open my eyes. Not regular darkness — the pervasive, personified kind of dark that almost seems alive; where shadows slither along the walls and any corner might be hiding monsters. The kind that keeps children awake at night, weeping into pillows with blankets clenched tight, calling out for someone to comfort them.

I'd take a monster under my bed over this nightmare any day of the week.

My head aches like someone's taken a jackhammer to it — lingering effects of whatever drug he slipped me. I can feel the rope wrapped tight across my midsection, binding my wrists to the arms of the steel-backed chair, looped fast around my ankles. My tongue pushes uselessly at the duct tape covering my mouth.

I thrash for a few moments until my strength runs out.

Scream until my throat goes raw and I'm out of breath.

For all my trouble, nothing but muffled cries escape the thick tape. My wrists chafe until the skin breaks, but my binds never loosen.

No one hears me. Or, if they do, they don't bother to come.

As the drug haze slowly clears, my mind swims with questions.

How did I get here? Did Cormack carry me from that bench to his car? Was he working alone? Why on earth would he take me? And above all, why the hell was I so fucking stubborn when Nate told me not to go out with him?

I don't have answers to any except the last.

Pride.

Nate crashed back into my life out of nowhere, a rogue meteor disrupting my carefully-balanced orbit, and expected me to trust him like nothing had changed between us. Like no time had passed and I still thought he hung the moon.

Except I wasn't six years old anymore, that day he'd stolen a screwdriver from the gardener's shed and unscrewed my training wheels when Dad wasn't home and Parker was inside playing some video game.

Trust me, he'd said, both hands on the handlebars of my sparkly pink bike. *You can do this, little bird.*

And I had. I'd trusted him, a ten-year-old kid, with every fiber of my being because I knew he'd never let me fall.

But he isn't that boy anymore and I've long since stopped being the girl who puts blind faith in other people to protect her.

Trust isn't transferrable. It doesn't leap over years, cut through hurt and heartbreak. Once its foundations are shaken, the whole damn structure is destroyed. You have to demolish it with a wrecking ball and build it back up from ground level.

Nate expected me to ignore the rubble. To trust him without ever giving me a reason.

I can't.

It hurt too goddamned much last time he disappeared to let him waltz back into my life and give orders like he's earned the right. Call it pride, call it self-preservation, call it whatever you want — bottom line is, leaping into anything involving Nate before I look long and hard at the consequences... well, that felt like the biggest threat to my heart in history.

I just wish I'd been a bit more concerned with the looming threat to my life.

A LONG TIME PASSES.

So long, the pressure starts to build in my bladder until I can't hold it anymore. Tears trickle down my face as wetness seeps into my favorite little black dress, now dirty and wrinkled. My nostrils sting as the scent of humiliation reaches them.

If I ever get out of this godforsaken dungeon, I'm going to burn this dress to ashes.

I try to imagine I'm somewhere else. Somewhere safe and warm.

Like Tahiti. Or curled up with Boo on my couch.

But for some unknown reason, when I crave safe and warm, all my mind conjures up is Nate. He's neither of those things, but I can't stop thinking of the look in his eyes when they crinkle up against his better judgment. The electric feeling of his hand on my arm. And mostly, the way his voice cracked when he finally used my first name.

My name on his lips — I feel it everywhere, like the first strike of my violin bow across the strings. It vibrates through my every atom until I'm charged with it.

Phoebe.

Phoebe.

Phoebe.

One word. I hang onto it like a lifeline.

He'll find me. He'll come.

I have to believe that.

I must have nodded off at some point, sagging against my bonds like a marionette on weak strings, because I jolt awake when the lights flip on.

It takes a minute to adjust to the sudden brightness — I squint in pain until the room comes into focus. My eyes widen as my gaze sweeps the space around me.

Definitely a basement.

Mold on the rough-hewn stone walls. Dirt floor. Bare bulb hanging from a cord overhead. There's a dusty graveyard of bar stools in one corner, broken legs and torn cushions rendering them useless. A few boxes are stacked along the far wall, by a set of rickety stairs leading god only knows where. And there are two men standing in front of me — legs planted firmly, arms crossed over their chests, eyes locked on my face.

Cormack and Padraic.

My eyes narrow. If looks could kill, they'd both be dismembered and dying on the dirt floor at my feet.

"Good." Cormack's voice is as cold as his smile. "You're awake."

My eyes must widen fractionally when his voice — thick with an unmistakable South Boston accent — reaches my ears, because he laughs.

"Oh, the accent?" His lips twist into a smirk and he shakes his head in amusement. "Yeah. Born and raised in Southie. But snotty bitches like you wouldn't give me the time of fucking day if I talked like this. Slap on a shitty Irish accent, though, and you're practically begging for it."

Me? Begging for it?

I fight the urge to roll my eyes.

He steps closer, gaze dropping to scan my body. "Too bad your little boyfriend started digging. I thought we'd have more time to..." He licks his lips and I try not to squirm in my seat. "... get to know each other."

Gone are his silver cufflinks, his two thousand dollar suit, his designer tie. He's in a tight fitting green t-shirt, dark jeans, a Carhartt jacket, and work boots. His clothes aren't the only things he's changed — his entire demeanor has shifted from charming to caustic in a matter of hours. It's like staring at a stranger.

"Enough," Padraic says, speaking for the first time. "Get on with it. We don't have a lot of time."

Cormack shoots his friend a dark look. "This was my idea, jackass. Don't forget it. If I hadn't brought you in, you'd be a bottom feeder for the rest of your life."

Padraic bristles. "You'd never have gotten close to her without me. The only reason any of your shitty fucking plan worked is 'cause I scored with her friend and got you an intro. Without me, you'd be nowhere."

"Just give me the fucking paper."

Padraic shoves a newspaper against Cormack's chest with so much force, he rocks back a few inches.

Trouble in paradise?

Cormack's eyes narrow as his hands come up to clench the paper. "Just go call Smithy. Tell him we've got West's balls in a vise so tight, he'll pay double Mac's normal commission if we ask. Hell, he'll pay a king's fortune."

Padraic's arms cord with tension — he likes being bossed around about as much as a steroid-abusing body builder enjoys testicular shrinkage. He holds his tongue, though, giving a curt nod and turning for the stairs without protest.

Leaving me alone with my caring, compassionate almost-boyfriend, who drugged me and tied me to a chair in a basement that makes the *Silence of the Lambs* set look downright inviting.

Christ. The first time in my life I try dating, and this is what happens. First Brett, now Cormack.

What are the odds of that? Approximately a gazillion to one, I'd guess.

Am I some kind of psychopath magnet? Am I putting out some kind of beacon to attract the crazies? Emitting signals on a frequency only heard by those who score high on the Levenson Psychopathy Scale?

Oh my god.

My vagina is a dog whistle for sociopaths.

Perfect. Just *perfect*.

Spinsterhood never sounded so good.

Cormack is eyeing me with a flat, measuring look. Before I can wonder what he's planning or even flinch away, he takes two strides in my direction, reaches out, and rips the duct tape off my mouth in one sharp tug.

"Fuck!"

The curse bursts out before I can stop it — an involuntary reaction to the tape tearing at my skin. Pain stings my chapped,

CROSS THE LINE   153

bleeding lips. My head falls forward, hair cascading in a tangled, dark brown curtain around my face as I gasp for much-needed air. Breathing through my nose for the past few hours has left me lightheaded. Without the tight loops of rope around my midsection I'd slide to the floor like a wet piece of linguine, boneless and weak.

God, my mouth is drier than California in a drought, now that whatever sedative he slipped me is wearing off. I'd give my virginity for a single glass of water. My tongue darts out to catch the trickle of blood oozing from one of the cracks in my split lips. Sticky tape residue coats my skin like superglue.

"Take this and shut the fuck up." He shoves a copy of today's *Boston Globe* into my tethered hands. "And don't cover the fucking date."

My fingertips curl awkwardly around the top edge, arms gawking at an odd angle against their bonds as I try to maintain my grip without blocking the bold typeface at the corner. My eyes scan the headlines briefly — nothing exceptional jumps out.

Sox Sweep: Red Sox take Orioles 4-0 in Fenway Victory

Mayor Walsh Approves Anti-Tobacco Bill

Spring Storms Cause Citywide Power Outages

There it is — the rest of the world, carrying on as though nothing happened. As though I'm not tied to a chair in a dark basement somewhere, breathing in toxic black mold spores — they need to get an exterminator down here *pronto*, this stuff can't be healthy — all while praying to god they don't kill me.

Because, well.... I can't die. Not when I've barely *lived*.

I'm only twenty-three. I haven't gotten to go skydiving or ever been kissed passionately in the rain. I haven't had the chance to try out a surely-disastrous pixie cut or tan topless on a beach in the French Riviera. I've haven't gone cage-swimming with sharks or told the man I'm crazy about that I ~~love him. Hate him. Want him.~~ Want to kill him?

Oh, who the hell knows.

I've never been in a committed relationship. Hell, I've never even had an orgasm.

Seriously, I can't go to my grave without at least *one* Big O on my record. That's a crime against humanity.

"Your daddy will want proof of life," Cormack sneers, snapping me back to reality. "Hold it up so I can see it. You cooperate, you go home. You don't..."

He doesn't fill in the rest; doesn't need to. It's pretty self-explanatory, as threats go.

I contemplate tossing the paper to the floor at his feet, but I'm not exactly in a position to fight back. I try to lift my arms higher, but it's not easy to do much of anything with the cord wrapped so tight around my wrists. The skin has gone raw where the rope digs into my flesh and my fingers feel tingly from lack of circulation. Unable to shift on the cold metal seat, everything below the waist is pretty much numb.

Once, I watched a YouTube video showing how to escape if your hands are ever bound with duct tape. Just my luck I'd end up with the one kidnapper in the freaking world who still uses rope.

He strides across the room and flips on a set of overhead track lights, the sudden flare of the bulbs making my eyes water. I squint to keep him in focus as he sets his iPhone on a tripod and aims it at me.

"Smile for the camera, love." His lips twist in a cruel grin and I wonder for the thousandth time how I missed it — the sociopathic gleam in his eyes, the dark edge to his charm. How could I have been so blind?

Oh, right.

The accent. The dimples. The muscles. And dear god, the way he fills out a pair of dress pants...

Frankly, I never stood a chance.

"Come on, Phoebe. You can do better than that." His eyes narrow. "Daddy will be wanting an update on his darling daughter's safety."

"Fuck you," I spit, glaring at him.

"That can be arranged," he volleys back flatly, the threat sending a cold tingle down my spine.

"You won't get away with this... This... whatever you're planning." My words sound remarkably steady, considering my insides have dissolved into jelly. "He'll never pay the ransom."

"He'll pay with his money or you'll pay with your life. " He leans toward me, face dark with anger, those stunning eyes narrowed on my wide hazel ones. "Either way, the Wests are going to fucking pay."

My throat convulses.

I'm totally going to die a virgin.

I steady my shoulders and force my face into a sneer, praying none of my fear shines through the thin mask of bravado. "You're an idiot. You really think you'll get away with this? The cops are going to be all over your ass." I narrow my eyes at him. "And I have a feeling your cellmate at Walpole is going to be all over it, too."

"Shut the fuck up."

"You think you can just kidnap someone and get away with it? Seriously? Have you never seen CSI?" I snort.

"I said *shut up.*"

"People know I was out with you," I can't help but point out. "Are you on crack, or something? Seriously, I've heard that shit really messes with executive functions—"

He moves so fast, I never see his fist coming. Suddenly it's just *there*, cracking against my right eye socket so hard my head snaps back like a Pez dispenser. For a few sluggish seconds I stare up at the ceiling, waiting for the bright spots to clear out of my vision.

He hit me.

He actually *hit* me.

Holy fucking shit. If Parker finds out, there'll be hell to pay. If *Nate* finds out...

They'll never even find the body.

"Bitch," Cormack spits, grabbing my chin and pulling my eyes up to meet his furious blue-green ones. With his other hand, he grabs the thin gold chain around my neck and snaps it off my neck in one sharp tug.

I cry out from both the pain of the necklace cutting into my skin and the horror of my most treasured piece of jewelry being destroyed with one careless snap of the wrist.

He's still gripping my face. My eyes water helplessly as he swings the sunshine pendant in front of them like a metronome. "Maybe I'll keep this as a memento. Or maybe I'll send it to Milo as a reminder of you, wrapped up with one of your severed fingers in a pretty little box..."

"I'm going to kill you," I yell, thrashing against his hold, tugging at my bonds.

He laughs as though he finds me hilarious. Leaning close again, he repositions the newspaper in my hands.

"Sit still, hold the paper, and keep your mouth shut until I say otherwise. Your father owes my boss a fuckuva lot of money. If he gives a shit about you, he's going to pay up. And if you're counting on the police bursting in to save the day — don't. Your father is a smart man. He knows if he calls them, you'll never get out of this basement alive."

A shiver moves through me, at that. When he feels it, he smiles.

"Good. You're scared. You should be." His voice drops lower. I can feel his breath on my lips, stale and too warm. "The BPD knows better than to interfere with Bunker Hill's business. Your father is barking up the wrong fucking tree with his plans to gentrify our town without Mac's go-ahead."

Who the hell is Mac?

I try to jerk my head away, but he holds fast. I'll have bruises on my chin tomorrow.

If I'm alive tomorrow...

Cormack leans so close we're practically kissing.

"You fuck with Mac's territory, there's a price. He owned this town long before your daddy ever bribed the city into zoning it for his precious little development. He won't last a day without Mac's blessing. And Mac's blessing don't come free."

This is about the Waterfront project?

Is he screwing with me? He must be screwing with me.

"Now hold up the newspaper like a good little girl, so I can take the fucking video. Unless you want to stay here with me." His tongue slides out of his mouth like a slug, dragging up the length of my cheek and leaving a trail of saliva in its wake.

I try not to gag.

"No?" He chuckles. "Shame. We could have fun, you and me."

"I'm going to vomit on you," I snap sweetly through clenched teeth.

He pulls back so quickly it's clear he believes my threat. A second later, he's behind the tripod, pushing a button on the iPhone screen to activate the camera.

"Tell him to pay, princess."

I stare into the camera for a long, suspended slice of time. I can feel my heartbeat pounding behind my eye, which is rapidly swelling. I'd bet Boo's life it'll be black as Cormack's soul by tomorrow morning.

"Dad." I clear my throat. "Whatever they're asking for, please..."

Cormack goes tense with anticipation.

"Don't give them a goddamn thing."

I smile.

Cormack doesn't.

When his fist flies out again, this time I see it coming. But as it cracks against my temple, shattering my consciousness, the world disappears before my eyes.

And for a while, I don't see anything at all.

CHAPTER 14

I'VE HAD HUNDREDS OF BOYFRIENDS.
SO WHAT IF THEY'RE FICTIONAL?
DON'T YOU DARE JUDGE OUR LOVE.

Phoebe West, on the many merits of book boyfriends.

"CHRIST, you're heavy. Dead fucking weight." A feminine grunt sounds close to my ear, pulling me reluctantly back into the world of the living. "If I'd known you were this heavy, I would've brought a fucking sherpa."

I groan as pain rushes through me.

Holy hell.

Did an elephant sit on my head? A rhino? Some other large-boned creature with a god-complex?

Judging by the excruciating pain needling through my

temple, whatever brains I once possessed have been irreparably damaged. I'm having full-on auditory hallucinations, for god's sake.

"We don't have a lot of time so if you could snap the fuck out of it, that'd be great. Thanks."

My hallucination is speaking again and now she's *shaking* me.

I kid you not — there are two hands wrapped around my shoulders. I can feel tiny fingertips digging into my flesh.

"Come on, come on, come on." Another girlish growl erupts. "They'll be back any minute and then you're on your own."

My eyes sliver open and I see my delusions have surpassed the auditory stage and entered the physical plane. *Wow.* You know your brain damage is pretty freaking serious when you're imagining a petite fairy princess verbally berating you while jostling your shoulders.

"Finally! I was beginning to think you were dead," she hisses, her eyes locking on mine. The shaking stops momentarily. "Come *on*. Move your ass!"

I must say I'm surprised. I figured if my damaged psyche were able to conjure up anyone after twenty-four hours alone in a basement without food or water or use of a bathroom facility, it'd be Nate. Not a foul-mouthed pixie with navy eyes and a seriously great head of unruly blonde hair, currently pulled back in a high ponytail. Bitch could be a Disney Princess, with hair like that.

A fairy godmother, come to save me. How quaint.

"What are you supposed to be? Tinkerbell?" I mutter at my disturbingly vivid delusion, moaning as pain crashes through my head in a wave. "Ow. Crap on a sesame seed bun, that hurts."

"Keep it down!" She shakes me again. "Jesus, do you *want* to get caught?"

I shoot her a skeptical look. "Fairy godmothers are supposed to be round, old, and kind. You are none of those things. You don't even have a wand," I inform her, albeit in a quieter tone. "This is *my* hallucination. Where is your freaking wand? And why are you in jeans and a hoodie? I'm pretty sure fairy godmothers wear magic cloaks and stuff."

Her eyes narrow on me. "I can't decide if you're brain damaged or just plain stupid. Frankly, even if we had the time to figure it out —spoiler alert: we don't — I wouldn't give a shit." She grabs my hands and pulls me from the chair in a surprising show of strength for such a tiny thing. "Now let's *go*, you cotton-headed ninny muggins, before I change my mind and let you rot down here."

"Was that an *Elf* reference?" I ask, feeling some of the haze clear from my brain when I'm back on my own two feet. It's only then I notice the bonds are gone from my rubbed-raw wrists and ankles. Tink must've removed them.

Her eyes cut to mine. "So?"

I shrug, swaying a little. *Whoa.* Woozy. "I mean... I'm just surprised. You say fuck a lot."

"So?" she repeats, impatience saturating her tone.

"So, people who say fuck a lot don't usually quote children's movies."

"I'm a classy bitch who happens to enjoy cursing and kid's flicks. You can ruminate on it later. But right now..." She starts pushing me toward the back of the basement. "You need to *fucking* move your *fucking* ass before Mac's boys get back or you will be dead *fucking* meat. Comprende, chica?"

"I never took Spanish, actually. My boarding school encouraged everyone to take Latin, said we'd do better on the SATs if—"

"Just shut the fuck up and follow me." She starts moving along the wall, into the pitch black. "Christ, it was way easier to convince myself to help you when you were unconscious."

My lips snap shut. Not because of what she said, but because at some point in the past minute I've realized I am not, in fact, delusional or brain damaged. (Well, maybe a little...)

Point is, Tinkerbell isn't some figment of my imagination.

She's actually here. Alive. Real. And currently saving my ass.

Crap on challah, hold the mayo.

"The stairs are the other way," I call quietly, when I realize she's moving away from our only escape route.

"There's a storm entrance in the back. The door jams but if you're small enough, you can wiggle through. Perks of being petite."

"How do you know?" I ask, voice cracking. God, my throat is dry.

"Because that's the way I got in here, genius."

"But how did you even know I was here?"

"Are you reenacting the Spanish Inquisition? Enough with the questions." Her voice is moving farther away by the second. "And FYI, I'm not waiting for you. So unless you want to stay down here alone..."

She trails off. With no other choice, I follow her into the dark. We move quietly through the vast space, trying not to trip over stacked boxes and broken furniture. It's slow going.

"But—" I start again.

She groans. "This is what I get for trying to save a life. The most annoying fucking rescue victim of all time."

"You're kind of mean, you know."

"So I've been told."

"Who are you?" I whisper-yell as we slither through the dark, hands thrown out to the grimy stone wall for guidance.

"Someone who's tired of watching Mac and his boys steamroll over everyone in this goddamned hellhole of a neighborhood. Between the yuppies on the west side and the mobsters on the east, the whole place has gone to shit."

"Why are you helping me?

She pauses. "Does it matter?"

"No. But it'll make it much harder to send you a *thanks-for-saving-my-ass* fruit basket if you don't tell me your name."

She snorts. "Is that the going rate for saving the life of an heiress, these days? A fucking fruit basket?"

"Don't knock it till you've tried it, Tink. Those edible arrangements are surprisingly—"

My words cut off abruptly as she slaps a hand over my mouth and stops in her tracks, stiller than a statue. I'm about to ask what the hell she's doing when I hear them.

Footsteps.

The floorboards overhead are creaking with the weight of slow, measured footfalls as someone moves through the space above us. Dust drifts down onto our heads, coating our hair like snow. They come to a stop almost directly over us. There's a sharp ringing sound, then murmured conversation fills the air.

They're on the phone.

Saved by the bell-tower ringtone...

My heart starts to pound so loud I worry whoever's upstairs will be able to hear it from a floor away. After a few breathless seconds, Tink's eyes meet mine through the darkness, wide and alert. She nods slowly, and we start to edge backwards in unison toward the wall.

We've made it only a few feet when the conversation upstairs falls silent and footsteps start up again.

He's moving away — I can hear his steps getting fainter. That would normally be a relief, except he's heading straight for the door at the top of the basement stairs.

My heart pounds faster.

Any minute that door will open, the lights will flicker on, Cormack will walk back down here, and we'll be more thoroughly screwed than the cast of Sex and the City.

"Fuck." Tink's curse is so low, it barely reaches my ears.

There's a muffled scraping sound, like wood being dragged across stone. "Help me, idiot. It's stuck."

I unfreeze, spinning to see she's reached the storm door. Her hands are gripping the wood, trying to pry open the narrow sliver of space until it's large enough to squeeze through. Before I've had time to blink, I close the distance between us, align my hands next to hers, and pull.

The footsteps are practically to the stairs.

We yank harder — muscles straining, sweat beading — and are rewarded when the door screeches open an inch.

Still not wide enough.

"What, are you afraid to break a nail?!" Tink hisses. "*Pull* the damn thing!"

"I'm trying!" I snap. "Maybe if your arms weren't the approximate width of toothpicks—"

"That's rich, coming from a girl who probably thinks yoga is a sport."

"*You* try balancing your chakras in a 98 degree sweat box, then we'll talk."

I hear the sound of a boot hit the top step.

The storm door creaks a half-foot wider.

Just a few more inches.

The overhead light flips on, burning my eyes with sudden intensity.

Fuckfuckfuckfuckfuck.

"Hey — what the hell?" A man's voice rings out with alarm at the same moment the door finally gives beneath our collective weight.

"Go, go, go!" Tink's words are intent and her hands are rough as she pushes me bodily through the tiny opening.

"STOP!" I hear the man call, pissed beyond belief. The sound of running footsteps reaches my ears. "Stop right fucking now!"

Does he really expect us to listen?

Tink gives me a final shove and I fall through the gap, flailing as I go. Thankfully, my face breaks my fall. (Because it wasn't already bruised *enough.*) I moan as my head smashes against the storm steps but before I can gain my feet, the weight of a small body lands on my back, knocking the breath from my lungs and flattening me back against the concrete.

"Ugh," I grunt as Tink scrambles off me, grabbing my hand and dragging me up. Mere inches away, the man is struggling with the door, trying to squeeze through the sliver of space. His arm snatches at the air above our heads.

"Let's move!" Tink tugs at my hand. "He can't fit through there, but he'll be out the front in less than a minute and you can bet your ass he won't be alone."

Ignoring the pain in my shredded palms, scraped knees, and battered head, I drag myself into a semi-vertical position and make my way up the stairs after her. Our fingers stay twined tight until we hit the asphalt of an abandoned parking lot, its every streetlamp shattered and dark. I barely have time to look around, because we're running. A dead sprint, faster than I've ever run in my life and still somehow not fast enough. My arches ache as my stilettos crash against the pavement without mercy.

Maybe Nate was right about my impractical shoes, after all...

We cut past dumpsters, through ditches, across lawns — never slowing, barely breathing, not once looking back to see if we're being chased. Buildings pass in a blur — dilapidated row houses with lights long dimmed for the night, run-down businesses with metal grates dropped fast over their glass windows. I can see the Tobin Bridge, glowing dim over the water in the distance. Its presence grounds me, and I suddenly know exactly where I am.

Charlestown.

I'm in Charlestown. Less than a mile away from the zoning site for my father's new development.

I don't have time to think about that — there's no room for it in my head, what with all the terror and adrenaline monopolizing the space.

We run.

Arms pumping, feet lifting, one step after another until I think I'm going to die right there on a cracked sidewalk in one of Boston's most notorious crime neighborhoods.

"How do you...run in...those damn...shoes," Tink wheezes, rounding a corner at breakneck pace, her black Toms never losing stride. "Take...them...off."

"These...are...my...best...Manolos," I gasp, outraged and breathless. "No...freaking...way."

"Idiot," she pants.

"Bitch," I croak.

After a few blocks, the rough edges of the neighborhood give way to something a bit softer, more gentrified. We pass houses with small, well-manicured lawns, businesses with flower boxes lining their windows. In the space of a few streets, we've entered civilization again.

"Think we... lost them..." Tink's voice is choppy. "Fucking... finally."

She finally slows to a walk by a covered bus stop on a narrow side street, pacing in tight circles so her limbs don't cramp up. I have no such patience or perseverance — limbs be damned, I collapse onto the stained wooden bench, uncaring whether there's lactic acid building up in my joints or gum clumping in my hair or a gazillion germs crawling onto my body. One more second on my feet and my heart is going to give out.

If Cormack catches us right now, so be it. I couldn't find the energy to move if Tom Brady himself pulled up to the curb and offered me a ride in his Escalade.

My eyes slip closed and I try to regulate my breathing. I'm panting like a sex-line operator. My lungs ache with each inhale and every muscle in my legs burns like my veins are on fire. I can't tell whether the buzzing in my ears is from lack of oxygen, permanent brain damage, or the flickering street lamp down the block.

I don't know how long I lie there — not nearly long enough to recover — before Tink interrupts me.

"Take this." Her voice is close. When I open my eyes, I find her crouched down at eye level with me. Her breaths are perfectly even, her face is a mask of composure.

"What?" I whimper, barely able to get out the word.

She rolls her eyes, grabs my hand, and presses a slim black cellphone into my palm. "It's a burner. Call whoever it is you need to call, then toss it. Do not, under any circumstances, call the police. You got me?"

My eyes widen and I drag myself up into a sitting position, abs burning the entire way. My fingers curl around the phone. "Why?"

"This neighborhood..." Her eyes shift to scan the empty street. "You call the cops, you're just as likely to get an officer in Mac's pocket as you are an honest one."

"Who *is* Mac?"

She stares at me a beat. "God, you really don't know anything at all, do you?"

"I know I was just kidnapped by a guy I thought was really cute, until he turned out to be a sociopath. I know you're a lunatic, who happened to save my life just now. I know this all has something to do with my father and his waterfront development." My voice is rising and I think I'm getting a little hysterical, now that I'm not tied to a chair in a basement or running for my life. "I know I would really, really like a shower, because I smell like sweat and dirt and tears and my own pee, and now there's a wad of gum in my hair and I'll probably have to chop it all off and get a pixie cut — which I realize is something that's always been on my bucket list but, I mean, it's a big commitment. It's not like I have Emma Watson's bone structure. It could be a total disaster. Do you know how long it takes a pixie cut to grow out, Tink? *Months.* Months! I could be dead by then! I could get kidnapped again tomorrow by a cute guy with dimples who's actually a psycho in disguise and then where will I be? In a *coffin.* With a *pixie cut."* I think I laugh, but it sounds more like a sob. "I'll have to have a closed casket funeral. Or maybe they should just cremate me and call it a day."

I stop talking at that point because I literally run out of breath.

Tink stares at me in silence, her brows raised, waiting for me to go on. I don't. Instead, I pull a deep gulp of air in through my nose and try to collect myself. Rambling like a schizophrenic off her meds isn't exactly my best look.

"Should I slap you, or are you good now?" she asks eventually.

I swallow. "I think I'm good."

"Great." She rises to full height — barely hitting five feet — and glances down the street again, as though she's not quite convinced we're in the clear yet. "I've gotta jet. Stay out of trouble, princess. You owe me one."

Then, she turns and walks away. Just like that.

No explanation. *Nothing.*

"Wait!" I whisper-yell after her. "*Tink!*"

Just before she rounds the corner and disappears from sight, she glances back over one shoulder at me with an exasperated *what the fuck do you want* expression.

"Thank you," I call quietly, hoping the sound carries to her.

It must, because she tilts her head in acknowledgement and

tosses a wink at me a second before she melts into the night, leaving me utterly alone.

MY FINGERS TREMBLE against the illuminated buttons. I can count on one hand the phone numbers I've got memorized. Of those few, there's only one sure-bet who I know will answer day or night, even if she doesn't recognize the caller.

I dial and press the speaker to my ear, wondering if I should move from the bench, find a bush to hide in or something, like they do in the movies.

Am I safe here? Is Cormack out looking for me?

It barely rings before the call connects.

"Phee?!"

"Lila, how'd you know—"

"*IT'S HER!*" she screams, and I know she's not talking to me. There's a muffled sound, like the phone's being ripped out of her hand, and then his voice breaks over the line.

"*Where are you?*"

His words are guttural, harsh. The sound of a man at his breaking point.

My eyes move to the sign at the intersection and I hiccup out the cross street. The words are barely out when he barks again.

"Are you okay?"

"Yes," I whisper, my voice small.

"Stay there. Don't move a single fucking inch from that spot." He's breathing hard, like he's running. "I'm coming."

CHAPTER 15

ENOUGH WITH THE SEX POSITIONS. WHY CAN'T
MAGAZINES PUBLISH AN ARTICLE ABOUT *READING*
POSITIONS THAT DON'T GET UNCOMFORTABLE AFTER
FIVE MINUTES?

Phoebe West, while perusing an issue of COSMO.

I DON'T KNOW what speeding laws he breaks or how he
manages it, but five minutes later a black Viper screams around a
corner and slams to a halt in front of me. He's out of the car and
around the hood before I can even gain my feet. His expression is
scarier than I've ever seen it — taut with tension, dark with fury.
It makes his Badass Mercenary look seem downright friendly. His
eyes though — they're the most frightening. Because when he
catches sight of me, shaking like a leaf in my little black dress,

CROSS THE LINE 171

bruised and battered and bleeding... the unrelenting wrath burning on the surface of his irises shifts to reveal something else.

Fear.

Pure, unadulterated fear.

Nathaniel Knox is afraid.

The realization hits me like a ton of bricks. I always thought the day I saw Nate afraid of something would be the day Satan enjoyed a nice, cold ice cream sundae in Hell. And I certainly never thought it would be because of *me.*

"I'm fine," I murmur, a second before he reaches me.

He doesn't respond. He's too busy running his hands over my limbs, checking for injuries, scanning to see if the scrapes on my arms need serious medical attention.

"I'm fine," I repeat, my voice stronger as he crouches to move his hands down my legs, pausing to examine my ravaged knees. "Nate, I said I'm okay."

He doesn't respond. I don't even know if he can hear me, he's so far gone right now. Which isn't good — not when we're standing out on a street corner, exposed and vulnerable.

I take a deep breath and gather my courage. Too weary to talk myself out of it, I lift one shaking hand and thread it through his hair. My fingers are dirty - the nails ripped from falling on concrete, the cuticles torn and bleeding, the skin coated with dust and grass stains. I barely register any of that as my hand twines through his short, dark locks, just as I've dreamed of doing for years.

He freezes the instant I touch him.

"I'm fine, Nate," I whisper again. "I'm *fine.*"

A sound, almost like a growl, slides from his lips as my hand moves lightly through his hair. To my surprise, it's soft. Silkier than I'd imagined.

After a moment, he moves. His grip is a little too rough, his touch a little too furious, as his hands slide from my knees around to the back of my thighs, pulling me into him until there's no space between us. There's desperation in his touch, like he can't quite believe I'm in his arms. His fingers dig harshly into my skin, sending tiny aches flaring through me.

I don't mind. I'm not even embarrassed about my stained clothes or dirty body. Right now, I get the sense he needs to touch me. To reassure himself that I'm real.

His face hits my stomach, his hands find the small of my back, and then... he's *hugging* me.

Nathaniel Knox is on his knees on a littered street corner, hugging me like he thinks I might disappear. Like the slightest loosening of his hold will let me vanish into thin air.

"Nate," I whisper, both my hands in his hair, now. His face presses tighter against the fabric of my torn dress, forehead digging into the soft flesh just below my ribcage.

This moment — this *man* — does something to me. Sends a pang through my heart, a knife of longing through my soul.

"I'm fine," I say for the millionth time, like a mantra, even though it's a lie. "I'm fine."

He ignores me. He's receded into a place I can't reach. A place where words are meaningless and touch is all that matters. All that's real.

My hands move to cup his cheeks, feeling stubble and sharp angles beneath my stained fingertips.

"Nate..." I whisper, wishing he'd look at me. "I'm okay. I'm alive. Bruises will fade, cuts will heal. But right now, we really need to go because I don't know if they're going to come back, or if—"

"*I'm going to kill him.*"

His words are muffled but that doesn't dilute their ferocity in the slightest.

Okay. He's speaking. That's progress, right?

Yes, the things he's saying are really freaking scary, *but...*

"Nate, really—"

"He's a fucking dead man."

Hooooooooly shit.

My heart pounds at the total calm in his tone. He's not bluffing or exaggerating. He's deadly serious.

This man could kill with his bare hands, without flinching.

And it doesn't change how I feel about him in the slightest.

What does it say about me?

I swallow hard and push the thoughts away.

"We have to go, love," I whisper, voice cracking on the endearment I didn't mean to let slip out.

He flinches when it hits him. Like I've struck him.

I sigh. "Nate."

He's a statue at my feet.

"I told you I was fine, but that's not exactly true," I say, needing to get him to focus.

It works. He goes totally tense again, arms turning to steel around me. His face pulls back and tilts up, so his eyes are on mine for the first time in minutes. I stifle a gasp at the ghosts swimming in his gaze.

He's not pretty — he's haunted, Lila's voice whispers in my head.

She was right.

His eyes are a black hole — infinite, bottomless, and teeming with darkness.

"You're not fine," he repeats finally, his voice low, thick with emotion.

I shake my head. "See, I have to pee. I'm thirsty. I could really use a shower. And I also have to check on Boo, because I'm worried no one has taken him for walkies or fed him the entire time I was kidnapped, and he's probably pooped on my new Anthropologie rug. Which would suck, because they have a really strict return policy, and—"

"You're fine," he says, some life coming back into his eyes – as though he's witnessing a miracle firsthand.

"I'm fine," I echo, trying to smile at him. The movement makes one of the splits in my lips reopen, and I feel a trickle of blood drip down my chin.

He's on his feet, looming over me, before I've had a chance to blink. His eyes watch the trickle as his hand comes up to cup my face. I feel the swipe of his thumb against my chin as he wipes it clean. When he pulls his palm away, he stares at it for a long time — my blood on his hand.

"He'll never touch you again." The words hold a dark promise. "Never."

I shiver. "Nate—"

His eyes lift to mine as he takes a careful step back from me, relinquishing his hold for the first time since he arrived.

"We should go." His words are flat.

"We should," I agree.

Neither of us moves. We stare at each other for a long moment, not knowing quite what to say or where to look or how to deal with the crushing memory of his arms around my waist and my hands in his hair still crowding out every other thought. I'd seen his ghosts swirling in his eyes; he'd heard mine in the cracking endearment on my lips. In that desperate, aching moment, with all the bullshit stripped away, we'd come together and crossed an irrefutable line of demarcation.

I worried there was no going back.

"You were wrong, you know," I murmur after a while, because there's nothing else to say.

His brows lift in question.

"I actually *can* run for my life in these heels." My voice is smug. "Like a pro."

His eyes crinkle a tiny bit at the corners and I know I've brought him back from whatever dark place he was stuck in.

There he is.

"Let's get you home," he says, grabbing my hand and pulling me toward the passenger side.

"Okay," I whisper, not knowing if he's talking about his place or mine, and not caring one bit either way.

I MUST'VE FALLEN asleep in the car, because when I wake up I'm in bed.

Not my bed, either.

A man's bed. Dark gray sheets, sparse wooden headboard, not a single decorative throw pillow to be found. My face turns on the pillowcase and the scent of smoke and leather and *Nate* floods my senses.

I'm in his bed.

I sit up abruptly, sending the sheets flying. Chilled air hits my skin and I look down to discover I'm practically naked except for my strapless black bra and a pair of what looks like men's boxers. They're huge on me — rolled at least three times at the hips to keep them in place — but that's the least of my concerns.

I'm wearing Nate's boxers.

Which means... someone took me out of my panties and *put me* in Nate's boxers. And that someone was probably...

"You're awake."

At the sound of his voice, my gaze flies toward the doorway where he's leaning, arms crossed over his chest and intent eyes locked on my face. When they flicker down to my exposed body for a fraction of an instant, I squeak like Boo's favorite duck toy and scramble to pull the sheet up over the girls.

I lift my eyes back to Nate's, fully expecting to find them crinkled up at the corners. Instead, there's a look in them that makes my breath catch and my throat close.

Fearlustangerhopesadnessguiltrelief.

"Nate..." My voice catches on his name and his eyes shutter.

"How are you feeling?" The words are halting.

"I'm fine."

He stares at me, calling my bluff.

I sigh. "Fine. I'm tired. Somewhat sore. My eye feels about six times its normal size," I admit. "Nothing that won't heal."

"We need to talk about what happened."

"I know," I say softly, eyes dropping to the sheet spread over my legs. "Can I clean up first?" I ask, voice shaky.

I hear a sound — half sigh, half curse — and then he's there, sitting on the edge of the bed just inches from me. Without lifting my eyes, I can see his thigh, encased in black denim, so close I could reach out and stroke it.

He clears his throat harshly.

"Do you..." He breaks off. When I lift my eyes again, I see his hands are tight fists at his sides. "Do you need help? I can call someone. Lila, Gemma... Or I can..." He pulls in a breath. "I can help you shower."

He's trying to be considerate, but I gulp at the idea of Nate running his hands across my wet, naked skin.

"I'll manage," I say shakily, eyes on his.

He nods and rises to his feet.

"Bathroom's through there." He gestures at the door. "Fresh towels on the shelf. Some clothes you can borrow."

"Okay."

He disappears without another word.

———

"DRINK THIS."

He slides a glass of water across the butcher-block counter.

It's a thick slab of dark-stained wood, matching the other oak accents throughout his loft. As I drain my glass, I look around.

The space is an open plan — a former industrial building, most likely — with big glass-block windows, exposed brick walls, and matte-black painted air ducts crisscrossing the ceiling. The furniture is sparse — only his bed, a black leather couch, and some bar stools pulled up to the kitchen island, with a tiny bathroom tucked into the far corner. No photographs, no knick-knacks, no clutter.

I've seen monks' quarters with more personality.

Soft track lights illuminate the space. It's still dark outside, which means I only slept for an hour or so before my shower. I should've slept longer, but my dreams were full of images that made me shiver awake.

I set the glass down on the wood counter and he quickly refills it.

"Another," he orders, sliding it back to me.

I don't protest — I'm thirsty. I drain the glass in a few gulps. When I finish, I catch him staring at my eye. I know it's swollen. I saw it in the bathroom mirror after my shower and almost screamed. My eyes haven't been this black since my preteen emo-punk phase.

"One more," he says, reaching for the glass again and filling it to the brim.

"I'm good," I tell him, feeling more myself. And by *more myself* I mean *not in the mood to be bossed around.*

"West—"

"Back to last names, are we?" I roll my eyes. "I'm not thirsty, *Knox.*"

He stares at me, eyes hard. "You spent twenty-four hours without fluids. You're dehydrated."

"I was in a damp basement, not the Sahara. I'll live."

His eyes narrow. "Where?"

"What?"

"Where was the basement?"

I sigh. "I don't know. We ran for a long time, when we got out. Blocks and blocks. Over a mile, I'd guess."

"We?"

"Me and Tinkerbell."

He gives me a skeptical look.

"I'm not crazy." I sigh again, louder this time. "There was a girl. Tiny, cute as a button, cursed like a sailor. She got me out through a storm door, we ran like hell, and then she gave me the burner phone and told me to call for help."

"And where is..." His teeth saw back and forth, jaw clenched. "*Tinkerbell* now?"

I shrug. "Beats me. She took off a few minutes before I called you."

His hand curls into a fist and begins to pound against the countertop in rhythmic strikes. "And you'd never seen her before?"

"No."

"She didn't tell you who she was?"

"No. And I don't think *Tinkerbell* is her given name, if that's what you're asking." I roll my eyes. "I just didn't know what else to call her."

He's quiet for a moment. "Start at the beginning. Tell me all of it."

"The *beginning* beginning? Like, how far back are we talking? The gallery opening? The date? Or the part when I woke up in a mildewy basement, was held for ransom, and got punched in the eye socket twice?" My head tilts. "You know, I look kinda like Ronda Rousey after a cage fight. Or a raccoon." I shrug lightly. "All in all, I think it's a good look on me. Dark shadows are really *in* this spring, you know?"

His face turns to stone when I say that.

"Sorry," I murmur. "Too soon?"

His jaw ticks. "I called you. Your voice was slurring, you were drunk. I knew something was off, but I didn't know where you were. Why don't you start with whatever happened when we got disconnected."

It's not a suggestion.

"I wasn't drunk. I was drugged." My voice is barely audible.

He goes still. "What was that?"

"He slipped something in my drink. I don't..." I swallow. "I don't remember anything from the time he grabbed my phone until I woke up in that basement."

"Did he—" His words break off abruptly and I know he's fighting for control. His fist picks up pace as it smacks against the countertop.

Bang. Bang. Bang.

I flinch with each hit.

"Did—" He starts again. "Did the motherfucker *touch* you?"

I know he's not talking about the bruises around my eyes. The worry in his voice, buried not so deep beneath the anger, makes me reach across the counter and lay my hand over his clenched fist. My fingers look tiny against the broad width of his grip. The pounding stops when our eyes meet.

"No." I hold his stare. "He didn't touch me. Not like that."

Some of the tension slips out of him and he nods sharply for me to continue.

"When I came to, I was in a basement. There was nothing around — just a few broken bar stools, some dusty boxes. Padraic and Cormack were there." I know I should move my hand away, but I can't seem to let go. "They talked about a man named Mac."

The name means nothing to me, but it clearly means something to Nate judging by the way he goes still.

"You're sure they used that name?" he asks, eyes active.

I nod.

"Fuck." He pushes away from the counter, disengaging his hand from mine in a swift move, and starts to pace. "Fuck. I figured they were acting alone, but if Mac's involved..."

"Who the hell is Mac?"

He doesn't even glance my way. "No one you want to know."

I hop off my barstool and circle around to him. When he doesn't look at me, I plant myself firmly in his path with my hands on my hips. I'm sure I don't look very intimidating barefoot, braless, and dressed in one of his giant black t-shirts, but I hold my ground anyway.

He stops pacing a half-foot from me and a silent stare-down ensues.

"Tell me." My words are icy as my glare.

"You don't need to know."

"I'm the one they kidnapped. I'm the one they came after." I step closer, until I'm practically in his face. "Pretty sure that means I deserve to know who they are."

He hesitates a beat, eyes scanning the stubborn set of my jaw, then finally relents. "Keegan MacDonough."

My brows go up — the name still means nothing to me.

"He's the head of the Bunker Hill gang."

Still not ringing any bells.

Nate sighs. "The Irish mob."

A sound flies from my mouth. It might be a snort. "The *mob*? As in *the mafia*?"

He nods tightly.

"As in *let's give him some cement shoes and make him swim with the fishes*?" My nose wrinkles. "*That* Irish mob?"

"This isn't a joke." His voice is flat. "O'Pry and Fitzpatrick are just underlings, they don't have any real power. Mac, on the other hand... He's the real deal. Controls half of Charlestown. Runs drugs, guns, counterfeit cash. Keeps a few dirty cops in his pocket, for insurance. The MacDonough family has held those streets since the 1970s, when the Feds cleaned up shop and tossed the former bosses in the big house. Mac was only too happy to quietly pick up the reins and fill the void they left behind."

"Who the heck are O'Pry and Flannery?" I ask, trying like hell to keep up. It's hard, considering I've been transplanted into a Matt Damon movie overnight, but I'm doing my best.

"Cormack O'Pry — alias *Cormack O'Dair*. And Petey Fitzpatrick — also known as *Padraic Flannery*." Nate's eyes are unwavering on mine. "They saw an opportunity with you and they took it. Probably hoped it would get them in Mac's good graces if they could make your father squirm."

"But I still don't understand *why*." I shake my head, grab my water glass, and take a big sip. "What does this have to do with the West Waterfront? Why would they target me? My dad? Seems extreme, just for a little ransom money."

"Twenty million isn't chump change."

"Twenty million?" I repeat dumbly, eyes wide. "For me?"

Nate nods.

I laugh — I can't help it. "If only they knew my father doesn't give a shit about me." A snort pops out. *Attractive.* "Man doesn't even answer my damn phone calls, he sure as shit wouldn't pay a royal fortune to get me back."

Something dangerous flashes in Nate's eyes when he hears that.

"He would've paid."

I roll my eyes. "Right."

"You should really call him. He needs to know what's happening—"

"Do you have something stronger than this?" I lift my water glass. "If we're going to discuss my father, I really need some liquid courage."

"West—"

"*Knox,*" I mock, cutting off his protest. "Bourbon. Now. I know you have a bottle lurking in one of these cabinets."

He shakes his head, not liking it, but follows my command. A second later, he's got a bottle of Buffalo Trace in one hand, two short glass tumblers in the other. When I reach for the whiskey, he shoots me a look and walks to the other side of the island, out of reach.

I watch, mystified, as he moves from fridge to cabinet to counter, pulling out all the ingredients for my favorite drink. With the expert efficiency of one of Boston's best bartenders, he drops a sugar cube into the bottom of each glass, then adds a splash of bitters and a dash of water. There's the muddled sound of stirring, the clink of ice cubes, the snap of a bottle cap twisting.

Less than a minute later he sets a perfect Old Fashioned in front of me — all that's missing is a cocktail cherry and an orange slice. (Which just so happen to be the only fruits I consume on a regular basis.)

He leans one hip against the island, watching me carefully.

"You made me an Old Fashioned." I say, eyes moving from his face to the glass.

He nods and takes a sip. I watch him swallow, fascinated by the simple action of his Adam's apple bobbing.

"It's my favorite drink."

He nods again. "I know."

He knows?

My mouth opens, closes, opens again. I can't find any words, so I just grab my glass and take a swig.

Damn, that's good. There is nothing sexier than a man who knows how to mix a good drink...

Pushing that perilous thought to the far reaches of my brain, I move away from the kitchen and head for the couch. I'm too tired to stand upright any longer. Balancing my drink precariously, I fold my limbs into a tight pretzel and settle on the corner cushion, like I'd do when I was home sick with the flu in elementary school. Nate watches me intently, never moving from his place by the barstools.

"What?" I ask, feeling his eyes on me.

He shakes his head.

"You're staring." I take a breath. "It's creepy."

It's not remotely creepy. It's... *intense.*

His eyes don't shift. "Sorry," he murmurs, sounding like he's not sorry at all.

"You know, this is going to take forever if you refuse to answer a single one of my questions and only speak in monosyllabic sentences," I point out. "And then I'll be here in your lair for a long ass time, being too loud and touching all your things. Which I'm sure is not what you want. In fact, it's probably the exact *opposite* of what you want."

His eyes crinkle. "My lair?"

I gesture at the space around us.

"We're in Seaport, not Middle Earth."

I snort. "Well, maybe I'd know that if you'd spoken more than five words since I woke up here."

"West, I've been a bit busy trying to figure out how to save your ass." His voice is getting exasperated. "What do you want from me?"

Oh, isn't that the question of the decade...

"I want a conversation. Not this... this... *thing* we've been doing for the past ten years."

His eyes narrow. "And what would that be?"

"Ignoring each other's existence except when absolutely mandatory. Hating each other the rest of the time."

"I haven't been ignoring you." His forehead furrows. "And I don't hate you."

"Excuse me?"

"You heard me." He strides away from the counter and walks

to the middle of the room, arms crossed over his chest. His eyes never leave mine. "Why would you think I hate you?"

"Um... maybe because you haven't spoken to me in years, with the exception of the last month? And even then, most of the time it's less *speaking* than *yelling*."

"That's not true."

I make an incredulous noise.

He steps closer. "I talked to you at the launch party three years ago on Parker's boat."

"You told me I should wear a life preserver if I was going up on deck. One of the big, puffy orange ones. Over a vintage Chanel mini-dress, no less."

His eyes crinkle up — not in amusement, but something else. I've never seen those chocolate eyes look *warm* before, but they are when he mutters, "I remember that dress."

What?!

Forcing myself to breathe, I carry on. "Well... it wasn't exactly a conversation between pals."

"There have been other times." He steps closer. "The West-Tech Christmas party two years ago. You were wearing those ridiculous heels with the straps that wrapped all the way up your calves."

WHAT?!

"You asked me if I was planning to carry a taser when I moved off campus after graduation." I shake my head, trying not to have a heart attack. "Not exactly small talk."

I think his lips twitch. "Maybe I'm not good at small talk."

"Then talk about something big."

"How big are we talking?" he says, voice low and amused.

"'Cause it's *big*. Legendary, even."

My mouth threatens to drop open. "I can't tell if you're being funny right now or just trying to make me uncomfortable."

He takes another step toward me. "Is it working?"

Yes.

"No," I snap.

His lips *definitely* twitch, this time. "West, anyone ever tell you you're a shit liar?"

"Knox, anyone ever tell you you're an arrogant bastard?" I smile sweetly.

He stands there for a while, almost smiling at me with those warm eyes and upturned mouth, and it's all I can do not to hurl my body from the couch and kiss him.

"You feel better, now?" he asks after a while.

I nod. "A little, actually."

"Good, 'cause we still need to talk about shit."

A deep sigh slips from my mouth. "Fine. Fire away."

CHAPTER 16

THE SENSATION of arms lifting me from the couch stirs me
back into consciousness.

"Nyuuggghh," I grunt. Adorable as always.

I feel a chuckle move through the chest I'm cradled against.
"Shhh. Go back to sleep."

My eyes open because, of all the times I could start listening
to Nate's orders, it's not going to be *this* one, when he's got his
arms wrapped around me. There's a tanned slice of skin two

millimeters from my eyeballs. *Hello there, source of all my nighttime fantasies...*

"What are you doing?" I whisper to his throat.

"Putting you in my bed," he answers, like it's the most obvious thing in the world.

I blink hard.

The last thing I remember is telling Nate about the kidnapping. He wanted to know everything — the exact wording Cormack used, minute details about the landscape, the angle of my view of the Tobin bridge, the color of the barstool cushions scattered around the basement. Things I never would've imagined were important.

By the time I'd drained my Old Fashioned, my eyes were drooping closed and my brain felt limp in my skull from being so thoroughly picked apart. I must've fallen asleep on the couch, mid-interrogation.

"Is the cross-examination over, prosecutor?" I ask sleepily.

He chuckles again — a silent vibration that makes my body hum against his. "For now."

I stare at his neck as he carries me, thinking this is the closest I've ever been to him.

It's still not close enough. Not remotely.

His body bends as he sets me down on his bed. His hands are gentle — what a strange thing, Nate being *gentle* — as they pull the black duvet up over me. It's still dark, but his eyes find mine.

"What time is it?" I ask.

He glances at his watch. "Almost five. Sun will be up soon."

"I'm never going to be able to sleep, now."

"Try," he commands softly, tucking the blankets tighter around me.

Bossy, bossy, bossy.

Right now, I kind of like it.

His hands pull back. "You need anything before I go?"

I sit up, sending the blankets tumbling. Panic sluices through me. "Go?"

Very abruptly, I realize that I don't want to be alone in the dark again. Not for a long time. Maybe not ever.

His eyes soften as they read the fear in my expression. "To the couch," he clarifies gently. "I'm not leaving you, West. I promise."

Something expands in my chest, when he says that with those dark eyes locked on mine. So steady. So sure. So safe.

I'm not leaving you.

Suddenly I can't stop myself. I don't *want* to stop myself. I fling my body forward and wrap my arms around his neck. The impact is hard – he jolts two inches back when we collide. I feel him freeze, uncertainty filling his every atom, but I don't care.

My face finds that spot in the crook of his neck where muscle bunches and veins cord tautly, nestling in so we're skin on skin. My arms twine around his back until I'm plastered so tight against him, I'm not sure where he ends and I begin. He doesn't return my embrace, so I hug him hard enough for us both.

"West—" he starts.

"Please," I whisper, voice breaking on the word. "Don't push me away, Nate. Not right now." My throat is constricted by the lump of emotion gathering there. "I just.... I need a minute of this — of *you* — so I know everything's going to be okay. Then... I promise I'll let go."

Something shifts in the air around us, when I say that. I can't see it, but I sense it with every single part of my being. He stops fighting — me, himself, those demons that lurk in the back of his eyes. And then, before I can process it, his arms come up around me and he's hugging me back.

So tight my ribs ache. So hard I think he'll never let me go.

My tears drip against his skin and his head ducks to rest on my shoulder. It's not about sex or lust or even love. It's pure comfort between two people who've always walked the line of misery. Who've always carried the burden of their broken pieces in total solitude.

The shattered fragments of my heart find solace against the jagged edges of his soul. We breathe each other in and exhale out everything that makes us damaged, consoling each other in the dark in a way we haven't since we were kids.

I can't say who moves first. I can't define the exact moment that this stolen embrace changes from one of simple comfort to something entirely different. I can't tell you if it's my hands, sliding into the curling hair at the nape of his neck... or his lips, brushing the skin where my shoulder meets my neck. I can't tell you if the thrumming in my body, the heat between my legs, or the fire in my heart are responsible for the way I shift against him, until I feel the length of him hard against my stomach.

All I can tell you is that when that shift happens — when lips hit skin and our bodies align like two lost puzzle pieces — the electricity that always crackles through him like a live wire jumps over to me.

One bolt of lightning. A single spark.

We combust into flames.

My mouth finds his, or maybe his finds mine. It doesn't matter. As soon as they brush, we're both lost. His tongue spears into my mouth without hesitation and then he's kissing me. I've never been kissed like this before — like I'm being claimed, branded, marked as his. Every fumbling high-school boy and drunken college crush falls away in the wake of Nate's kiss. Teeth, tongues, hands, lips. We devour each other.

I taste bourbon and blood as my lip cracks open again beneath his onslaught. A growl rattles from deep in his chest as he tastes it, but he doesn't stop. I wouldn't let him if he tried.

My hands work into his hair and pull him closer, deepening the kiss. His stubble scrapes my cheeks as our mouths consume each other — a decade of lust pouring out in a torrent, fueling the fire. His hands roam my back, my ass, my sides. They slip up under my borrowed t-shirt, seeking skin and heat. I moan at the sensation of his callused hands against me, writhing to get closer.

Not close enough. Never close enough.

We are the most treacherous of fault-lines, long overdue for a quake. The pressure has built and built and built between our opposing sides for years, until finally, the very earth cracks open beneath us.

We are a natural disaster.

We are a perfect storm.

We will ruin lives and level cities and destroy everything in our wake.

And none of it matters. Not now. Not here, in his arms.

He kisses me deeper, like he can't get enough, his hands finding the sides of my face, holding me there without tenderness. Winding into my hair, tugging until my head falls back, totally at his mercy. He's playing rough.

I can play rough, too.

I slide my hands down his back, around his hips, up his thighs. When I find the length of him, he's hard as steel encased beneath the denim of his jeans. I stroke my fingers against the ridges there, reeling when I hear a needy sound rattle from his throat.

I did that. One brush of my fingers did that.

It's a rush — knowing he's just as affected by me as I am by him. I do it again, harder this time, feeling bold with his hands in my hair and his tongue in my mouth. He breaks away, panting, his forehead resting on mine.

"Fuck." The sheer need in his voice is barely leashed. "We shouldn't—"

I meet his eyes as my hand grips him. His gaze is stormy, filled with guilt and lust and a million other emotions.

"Nate," I whisper, hand running the length of him again. Except for the ragged inhales moving his chest, he's entirely still. "Make love to me. Please."

He groans. His forehead hits mine again, and I feel his breaths against my swollen mouth. I press my lips to his in a lingering kiss.

"You're going to kill me." His voice is tight.

"I'll make sure you die happy," I whisper.

That's all it takes.

His control snaps like a twig beneath the weight of our desire. His mouth hits mine, his hands find the bottom of my t-shirt, and then it's simply gone, tossed across the room somewhere, and I'm practically naked in his hands. His palms find my breasts, rough like sandpaper on my skin, and I almost come apart at the sensation.

"So responsive," he mutters against the skin of my collarbone. When his face drops lower, I nearly come up off the bed. "Like a live wire in my hands."

My head falls back.

I feel incredible. Every part of my body feels alive, burning up with need for him. I can't believe, after so many years of waiting and dreaming of this moment, it's finally happening. I want to savor it, embed it in my memories so I never forget what the scratch of his stubble against my cheek feels like, or the hot breath of his sighs against my neck, or the way he touches me, like I'm glass and he's fire, forging me into something beautiful.

His hands slip lower, to trace the band of the borrowed boxers rolled over my hips. I push up against him, so my breasts drag against his chest, and then his hand is there, against me, exploring uncharted territory with deft fingers.

"Fuck," he groans, feeling the heat between my legs. He's cursing but somehow, it sounds almost like a prayer on his lips. "So ready for me."

I'm totally lost in the feeling of him. His fingers are moving faster and faster, and I feel something start to build inside me, something powerful and unfamiliar, and all I can do is cling to his shoulders as it overtakes me. I'm being swept up in a tidal wave of need. His lips find mine again and the wave starts to peak and then—

Bang, bang, bang, bang.

Someone is pounding on the door. In fact, judging by the number of strikes, it sounds like *several* someones.

"Goddammit," Nate curses, pulling his hand out of my boxers.

"No!" I wail, feeling the wave recede.

So close.

"Open up, Knox! I want to see my goddamned best friend! And then smack the hell out of her for scaring me to death!"

Lila.

"We know she's in there! You said we had to wait until morning to see her. Look outside — the sun's coming up!"

Gemma.

"Sunshine, calm down. He's not holding her hostage. They're probably sleeping."

Chase.

There's a brief pause during which I imagine she weighs his words, then, "Open up!"

Bang, bang, bang.

Chase's sigh is so loud, I can hear it through the door.

I laugh lightly and look up at Nate, surprised to find he's already watching me. His eyes move over my face like he's memorizing its every feature.

"What?" I ask, patting down my bangs. "Do I have sex hair?"

His lips twitch. "No."

"OPEN UP!" Gemma yells. "Don't make me break open this door."

CROSS THE LINE 193

"Sunshine, have you been working out?" Chase's voice is amused. "Last I checked, you couldn't even break open the paint cans to redecorate the living room."

"Whose side are you on?" Gemma hisses.

"Yours." I can hear the smile in his voice. "Always."

She pauses. "Knox! Don't make Lila break down this door!"

Lila giggles.

I snort. When I meet Nate's eyes, I see they've gone crinkly again.

"Do we have to let them in?" I ask.

"You really think they're going to give up?" He winces as the pounding continues.

I sigh. "Where's my shirt?"

A FEW HOURS LATER GEMMA, Chase, and Lila have been filled in on everything that happened to me. Lila feels horrible for introducing me to Cormack — she's apologized approximately seventy billion times since she got to Nate's, despite my assurances that she's just as much a victim as I was. If she ever sees Padraic — or, *Petey* — again, he's in for a serious ass-whooping.

"I'm the worst friend ever," she announces, collapsing back against the cushion beside me. "It's official."

"You took care of Boo while I was gone." I bump her shoulder with mine. "That means you're not the worst friend. Maybe in the top ten, but not the absolute *worst*."

"Not funny," she grumbles. "Would this be a bad time to mention we ate all the Cheez-ITs in your pantry?"

I gasp in faux outrage.

"You didn't have cupcakes," Gemma says unapologetically from my other side. "It was the only option."

Apparently, they'd used my brownstone as a gathering place

in the hours after I disappeared — which explains why Nate was with Lila when I called from the burner phone.

I smile and stare at my hands, doing everything in my power to keep my eyes off him. He and Chase are by the kitchen island, talking in hushed tones, no doubt plotting revenge against Mac and his boys. He's barely glanced my way, since they arrived.

There's a strange tension between us, now. Different than before.

In the past, we've circled with a caustic kind of caution, careful not to get too close for fear of ripping each other's heads off. Now, I'm afraid if I get too close I'll rip off something else.

Namely, his clothing.

"You look like crap," Lila says, staring at my swollen eye. "Have you been to bed, yet?"

To bed? Yes.

To sleep? No.

Do not look at Nate. I repeat, do *not* look at Nate.

I stare harder at my fingers, which have knotted together. "Not exactly."

"Well, we're going back to my place, then. I'll make you a big cup of tea, give you a valium, and you can recuperate with a nice drug-induced coma."

"No drugs," I say immediately. I'm surprised she'd even suggest such a thing – she knows how I feel about prescription pills.

She sighs. "One Valium won't kill you."

"Lila."

She rolls her eyes. "Fine, fine."

Gemma's hand lands on mine. "You can come to the penthouse, if you want. It's safe there. Chase's security guys won't let anyone in."

"Thanks, but I just want to go home. Sleep in my own bed, and all."

An uncompromising voice cuts in. "You're staying here, where you can't get into any more trouble."

I go still at the ice in his tone. My eyes fly in Nate's direction, surprised he was even listening to our conversation, and I find he's glaring at me with hard eyes.

"What did you just say?" I snap, not liking that look one bit.

"Did I stutter?" He takes a few steps across the room in my direction. "You're not leaving until this is over."

"That sounded an awful lot like an order."

"Probably because it was one."

My mouth falls open. "Are you fracking kidding me?"

I admit, I may be a *bit* cranky, what with the lack of sleep and the near death experience and the coitus interruptus just before the Big O finally made her debut... So, there's a chance I'm more irritable than usual.

Whatever. He still shouldn't boss me around like I'm seven years old.

His eyes narrow. "I told you not to go out with O'Pry. You didn't listen. You never listen." His voice gets low, lethal. "This time, you're going to listen, West, even if I have to handcuff you to my fucking bed."

"Hot," Lila whispers under her breath.

"Seriously," Gemma agrees.

I ignore them.

Huh. Turns out we still want to rip each other's heads off, after all...

"You can't keep me here like some kind of prisoner." I scoff. "I have a life. A house. A dog. A job." I rise to my feet. "I'm not staying here."

He smirks. "You're not leaving."

"You can't tell me what to do!" I whirl around and pin my friends with a look. "Come on. We're going."

Gemma blanches. "Phee, I really don't think—"

I glare at her and the words die in her throat. My gaze shifts to Lila. She's inspecting her cuticles, looking bored.

"Lila!" I snap.

"Mmmm?"

"Get up and come with me."

"Why?"

My voice lowers. "It's much more effective if I storm out of here with a posse."

I hear a muffled chuckle from Chase. When my glare swivels in his direction, he adopts an innocent expression.

"Don't look at me," he says, holding up his hands. "I've got nothing to do with this."

"I was just kidnapped," I point out. "You guys are supposed to be catering to my every whim."

"Really?" Lila's nose wrinkles.

"I don't think that's a rule," Gemma adds, voice speculative. "It wasn't in the guidelines of Operation SPANK."

"Nope," Lila agrees. "Sure wasn't."

I shoot them my iciest glare. Neither seems to be affected.

"Operation SPANK?" Nate asks, full of curiosity.

"I think what Lila and Gemma are trying to say is..." Chase's green eyes are steady on mine. "We just want you to be safe, Phoebe. And you're safest here. There's video surveillance at all the doors and windows. State of the art tech." His eyes soften. "As long as those men are out there, you're a target."

Damn. Why does he have to be so kind and chivalrous and logical?

I look at Gemma. "How do you win any arguments, with this guy?"

She shakes her head miserably. "I don't."

Chase grins. It's a good grin. I know right then, I'm not going to get my way.

"Fine." I collapse back onto the sofa with a huff. "I'll stay. But I won't be happy about it."

Chase buries a laugh beneath a cough. Lila giggles outright. Gemma lays her head on my shoulder. When I catch Nate's eyes, they're crinkled up in amusement.

Bastard.

If I didn't love him so much, I'd hate him.

CHAPTER 17

PEOPLE SAY GOD ONLY GIVES US AS MUCH AS WE CAN
HANDLE.

I SAY, HIS HOLINESS THOUGHT SPIDERS WERE A
GOOD IDEA.

POINT ME TOWARD A DIFFERENT AUTHORITY.

Phoebe West, contemplating a higher power.

I CAN'T SLEEP.

I know it's been days since I properly rested and my wounds
need time to heal, *yada yada yada*, but it's the middle of the day
and no matter how tight I pull the light-blocking curtains, my
body isn't fooled. Plus, it doesn't help that whenever I so much as
look at Nate's bed, memories of what we almost did there start
playing in my mind like a movie. An X-rated, slow motion movie.

Gemma and Chase left for work a few hours ago, her to the gallery and him to Croft Industries. *Damn power couple.* They promised they'd be back to visit tomorrow.

Lila left to pick up Boo and bring him here, along with some clothes and my laptop. If Nate's going to hold me hostage, I need basic supplies.

Speaking of my captor — he's gone, too.

A few minutes after our friends filed out, he pulled on his boots and a black leather jacket, shoved a "for emergencies only" cellphone into my hands, and headed for the door.

"Where are you going?" I called after him.

He froze in the doorway, head turning over his shoulder so I could see his face in profile. "Hunting."

With that, he set the security system to ALARM mode, slammed the door, and disappeared without another word.

Rude.

I'm under strict orders not to leave the loft under any circum-stances. Hell, I wasn't even allowed to let Lila and Boo in without an escort in the form of one of Nate's *men* — the scary, commando-type dudes who work at Knox Investigations. I found this utterly ridiculous.

Lila, on the other hand, didn't seem to mind spending time with Alden, the ripped blond with a crew cut and dimples, who escorted her to and from the loft. The dreamy smile on her face told me she's already moved on from the heartbreak of Padraic.

Shocking, I know.

Boo was happy to see me, at least. We snuggled for a solid thirty seconds on the couch before he got tired of me and decided he'd rather sniff every square inch of the loft. Which means, for all intents and purposes, I'm alone again until Nate gets back.

God only knows how long his *hunting* trip will take.

A small part of my mind protests that I shouldn't be so easily accepting of his... shall we say... *extracurricular* activities. He's never exactly been a Boy Scout — but there's a difference between breaking into our neighbor's guesthouse as a reckless teenager and tracking down thugs to teach them the meaning of the word *pain*.

It should scare me, right?

I should want to change him, tame him, make him into someone with softer edges — like a wild hawk with a broken wing you slowly nurse back to health, hoping someday he'll stop snapping at you for daring to come close.

But loving someone isn't about wanting them to evolve into someone better. My mom taught me that.

Real love is saying: here, take my still-beating heart and hold it in your hands and please, please, please, promise not to squeeze too tight or drop it on the pavement. Love is being naked and afraid, but refusing to flinch.

It's not asking that person to change; it's trusting them enough not to. And it's not even about needing them to love you back equally; it's just about loving them for who they are.

And I do, I realize. *I love him.*

Despite all my attempts to push him out of my thoughts, to convince myself all I felt was lust or hate or a burning need for revenge...

I love him.

Even if he never loves me back.

Even if it only leads to heartbreak.

So, I make peace with the thought of Nate going up against the entire Irish mob for me. And I do the only thing I can think of that'll let me feel like I've got even the slightest bit of control over my own life.

I make cookies.

I BLINK AWAKE SUDDENLY.

I don't know why, exactly. There's no noise, no sudden light, no alarm pulling me out of my dreams. But something causes me to stir.

My eyes flutter open and I find I've passed out with my face on the kitchen island. It's a miracle I didn't fall off the stool and crack open my head. I'd been battling exhaustion all day; looks like exhaustion won.

My cheek is resting on the sticky butcher block, inches away from the empty bowl of cookie dough. Turns out *making cookies* turned into *eating half the batch raw* before baking a single tray of them. Oops.

The kitchen is a war zone of bowls and utensils and greased baking sheets. I was surprised to find Nate had all the ingredients I needed — sugar and flour and baking powder and even vanilla extract. I'd pegged him for a takeout-menu connoisseur, but I suppose his cooking skills must've advanced some since the days he'd make me burned macaroni and cheese after school.

I lift my head, groaning at the crick in my neck. I catch sight of him all at once, appearing out of nowhere like a ghost in my peripherals.

He's so still, you'd think he was a shadow if you looked too quickly. His face is silhouetted; the dim shafts of twilight leaking through the loft windows barely illuminate him. I'm thrown back in time to the night he showed up at my brownstone and scared me half to death in the dark. If someone had told me then that a few weeks later I'd be here, in Nate's loft, wearing one of his t-shirts and considering the repercussions of kissing him, I would've smacked them upside the head.

"Hey," I murmur sleepily, wiping cookie dough off my cheek with the back of one hand. My long brown bangs are dusty with flour.

"Hey," he returns, stepping into the light. His eyes are careful as he looks at me.

"Must've passed out between batches. Sugar coma, and all." I slide off my barstool and grimace as I take in the disaster site that was once his kitchen. "Sorry about the mess. I'll clean it up."

"We'll get it tomorrow." He steps closer, still watching me.

I swallow. "How was hunting? Catch anything?"

He shakes his head. "Nothing. O'Pry is smart enough to go to ground, for the time being, but he can't stay gone forever. I'll keep looking." He exhales sharply. "I'm going to find them before..."

"Before they find me?" I finish softly.

A dark look crosses his face. "That's never going to happen. I told you I won't let them touch you again. Don't you believe me?"

I nod and try not to shiver when he closes a bit more of the distance between us, until there's only a foot or so dividing his chest from mine.

"You're a shit liar," he murmurs, eyes on my mouth.

I nod again, mesmerized as he comes closer. I open my mouth to speak, even though I have no idea what I'm about to say, but nothing escapes because his hand is lifting from his side. There's a tiny instant of time before his thumb hits my cheek — the moment before the lightning strike, when the whole damn sky seems to hold its breath in silence, waiting for impact.

"Cookie dough," he explains as the pad of his thumb lands on the corner of my mouth, his touch bolting through me like electricity. I'm totally still as he brushes my skin, barely daring to breathe. When the crumbs are gone, his hand stays on my cheek and his eyes stay fixed on my mouth.

Holy frack.

"Are you going to kiss me?" I ask quietly.

He pauses. "Thinking about it."

I gulp and hope it's not too obvious. I'm thinking about it too.

And about earlier, in his bed, and the fact that there's no one to interrupt us this time.

"Are you weighing the pros and cons?" I ask, leaning into his touch.

"Only cons here, West." He shakes his head. "You and me... we're a story that won't have a happy ending. A tragedy. Nothing good comes from a tragedy."

"Well, maybe..." I grit my teeth so I don't say something I'll regret, and take a steadying breath. "Maybe I'd rather live in the wreckage with you for while than fake a fairy tale with someone else forever."

Those dark eyes search mine, searing into me like fire. "What do you want from me, little girl? Because I'm almost certain I can't give it to you."

"For starters... stop calling me *little girl*. I'm not one. I haven't been for a long time."

Gathering my courage, I swallow, take a deep breath, and step into him. Our chests collide — I have to crane my neck to keep his eyes on mine.

"And after that?" he asks, voice huskier than normal as I press against him.

"After that..."

Everything, my mind screams. *I want everything!*

If I tell him that, he'll run from me so fast, Usain Bolt will look sluggish in comparison.

I shrug. "I barely know what I want for breakfast tomorrow. Hell, I might not even be alive tomorrow, if Mac gets his way. So... maybe I just want this. This moment. One single moment with you, where we lay down our weapons and stop trying to kill each other. A truce on the battleground. Nothing more."

His jaw clenches as he looks at me. I can see the struggle playing out inside him. He wants me — so bad it's nearly killing him — and he's not exactly thrilled about it. In fact, judging by the scowl on his face, I think it's safe to say he's downright pissed about it. So pissed, I actually think he's going to walk away.

Which explains why I nearly have a heart attack when his arms shoot out and he lifts me up onto the messy, dough-covered countertop in one swift motion, spreading my legs apart so he can step between them. I've barely had time to catch my breath when his mouth lands on mine in a crushing kiss.

"You taste like cookies," he mutters, groaning a little as his teeth nip at my bottom lip.

I grin against his mouth, laughing as I deepen the kiss. All it takes is a few seconds, a quick stroke of tongues, and we're back exactly where we were earlier. *Combustible.* My shirt disappears. My legs wrap around his waist. Our mouths cling and gasp until I taste the coppery tang of blood instead of sweet sugar and chocolate.

It's almost violent.

I was wrong, when I said I wanted a moment with him where we weren't trying to kill each other. I realize now, there'll never be a moment like that. Nate and me... we aren't built for truces, for good times, for light jokes and giggles. We're meant for the shadows. For the dirty, ugly, secret parts of our souls, the parts we can't hide because we know each other too well.

There's never going to be a Honeymoon Phase with him. I can't pretend not to see his flaws — I know them almost as well as my own. He won't deny my imperfections — he's seen them since we were kids. We cut straight through to the heart of each other long ago. I've got my finger on his pulse point and he's got his hand wrapped around every chamber of my heart. One squeeze, we're both dead. Mutually assured destruction.

The kiss builds into something I can hardly describe. We're at war — fighting for the same thing but unable to lay our weapons down and get there.

He growls as he pushes himself up onto the counter, shoving

me back against the butcher-block and stretching out above me. There's flour in my hair, on my hands, streaking his skin everywhere I touch him.

I barely notice.

My nails scratch down his back, his teeth scrape at my ear. He's barely touched me and I'm coming undone. In another minute, I'll—

Bang, bang, bang.

I freeze at the sound of a fist against his door.

"No... fucking... way." His words are a grunt against my neck.

"Don't answer," I beg, arching up into him. "I don't care who it is."

He seems to agree, because his mouth returns to mine an instant later, the kiss just as intense as before.

"Knox! Sweet P!" A male voice calls through the thick wood, filled with concern. "Are you there?"

We both go completely still.

"Lemme in, or I'm using my key."

"Frack!" I hiss, pushing Nate off me. He practically falls off the counter, for once not in total control of himself. I'd smile, if I weren't about to pee my pants in utter panic.

"Fuck!" he curses, scrambling to find my shirt. "Here." He tosses it in the general direction of my head. I pull it on without looking.

"Inside out," he says, watching me. His eyes are crinkled in amusement but his lips are set in a serious frown.

"Huh?" I ask dumbly.

He reaches out, whips the shirt up over my head, and puts it on correctly. "There."

I nod, feeling off-balance. "You have flour on your nose," I inform him quietly.

He scrubs at it, then looks at me in question.

"Gone," I confirm, lips twisting at the sight of him so thrown from his normal, tightly controlled equilibrium.

"That's it!" The voice calls from the hallway. "I'm coming in!"

The smile falls off my face. Nate hurries toward the door, flips the deadbolt, and yanks it open.

"Dude!" The man in the hallway is grinning ear to ear. His dark blond hair is disheveled from travel, his hazel eyes are warm but tired, and he's got a messenger bag slung over one shoulder. "What took you so long? Don't tell me you're banging some chick in there..."

Holy frack.

Parker is here.

CHAPTER 18

I USED TO THINK IT WOULD BE COOL TO READ OTHER
PEOPLE'S MINDS.
 THEN I JOINED FACEBOOK.

Phoebe West, defending her techno-phobic life choices.

"SWEET P!" Parker's voice is a mixture of concern and glee as he sweeps me up in a hug. "Little sis, you look like shit."

"Thanks, bro. Nice to see you too." I hug him back until my ribs start to ache.

"God, it must be six months since I've been back here."

"Eight," I correct, trying not to infuse my voice with accusation.

He pulls back to look at me, a guilty expression twisting his features. "Missed you, kiddo."

I narrow my eyes at him. "I'm not a kiddo."

"You'll always be my kid sister. Even when you're old and fat and wrinkly."

"I'm not going to get fat!" I whack him on the arm playfully. "You, on the other hand..." I grimace. "I see a beer belly in your future."

He makes an outraged sound and pulls up his shirt. "Washboard, baby. You could crack an egg on these."

"Ew."

He grins, a boyish smile lighting up his whole face. "The ladies don't complain."

I feign gagging noises. "Sorry, I just threw up in my mouth."

"Sweet P, don't make me give you a noogie."

I roll my eyes at his childish threat. "Oh no! What's next? An Indian sunburn? I'm *so* scared."

He laughs, then turns to Nate for some kind of weird man-hug ritual, which involves unintelligible grunting and back-slapping.

Ah, bromance.

I watch their reunion, a happy smile stretching my cheeks wide. It's great to have Parker home, even if he spends the whole visit calling me names and giving me a hard time.

Sweet P.

The old nickname hits me with a wave of nostalgia.

When I was two, I couldn't for the life of me pronounce *Phoebe* — the closest I could get was *Pee-Bee*. So Parker, loving big brother that he is, took to calling me *Pee-Pee* — insert six-year-old boy giggles here — which was eventually shortened to *P* and finally, transformed into *Sweet P* when we were old enough to stop fighting over LEGOs and blaming each other for pilfering the last Hostess cupcake from our nanny's secret stash above the fridge.

"Knox, you got a kitten and didn't tell me?" His voice is

teasing as he bends to scratch Boo behind one tiny white ear. The poor thing has been running circles around his legs, seeking his attention since the moment he arrived.

"Shut up," I say sweetly. "You remember Boo, your nephew-in-paw. You met last time you were home."

"Must've blocked him from my memory." Parker grins wide as he greets the small Pom. He's so full of shit. He may act like a macho man who only likes dogs over a hundred pounds, but last time he came to visit I caught him napping on my couch with Boo snoring on his chest. They're best buds.

"I didn't know you were coming home," I say, scooping up the Pomeranian. He licks my cheek, then proceeds to squirm until I release him. *So* affectionate, my demon-dog. "You could've called."

"You know who could've called? *You.* When you were kidnapped by the fucking mob." Parker crosses his arms over his broad chest and levels me with a look that probably strikes fear into the hearts of cheating bimbos worldwide. "Did you really think I'd stay away, when I heard?"

I drop my eyes from his, watching as Boo hops onto Nate's couch and settles in like he owns the place. "I didn't want to bug you."

"You're my sister. Your life was in danger." He glares at me, hazel eyes serious. "You think I give a shit if you *bug me?*"

My mouth opens as I try to think of a good response. A morose "sorry" is all I can come up with.

Parker nods. "You need me, I'm on a plane home. No questions asked. You should know that."

I sigh.

"Hey, you thirsty?" Nate asks Parker, walking toward the kitchen. "Want a beer?"

I try not to blush as I turn and catch sight of the counter. If

I'm not mistaken, there's a faint outline of my body in the flour still scattered there.

"I'm on Australia time." Parker grins. "How 'bout some caffeine instead?"

Nate reaches for the filters. "How do you take your coffee?"

"Very seriously." Parker's voice is solemn.

"I see your jokes haven't improved," I say, trying to shove him and nearly falling on my face when he dodges at the last second.

"I see your aim hasn't improved." He darts away nimbly when I take another swipe at him.

Nate watches us from across the kitchen, eyebrows raised.

"Jesus, Knox, it's a mess in here." Parker surveys the disaster on the counter, snatching up a cookie off the cooling rack as soon as he spots them. "Since when do you cook?"

"I'm not the one who stress-bakes." Nate meets Parker's eyes, then tilts his head in my general direction.

"Ahhh, I should've known." Parker laughs. "Remember how many brownies she made when we put her paper maché volcano on the roof and filled it with fireworks?"

"That was my science fair project!" I hiss. "I got a zero, because of your little stunt! If any time has ever called for double-fudge brownies, it was that day."

Nate's mouth twitches. "What about the time we covered all her bedroom furniture in wrapping paper over the holiday break?"

"It looked like the Christmas Tree Shop threw up on my walls. It took me days to get all the tape off!" I glare at them both. "I needed cookies to recover. And I donated most of them to the church bake sale, anyway."

Parker grins wider. "Wait, what about—"

"Enough!" I snap. "So, I bake when I'm nervous. It's not like I do hard drugs, or have crazy monkey sex, or jump out of airplanes."

"Monkey sex?" Nate asks, voice thick with amusement.

"Sweet P, you gotta come skydiving with me next time. You haven't lived till you've felt the air at 12,000 feet."

"I hate you both."

They grin in unison and, for a brief second, it's like we're all kids again. Eating cookies and joking around, back in the days when everything was fun and there weren't things like mobsters or broken hearts or brothers who only visit twice a year.

"You've got flour in your hair," Parker says, leaning forward to tug on a tendril. "But these cookies are damn good, I'll give you that."

I roll my eyes as he shoves another into his mouth.

"What?" he asks, unapologetic. "I'm hungry. The plane food sucked ass. Milo's gotta look into a new catering company for the jet."

"I wouldn't know. I don't use the jet."

He sighs. "Your loss, sis."

"Speaking of Daddy dearest... did you tell him you were coming home?"

"Nope." Parker shrugs. "If I did that, we'd have to have a 'talk about my future.' And I already know exactly what he'd say."

My brows lift.

"That I have *obligations* here with WestTech." Parker pulls out a barstool and straddles it, elbows on the butcher-block. "That I should stay for good."

Would that be so terrible? I think but don't say, hopping up to sit on the counter. My bare legs dangle — I catch Nate staring at them for a brief second before he turns to pour coffee into three black mugs.

"What are you wearing?" Parker asks abruptly, seeming to notice my outfit for the first time. I tug at the hem of Nate's too-big t-shirt, fighting off a blush.

"Um. I borrowed a shirt from Nate." I strive for a casual tone.

"He's been holding me captive since the whole kidnapping thing. He says it's to keep me safe, but I'm pretty sure he's just trying to annoy me to death."

"Oh." Parker's gaze moves from me to his best friend and back.

"Yeah." I clear my throat. "I can't wait till this is all over, and I can get back to my place."

Nate slides a mug across the counter to Parker, then passes one to me. I take a sip so I'll stop talking and am surprised to find he's made it exactly how I like it — dash of cream, no sugar.

How did he know? How does he always *know?*

I glance at him, surprised and grateful, but he's not looking at me. His eyes are on Parker.

"You want milk?" he asks my brother.

"Nah." Parker sips his mug, watching Nate carefully. "I like it black as my soul."

I snort, to cover my nervousness.

Parker's gaze flips to me. "You're never going to catch a man if you keep snorting. I'll have to call you Miss Piggy instead of Sweet P."

I shoot him a death glare. "How's the parade of Victoria's Secret models treating you, Parker? Have you figured out that happiness does not reside at the end of the bimbo rainbow?"

His grin is shameless. "You know what they say about that rainbow, kiddo?"

My eyebrows lift.

"*Taste* it."

I gag again. "I think that pertains to Skittles, not slut-bags."

Nate chuckles under his breath.

"Tom-a-to, tom-ah-to." Parker takes another sip of coffee. "At least I *have* a love life."

"Love?" I scoff. "*Lust*, maybe."

"That's quite a high horse you're riding, P." His eyes narrow. "Are you still dating that guy? Diego, is it?"

I sense Nate go suddenly tense. Just a tiny shift — his fingers curling a little tighter around his mug, his stance widening a fraction of an inch. If I weren't so attuned to his presence, I wouldn't notice it at all.

Swallowing hard, I try to keep my voice steady. "Not really."

"What does that mean? *Not really?* You're either dating the guy or you aren't." Parker's eyes are fixed on my face, searching for signs that I'm lying.

Crap on whole wheat, extra pickles.

Truth is, everything about Diego is a lie. There never *was* a Diego. Not one that I dated, anyway.

See, Parker called me one night last spring from whatever tropical island he was exploring, and I happened to be in class at the time. Naturally, I told him I couldn't talk because I was with Diego, but that I'd call him back later.

It's not *my fault* that Parker assumed Diego was my boyfriend instead of, uh, the TA of my Senior Design class.

It may or may not be my fault that I've failed to correct his assumption for the past year, though — which, let me tell you, was pretty freaking tricky when Parker flew in for the MIT graduation and wanted to meet my imaginary boyfriend. (Unfortunately for Parker, my beloved Diego joined Doctors Without Borders and shipped out just days before the ceremonies. *Shame.*)

I know, I know — I'm a dirty rotten liar. But I was tired of listening to Parker make those concerned big-brother noises every time he called and asked if I was dating anyone. There's only so many times you can lie and say, "No one serious!" before people start to wonder if you're asexual.

"Well?" Parker prompts.

"We broke up," I say, trying not to fidget.

Both men stare at me for a moment, expressions unreadable.

"Do I have to beat him up?" Parker asks, entirely serious. "Because if he hurt my baby sister, I will kick his ass."

"No! No." I swallow a nervous sip of coffee. "Definitely not necessary. We parted amicably."

Amicably?

What am I, a cast member of Downton Abbey?

"Amicably," Parker repeats slowly, like he doesn't quite believe me.

Probably because I'm lying through my teeth.

"Uh, yeah." I take another sip, mind racing. "He, uh, left. For Doctors Without Borders!" I exclaim, latching onto the thread of my previous lie in desperation. "I'm here and Diego, well, he's off... saving people... and stuff." Are my cheeks on fire? I think they're on fire. "So... we had to break up. But it was..."

"Amicable," Parker finishes for me.

"Yeah," I confirm weakly.

Nate's grip tightens even more on his mug. I wish I knew what that meant.

Parker stares at me like I've gone mad. "O-*kay*. Now that that's all cleared up..." He turns to Nate. "What about you, my friend? Still flying solo? Last time I was here, you were basically celibate."

I choke on my coffee. I'm so surprised, the sip in my mouth shoots straight up my nasal passages and out my nose. I sit there, spluttering like a fool, and Parker bursts out laughing, the bastard.

"Need a sippy cup, sis?" He slaps me on the back.

Nate silently hands me a napkin, mouth twitching in a dangerous approximation of a smile as I continue to cough.

This makes him smile? *Seriously?*

I wipe my dripping nose and pray that this is all a dream. With Parker here, everything feels alarmingly like middle school all over again.

LATER THAT NIGHT, I clean the kitchen while the boys talk, their voices hushed low. Every now and then, Parker will glance over at me with concern in his eyes, so I know they're talking about me.

I do my best to ignore them.

My hair, still wet from a shower, is up in a towel. I'm finally back in my own clothes, looking sleek and sophisticated in a pair of ultra-slim black chinos, a fitted Gucci blouse, and coral Brain Atwood heels. I tell myself if I dress normal, I'll feel normal.

For some reason, I'm not half as comfortable in the designer getup as I was in Nate's simple black t-shirt.

I took my time beneath the water, examining the damage to my body. There's a burn on the back of my neck, where my necklace was yanked off. My raw wrists, knees, and elbows are starting to scab over, though it'll be a few days before they're back to full working order. For the most part, my body looks totally fine.

My face is another story.

A dark bruise blooms from my right eye socket all the way to the hairline by my temple. It's an ugly blue-black color — mottled red at the edges where my blood vessels burst. In the coming days, I expect it'll run the full gamut of colors, from purple to green to yellow, before finally fading away.

How delightful.

Stomach rumbling, I raid Nate's fridge in search of dinner. He's got plenty of standard boy-fare — more beer, some leftover pizza, two uncooked steaks, seventeen thousand different kinds of hot sauce — but I'm also pleasantly surprised to find chicken breasts, milk, cheese, and even — *gasp* — vegetables.

I grab the chicken, a lemon, and fresh parsley from the fridge, then root around his cabinets for the rest of my ingredients.

Twenty minutes later, I've got water heating on the back burner and a simple chicken piccata — without capers because A. Nate didn't have them and B. *Ew*, capers — sizzling in a skillet up front. I lower the heat, add another dash of chicken broth, and toss in a handful of chopped parsley for flavor. A peek into the back pot shows the water has reached a rolling boil — I dump in a generous handful of pasta.

Unless there's been a drastic change in the boys' eating habits, I'm guessing every morsel of this meal will be devoured in less than twenty minutes.

I don't bother calling them. The aroma of dinner does that for me.

They both wander over and lean against the counter, drawn like bloodhounds to a fresh kill. When I turn to look at them, they're both eyeing my skillet with hungry gazes.

"Whatcha cooking there, sis?" Parker asks, fingers darting out to nab a piece of chicken from the pan.

I smack his hand with my spatula before he makes contact.

"Hey!" He glares at me and pulls back his walloped fingers.

"It'll be done in five minutes, grabby." I glare back at him. "This is not a free for all."

"I just wanted to taste test it. Check it for poisons." He grins like a scolded child who isn't particularly sorry. "I was protecting your life."

"Uh huh." I roll my eyes. When they come to rest on Nate, he ducks his head quickly.

Not quick enough that I don't notice the telltale movement of his jaw, though.

"Nathaniel Xavier Knox — did you steal a piece of my chicken?" I hiss.

He shakes his head. "Absolutely not," he says, voice muffled by the chicken still in his mouth.

I throw a dishtowel at him. "Get out of my kitchen! The both of you!"

Nate's head comes up and my breath catches at the look on his face. There's a playful light in his eyes that I've missed, these past few years — missed so much it sends an ache of longing shooting through my chest. When he leans a few inches closer, mouth twitching in amusement, and asks, "Oh? *Your* kitchen?" it's all I can do to remain upright.

I fight a blush. "For the next ten minutes, yes. It's mine. I'm claiming it."

Something changes in his eyes when I say that. Something so intense I'm too scared to define it, so I turn back to the stove and stir the pasta.

"Parker, come taste this," I order, fishing a strand of spaghetti out of the water and handing it to him. "Done?"

He chews for a few seconds, swallows, then nods. "Yep."

"Are you just saying that because you're hungry?"

His grin twitches wider. "Thirty more seconds. Then it'll be done."

"You're impossible."

"Admit it, though." He slings an arm around my shoulders. "You've missed the hell outta me."

I smile. I'll never admit it...

But he's absolutely right.

CHAPTER 19

THERE'S A TIME AND A PLACE FOR STILETTO HEELS.
ALWAYS AND ON MY FEET.

Phoebe West, justifying her fashion choices.

"DAMN, Sweet P. That was incredible. I could be convinced to move back to the States, if you'd promise to cook for me every night." Parker pushes back his barstool, hands on his stomach. He's had two helpings and practically licked his plate clean.

"If you want to keep those washboard abs, you better not," Nate says, shoving another bite of chicken into his mouth and letting out a small sound of pleasure.

I swirl pasta strands around the tines of my fork so I have something to do other than watch Nate's mouth move.

God, I even think he's hot while chewing.

There is something seriously wrong with me.

"Believe me, this isn't an every day occurrence. I don't cook very often." I hop off my stool, grab Parker's empty plate, and stack it on top of my own. When Boo barks at me, I shoot him a look. "No chicken piccata for you, demon-dog. Eat your kibble."

He glares at me before going back to his food bowl.

"That was seriously the best meal I've had in about ten years." Parker belches.

"Cute." I roll my eyes at him as I move to the sink.

"It's a sign of appreciation," he says, totally shameless. "Gotta hit the head. Don't miss me too much while I'm gone, kids."

"I think we'll manage," I call after him as he disappears into the bathroom. Less than a minute after I hear the door close, I feel Nate's presence at my side. I hope he can't see my hands shaking beneath the stream of water as I rinse the plate clean.

"If you can cook like this, why does your pantry contain nothing but snack foods and cobwebs?" he asks quietly.

I don't look at him. My voice is equally quiet when I say, "Not much point, cooking some elaborate meal when there's no one to share it with."

There's a sharp intake of air. A lengthy pause. Then, "Maybe—"

I don't get to hear what he's going to say because at that moment, the bathroom door swings open and Parker strides back into the room.

"Man, I'm beat," he announces, flopping down on the couch. "Jet lag is killer."

I turn to arch an eyebrow at him. "Imagine if you actually had a job to get to tomorrow, rather than freedom to just sleep the day away!"

He makes a disgusted face. "Why would I want to imagine that? That sounds terrible."

I snort and finish washing the dishes, passing each one to

Nate when it's clean. He accepts them wordlessly, dries them with a dishtowel, and puts them back in the cabinet. For a few unspoken moments, we're totally in sync.

Weird.

"I was going to catch a cab down to the harbor and sleep on my boat, but I'm not gonna make it. I'm crashing on your couch, man." Parker stretches his long frame across the sofa cushions, eyes already closed. "You guys can fight to the death over the bed. Just keep it down, will ya?"

"Parker—"

"Shhh." He turns onto his side, facing away from us. "Tell me tomorrow."

"But—"

"Night, Sweet P."

Approximately two seconds later, his breathing slows into the rhythmic patterns of sleep... leaving Nate and me staring at each other in horror, looking anywhere but at the bed we will now be sharing ten feet from my big brother — the same big brother who would probably have a heart attack if he ever suspected his best friend had his hands on his little sister's boobs mere hours earlier.

Well. This isn't awkward at all.

I TOSS.

He turns.

I huff.

He sighs.

Boo glares at both of us from the end of the bed.

Needless to say, none of us is getting any sleep. (Besides Parker, who is snoring away happily on the couch.)

I don't think my eyes have stayed closed for more than five consecutive seconds in the forty-five minutes since climbing beneath the sheets. I changed for bed while Nate took Boo out for a quick walk. If he noticed I chose to sleep in one of his t-shirts again instead of the skimpy nighty Lila packed for me — in a painfully transparent move to help me get laid — he didn't mention it.

I toss again and hear him grumble under his breath from the other side of the pillow barrier between us.

Something happens, when you lie next to someone in the darkness. Both awake, both afraid to look at each other or brush limbs beneath the blankets. The air grows thicker with every moment that passes. After an hour, the weight of our silence is so heavy, I can barely pull a breath into my lungs.

I'm about to slide onto the hard, cold floor and sleep there rather than endure another second of this, when I feel the mattress shift. My head turns in time to see Nate sit up, climb out of bed, and walk around to my side. I stare up at him in confusion, clutching the sheets to my chest like I'm five years old and he's the monster in my bedroom closet, come to destroy me.

His mouth twitches and he holds out one hand.

"Come on."

The words are so low, I almost miss them.

"What?"

He sighs deeply, grabs my hand, and pulls me out of bed. Boo glances up, seems to contemplate following us, then decides against it, cuddling deeper into the blankets.

So loyal, my demon-dog.

"Hey!" I hiss quietly at Nate's back as he tugs me across the loft, past Parker's sleeping form, toward the doorway. "Where are you taking me?"

He doesn't answer. He just twines his fingers tighter with mine as he leads me out the front door of his apartment into a low-lit hallway, tows me toward a service elevator, and slides open the gate so we can clamber inside. There are only three buttons on the panel — **1**, **2**, and **B**. He hits **B** and the elevator rattles into motion a few seconds later.

"Hello?" I yank at my hand, trying to get free, but he's latched on tight. "I'm barefoot. Braless. My butt is barely concealed by these boy-short undies. And I would really not enjoy meeting your neighbors while practically naked."

"No neighbors." Nate's eyes flicker down to my chest as if to confirm I am, in fact, braless, then move slowly down my body. "I own the whole building."

I cross my arms over the girls, feeling my heartbeat pick up speed as his eyes slide down to linger on my bare legs.

He owns the building? The whole *building?*

Does that mean we can hook up in this elevator?

Eeek! Danger!

I push the thoughts away and take a step back, so I'm pressed against the wall as far from him as humanly possible. His eyes never leave me as we descend.

It's easily the longest thirty seconds of my life.

"Well." I swallow, searching for composure. "Where the hell are we going? It's, like, one in the morning. I could be sleeping right now."

Not.

He runs his free hand through his hair, expelling a harsh breath. When his eyes lift to mine, I see frustration in their depths. "Neither of us is going to get any sleep, and you know it."

My mouth opens, closes, opens again. I can't really protest — he's right.

"So you're taking me where, exactly?" I adopt a haughty expression. "You hit **B** — is that basement? Batcave? Bottomless pit into which you will throw my lifeless body?"

"You'll see."

I roll my eyes. "Could you be any more cryptic?"

"Probably." His eyes crinkle. "If I tried."

CROSS THE LINE   223

"You're annoying," I inform him.

Annoyingly good-looking.

Annoyingly funny, in your own smart-ass way.

Annoyingly charming, when you look at me like that.

"Uh huh," he says, like he doesn't believe a word I've said.

"I don't like you."

"Boo likes me." He shrugs, as though that makes everything balance out.

"He likes anyone who takes him for midnight walkies," I say, lying through my teeth.

Boo barely likes anyone. Even me.

Yet, for some ungodly reason, he's taken a shining to Nate.

"Uh huh," Nate says again. *Damn.* He knows I'm full of shit. "Whatever you say, West."

Wherever we're going, I know one thing: I'm totally screwed.

———

ON THE RIDE DOWN HERE, I made jokes about the basement level of his building being a Batcave — turns out, I wasn't that far off. In addition to a stockpile of weaponry and electronics in a massive locker on the far wall, there's a sparring area with a punching bag and mats, and an honest-to-god shooting range set up on the other side of the space. It looks like a bowling alley with four separate lanes, except instead of pins there are hanging paper targets at the end of each strip.

"Do you live above Knox Investigations?" I ask after a few seconds of looking around with wide eyes.

His gaze cuts to me and he nods sharply.

"Sleep on the second floor.... Batcave in the basement...." I tilt my head. "What's on one?"

"Control room," he says succinctly. The stubborn set of his jaw tells me I'll get no more out of him on the subject.

"What are we doing down here?"

His arms cross over his chest, making his muscles bulge. "I'm going to teach you how to protect yourself."

"What?" My heart beats too fast as I eye the sparring matts, picturing me and Nate rolling around there, hands all over each other as he teaches me his moves.

In my fantasy version of this scenario, we may or may not be naked. And his *moves* have very little to do with the rules of jiu-jitsu.

Danger!

Realizing I've been lost in my lusty thoughts, I force myself to tune back in.

"...just a few basic defensive techniques," Nate is saying. "How to break out of an attacker's hold, how to use your stature to your advantage, things like that."

"My *stature*?" My eyes narrow. "Was that a dig at my height? I'll have you know, I may be petite but I'm agile. Must I remind you of my karate chop skills?" I drop into a crouch, hand-blades extended. "Ninja, remember?"

His lips twitch and he shoves his hands in the pockets of his sweat pants, tugging them further down his hips so a slice of taut flesh appears beneath the hem of his tight black t-shirt. I catch a flash of tan skin and dark hair before I force myself to look away.

Oh boy.

"Yeah, comforting as that is...." He suppresses a laugh. "You're tiny. You're never going to overpower a full grown man." His eyes narrow. "But that won't matter if you know how to outmaneuver them."

I stare at him for a long moment, saying nothing.

"You're uncharacteristically quiet," he points out, after a minute passes in silence. "I expected more objecting. A temper tantrum. Some whining. A little foot-stomping."

Well!

"I don't have temper tantrums," I mutter. "And I only have one question."

His eyes are crinkly and warm. "Yeah? What's that?"

I take a step toward him, eyes never shifting from his face. "Just to be clear... you're going to teach me defensive techniques."

He nods, looking at me like I have a few screws loose.

"And to teach me these moves... we're going to be on those mats." I gesture at the sparring area.

He nods again, but awareness is creeping into his eyes.

I step closer and drop my voice to a sultry whisper. "Just you and me."

His mouth parts a little as he watches me move toward him. "Yeah," he says, voice a little more ragged than usual.

Serves him right, after that temper-tantrum comment.

"You and me, on the mats. Your hands on my body, guiding me into different positions." My words are breathy as I take the final step, until I'm practically pressed against his chest. I'm barely holding my laughter in check. "Are you going to show me some things I've never done before, Nate?"

He swallows, body vibrating with tension as he stares at my mouth. "Fuck." His eyes drift heavenward, seeking guidance.

I trace a fingertip down his chest — just one, tiny graze — and his entire body rocks back like I've punched him in the gut.

"Come on," I whisper, feeling devious. "Teach me."

He groans and takes a step away, breathing harder than Gemma at yoga class. Which is really saying something.

"Fuck it." He grabs my hand and pulls me from the mats, toward the shooting range. "We'll start with guns instead."

I laugh.

BEFORE I KNOW IT, he's strapped me into a vest, handed me a set of glasses and soundproof earmuffs, and shown me the basics. Now, thirty minutes and one too-brief crash course later, I'm standing at the end of a gun lane with my eyes on a distant target and my hands locked tight around a sleek black handgun.

My veins are thrumming with adrenaline — thanks in part to the gun, but mostly to the man who handed it to me. I thought target practice would be easier to withstand than sparring, since I wouldn't have to touch Nate as much.

I was wrong.

"Adjust your grip. No, not like that." His arms wrap around me from behind, bringing his entire front up against my back. His head ducks so his chin rests almost on my shoulder. His hands close over mine, moving my fingers so they fit around the Beretta right. I can feel every muscular contour of his chest.

Crap on pumpernickel with peanut butter.

"That's it," he whispers when my hands are positioned correctly, the heat of his body radiating through the back of my sleep shirt. "Just like that."

I hold myself perfectly still, so I don't do something stupid. Like squirm against him. Or press back, to see if he's as affected by our proximity as I am.

One tiny shift of my stance and I could feel his...

Danger!

"I'm not sure about this," I say, wishing my voice wasn't so goddamned breathy, even if the words are true.

I'm not sure about *any* of this.

About his gun in my hands.

About his arms around me.

About the way my heart is racing inside my chest.

His mouth brushes my neck and I shiver.

"We should've done this a long time ago," he says, voice husky.

"Wha... We... Wha... *What?!*" I gasp out finally.

My brain has officially stopped working.

"Shooting lessons," he clarifies.

Right. Shooting lessons. What did you think he was talking about, lunatic?

I swear, he's laughing under his breath as he drops his arms and steps away from me. Pushing a button on the side of the booth, he activates an overhead pulley to bring the hanging paper target closer, until it's less than ten feet away.

I glance at him, somewhat offended. "Really? I can almost *lick* the bullseye from here."

He smirks and pushes a button to move it farther out, until it's about fifteen feet away. "Better?"

"Slightly less insulting, yes."

He moves in close again, eyes on mine. "Focus on the target."

I turn my head back, pulse pounding.

"Take aim."

I narrow my eyes down the sight of the gun, focusing on the tiny red circle at the center of the paper.

"Don't forget to breathe, West." He chuckles. "If you pass out from lack of oxygen before you get off a single shot, the bad guys win. Got it?"

I force a breath into my lungs. "Got it," I mutter.

"Don't forget—"

"You don't have to lecture me!" I cut him off. "How hard can it be to hit the damn thing?"

He's silent, but I can almost *feel* waves of amusement rolling off him into the air around us.

Whatever. I've so got this.

I steady my arms in preparation for the recoil, cock my head a tiny bit to the left, and pull the trigger, wincing in anticipation of the loud bang.

Except... it never comes.

No bang. No bullet. No recoil.

Fine. I so don't got this.

"What the...?"

Nate leans in until I feel his breath on my earlobe. "As I was saying before," he murmurs. "Don't forget the safety."

I shoot a glare in his direction, nearly bumping noses with him in the process. Damn, he's close. My heartbeat picks up speed again when I see his eyes are on my mouth.

"I knew that," I snap, hoping my bitchy tone will cover the fact that I'm about two seconds from mashing my lips against his.

Down, girl.

"Uh huh," he says, leaning back to give me room. Then, he grins. A real, genuine *grin*, with teeth and everything. The sight makes about three trillion butterflies burst into flight in my gut.

"I... uh..." I swallow hard, trying to convince myself to look away before I start to drool. "I..."

The grin widens. "You gonna shoot me or the target, West?"

I pivot swiftly so he won't see the blush creeping across my cheeks. Adjusting my stance once more, I lift the gun back to eye level, lock my arms, and adjust my grip.

This time... this time I've *totally* got this. I'll show him.

Him and his stupid, sexy, grinning mouth. And biceps. And dear god, those leg muscles...

Focus!

I swallow, move my thumb along the barrel of the gun like Nate showed me earlier, and grin victoriously when I find the small raised lever.

"Ha! Found it."

"West, you—"

"Shh! I'm concentrating. You don't need to baby me, Nate."

An amused sound rattles in his throat. "Whatever you say."

I ignore him, mouth twisted in a smug smile as I press the button to release the safety.

...Which makes it really freaking embarrassing when the magazine drops out the bottom of the gun and clatters to the cement floor.

Perfect. Just *perfect*.

I didn't hit the safety at all. I hit the clip-release button.

"Frack!" I yell, stomping one bare foot against the cement. I yank the shooting glasses from my eyes and toss them onto the booth.

There's a choked sound from my side. I turn in slow motion, eyes narrowed, and find Nate watching me with a strange, strangled look on his face.

"Okay... so maybe I need a little more practice," I admit warily.

At that, he loses it completely.

CHAPTER 20

I'LL NEVER LOOK AT A DAMN CHOCOLATE CHIP COOKIE
THE SAME WAY AGAIN.

*Nathaniel Knox, whose sweet tooth is more inclined
toward brunettes than brownies.*

LAUGHTER BURSTS from Nate's mouth — loud, roaring
laughter. The kind that makes you bend at the waist and clutch
your knees and gasp for air. The kind that makes your eyes tear
and your stomach hurt.

I want to laugh too — because even *I* can admit my abysmal
show of marksmanship is pretty funny — but I can't take my eyes
off him. Not yet. Because watching Nate laugh has to be the most
beautiful thing I've seen in my twenty-three years and three
hundred sixty-three days of life on this planet.

"Stop laughing at me!" I protest, setting the useless gun on the booth. "Or I'll shoot you."

That threat just makes him laugh harder.

"I hate you," I inform him sweetly.

"No you don't," he gasps, straightening to full height again.

"I do," I say, stepping closer. "I really, really, *really* hate— Eeek!"

My words are cut off when his hands shoot out from his sides and pull me into his chest. I watch as the laughter dies out of his eyes, replaced by something else. Something that looks a lot like lust.

"What did you just say to me?" he asks, voice intense.

I feel breathless, pressed against him so tightly. All the air has been forced from my lungs, like I've just run the Boston Marathon and his arms are the finish line.

I stare into those dark eyes and try not to sway closer. "I said I hate—"

The words are swallowed up as his mouth lands on mine. His kiss is hard, uncompromising, stealing my breath and sending my mind into a tailspin. His hands find the small of my back, pulling me closer as his lips overtake mine. It's all-consuming. The kind of kiss you can't even return properly — you just hang on for dear life and hope you're still breathing when it's over.

When he's finished, my arms are looped limply around his neck, I'm panting like Boo when he takes on the stairs, and I'm pretty sure if Nate lets go of me I'll slide to the floor in a heap of limbs, because my legs are made of Jell-O.

"I grew up with that — *I hate you*." His forehead rests against mine; his eyes are closed tightly. "My parents would shout it at each other, in the years before they became so indifferent to their marriage they couldn't be bothered to work up any feelings at all. Even hate. They didn't always use the words, necessarily, but it was there in their eyes. In the way they snapped and snarled." He exhales sharply. "I've never met two people more toxic for each other."

"Nate," I whisper, not knowing what to say.

His eyes flicker open. "Don't say you hate me. Even if you're joking. Even if you don't mean it." His forehead presses tighter against mine. "Don't ever say that to me, West. Because the day you hate me is the day I know I've finally fucked things up for good."

I look at him, feeling confused and hopeful and maybe even scared by his words. My hand lifts to trace the stubble shadowing his jawline. He sucks in a breath of air as soon as my fingertips make contact.

"I don't hate you," I whisper, staring at his mouth. "I don't think I could ever hate you. Trust me, I've tried."

His eyes crinkle. "You've tried?"

"Plenty of times."

"When?"

I tighten my arms around his neck and crane back to look up into his eyes. "Hmmm, let's see..." I tilt my head. "Definitely that time in second grade when you and Parker cut all the hair off my favorite Barbie dolls."

His lips twitch.

"And the time you put bean sprouts in my dinner and told me they were worms."

He snorts.

"And!" I say, narrowing my eyes at him. "When you turned me down for the Sadie Hawkins dance in eighth grade."

His eyes are glimmering with humor. "That's it? That's the best you've got?"

"No." My voice gets smaller but I force myself to hold his gaze. "The time you pretended I didn't exist for ten years." I swallow. "I hated you then."

He goes still, watching me carefully for a long, suspended moment. "You always existed for me, little bird."

The endearment is a shock to my system. He hasn't called me that for years, not since we were kids. I didn't realize how much I missed it until it slips from his mouth.

I try to duck my head so he won't see the emotion swirling in my eyes, but his hand finds my chin and he tilts my head up, refusing to let me escape.

"Every damn day," he whispers, eyes locked on mine. "Since you were no more than five years old, that day I climbed over the fence from my yard into yours and saw you sitting on the grass, perfectly still, crying your eyes out over those damn turtle doves... Every second of every day since that moment, you've existed for me."

"Then why..." I trail off.

His fingers stroke the tender spot where my jawline and ear connect. "Why what?"

"You wouldn't talk to me. You wouldn't even look at me. And then you disappeared." I bite the inside of my cheek so I won't cry. "I needed you, and you disappeared."

His eyes get soft and a heartbreaking look drifts across his face — full of longing and regret and sadness. "I had to leave. The things my father wanted for me — a Harvard law degree, a cushy job in the DA's office. ... I couldn't do it. I couldn't become him. That life I watched him live, full of hatred and greed and self-obsession — it was never what I wanted for myself." He pauses. "The only thing I ever really wanted was off limits."

My breath catches in my throat. "And what was that?"

Me. Me. Me. I repeat it over and over, like a prayer to the heavens. *Please, say it was me.*

He doesn't answer right away. After a minute, I realize he's not going to at all.

His thumb moves to stroke the fragile place beneath my eye,

where bruises stain the skin black and blue. "I wish I could erase this," he says softly.

"Why?" I ask, only slightly offended. "Is it grossing you out?"

He stills in surprise, then lifts his eyes to mine. "No, it's not *grossing me out*." He pauses and I know he's weighing his words, deciding how much of himself he wants to reveal. When he finally speaks, his words are halting. "You're beautiful. Always. In a ratty t-shirt with messy hair or in those goddamn six inch stiletto heels with a gorgeous dress."

Beautiful.

Nate thinks I'm beautiful.

His mouth touches the tip of my nose in a fleeting kiss so tender, it makes me want to cry. When his lips move to the aching spot above my eyebrow, then over to my bruised temple, depositing tiny kisses in their wake, I have to fight the tears building behind my eyes.

"I want to erase it because it's a reminder of the man who hurt you. I don't want his mark on your skin. Every time I see it, I'm reminded that I failed to keep you safe. Failed to protect you when you needed me most." His jaw clenches. "And every time you look in the mirror, you're reminded of the worst day of your life."

The tears I was fighting win the battle — they gloss over my eyes as I lay my hands on his chest. I can feel his heart pounding beneath my palm.

"You didn't fail me," I whisper to his mouth, because I can't look into his eyes — if I do, my tears will spill over.

"I did. If you'd trusted me when I told you he was dangerous, you wouldn't have gone with him that night."

"Exactly." I shake my head. "That's not your fault, it's mine."

"No." His voice is firm. "That's on me, West. I didn't give you a reason to trust me. I fucked up. And you got hurt because of it."

"You can't blame yourself for this, Nate." I press my fingertips harder into his chest. "I was angry at you. Angry and stubborn and too proud to admit you might be right. That's not on you. That's on me." My voice gets smaller — I'm ashamed of the next part. "And, if I'm honest, there was a part of me that enjoyed thinking you might be jealous. That it might hurt you, seeing me with him."

There's a loaded silence when my words trail off. I'm suddenly terrified to look at him, which is unfortunate because his thumbs find the soft spot beneath my chin, and then he's tilting my face up to look into his. As soon as our eyes meet and he sees the tears gathering there, a look flashes over his face. It's possessive, almost predatory.

"I hope those tears aren't for me, little bird."

"What tears?" I ask shakily, as they track down my face. "I don't see any tears. You should get your vision checked."

Denial is always the answer.

A soft smile tugs at his mouth. It's new and old at the same time — a revolutionary look for *this* Nate, the hardened man with too many memories in his eyes, but not for the Nate of my youth. I remember that same gentle smile on the lips of a ten-year-old boy when I'd trail after him and Parker on one of their adventures; that same look on his face when I'd ask for help with math homework at the kitchen table and he'd grudgingly show me how to do fractions. (For the third time.)

"Must be my imagination," he murmurs, wiping away an escaped tear with the pad of his thumb.

"Definitely," I agree, still weeping steadily.

His arms slide around my back, my hands slip up over his shoulders, and for a few minutes, I let my tears drip into the fabric of his t-shirt. He doesn't say anything — he just holds me.

"I don't even know why I'm crying," I hiccup after a while, voice muffled against his body. I pull back and see I've made a mess of his shirt — dark wet splotches cover the entire shoulder section. "I'm sorry, I didn't mean..."

"Don't apologize." He ducks to catch my eyes. "It's just a shirt. It'll dry."

I shake my head. "I don't know what's wrong with me."

"You went through a trauma. This is normal." He runs a hand through my hair, petting me like a scared child. "You acting like everything's fine and baking cookies and wanting to go back to your place right away — that's *not* normal."

"But you shouldn't have to deal with me being a mess. You've got enough to—"

"West." His voice is stern. "I can handle it."

I glance up at him from beneath my eyelashes, still wet with traces of my tears. "You were wrong, before."

His eyebrows go up. "About?"

"It wasn't the worst day of my life, when Cormack took me."

Dark eyes scan my face, a question in their depths.

"The day my mother died," I clarify. "That was the worst day."

His expression softens.

I clear my throat. "I'm the one who found her, you know."

"I know."

"I remember every detail of that day. Every single one. They're etched into my head and I'll never get them out."

"Little bird..."

I almost fall apart, when he says that. But now that I've started, I can't seem to stop the words from flowing. I stare at his Adam's apple and let the words pour from my lips, not thinking about the consequences. Just knowing I have to tell him, tell *someone*, because if I hold it in another moment I'm going to explode.

"If I close my eyes and think back, I can still smell the ocean that day. Seaweed and salt and that indescribable scent of summer. I can hear sound of shorebirds calling out overhead. Feel the whip of the wind against my face as I ran down the beach toward her. And the colors — the colors I remember most of all. The sand was so white, the sky so gray, the waves so green. And her skin. So blue. Like ice." I swallow hard when my voice breaks. Nate's arms tighten around my back but he doesn't interrupt me. "I knew she was dead before I reached her. Even at seven, I knew what death looked like. I knew she was gone."

I look up at him to see concern and sadness twisting his features.

"There wasn't anything you could've done." His words are intent. "You were a little girl. A baby."

"I know," I whisper, wishing I believed it. "But... seeing her like that... it did something to me. Most people spend their lives waiting for The Worst Day to happen. But when it happens to you while you're still a kid... every other bad thing that happens to you for the rest of your life seems a bit anticlimactic. I mean... *Failing grade on a test? Humiliating pool party? Date throws up in your purse?* Still not as bad as finding your mother's dead body." I take a deep breath. "Maybe that's why I haven't really processed the whole mobsters-kidnapping-me thing. Because, as scary as it was..." I stare into his eyes.

"It still wasn't The Worst Day," he finishes for me.

I nod. "You know, I've always thought I'll die young, like she did. That my timer is going to run out sooner than later. Maybe that's why I wasn't more freaked out when Cormack grabbed me. Because, in a way, I've kind of been expecting it for years now."

His hands tighten suddenly around me, and his voice gets intense. "Don't say shit like that. Get it out of your head. You're not going anywhere. You're not fucking dying on me." He shakes me gently, as if he might force some sense into me. "I won't let you."

There's a long pause where we simply stare at each other,

eyes locked, breaths mingling. His words wash over me, seep into my soul like balm on a long-aching wound I thought would never close.

I won't let you.

"Promise?" I ask finally, voice shaking.

That possessive look flashes over his face again.

"I promise, little bird."

———

WE DON'T SPEAK as we ride back upstairs and cross through the darkened loft to his bed, but his hand never unlaces from mine and when we climb beneath the sheets there's no pillow barrier between us. He holds me close, his big hands on my stomach beneath the large t-shirt, his body curled around mine perfectly, like we were made to fit together.

Nothing's changed — not really. Not on paper. I can't pinpoint the exact moment everything between us shifted. But somehow, in the space of an hour, my whole world has flipped upside down and I'm living in an alternate universe where Nate and I hold each other close and aren't afraid to show weakness.

I fall asleep in his arms and, for the first time since I got out of that basement, I sleep soundly.

CHAPTER 21

LET'S BE HONEST: IN TEN YEARS, THE MAN-BUN OF
THE 2010S WILL BE EQUIVALENT TO THE RAT-TAIL OF
THE 1980S.

*Phoebe West, whose tastes sway more toward clean cut
men with short, soft hair and deep chocolate eyes.*

"WELL, ISN'T THIS COZY."

Parker's voice is the first thing that permeates my subconscious — followed quickly by the realization that there is a large hand under my shirt, nestled warmly in the space between my boobs, along with a male thigh sandwiched firmly between my legs.

Nate.

"I guess you didn't mind sharing the bed after all," Parker says dryly.

Frack!

I spring away from Nate. Well, I *try* to spring away from him. His arms are so tight around me, I only make it about half an inch before he pulls me back into his chest and buries his head deeper in the space between my neck and the pillow.

"Piss off, we're sleeping," he grumbles against my skin. He's not talking to me.

There's a scoff from the end of the bed.

I turn my head and catch sight of Parker, who's got Boo cradled in his arms like a stuffed animal and is staring down at us with a knowing look. My wide eyes meet his amused ones.

"He's half asleep," I explain desperately, doing my best to squirm away from Nate. "He doesn't know what he's saying."

"Sure he doesn't." Parker's voice is skeptical.

"Nate!" I hiss, elbowing him in the side. "Let go of me."

With a deep sigh, he unwinds his arms from my frame and rolls onto his back. His hair is mussed and his eyes are sleepy when they peel open to meet mine.

"Christ, West, it's not even seven. You always wake up like this?"

I glance from him to my brother and back again in total confusion.

Parker just caught Nate and I twined together like wisteria vines, and neither of them is acting like it's a big deal. In fact, they're both staring at me like *I'm* the crazy one in this scenario.

What the hell?

Before either of them can say another word, I hop out of bed and practically run to the bathroom, muttering a short, "Gotta pee!" under my breath before slamming the door behind me.

I stare at myself in the mirror for a few seconds. My eyes are bright with anxiety and something else — something I barely recognize.

It looks a lot like hope.

Unfortunately, that does very little to detract from the ugliness of my black eye which, while slightly less swollen today, still makes me look like Hilary Swank in *Million Dollar Baby*. I'm not going to be winning beauty pageants anytime soon.

I can hear murmured conversation through the door, but I can't make out any of the words. I quickly decide I don't *want* to hear any of their words, especially if they concern me, so I strip down to my skin and pull open the shower door. Nate's shower is ultra-modern — opaque glass extends down to the tile floor and a chrome rainfall fixture drops a torrent of hot water straight down on my head. I stay in there for far too long, experimenting with the different settings, smelling Nate's shampoo like a creepy stalker, and generally pretending the world outside this glass cube of steam does not exist.

If only.

Then I wouldn't have to deal with the maybe-crisis of my big brother knowing about my not-so-secret feelings for his best friend of all time who, coincidentally, is forbidden from ever so much as touching me.

I think I'm developing an ulcer.

I dig through my bag until I've located my toothbrush, some makeup, and a fresh outfit. My choices are severely limited, but I eventually settle on a red silk wraparound top that fits me like a glove and brings out the hazel in my eyes, a pair of slim-fit black jeans, and few simple silver wrist bangles. Staring at the burn on my neck, I mourn the loss of my sunshine necklace and wonder again if Cormack kept it as a souvenir or tossed it in the garbage.

Bastard.

Knowing it'll drive Nate crazy, I forego the practical Tory Burch flats Lila packed in favor of my sky-high classic Louboutins

— jet black with a cherry red sole. After a few swipes of mascara and a failed attempt at concealing the bruises around my eye, I steady my shoulders and take one last look in the mirror.

My hair's a bit wild — towel dried, since Nate doesn't own a blow dryer — and there's no missing the ugly black eye... but still. I'm not half bad.

Not half bad? I glare at myself. *You're hot. Go out there and show Nate what he's been missing all these years, the idiot.*

If my hands weren't shaking so much as I reach for the doorknob, I'd almost believe it.

OF COURSE, Nate's not even there when I get out of the bathroom. Only Parker and Boo, who watch me from the couch as I wander into the kitchen and fix myself a cup of coffee. When I settle in on the chair across from them, two sets of eyes follow my every move.

"What?" I ask, taking a sip.

"How long have you and Nate been screwing?"

I splutter, sending coffee shooting up my nose. "*What?*"

He looks at me. "You really want me to ask again?"

"No." I shake my head swiftly. "Definitely not."

"So?"

"We aren't... it's not..." I take a deep breath. "You're way off, Parker."

"Really?" His eyes narrow. "That's not what he told me."

"Nate told you we were *screwing?*" I wince at the sound of my own voice — I'm yelling so loud, I bet they can hear me in the control room.

"No. He didn't say screwing. He just didn't deny it when I asked if he was crossing a line with you."

"He's not," I deny immediately. "*We're* not."

"Uh huh."

"Where is he?" I ask.

"Downstairs grabbing a shower and checking in on things in the control room." He grins. "Why? You missing him already?"

"No. I'm going to kill him."

Parker laughs. "Don't do that. Then I can't punch him in the face."

"Why would you punch him in the face?"

"For screwing my little sister."

"Ugh!" I scream. "For the last time — *I AM NOT SCREWING NATHANIEL KNOX!*"

"Good to know," a dry voice says from the doorway.

Crap on wonder bread.

I turn slowly from Parker, who's grinning like an idiot, to Nate, who's leaning casually in the door frame, looking serious and badass with still-damp hair and that wicked looking leather jacket I've been plotting to steal for years. I'd think he was pissed, if not for the way his eyes are crinkled up at the corners.

He's so gorgeous it takes my breath away.

Dammit.

"You're annoying," I tell him, then turn to my brother. "And so are you."

Parker's grin widens. "You'll miss me when I'm gone."

"Doubtful," I lie. My eyes drop to my dog, who's perched on Parker's lap. He's licking my brother's hand with such reverence, you'd think it's made of rawhide. "Come on, Boo. Come see me." I pat the cushion next to me. "Come on."

His tiny head cocks to one side, considering my words, before he yawns, closes his eyes, and snuggles closer to my brother.

"Traitor," I hiss, rising to my feet and stalking toward the kitchen. I need more coffee.

I swear, all three of them laugh at me as soon as my back is turned — Boo included.

SEVEN HOURS LATER, I'm so bored I've skipped passed regular old stir-crazy and gone completely insane. Parker and Nate both left hours ago — Parker to check on his yacht, Nate to deal with some of his existing clients and continue the search for Cormack. Which means I'm sitting in the loft for the second day in a row, going totally out of my mind.

Within the first two hours, I finished every bit of work I had outstanding for WestTech, cleared out my junk folder of several dozen male enhancement emails, and watched four consecutive YouTube video compilations of people nailing their X Factor auditions. Hour three, I did the dishes and brushed out Boo's coat, much to his chagrin. Hour four, I finally remembered Nate left me a phone for "emergencies only" and texted Lila.

Dying of boredom was technically an emergency. Right?

PHOEBE: Hey! It's me.
    Lila: Darren?
    Phoebe: No.
    Lila: Oh. Tom?
    Phoebe: No.
    Lila: Well, this is awkward. Um... Martin?
    Phoebe: How many dudes are you texting at once, Lila?
    Lila: OH, it's you. Hi Phee.
    Phoebe: How'd you know it was me?
    Lila: I'd recognize that semi-judgmental-but-loving tone anywhere. Even in text form.
    Phoebe: Cute.
    Lila: So, you're still alive? I haven't heard from you.
    Phoebe: I saw you yesterday.

Lila: Yesterday *morning*. You could've called last night.

Phoebe: Phone was swallowed by the Atlantic, remember? That time mobsters kidnapped me?

Lila: Excuses, excuses.

Phoebe: If you're free now, I can call.

Lila: K.

OH NO. She texted me the letter *K*.

That's never good.

In BFF-code, there's nothing quite as terrible as the *K* text. It's the DEFCON 1 of texting. The holy grail of passive aggressive communication.

She's pissed.

I chew my lip as I dial her number and hit the call button.

"Well, well, well," she snaps through the speaker. "If it isn't my former best friend."

"A little harsh, Lila."

"Maybe, but you know what else is harsh?" she asks. "Being totally out of the loop about the things going on in your best friend's life."

"Aw, were you concerned about me? Don't worry. I'm okay. The bruises are healing and Cormack hasn't made contact—"

"I don't care about *that*, idiot. I want to know about the important stuff."

"Threats to my life aren't important?"

"Clearly not." Her voice is exasperated. "I want to know about Knox."

I roll my eyes. "Seriously?"

"Did you wear the nighty I packed? Did you jump his bones?" she hisses. "I was picking up a serious vibe yesterday morning. Tell me I'm not wrong."

"Lila—"

"Phoebe Evangeline West." Her voice is rising. "After all the things I do for you, you're going to hold out on me?"

"What do you do for me?" I ask, genuinely curious.

"I give you hair ties whenever you need them, even when it's taken me two solid weeks to stretch them out to fit my wrist perfectly."

"Are you kidding?"

"Why would I kid about that?" She huffs. "Not to mention the fact that I always tell you when you've got food stuck in your teeth or a weird, rogue eyebrow hair."

"Lila—"

"And I bought you a ticket to Burning Man." Her voice drops lower. "You owe me $1500 for airfare, by the way."

"*What*?!"

"My point is, you owe me. So spill about Nate. If there were sexy-times, I need to know about them."

"It's possible there were..." I hedge. "...A few moments."

Silence blasts over the line and I realize she's waiting for me to continue.

"He kissed me. Or maybe I kissed him..." I shake my head. "There was definitely kissing."

"Just once?"

I hesitate.

"More than once!?" I can hear the smile in her voice.

"Yes," I say, groaning. "And I think we almost did it on the counter, but then Parker showed up. And honestly it's kind of a mood killer when your big brother almost walks in on you getting naked with his best friend."

Indecipherable squealing erupts through the phone. I stare at it, baffled, and wait for Lila to contain herself.

"You done?" I ask, when the squealing stops.

"For now."

I sigh. "I don't know why you're so excited."

"I don't know why you're not doing cartwheels down Summer Street," she counters.

"Because I don't know what any of it means." I tap my fingers against my kneecaps. "And I know your genius plan is for me to just have sex with him and walk away but..."

"Oh, honey." Lila's laughter is so loud, it hurts my eardrums. "You really bought that bullshit?"

My eyes widen. "What?"

"Swear to god, Temperance Brennan on *Bones* is more in touch with her emotions than you are. And it took her *seven seasons* to tell Booth she loved him. *Seven.*"

"Can we get back to the part where you said Operation SPANK was a complete and total lie?"

She snorts. "Still the best code name ever. But yeah... I hate to break it to you, but there's no *severing* anything. Especially not your attachment to Nathaniel Knox."

My fingers grip my kneecap so tight the knuckles go white. "Your exact words were *the best way to get over someone is to get under them.*"

"Phoebe. Honey. I knew from the start you'd never be able to make it *just sex* with Nate. You love him. You've always loved him. That doesn't just go away, especially if you take it to the next level."

"Then why the hell would you push me to go after him?" I practically scream. "Do you want me to get my heart broken?"

"No! Of course not." She sighs deeply and adopts a rare, somber tone. "I want you to be happy. And for the past ten years, you haven't been."

"That's not true," I protest weakly.

"Being content and being happy are not the same thing," she says. "Do you know how sad it makes me to see you pining away, year after year, over the same guy and refusing to go after him because you're too scared to take a chance? Scared to get hurt again?" Her voice breaks. "Do you know how freaking heart-breaking it is to see someone you care about paralyzed by their own self-doubt? To hear them question that they're worthy of love?"

"Lila—" I try to interrupt, but she plows on.

"I knew the only way I'd get you to even *talk* about the Knox situation was if I framed it as a plan to help you get over him," she says, exasperation in her tone. "And I also knew as soon as you walked back into his life, once you gave him a tiny indication that you were still interested in him... he wouldn't be able to push you away."

"You couldn't possibly know that," I snap.

"Except I did." She sighs deeply. "Don't you get it? The two of you are so alike — so stubborn, so hot-tempered, and so, so utterly blind to the fact that you need each other like normal people need air."

"But—"

"Has he pushed you away, since this whole thing started?" she asks. "Has he been distant and cold?"

"Well—"

"No." She answers her own question. "He hasn't walked away. He's shown up more than ever. He's been intense. Angry. Passionate. Domineering, even. But not cold. Not distant. Because he knows deep down, even if he doesn't want to admit it, he needs you just as much as you need him."

My throat contracts. I'm so mad at her I can barely breathe, at the moment, but there's an insistent voice at the back of my head telling me maybe, just maybe.... She's right.

"You played me," I say finally. "Best friends are supposed to be honest with each other."

"Maybe." Her voice is small but full of sincerity. "But best friends also do everything they can to make the other happy. Even if doing it gets them in trouble."

"Lila..." My voice shakes as I force myself to confront the real reason I'm so upset. "What if you're wrong? What if he doesn't want me? What if it really is just sex to him?"

"I'm not wrong." Her voice is confident.

I chew my lip. "How can you be sure?"

"Because the only time the ghosts disappear from his eyes is when he's looking at you."

CHAPTER 22

CAN WE ALL JUST AGREE THAT PEOPLE WITH PET BIRDS ARE WEIRD?

Phoebe West, genuinely curious why everyone on earth doesn't own a teacup Pomeranian.

I'M quiet when the boys come back that night. I know it freaks them out — I'm many things, but *introspective* isn't typically one of them. They don't say anything, but I feel their eyes on me as we eat dinner at the kitchen island — Nate on the stool beside mine, Parker straight across from us.

"You feeling okay, Sweet P?" Parker asks.

I nod and take another bite of mashed potatoes.

"I only ask, because the last time you were this quiet was

when we picked you up from the Sadie Hawkins dance with the purse-puker. What was his name, again?"

"Duncan," Nate mutters quietly.

I glance at him, surprised he even remembers that night let alone my date's first name. He stares searchingly at my expression and I know he's trying to figure out what's wrong with me. I force my gaze back to my plate so he can't read the emotions in it.

"Right. D-bag Duncan." Parker shoves another hunk of steak in his mouth.

"He's not a d-bag. Even if he did puke in my favorite clutch and fail to ever call me again."

"Well, it's not exactly a surprise he didn't call you," Parker says.

My eyes lift to shoot daggers at my brother. "What the hell does that mean? It's *no surprise* a guy wouldn't call me back? Are you saying I'm not worthy of common courtesy? That any guy wouldn't be *lucky* to date me?" My voice is icy.

"Whoa, whoa, whoa. Sweet P, *chill*. That's not what I meant at all." Parker looks from me to Nate and back again. "I just meant I'm not surprised he didn't call you, considering Nate gave him a black eye the day after the dance and told him to stay the hell away from you."

My eyes widen. "What?"

He nods.

My gaze moves to Nate, who's scowling at his plate. "You did *what?*"

"Shut the fuck up, Parker." Nate's voice is cold. "Why are you digging up ancient history?"

"How did I not know about this?" I ask.

Parker shrugs. "I don't know. Could've sworn you knew. Lila never told you?"

"No."

"Maybe she doesn't know either, then."

I shake my head, torn between awe and mortification. "But..." I stare at Nate. He ignores me. "Why the hell would you do that?"

There's a long pause before his eyes finally flicker over to meet mine. "He deserved it."

"It was just a purse," I whisper, voice shocked.

"It wasn't just a purse." Nate's jaw clenches. "The next day I heard he was bragging about how he was going to be the first to...."

My eyebrows go up when he trails off.

He sighs. "The first to nail Phoebe West."

I glance at Parker.

"It's true," he confirms. "Believe me, if Nate hadn't gotten there first, I would've beaten the shit out of him myself."

I sit there in stunned silence. "What a dick," I murmur finally. "He never even danced with me, you know. Not *once*. Which was bad enough. Then he puked in my purse, which just added insult to injury. And now you tell me he was bragging in the locker room about *nailing me*?"

"It wasn't actually in a locker room—" Parker starts.

"It's a figure of speech!" I snap. "I can't believe he had the nerve to ask Lila to set me up with him again this year! Did he think he could finish what he started ten years ago? *D-Bag Duncan strikes again*?!"

"He did what?" Nate asks, voice dark.

When I glance over at him and see the ominous look on his face, I quickly backtrack. "Nothing! Nothing."

His eyes narrow.

"Please don't kill him," I whisper. "He may be a douche, but he's my best friend's older brother. And it was about a million years ago. It doesn't matter."

"You still think about that night?" Nate asks intently. "Still remember being sad, getting your feelings hurt?"

Maybe, but not for the reasons he thinks I do. I don't dwell on Duncan when I remember that night — instead, I remember how in love with Nate I was at fourteen. How much I wanted it to be *him*, slipping a corsage around my wrist, leading me out onto the dance floor. But I can't say that now. Not without sounding like some kind of crazy person.

"Do you?" he prompts.

"Sometimes," I admit, shrugging. "But—"

"Then it matters." His voice is intent. "Someone hurts you, it matters. Always."

Staring into his eyes, so bright with passion, I have to remind myself to breathe. The moment stretches on with our stares locked together, lengthening into something heavy and hard to swallow. He shifts on his stool, I sway on mine, and for a crazy instant I wonder what would happen if I leaned forward and closed the distance between us right here during dinner...

"Well, then." Parker's voice is wry as he interrupts the moment. Frankly, I'd forgotten he was still sitting there. "How 'bout them Red Sox, huh?"

When I glance his way, cheeks flaming bright red, I see he's fighting to hide a smile.

I can't seem to formulate a single word, at the moment, so I take another bite of mashed potatoes and order myself not to think about eighteen-year-old Nate beating the shit out of my Sadie Hawkins date all those years ago. Because thinking that he was looking out for me back then, when I've spent years convincing myself he didn't know I existed... when I've always thought I was totally invisible to him....

That may just make me fall even harder for him.

Thankfully, the conversation shifts as Nate and Parker begin a semi-heated debate about the new Sox pitcher. After a few minutes, I'm pretty sure they've forgotten my existence.... until I feel Nate's hand slide onto my thigh beneath the counter ledge,

254   JULIE JOHNSON

out of view. His grip is firm, but casual. Natural. Like he does it all the time.

I suck in a breath and try not to fall off my stool.

He doesn't look at me, doesn't say a word. But his hand never moves for the rest of the meal.

———————

THE SOUND of the faucet drowns out Parker and Nate's hushed conversation across the loft, which makes it nearly impossible to eavesdrop while I'm washing the dishes. So, I'm surprised I'm able to hear the slight buzzing of a cellphone against the wood counter on the other side of the kitchen.

Lured toward the sound like a moth to flame, I narrow my eyes when I see it's the burner phone Tink gave me, its screen illuminated with an incoming call. A glance behind me shows the boys are still deep in conversation across the loft.

Before I have time to ponder all the reasons it's a terrible idea, I lift the phone to my ear.

"Hello?"

"Thought I told you to toss the burner phone."

"Tink?"

"Listening isn't your strong suit, huh?"

Sigh. "If you thought I'd tossed it, why bother calling at all?"

"Because I knew you wouldn't listen to me." I can almost hear her eyes rolling in their sockets. "You're a pain in the ass."

"You barely know me!"

"I know enough."

"Did you call to harass me?" My words are snippy.

"No, I called to warn you."

"Do you have some kind of savior-complex I should know about, Tink?" I press a hand to my chest and gasp. "Are you my fairy godmother!?"

"Just shut up and listen to me." I hear a sound in the background, like fingers clacking against a keyboard at hyper-speed. "You wouldn't happen to be at your boyfriend's place in Seaport?"

"He's not my boyfriend," I hiss.

"So you're there." Her voice gains an edge it didn't have before. "Listen, you have to leave. Pronto."

There's a sudden presence at my side. I turn and see Nate looming over me, eyes narrowed on the phone in my hand.

"Who is it?" he asks, voice ominous.

"That your boyfriend?" Tink asks through the phone.

"He's not my—" I break off when I catch sight of Parker hovering close behind Nate. "It's Tinkerbell," I inform them wearily.

"Yo! Princess!" Her voice is impatient. "Heads up or I'm hanging up."

"Put it on speaker," Nate commands. His voice books no room for argument.

I sigh and hit the button to trigger the speaker.

"Gang's all here," I inform Tink. "You've got the floor."

There's a furious sound of typing, then a low curse. "Great. Let's hope at least one of you has a brain." She curses again, distracted by something. "Turns out we stepped on a few toes the other night, when I broke you out. O'Pry and Petey are pretty fucking pissed we got the jump on them. Ruined their plan to make good with the big boss and all. They've been trying to track you down. Paid a visit to your place in Back Bay earlier."

"How do you know where I live?" I ask, surprised.

"I have men stationed at the brownstone." Nate answers before she can. "No one's getting in."

My eyes fly to his face. "How many *men* do you have, exactly?"

His lips twitch at the incredulity in my tone. "Enough."

"Focus," Tink snaps. "I don't have all day to listen to your inept sexual foreplay."

I roll my eyes. "You're a jerk."

"I prefer ball-buster, but I'll take what I can get." Her smile is audible. "Anyway, no luck at your place means they're casting their net wider. Cell pings say Seaport is their next stop — unless their phones have grown legs and decided to go for a stroll through Fort Point on their own."

A thought suddenly occurs to me. "Are they coming after you, too? If they know you're the one who helped me..." I can't help but be worried for the little blonde imp.

"I can take care of myself." The confidence in her tone is unshakeable. "I tapped into Mac's server. His boys are headed your way, not mine."

"You're a hacker?" I ask, surprised.

There's a brief pause. "I prefer hacktivist."

My head tilts. "Isn't that like calling a garbage man a *waste management official?*"

"Detritus disposal technician," Parker offers, grinning.

Nate glares at us both. I bury a laugh.

There's a pause from Tink's end, then, "Who's that?"

"My brother." I glance at Parker. His eyes haven't shifted off the phone once since she started speaking.

"Just what we need right now — a man-whoring party boy." She grumbles under her breath. "I don't even know why I'm bothering with you people. Maybe I should just let natural selection take its course..."

"Because you're such a kind hearted soul?" I offer.

She laughs outright at that — a light, joyous sound that's totally at odds with her personality. "Yeah, that's it." Her sarcasm is thick. "Now shut up and listen. I've been tracking some of Mac's boys since the other night. They're headed your way and I don't think they come bearing fruit baskets, if you catch my drift."

"They'll never get inside." Nate's voice is cold. "My security system is impenetrable. And even if they somehow managed to breach it..." His eyes narrow further. "I'd take care of it."

Shiver.

"Okay, macho-man. We get it. You're packing heat." Tink snorts. "Point is, Mac's boys have put a hit out on your girl. You're standing in their way. That means they're coming for you, and they won't stop until they've got what they want."

"And they want me?" I sigh. "*Again?*"

"They tried that. Didn't work. Now, they're pissed. They want their money or they want West blood," Tink clarifies. "You need to talk to your father. Get him to pay up. Otherwise..." She trails off, keys clacking again.

"You could be making all of this up. How do we know we can trust you?" I ask.

"Sweetie." She laughs. "I don't give a fuck if you trust me. All I know is, you should leave that loft. When Mac's boys are involved, things have a tendency to go up in flames."

She clicks off.

My eyes move from the phone to Nate to Parker. We're all totally silent for a full minute, contemplating her words.

"Is she as hot in person as she sounds on the phone?" Parker asks eventually.

I whack him on the arm. "Don't even think about it. She's totally out of your league."

"No one's out of my league," he mutters, rubbing the spot where I hit him.

"Question is, do we believe her?" I ask, looking at Nate.

His eyes are active, face hard-set. After a moment, he nods. "We don't have a reason not to."

"She did save my life," I concede. "Even if she complained the whole time."

Parker grins. "Personally, I think we should track this Tinker-bell down."

"Why, so you can ask her out?" I snort. "Fat chance."

"We'll find her." Nate crosses the kitchen and grabs a set of car keys. "One way or another."

"Yes!" Parker pumps a fist into the air. "Knew you'd have my back, bro."

My eyes are suddenly a little too focused on Nate. "Don't tell me you want to date her, too."

Seriously, don't tell me. I can't handle it.

"Hardly." He pulls on his leather jacket and meets my eyes, a playful light dancing in his irises that I've never seen before. "I want to hire her."

"WHERE ARE WE GOING?"

"WestTech." Nate's hands tighten around the steering wheel as we race past the Convention Center toward the financial district at well above the legal limit. "Your father is overdue for a visit."

It's getting dark outside — well past six o'clock — but we all know Milo is still at his office. He's there till midnight, most nights.

"Fuck." Parker glowers in the passenger seat. "The old man isn't going to be thrilled to see me."

"He'll probably be a bit preoccupied with the twenty million dollar commission the Irish mob wants in exchange for not slaughtering his only family," I point out. "I doubt he'll have time to admonish you about your many failings."

"He's surprisingly good at multi-tasking," Parker says darkly.

I roll my eyes and look out the window as the city blurs by. Maybe I'd feel more sympathy for him if, as soon as we left the loft, he hadn't called, "Shotgun!" like we're still adolescents and shoved me toward the back seat. Now, Boo and I are sitting in the back of Nate's giant SUV, the kind with blacked-out windows I imagine Secret Service members use to escort the President. I would've preferred the Viper, but it's a two-seater and Parker was surprisingly unenthusiastic about my suggestion that he squeeze into the trunk.

Go figure.

Twenty minutes later, Boo's tugging his leash so hard, I'm practically running to keep up as we move through the lobby of a gleaming glass skyscraper in the heart of the South End, where the WestTech executive offices are housed. I nod to Bill, the security guard behind the front desk, when we reach him.

"Hi, Bill. Empty in here, tonight."

"Wednesdays – always quiet, Miss West." He folds his newspaper and peers over the counter. "Hello, Boo."

The little dog barks promptly at the sound of his name, sits in a perfect show of posture, and waits, his stare never wavering from Bill, his short tail wagging furiously.

Bill isn't just my favorite lobby guy — he's Boo's, too.

After a second, the aging security guard reaches beneath his desk and retrieves one of the mini milk bones he keeps there. It's become a tradition of sorts, since the first time I brought Boo with me to work last year.

"Speak," Bill commands, his kind eyes locked on my dog.

Two short barks erupt from Boo's mouth.

"Paws."

Tiny white paws shoot into the air, as the dog balances on his back feet.

"Lie down," Bill says, nodding.

Boo's front paws slide across the marble until he's totally flat on the floor.

"Roll."

Boo flips onto his back in one swift move.

"Good boy," Bill says, smiling as he tosses the tiny bone into the air. Boo's back on four paws as soon as it leaves his hand. He catches it before it hits the ground and devours it with glee at my feet.

Hell. I buy him food, give him toys, take him out at midnight when he needs to pee, brush his coat until it's shiny... and in return, the little demon uses my Manolos as chew toys, ignores my every command, and will barely walk straight for me on a leash. Put him in front of a virtual stranger with a milk bone, though, and he'll do circus tricks.

I look from the dog to Bill, whose smile is as warm as his eyes.

"Brought some friends with you today, Miss West?" he inquires, looking at the men flanking my sides like bodyguards.

"Bill, come on now." I shoot him a look. "It's *Phoebe* and you know it."

"Uh huh." His mustache twitches when he smiles.

I shake my head, knowing he'll never comply with my wishes. "This is my brother, Parker, and my..." I glance at Nate. *What is he?*

Friend? Enemy? Alien?

"My acquaintance, Nathaniel Knox," I finish.

Acquaintance. See? I'm so diplomatic.

I can feel Nate staring at me; I studiously ignore him.

Bill nods politely in greeting.

"Is the old man in?" I ask, jerking my thumb toward the ceiling.

"Should be."

"Cool." I grin and waggle my fingers. "Bye, Bill."

"Until next time, Miss West."

We glide past the desk, I scan my company badge, and we head for the elevator bank. Boo follows grudgingly, casting adoring puppy-dog looks back at Bill on regular intervals. We're almost there when a thought pops into my head and I turn back.

"Hey!" I call.

Bill looks up from his paper.

"Did Sadie have her puppies yet?"

He smiles, gray mustache twitching. "Sure did. Six little German Shepard runts, running around like miniature tornados. They're driving my wife crazy."

"I'll bet." I laugh.

"Any chance you want to take one off our hands?"

I glance down at Boo dubiously. "This little guy gives me enough trouble. But if I think of anyone in need of a fur-baby, I'll send them your way!"

He nods and goes back to his paper.

The elevator doors slide open a second after I hit the button. When I turn, I find Parker and Nate both watching me, identical expressions on their faces.

"What?" I ask, walking inside.

"How long have you been friends with the lobby guy?" Parker asks under his breath.

I shrug. "A few months. Why?"

"You always befriend total strangers and let them into your life without question?"

"No," I lie.

"Uh huh." His hazel eyes, so similar to my own, move over my face. "And you wonder why you were so easy to kidnap?"

"That was totally different."

"How?" Parker asks, finger jabbing into the 27 button.

"Cormack was an anomaly. I usually don't trust just anyone off the street."

Nate snorts and glances at Parker. "She splits her lunch with a homeless guy at the park every time she works from the office."

I gasp. "How do you know that?!"

Nate ignores me. "She let two guys who live in the building next to hers use her kitchen last Thanksgiving, just 'cause they said theirs wasn't working."

"They couldn't cook their turkey!" My voice is defensive. "What was I supposed to do, let them starve on a national holiday?"

"She also made dinner for the guy fixing her cable last month, when the job took him longer than expected." Nate shakes his head.

"That was *one* time," I point out.

He makes a frustrated noise. "Frankly, it's a miracle she hasn't been kidnapped long before this."

"Christ," Parker mutters, looking up at the elevator ceiling as we ascend.

"How do you know all that?" I squeak, narrowing my eyes at Nate. "Have you been spying on me?"

He doesn't answer. He just watches me with those steady brown eyes, and I can't help but notice they're crinkly and warm as they move over my face.

"You're an odd duck, Sweet P." Parker hooks one arm around my neck and pulls me in for a half-hug. "But I still love you."

"Gee, *thanks*," I mutter sarcastically. "I feel so cherished."

My eyes catch Nate's as the words leave my mouth and the sarcasm in them seems to float away.

He's as far from me as possible, on the exact opposite side of the elevator, but as the moment stretches on, I hold my breath and marvel at the power of this man who can touch me so deeply without even using his hands.

The blush never leaves my cheeks the entire ride up to the twenty-seventh floor.

CHAPTER 23

IF I WERE A BETTER MAN, I'D BE ABLE TO STOP
PICTURING HER NAKED.

*Nathaniel Knox, keeping his eyes carefully averted at all
times.*

"PHOEBE."

Milo West rises from behind his desk as soon as I step
through his office door. His salt-and-pepper hair is meticulously
styled, his mouth is etched with frown lines from too many long
nights at the office.

"You haven't been answering my calls."

I roll my eyes at his stern words, bending to let Boo off his
leash so he's free to roam the office. As soon as the latch unclips

he's off like a shot, smelling every piece of furniture on the 27th floor.

"Yeah, well, it's been kind of hard to keep in touch, ever since a mobster chucked my iPhone into the Atlantic."

His face pales a little. He opens his mouth to say something else, but the words die in his throat as Nate and Parker step through the entryway behind me. I shuffle awkwardly into his hyper-organized domain to give them some room. The CEO suite is all white and glass — so sterile just stepping foot inside makes me feel like a bull in a china shop, liable to break something without even trying.

"Parker." There's surprise in my father's voice — a rare emotion from him. "I wasn't expecting you."

"Dad." Parker shoves his hands in his pockets and surveys the space, whistling under his breath. "Nice office. This *Wolf of Wall Street* act must be paying off."

"And what act are you playing?" Milo asks coldly. "The ungrateful son? The whore-mongering wastrel?"

A long-buried ache stirs in my chest, seeing the two of them at odds. I can't remember the last time they were in the same room.

Parker's hands fist inside his pockets and a chilling smile crosses his lips. "Don't hold back to spare my feelings." He scoffs. "Tell me how you really feel."

"Oh, believe me—"

"Believe you? *You?!*" Parker laughs, but it sounds almost like a snarl. "That's rich, Pop."

"You're just as disrespectful as I remember. I should—"

"Mr. West," Nate cuts in before the situation can escalate to bloodshed. "We're here to talk about Keegan MacDonough."

The power of that name alone makes everyone fall silent.

Dad's eyes move to Nate for the first time since we arrived. I can see the wheels turning in his mind as he tries to come up with a name to match the face of his children's closest childhood friend, a boy who spent more days at our Nantucket estate than he ever did. A name a normal parent could recall within nanoseconds.

"Nathaniel," Milo says finally, a smug smile playing at his mouth when he finally pulls the name from his memory banks. "Nathaniel Knox."

Nate nods tightly.

"I had lunch with your father a few weeks ago."

Nate says nothing.

Milo's eyes narrow. "He didn't mention you still lived in the area."

"He doesn't know." Tension stiffens Nate's shoulders. "We don't keep in touch."

My heart falters at that information and a pang of sympathy shoots through me. Nate's never been close to his family — his relationship with his father makes Milo and Parker's bond look like an ad for Hallmark — but I'm surprised to hear he's cut them out of his life completely.

The three men stare at each other, a trifecta of tension. It's so awkward, I'd like nothing more than to edge slowly backward out of the room and make a run for it. Unfortunately, that's not an option.

Clearing my throat, I step into the middle of the office.

"Enough. You're all acting like babies." I turn to address my father first. "I'm sure you already know the basics but, to recap — three days ago I was kidnapped by some seriously scary dudes who have a bone to pick with you. Personally, I would really not like to repeat the experience. One black eye is enough for a lifetime."

His face softens as he stares at the fading bruise beneath my eye makeup. "I didn't think they'd come after you. I'm sorry, Phoebe. Truly."

Parker scoffs. "Sorry doesn't mean shit when your daughter's been kidnapped and beaten."

"Parker," I admonish. "Blaming Dad won't help things."

"Why not?" he asks. "It's his fault."

"Parker. Not the time." Nate's voice is gruff enough that my brother falls silent. When he turns those dark eyes on my father, the older man shrinks back at the intensity in them.

I've been on the receiving end of that same stare more often than I'd like — I know exactly how Dad feels, at the moment.

"Care to share how you've managed to piss off the entire Irish mob?" Nate's words are clipped, totally controlled. Not an ounce of emotion slips out. "Mac made you his business for a reason."

My father tugs at his collar in an uncharacteristic show of nerves. When he collapses back into his leather swivel chair a few moments later, I just about fall over.

Milo West, showing weakness? Unheard of.

"I've made some mistakes," he admits, voice choked.

Parker laughs darkly. "Understatement."

I glare at him.

"Why does Mac expect a commission from you?" Nate asks, pinning my father to the spot with just the force of his stare.

"I don't know." Dad's face is flushed. "My development project has nothing to do with him. He doesn't own the land."

"Not in name, maybe." Nate folds his arms across his chest. "But that whole area is Bunker Hill gang territory. Everyone knows that. It's the reason the waterfront has never been developed. No one will touch Mac's land with a ten foot pole."

"Until now," I add softly.

"Only way a deal like that goes through is if there's some kind of arrangement in place," Nate says in a deadly soft voice. There's more danger in that gentle tone than I could muster screaming at the top of my voice.

When Nate yells, you know he's pissed... but when he whispers, you run and don't look back.

Milo shifts uncomfortably. "What exactly are you accusing me of, Nathaniel?"

Nate's eyes have a lethal gleam as he steps closer to the desk. "You got into bed with MacDonough."

I didn't think it was possible, but my father pales even more. "No," he whispers, though it's a weak denial.

"I've been looking into things. Every building constructed in that part of town in the last twenty years without Mac's blessing has either been burned to the ground, vandalized beyond repair, or run out of business because people are too afraid to go near there." Nate's gaze never wavers. "You're a smart man, Mr. West. You'd never have poured so much money into this development project unless you had assurances that he wouldn't give you problems."

"Christ," Parker mutters from somewhere behind me. "Perfect. Fucking perfect."

"How much did you give Mac?" Nate asks flatly.

My father sits there silently, too proud to lie and too weak too admit the truth out loud.

"Oh my god, Dad." I stare at him. He won't meet my eyes. "Tell me you didn't do this. Tell me this is some kind of mistake."

He swallows, staring resolutely at his desk. "I didn't think it would turn out like this."

"What? You thought if you made a deal with the head of Boston's biggest crime family, things would go *well* for you?" Parker's voice is incredulous. "You've got to be fucking kidding me."

"What did you promise him?" Nate's voice is colder than I've ever heard it.

A defeated sigh moves through my father.

My father.

The idealist. The self-made billionaire. The prince of the people. The philanthropist. The entrepreneur who truly *cares* about the fate of his fellow man.

What a load of horseshit.

God, I'm a fool for ever believing in him.

"If you care about your children, tell me." Nate's hands come down on my father's desk with a sharp smack. Milo jumps at the sound. "I can't protect them if I don't know what I'm up against."

Dad's eyes lift straight to me. They move over my face, no doubt reading the horror, confusion, and disappointment etched into my expression, and I see something inside him crumble.

"He wanted ten percent of the land value, plus interest, over the next ten years." I've never seen my father cowed before, but that's exactly how he looks right now as he lays out the terms of his deal. Utterly defeated. "It was a good deal. Fair. With the amount of revenue the new condos would bring in..." He swallows. "I'd still walk away with well over my bottom line."

Money. This was about *money*.

Nausea churns in my stomach. I feel Boo settle at my feet, perhaps sensing I need moral support.

"But then..." Milo drifts off.

"He changed the terms," Nate guesses. "Wanted more."

"Twenty million, on top of the millions I'd already paid him for access to the land." A spark of anger shoots through my father's eyes — a flicker of the uncompromising CEO that's built an empire on trade agreements and business mergers. "He tried to con me."

"That's what criminals do, Dad," I snap, voice shaking. "They extort and cheat and bribe and *kidnap people* when they don't get their way."

"I'm sorry," he whispers, eyes dropping back to his desk. "You'll never know how sorry I am. If I knew how to fix it..."

"Pay him," Parker says, all playfulness stripped from his tone.

"Pay him the fucking money or I swear to god, I will kill you myself for putting a target on my baby sister's back."

"He can't," Nate says, eyes alert as they watch my father. "It's not that simple."

Dad jerks his chin in response.

"What?" I gasp. "*Why?*"

"He'll just keep asking for more, don't you understand?" My father's voice is shaking. "It'll never be enough. Ten million, twenty million, fifty... it won't end. He won't stop. Not until we're bankrupt and the company's gone under. He'll take everything."

"Pull out of the project," I say immediately. "We haven't even broken ground yet."

"I've sunk millions into this development." His hands find his temples and he suddenly looks every bit his age. For the first time, my father looks *old*. "I can't just pull out now. And—"

"And money is more important than your family?" Parker snarls. "Guess that shouldn't come as much of a surprise."

"Dad." My voice breaks. "Please."

His eyes lift to mine and this time, they're red and watery with unshed tears.

Holy frack.

I've *never* seen my father cry.

Not once.

Not when Parker took off. Not at my graduation from MIT. Not when the crash of '08 made stocks plummet. Not even the day we found my mother, or when we lowered her casket into the earth.

But he's crying now.

I wish that somehow made all of this okay.

Nate turns his head to look at me. "Even if your father pulled out of the development, Mac won't let him walk away — not now that he's got his claws in him. He sees your father as a cash cow, his personal piggy bank to fund the mob. He's not going to give that up. Not easily."

"So..." I swallow. "He'll keep coming after us until he gets what he wants?"

Nate's jaw clenches tight. "Yes."

"What about the police?"

"No police." Nate's words are clipped. "Can't be trusted."

"The FBI then."

His eyes cut from me to my father, a knowing look in their depths. "I'm guessing if your father admits what he knows about Mac, it'll incriminate him, too."

Parker snorts. "Great. Fucking perfect."

My stomach clenches. I hadn't thought of that. Hadn't considered the possibility that my father's corruption might extend past shady bribes and business deals to actual criminal activity. Fraud. Extortion. Collusion.

White-collar crimes that could land him in federal prison.

"So we can't do anything." My words are shaky and so soft they barely make it past my lips.

My father's head drops into his hands. A sob rattles his chest.

I take a half-step then freeze, torn between wanting to comfort him and wanting to strangle him for doing this to our family. Parker steps to my side and wraps an arm around my shoulders.

"Don't worry, Sweet P. We'll fix it."

"How?"

"First, by putting you on the jet and flying you as far from here as possible," Nate says, barely containing his anger. "I want you out of this city until this is over."

My spine stiffens. "I'm not leaving. My family needs me."

"You're leaving."

"No. I'm. Not." I grit the words out between clenched teeth.

Nate stares at me for a long moment, then shifts his eyes to

Parker. "Call the airport. Tell them you both leave tomorrow morning, first thing."

My brother nods, reaches into his pocket, and walks to a corner to make the call.

"I'm not going!" I snap, glaring at Nate. Boo, likely hearing the edge in my voice, barks his support from the floor. "I'm not going to be carted off like some damsel in distress because you think I'm too soft to handle this. This is *my* fight, just as much as anyone else's."

"You can scream at me till you're red in the face, little bird." Nate's eyes never waver from mine and there's so much steel in his tone, I barely notice the endearment. "Your ass will still be on that fucking plane."

"You're a jackass," I snap at him. Boo barks again, for emphasis.

He smiles, and it's so cold it makes me shiver. Without another word, he turns back to my father, who's slumped in his chair like a broken mannequin.

"I'll have one of my men keep an eye on you in case Mac tries anything, but I have a feeling if he's going to target anyone, it'll be Phoebe, Parker, or..." His words cut off abruptly and his body goes tense. "Does Mac know about her?"

Her?

My father's head comes up. Something Nate said is important enough to pull him out of his pity-party.

"I don't think so." Milo shakes his head. "It's not public knowledge. Not yet." His eyes shift to me for a brief instant, then dart back to Nate. "I haven't had a chance to..."

He drifts off.

What the hell are they talking about? Who the hell are they talking about?

Nate nods sharply. "Still, I'll tell Chase to amp up security, just in case."

Chase?

Chase Croft?

"One of men will stay with your son. I'll stick with your daughter until she leaves. It's better if they're both away until this is resolved," Nate says.

A frustrated screech escapes my mouth. "I'm not leaving."

He ignores me. "Call if you get word from Mac," he tells Milo, his voice cold with disgust. "And don't do anything without clearing it with me first."

Before I can say goodbye to my father, Nate's turned, grabbed hold of my hand, and is tugging me toward the door.

"Wait just a goddamn minute!" I yell, tugging at his grip ineffectively. *God, he's strong.* Boo trots ahead of us, tail twitching happily as he goes to investigate a potted plant in the corner.

We come to a stop by Parker, who's shoving his phone back into the pocket of his jeans.

"Is it done?" Nate asks.

Parker nods. "Seven sharp, tomorrow morning."

A sigh escapes Nate — I'd swear, it sounds almost relieved. "Good. We're going to her place to pack her shit."

"No we aren't," I snap. "Because *I'm not leaving.*"

They both ignore me.

The sound of a chair being pushed back makes us all turn toward the desk. Milo's on his feet, looking more himself — all traces of weakness have been removed from his expression. If not for the faint redness around his eyes, you'd never know he'd been upset at all.

"I'll fix this." His voice is firm with false confidence. *This* is the father I recognize — the man who can sell any idea to anyone with a checkbook. "Everything in life is negotiable. I'll fix it. I promise."

Parker laughs. "Right. Because you've handled things so well up till this point."

"Parker." I sigh. "You're not helping."

"We have to go," Nate says, glancing at his watch. It's almost seven. "Your sister still needs to pack a bag, and we have..." He trails off, and a funny look crosses his face as his eyes meet Parker's. "...that *thing* at eight."

"I'm not packing," I insist. "And what *thing* are you talking about?"

"Nothing that concerns you," Nate says. "And if you don't pack, I'll do it for you, and none of your shit will match. I know how you feel about your goddamned shoes." He glances down at my Louboutins. "Can only imagine the horror if you were stranded without your perfectly coordinated outfits."

I glare at him. "Again: you're a jackass."

"Boo," he yells, ignoring my insult. "Come!"

The Pom comes running from behind Parker, skidding to a stop by Nate's boots with a look of adoration on his doggie face. *Traitor.*

An instant later, Nate's pulled the leash from my limp hands, snapped it back on Boo's collar, and is tugging us both toward the door. Parker's close on our heels.

"Parker." My father's voice is steady as he calls after us.

We turn to look at him.

"Stay behind a moment." Milo stares at his son. "I have something else to discuss with you."

Parker sighs deeply. "Dad, if you want me to set you up with one of my model friends, just send me an email."

"Must you turn everything into a joke?" Dad snaps, eyes flashing.

Parker shrugs. "I mean, it's not a requirement, but—"

"Enough. This isn't the time for foolishness." My father presses a hand to his head, as though this half hour conversation with his children has shaved years off his life.

I look at Parker, mouthing silent words in his direction like we used to do at the dinner table on the rare occasions Milo was home to eat with us.

Want me to stay?

"Save yourself," he murmurs, pushing me toward the door. "I'll catch up with you guys. If not at your place, then later. At the *thing*."

I roll my eyes and stomp out before the jackass who owns my heart can grab me again.

CHAPTER 24

SUPPOSEDLY, AN ORCHID WILL RE-BLOOM AFTER A 6-
12 MONTH RESTING PERIOD.
AIN'T NOBODY GOT TIME FOR THAT.

*Phoebe West, on her way home from the florist with a
trunk full of new plants.*

THE CAR IS TOTALLY silent as Nate steers us toward Back
Bay. Even Boo lies still on my lap, seeming to sense the intense
atmosphere between us. My fingers move absently in his fur as I
stare out the window, doing my best to ignore Nate's existence.

He thinks he can order me around? Shove me on a plane and
ship me off, out of the way, like some invalid? Like I'm an *incon-
venience?*

My teeth mash together as anger and frustration swirl in my stomach. I've never been so mad at him in my life.

When we approached the SUV, I actually contemplated climbing into the back seat, just to have some space from him, but doing so would've shown how much he affects me and frankly, I'm a little too proud for that.

His hands are clenched tight around the wheel and every time I glance his way, I see the muscle jumping in his cheek, a telltale sign he's pissed off. I don't know why *he's* so angry — he's not the one being shipped off like unwanted cargo — but by the time we pull up in front of my brownstone, I'm honestly surprised he hasn't spontaneously combusted. His rage — at me, at my father, at the entire situation — is apparent in every muscle in his body.

The engine shuts off and we sit frozen at the curb in total silence.

"This isn't your problem," I say finally, when I can't bear the quiet any longer.

He cuts a look in my direction that's so intense, I nearly pee my pants.

"Not my problem?"

I swallow. "You didn't have to get involved in this. So you don't have to act all pissed off and brooding, like I asked you to save me or something. I never *once* asked you to take this on your shoulders"

His eyes flash darkly. "Get out."

"What?" I ask, heart pounding.

"Get out of the damn car." His jaw tightens. "We're not discussing this here."

"Stop ordering me around!"

He's not listening. He's already out the driver's side, rounding the front of the SUV and pulling me onto the sidewalk. Before I have time to process what's going on, Boo's leash is snatched from my grip, a large hand lands on the small of my back, and we're up my front steps and inside my townhouse.

"What the hell do you think you're doing?" I shriek as soon as the door slams shut behind us. I take a few strides away from him, because I'm liable to smack him if he's anywhere within reach. The instant Nate unclips the leash, Boo scampers into the kitchen, out of firing range.

Wise dog.

"Trying to save your goddamn life!" Nate yells. "Though, at this point, I'm not sure why the hell I'm bothering!"

"Just leave, then. Go." My voice breaks on the last word. I ignore it. "Parker will take me to the airport tomorrow. And you and I will go back to how it was before."

"Before?" The word is so electric, it's giving off sparks in the air between us.

Oh boy.

I nod as I watch him warily, all my words fleeing along with my courage.

"Before what, West?" he asks in a scary quiet voice. "Before I had my tongue in your mouth? Before you were naked in my hands? Before I touched you and you almost came apart?" A smirk tugs his lips. "Can you really come back from that? I doubt it, little bird."

"Fuck you," I hiss.

"You were pretty damn close."

He steps toward me.

I step back.

"I'm not a robot. I had a physiological reaction. So, sue me." I jerk my chin higher. I'm not sure when this fight became about us, but now that it has there's no going back. "Just because *you're* an expert at blocking out every feeling you've ever had doesn't mean I have to be. Maybe that makes me weak, and maybe I'll get hurt in the long run, but I'd rather be like this than be like you."

"Like me?" he asks, voice rumbling with barely-contained anger.

My voice drops to a broken whisper. "Incapable of feelings. Of trusting someone. Of love."

"You wouldn't know love if it bit you in the ass, sweetheart."

I scoff. "That's rich, coming from you."

"And why is that, West?" he growls. "Please, enlighten me."

"Like you know anything about love, Nate?" I roll my eyes. "You've never loved a goddamned thing in your life."

He stares at me — hard, unflinching. "You don't know a damn thing."

"I may not know *everything*." I bite the inside of my cheek so hard I taste blood. "But I do know what love is."

"You know a definition in a dictionary. You know a fucking proverb — *love is patient love is kind*. That's bullshit. Because love, real love, the kind that lasts forever... it's not patient or kind. Not pretty or perfect. It's rough and hard as all hell. It's ugly." He steps closer, eyes never shifting from mine. "Love is holding someone's filthy, tarnished heart in your hands and claiming it as yours anyway."

My breath catches.

He takes another step. "And you don't like dirty, do you, West? You like everything pretty as a picture. Look at this fucking house!" He gestures around. "Not a rug out of place. Straight out of a Crate & Barrel catalogue. Perfect clothes, perfect dog, perfect job. Not a speck of dirt in your whole goddamned life."

"That's not true." I swallow. "My life is far from perfect."

"But that's the goal, isn't it? Perfect Phoebe West. Smile for the cameras. Hold it all together." His eyes are searing into mine. "You play pretend and think it'll make you happy. It won't."

"Yeah? Well, what about you, Nate?" I'm so pissed off, I can feel my heart hammering at my ribs. "The untouchable merce-nary — cold, calculated, always in control. You're so set on not letting anyone in, on never letting anyone get to you, one of these days you're going to turn to fucking stone."

"Is that what this is about?" His eyes narrow. He's breathing hard. "Is that what you need to hear? That you get to me?"

He crosses the room in two strides and then he's there, pressed against me full frontal. I gasp when I feel the unmistakable length of him, hard and heavy against my stomach.

His eyes lock on mine. *"You get to me."*

"Nate—"

"What? This is what you wanted, right? To know you affect me?" His voice rumbles from his throat like gravel. "To know I'm not a fucking robot?"

He grinds against me and it makes me shiver and groan at the same time.

"Well, here it is. Definitive fucking proof. You get to me. You feel that?" He presses harder against me. "It's yours. It's been yours for ten goddamn years, since you were fourteen in that little field hockey skirt. It's still yours."

I flounder for words as I stare at him, heart racing. In the end, all I can come up with is one.

"Mine?"

"Yours." He spits out the word like a curse. "You sunk your teeth in long ago and won't ever unclench, even if it kills us both."

We're both breathing too hard, our faces inches apart, our bodies pressed together. I'm not sure who moves first — I think it's me.

We crash into each other with so much force it knocks the wind out of me, but I don't mind at all because then he's kissing me and everything in my world boils down to the point of contact where his mouth consumes mine.

"NOT HERE."

He mutters the words against the skin of my neck, between kisses.

A frustrated sound slips from my mouth.

"Been waiting too long for this to do it on the floor of your entryway," he adds, scooping me up into his arms before I can protest. My limbs wrap around him, holding him close as he carries me up the stairs to my bedroom. When he sets me on the mattress, for a long moment he just stares down at me, breathing too fast. There's a look in his eyes I don't recognize. Something soft and warm, that makes my heart turn over.

"Come here," I whisper.

His hands curl into fists. "Parker's going to kill me if I fuck this up."

"You're thinking about my brother right now?" I ask, pushing up on my elbows.

His jaw clenches. "About his fist hitting my face, yeah."

I sit up fully, eyes on his.

"Well, let's see what we can do about that..." My words trail off as my fingers find the bottom hem of my shirt. In one swift move, I've tugged it up over my head and tossed it to the floor.

He stops breathing.

"Still thinking about Parker?" I ask, reaching for my bra clasp.

"No." His voice is hoarse. "Fuck no."

The clasp pops with a flick of my fingers. "Good," I say, letting the straps slide down my arms.

I don't see the bra hit the bed because suddenly Nate's on me, hands moving over my skin as his mouth crushes mine in a bruising kiss. We tangle together, equally ravenous as we tug at zippers and tear at buttons.

"I dream about this mouth," he says, kissing me. "This skin," he adds, fingers trailing a path down my stomach. "These legs wrapped around me." His hands hitch under my thighs as he pulls me closer. There's something like awe in his voice as he touches me with rough hands, kisses me with hard lips. "Did you know that, little bird? Do you have any idea what you do to me?"

I'm too busy working his shirt up over his head to respond. When it's off, I suck in a breath at the sight of his chest.

It's gorgeous. *He's* gorgeous. There's a scar I don't remember on the right side of his stomach. His abs are defined, his skin is tanned and warm. His hip bones form a perfect V, framing the strip of hair that leads down into his jeans.

"Holy frack," I murmur, tracing my fingertips against the scar on his stomach.

He chuckles against the skin of my collarbone. "What, never seen a man's chest before?"

"Not this close up," I admit foolishly.

I realize my mistake an instant after the words leave my mouth. Nate goes totally still. His face lifts from my chest to look into mine and I see something creep into his eyes that I don't like — partly because it replaces the lust there, but mainly because it looks an awful lot like apprehension.

"Just kidding," I lie, hands gripping his shoulders to keep him close. "Where were we?"

I'm no match for his strength — when he pulls back, my hands drop uselessly to the duvet.

"West."

I swallow. "Yeah?"

His eyes are steady on mine, but I can't discern any of the emotions in them. His expression is unreadable. "Are you... *Christ.*" He exhales sharply. "Are you a virgin?"

"No," I snap instantly, not above fibbing when I'm so close to finally getting what I want. (*What I want* being Nate naked on top of me.)

He stares at me, seeing straight through me like always. Something like shock flares in his eyes.

"You are." His voice is staggered. "You're a virgin."

The way he says it, you'd think I've just revealed I'm a unicorn or a fire-breathing dragon. Some kind of mythical, nonexistent creature.

"Yeah, well. So what if I am?" My voice is just the *teensiest* bit defensive.

He blinks. "How is that possible? What about..." His voice darkens. "...*Diego?*"

A scream of frustration pops out. "Diego was never..." I trail off, not wanting to get into that whole story right now. Or *ever*. "Can't we just forget I said anything and pick up where we left off?"

"No."

I huff.

"West—"

"You've had your face between my boobs," I bite out. "It's *Phoebe*."

His eyes flicker down to my exposed body for a second, as though he can't stop himself. If I weren't so angry, maybe I'd be embarrassed about sitting two inches from him wearing practically nothing. As it is, I gladly let him look. I hope the memory of me naked keeps him awake at night.

He sighs and runs a hand through his hair, a nervous habit I haven't seen in years. Not since before he joined the special forces.

"Why?"

"Why what? Use your words, Nathaniel."

He looks away from me, jaw clenching. "Why would you throw something like that away on someone like me, when you've been waiting so long?"

My mouth gapes. I've never wanted to yell at him more than I do in that moment.

Because I've been waiting for you, idiot! Because it won't be throwing it away. It will be sharing something incredible with the man I love. The man I've always loved.

He continues before I can say anything, not able to meet my eyes. "Why would you waste it on a night of meaningless sex?"

Meaningless sex.

Meaningless.

Sex.

All the breath goes out of me. The words I was about to say slither back down my throat into my stomach, where acids quickly destroy them. I feel nauseous. Physically ill. Worst of all, there are tears pricking at my eyes.

Damn him.

This thing between us isn't meaningless, and he knows it. He knows, and he's running because he can't handle it.

"I always thought you were brave, Nathaniel Knox, but you know what?" I ask, words scathing. "You're a coward."

I scramble to my feet and head for the door, not even caring that I'm half naked. At this moment, I'd rather parade bare-assed through Back Bay than spend another second in this room with him.

He stops me before I make it two feet. Arms wrap around me from behind, hauling me against his bare chest. I feel his mouth at my ear, rumbling with intensity.

"Phoebe," he says simply, undoing me with just one word. I feel his forehead hit my shoulder. "*Phoebe.*"

There's so much raw emotion in his voice it nearly sends me to my knees. I force my spine to stiffen, so he knows I'm immune to him.

Ha! I wish.

"I'm sorry." His words are low, hesitant. "I'm an ass. I know that." He presses closer. "I know I'm no good for you, that I should push you away, that I have no right to ask for a damn thing from you." He pauses, the silence humming with unspoken words. "But I can't help myself from wanting you anyway."

My heart skips a beat.

"You are the only person in my life who hasn't seen the worst in me from day one." His voice breaks and it damn near kills me. "The only person who's always looked at me like I could do anything, be anything, no matter how many other people said otherwise. And I know it's fucked up... but maybe the reason I push you away so hard is because I know it'll be easier to bear if I have some control over watching you walk away. Maybe I'm scared that if I let you look too close... you'll finally see what everyone else has always seen." He takes a breath. "Garbage."

There are tears in my eyes when I turn in his arms to look up at him.

"You are not garbage." My hands lift to cup his face. "You've never been garbage."

His forehead comes down to rest against mine. Our eyes meet and I see something move at the back of his irises — something stark and sad and saturated with longing.

"Phoebe," he whispers, that one word filled with so much hope it sounds almost like a prayer.

"I've—" I almost say *loved*, but stop myself at the last moment. "I've dreamed of you half my life," I whisper to him. "If you think you're trash, that means I threw my dreams away on nothing. If you think you're worthless, then you must think I'm worthless too."

"No." His reply is instant. "Never."

I take a breath. "Are we worthless, Nate?"

There's a sliver of silence as he stares at me. His hands come up around me, winding into my hair and pulling me closer.

"No." His voice cracks. "We're worth everything."

His mouth lowers, his lips find mine, and when he kisses me, it's not rough or hard or lust-fueled. There's a kind of tender desperation in the way he touches me, and the beauty of it steals the air from my lungs, makes my chest ache with need.

There's not an ounce of hesitation in the way his fingertips slide through the hair at the nape of my neck. No wavering uncertainty as he walks me backward toward my bed. No lingering doubts or dangling regrets when he fuses his lips to mine and kisses me until I can't breathe.

With every kiss, every stroke, every gasp, he embeds himself deeper in my soul. Until I can't think of anything but him, of the inevitability of this moment between us. It's been written in my stars since I was five years old with a crush on the older, off-limits boy next door.

My back presses into the blankets as Nate presses into me. And I know my fingers should be trembling, my courage should be crumbling, but instead of fear there's only the unshakable feeling that this is *right*. That he and I were always meant to wind up here together; that his hands were made to touch me, my body built to be explored by him.

"Phoebe," he mutters against my stomach a few minutes later. I can barely form words, I'm so lost in sensation. "We have to go."

"Shut up," I whisper back, fingers exploring his back. "We're not going anywhere."

"Phoebe—"

"Less talky, more touchy."

I hear the smile in his voice. "Phoebe—"

"Don't *Phoebe* me! We're naked. In my bed." I groan in frustration when his hands fall away from my body. "This is happening."

"Little bird." He kisses the sensitive spot between my breasts. "We're not doing this right now."

I make a sound — I'm pretty sure it's a growl. "I knew it! Knew it. I'm never going to have an orgasm. I'm going to die alone with several cats, one perfectly intact hymen, and two shriveled ovaries."

He chuckles, the bastard.

"Don't you laugh at me, Nathaniel!" I hiss, staring up at the ceiling and trying to regulate my breathing. "I dislike you."

His voice is amused. "You dislike me?"

"Yes." I nod sharply, not looking at him. "Immensely."

"You're aware you've still got your legs wrapped around my waist?"

I slowly unwind them, glaring at the ceiling. "I still dislike you."

He chuckles again. "And why is that?"

"Because you're backing out!"

"Phoebe." His head finally lifts and when I see the amount of desire swirling in his eyes, my words falter. "I'm not backing out. But I'm also not going to take your virginity in the twenty minutes between now and when we have to be at Gemma and Chase's place."

"The penthouse?" I ask, eyes opening to meet his. "Why do we have to be there?"

He hesitates.

I narrow my eyes. "Tell me."

"It's a surprise, little bird." He kisses my stomach again, soft and sweet. "You'll like it. I promise."

"But..." My voice is only a tad whiney when I moan out, "Are you sure we can't skip it?"

He chuckles. "I'm sure."

"How sure?"

"Very." He climbs up my body so our faces are parallel. His hands brace around me, holding the majority of his weight so I'm not crushed beneath him, and when he speaks, his voice is full of passion. "Because when I make love to you for the first time, I plan on taking my time. I don't want twenty minutes. I want hours. I want weeks. I want a fucking lifetime in this bed with you."

A pang shoots through my chest.

A lifetime.

I know he doesn't mean it like that. He's talking about a sexual marathon, not about spending forever with me. His *lifetime* doesn't involve things like first dates and marriage and teaching our son to toss a football in the backyard and dancing with our daughter standing on his feet.

Wow. That escalated quickly.

Still, that doesn't stop my heart from foolishly expanding at the thought of Nate wanting any kind of lifetime with me.

His mouth lowers and claims mine in a kiss. I feel one of his hands sliding down my body again and a second later, I gasp when his fingers land between my legs.

"I thought..." I'm panting a little. "We weren't..." *Oh my god.* "Doing this."

His fingers move faster. My head falls back.

"I said I wasn't taking your virginity." I feel his grin against my mouth. "I never said anything about orgasms."

CHAPTER 25

IF I WERE PRESIDENT, MY FIRST ACT WOULD BE
ADDING AN EIGHTH DAY TO THE WEEK, RESERVED FOR
LYING IN BED WATCHING BABY ANIMAL VIDEOS ON
YouTube.

Phoebe West, defining her political priorities.

A SECRET SMILE plays on my lips as I shove clothes into a Diane von Furstenberg duffle bag a few minutes later. I'm still basking in the happy glow of Big O, who finally made her Broadway debut, thanks to Nate. Let's just say, he earned a standing O-vation for his performance.

I snort at my own terrible pun, staring from a pair of very practical Toms shoes to my favorite, somewhat frivolous Miu Miu booties. I only have room for one of them.

Sigh.

This is torture for me. I'm the girl who starts packing two full weeks in advance of any trip, meticulously planning specific outfits before deciding *better safe than sorry* and stowing the entirety of my wardrobe in a large rolling suitcase. *Because, hey, it's entirely possible you'll need that full-length, sparkly Moschino gown, Phoebe.* Even on a ski trip to Vail, or an extended stay on the beaches of the Virgin Islands.

You simply never know.

After giving me the two best — and *only* — back-to-back orgasms of my life, Nate kissed me firmly, stalked into my walk-in closet, threw the smallest suitcase from my luggage set onto the bed, and ordered me to pack while he fed Boo and then took him around the block for a much needed walk. I was so sated and happy, I barely even glared at him when he grunted that I was — and I quote — "not to move a fucking inch outside this house" until he got back.

Bossy, arrogant, sexy son-of-a-bitch.

By the time I finish packing, the duffle bag is bursting at the seams. I have no idea where the plane is headed, so I stick with the basics — a few pairs of jeans, four of my favorite blouses, my Chanel wool coat, and three pairs of heels.

Flats are for sissies.

I'm sitting on the counter sipping a can of cranberry-lime seltzer, admiring the way my sparkly Kate Spade platform pumps catch the light, when Nate walks into the kitchen with Boo cradled in the crook of his arm like a football. The Pom looks happy as can be, nestled against him.

"Good walk?" I ask.

He nods and sets Boo on the floor. When his eyes find mine, they're ultra warm. Like melted chocolate.

"Did he sniff everything in a three mile radius?" I ask as Nate walks toward me.

"Yes."

"Did he poop?"

His hands land on either side of my neck. His thumbs push my chin up gently, so my face is angled toward his. "You really want to talk about dog poop right now?"

"Nope," I breathe.

"Good." A second later his mouth hits mine, delivering a lingering kiss that makes my mind spin. Things are just getting good when he breaks away. "We have to go."

My bottom lip juts out in a pout. "I still don't understand why I have to leave tomorrow."

His eyes find mine and there's no mistaking the serious look in them. "I can't do this with you here, little bird. The thought of them coming after you, hurting you again..." His head shakes swiftly. "When I think about that, I can't focus on anything else. Hell, I can barely fucking breathe."

My face softens. "Nate—"

"I need you safe." His voice is firm. "And you won't be, until you're away from here."

I sigh, frustrated but resigned. I'm not so pig-headed I can't see the logic behind his words.

"Fine," I whisper. "I'll go. But I won't like it."

He nips my bottom lip playfully. "I put Boo's water bowls, food, and leash in a bag by the door. Does he need anything else?"

"Stuffed duck toy," I say immediately.

"Okay. I'll make sure we grab the duck on the way out." Nate's eyes crinkle. "You finish packing your shit?"

"Yes." I tilt my head toward the bag resting by the fridge. "Though it wasn't easy, since I have no idea where you're sending me."

"Somewhere safe."

I give him a look. "Vague, much?"

His lips twitch as he strolls across the room and picks up my bag.

"Christ, this is heavy. What's in here? A grenade launcher?" Before I can say a word, he's unzipped the duffle and peered inside. "Three pairs of heels? Really, West?" He shakes his head in exasperation. "You're going to a safe house, not Paris Fashion Week."

"Don't you dare touch my shoes, Nathaniel Knox!" I hiss, hopping off the counter and striding toward him, tugging the hem of my black Prada mini-dress as I go. "I need those!"

"You don't."

"I do!" I screech, watching as he pulls out two pairs and sets them on the counter. "*Hey!*"

"Little bird, I'm telling you — you don't need the damn shoes."

"What if I have to go out somewhere fancy? What if some kind of formal engagement comes up out of the blue? What if...." I search frantically for reasons to justify my need for the shoes. "What if the President invites me to dinner at the White House? Or what if my invitation to this year's Academy Awards as Bradley Cooper's date — which was surely lost in the mail up till this point — arrives? Huh? What then, Nate?!"

He stares at me, mouth twitching. "You think that's likely?"

"Ugh!" I smack him with a Ted Baker slingback. "That's not the point."

"What *is* the point?"

"You never know what'll happen! You never know when a quality designer pump is going to be needed!" I glare at him. "Just because you're a barbarian with no appreciation for high heels—"

He removes the deadly weapon from my grip, locks his hands around my wrists like manacles, and backs me up against the fridge in one swift move. He's so close, I can feel each breath move through his chest as he presses into me. His mouth is millimeters from mine, his eyes never shift from my face, and I think he's going to kiss me again. Instead, he speaks. (To my vast disappointment.)

"I have the highest appreciation for them," he says, eyes on fire. "They've been driving me fucking crazy since I came home from my first tour and saw you'd switched from Sperry's to stilettos overnight. Do you know how many times those damn shoes have given me hard-ons in the past ten years? How many times I've pictured you wearing nothing *but* those damn shoes while I'm buried deep inside you?"

He's breathing hard — so am I. His admission is so hot, desire returns in a swift instant until every atom in my body is practically buzzing with it.

"Oh," I murmur, eyes on his mouth.

Kissmekissmekissmekissme.

"Yeah," he says roughly, barely in control. "Keep looking at me like that and we're going to miss your party."

My eyes flash up to his. "Party?"

His mouth tugs up at one side and he forces himself to take a step back. "Time to go."

"I still think I need to pack the shoes," I say, staring longingly at the Miu Mius on the counter. "Just *one* pair."

He grunts, the sound torn between amusement and lust. "You won't need them."

"You don't know that."

"Phoebe." He turns and lowers his head until his lips skim mine in the ghost of a kiss. "You won't need them. As soon as this shit is cleared up with Mac, I'm flying to meet you. And when that happens, you won't need any of your damn clothes because we're going to be naked for a week straight." His words send a delicious shiver through me. "Understand?"

"Um," I whisper, eyes wide and heart suddenly pounding. "Yep."

His mouth twitches. "Unless that's not what you want. If it's not, by all means, pack the fucking shoes and wait for your damn Oscar invitation. Either way, we're leaving now."

His lips land on mine in a too-brief, no-nonsense kiss and then he's gone, grabbing my bag and leaving me pressed limply against the refrigerator, with only my discarded heels to keep me company.

When I follow him to the front door a few seconds later and twine my fingers with his, the Miu Mius are still sitting on the counter in the dark, long-forgotten as thoughts of a naked week with Nate swirl through my head.

"SURPRISE!"

I squeak involuntarily and jump about a foot into the air as the elevator doors chime open, because the sound of ten people screaming at the top of their lungs is mildly terrifying, regardless of the situation. I nearly lose my footing, but Nate's hands land on my waist to steady me before I can fall on my face.

Phoebe West: queen of the elegant entrance.

"Breathe," he whispers against my neck, voice amused.

I try to follow his orders as we step into the penthouse and look around at the group of people beaming at me and clapping. Gemma and Chase are by the kitchen counter, where a massive platter of cupcakes rests, each bearing a candle. Lila and her new boyfriend-of-the-minute are leaning against the pool table, which has a bright red balloon tethered to each pocket. Shelby and a handsome man I don't recognize (who I assume is her husband Paul) are by the bookshelves in the corner, which have been strung end-to-end with streamers. Chrissy and Mark (Gemma's other married friends) are hanging by the sectional, trying to keep the adorable towheaded toddler at their feet from shoving confetti up his nose.

Every single one of them is grinning at me. And every single one of them is wearing one of those ridiculous conical party hats and blowing into a paper horn.

"Happy birthday, Phoebe!" Gemma says, grabbing me in a tight hug as soon as we step inside. "I know you said you didn't want a party, but I couldn't help myself. I hope you aren't mad."

"Mad?" I say, laughing as I embrace her. "No. This is..." I swallow so I don't start getting teary. "This is perfect."

"Told you so," Gemma says to Chase smugly. "I'm always right. Just in case you forgot."

He shakes his head. "Sunshine. Keep gloating. See what happens."

They trade a glance so heated, it's a wonder the room doesn't catch fire around them.

I hear Lila's voice only seconds before her body slams into mine in a full-on bear hug.

"Twenty-four! You old hag!" Her arms wrap around my frame, squeezing tightly.

"Technically not until tomorrow," I point out, returning her hug.

"The way things have been going lately, you could be dead by tomorrow," she says lightly. "We'd better celebrate now."

I roll my eyes and push her away with a playful shove. I've barely turned when Shelby appears, snapping a glittery party hat around my head before I can protest.

"If I'm wearing one of these things, you damn well are too," she says, slinging an arm around my shoulders in a half hug. "Plus, it'll distract from that impressive shiner you've got."

My nose wrinkles as I feel the elastic dig into my chin. "It's my birthday. Doesn't that mean I'm not required to wear the funny hat if I don't want to?"

"Technically, your birthday isn't till tomorrow," Lila reminds me, grinning. "Which means birthday requests are not yet valid. Try again."

Gemma plants her hands on her hips. "You have to wear the hat. It says *birthday girl* in silver glitter."

"Resistance is futile," Chase mutters under his breath, his green eyes catching mine. "Just go with it."

I sigh in resignation and, without thinking, lean back into Nate's chest for moral support. His arms slide around me immediately, palms flat against my stomach so I'm pressed tight against him.

Everyone in the penthouse goes completely still, wide eyes locked on us. Conversations fall silent. Even the music drifting through the overhead speakers seems to dim as every one of my senses hones in on the feeling of his hands on me, in a casual and unmistakably couple-like show of affection.

I hold my breath, waiting for Nate to realize we've become a spectacle and push me away. We aren't exactly public knowledge yet and, even if we were... he doesn't strike me as the PDA type.

To my surprise, he doesn't even seem to notice the eyes on us. Or, if he does, he doesn't care.

His head comes down so his lips are at my neck and his voice is soft when he whispers into my ear.

"I'm gonna grab a drink, little bird. You want something?" His breath is warm against my skin, sending goosebumps skittering down my nerve-endings. "Beer? Seltzer? Old Fashioned?"

I swallow and try — unsuccessfully — not to melt into him. I can't help it — he touches me and I turn into a puddle of hormones.

"A beer would be good," I breathe, wanting more than anything to turn and wrap my arms around him.

"Okay." He presses a kiss against the sensitive spot where my neck and shoulder meet and then he's gone, striding toward the kitchen as though we haven't just brought the entire party to a standstill.

I watch him walk away, smiling hopelessly at his back, before turning to Gemma, Shelby, and Lila. The three of them are grinning like idiots, practically bouncing up and down as they squeal in unison and throw their arms around me until I'm crushed in the middle of a girl-pile.

The sound of Nate's low laughter reaches my ears even across the loft.

THREE HOURS, two cupcakes, and one horribly off-key rendition of *Happy Birthday Dear Phoebe* later, I'm sitting on the counter with my legs dangling, drinking champagne out of a paper cup and trying to convince myself that three cupcakes is too many. I survey the room, feeling warmth spread through me as my eyes move over the people in it.

Gemma and Chase are across the penthouse, trying to beat Lila and Martin, her date, at pool. Paul and Shelby are camped out in a corner, talking in hushed, angry tones. Mark and Chrissy left early, needing to get their son Winston to bed and eager to check on their newborn, Summer, who they'd left with a babysitter for the first time since she was born. Boo, sad that his pint-sized new best friend Winnie is gone, has claimed a sectional cushion and is sprawled out snoring impressively.

It's not exactly a rave.

And yet, it's exactly the kind of party I've always wanted. Just a few close friends, some really stellar sugary confections, and the warm glow of knowing there are people who care about me in this world.

"Happy?" a rumbling voice asks from my side.

I grin wider as I turn to look at him. "Best birthday ever."

His eyes are soft as he reaches up to straighten my party hat, which has begun to droop crookedly on my head.

"Better than the year your mom rented that pony and you rode it around the backyard wearing a plastic suit of armor you stole from Parker's closet, yelling that you were Xena the Warrior Princess?"

My mouth falls open. "Oh my god, I totally forgot about that. I must've been, what? Five? Six?"

"Six." His lips are twitching. "Cutest damn thing I've ever seen, you with a sword instead of the princess wand your parents bought you."

"What can I say?" I giggle. "I'm a non-conformist."

"That was pretty much the end of your tomboy phase." His eyes narrow as he thinks back. "From that point on, you were all sparkles and glitter."

"Yeah, I think I discovered my mother's Jimmy Choo collection at age six." I shake my head. "There was no going back, after that."

He laughs.

"She had so many pairs," I murmur. "I used to sit on the floor of her closet and just stare at them. Row after row, all organized by color and designer. It was like a shoe museum." I smile softly. "I used to put them on and walk around in them even though they were inches too big. Even after..." I clear my throat. "Even after we lost her, I'd still sit in there and try on her shoes. Dreaming of they day they'd finally fit."

His eyes swirl with thoughts, then drop down to look at the Kate Spade heels on my feet. I see the moment comprehension surges through him.

"They fit now," he says, voice low.

"Yes." I swallow. "They fit now."

"Little bird," he whispers, voice thick with understanding and guilt. "I gave you such shit about those heels."

I shrug. "You didn't know. It's fine, Nate."

He exhales sharply. "You were fourteen."

"What?"

"When they finally fit." His eyes hold mine. "You were fourteen. I remember, because I came home from that first semester at college and you'd morphed into this little vixen overnight."

"The Sadie Hawkins dance," I say, laughing lightly. "That was the first night I ever wore a pair of my mother's heels. I remember worrying I'd have killer blisters, dancing in them all night. It didn't stop me from wearing them."

"Did you?" he asks.

"Did I what?"

He grins. "Have killer blisters."

"Oh." I sigh. "No. My date didn't dance with me, remember?"

His face darkens into a scowl. "Duncan."

"You know, if you'd just said yes when I asked you, all that drama could've been avoided." I tilt my head. "You were the one I really wanted to dance with, anyway."

He stares at me. "I was no good for you then, little bird."

I hold my breath. I have to ask. "And now?"

Our eyes lock for a long, suspended moment. Without saying a word, his hands wrap around my waist and he lifts me down from the counter.

"Nate?"

He doesn't answer. His hand entwines with mine and he leads me through an archway, across an empty bedroom, to a set of glass French doors. I lose my breath as we step out onto a rooftop terrace, taking in the sight of the city sprawled out below us. From up here, all the empty offices in the skyscrapers around us are illuminated against the night like glowing gemstones on a bolt of black velvet. It's magnificent.

"What are we doing out here?" I ask when we reach the railing, torn between staring at the beauty of the view and the man next to me. It's dark out here. Crisp air and total quiet.

Nate bends to brush his mouth across mine, wrapping his arms around my waist. His lips are gentle but greedy. I try to memorize this feeling – the pure bliss of his touch, his taste. When he finally breaks the kiss, it takes a minute for the fog to clear out of my brain... but when it does, I realize we're swaying.

Not swaying.

Dancing.

His body rocks mine back and forth, moving us in a slow rhythm across the terrace, and I feel tears gathering in the back of my eyes.

"What are you doing?" I ask, voice choked.

"I owed you a dance," he says simply, like it should've been obvious.

"There's no music."

His lips brush my ear. "Put your head on my chest."

I do.

"You hear my heartbeat?"

I nod, cheek rubbing the fabric of his shirt.

"It's beating for you, little bird," he murmurs, holding me closer. "That can be our music."

"But you can't hear mine," I whisper, voice cracking.

He pauses. "I can hear it, Phoebe. I hear it in my soul. I set my life by its every beat."

My eyes are glassy with unshed tears when I lift my head to look at him. I don't say anything as I stare into his eyes; neither does he. But I know, down to the marrow of my bones, that Nathaniel Knox has just told me he loves me.

And then his lips come down and he's kissing me against the most beautiful backdrop I've ever seen in my life, but not even a view like that can hold my attention when I'm standing in the arms of the man I love.

CHAPTER 26

I CONFESS: I DON'T LIKE PUMPKIN SPICE LATTES.
THERE, I SAID IT. TAKE ME AWAY, OFFICER.

Phoebe West, in a worrisome brush with the law.

NOW, the party don't start till I walk in...

"Is someone singing Ke$ha in the elevator?" Gemma asks, eyes wide.

Our group has dwindled to four: Nate, Chase, Gemma, and me. Lila and Martin bailed thirty minutes ago because Lila has to "get to bed early." Something tells me, she won't be going alone.

Insert eye roll here.

It's late, almost midnight, and the four of us are scattered across the sectional, counting down the minutes until it's officially my birthday. Boo is snoring on one of the couch cushions, totally exhausted by the events of the last few days.

"Parker!" I exclaim, recognizing his voice as the elevator doors chime open. He's grinning wide as he steps into the penthouse.

"Sweet P, you call this a party?" He crosses the space toward us, eyeing the few remaining cupcakes and semi-deflated balloons with amusement. "I thought you were turning twenty-four, not eighty four."

"Hardy har har," I mutter, standing to give him a hug before turning to face the rest of the group. "Gemma and Chase, this is my brother Parker." I smile. "Parker, meet my friends Gemma and Chase. This is their place, so try not to act like a total barbarian for the next few minutes, okay?"

My joke falls totally flat. Not even one pity chuckle.

"Jeeze, tough crowd," I murmur.

I soon realize no one in the room is even paying attention to me. Nate and Chase are occupied, staring from Parker to Gemma and back with wary eyes. My gaze lands on my friend and I almost gasp when I see how pale she is. Her skin is clammy white, her pretty blue eyes are wide with dismay and fixed firmly on my brother. I'm shocked when I glance his way and see he's glaring at her with vehemence.

"*This* is your friend Gemma?" he clips out, jaw tight.

My heart starts to pound. I've never seen him like this — so full of rage. He's not the type to take an instant dislike to anyone. I can't imagine what made his mood shift so quickly from playful to pissed.

"What's happening here?" I ask, totally at a loss. "Do you two know each other?"

Parker laughs, but it's bitter and cold. "Know her? No. Know *of* her? Yeah, you could say that."

Gemma looks at me and her eyes flash with sadness and worry.

"Gemma?" I prompt.

She remains quiet – which is totally unlike her.

Chase has one arm wrapped around her shoulders, and is staring at his girlfriend with concern. Parker's so busy glaring, he won't make eye contact with me. When I meet Nate's stare, though, I see cautious resignation.

"You know something." I pin him with a hard look. "What the hell is going on, Nate?"

"Phoebe—"

"Don't *Phoebe* me, Nathaniel."

He sighs and runs a hand through his hair, rising to his feet and stepping in front of Parker. "Come on, man. Let's go. This isn't the time."

"Oh, I think this is a perfect time." Parker's voice is colder than I've ever heard it.

"It's Phoebe's birthday." Gemma's voice is shaky when she finally speaks, rising to her feet. "Please... not now."

"Someone tell me what's happening here!" I hiss, getting angry.

"I'm not going to lie to my sister." Parker's jaw ticks. "Clearly, you don't live by the same morals."

Chase steps in front of Gemma when she pales further, his green eyes cold on Parker. "You should go. Now." He glances at me. "I'm sorry, Phoebe."

I ignore him and step closer to Parker. I feel the heat of Nate's chest close behind me.

My eyes lock on my brother's face. "Parker. Tell me what's happening, or I swear to god I'll never forgive you."

His eyes slide to mine. He swallows roughly. "She's not who she says she is. She's been lying to you."

"Parker," Gemma whispers behind me, a plea in her voice.

"Tell me!" I snap.

His eyes drift over my shoulder to her for a brief moment, before returning to my face. "Before Mom died...." He swallows and I swear, his voice is almost shaking. "Dad cheated on her."

"I know about the affairs." My spine stiffens. "What does that have to do with anything?"

Why are we talking about Milo?

"He..." Parker's eyes press closed, as if he's in pain. "Sweet P, he..."

Nate ducks to meet my gaze. His eyes are worried.

"Just say it," I whisper, heart pounding in my ears. "Rip off the band-aid. Knowing can't be worse than this — being kept in the dark by people who are supposed to care about me."

I hear what sounds almost like a sob from Gemma.

Parker's head is bowed and I see his fists clench tighter at my words.

"Phoebe." Nate tucks a strand of hair behind my ear. "The woman your father had an affair with twenty-seven years ago..." His voice is low. "He got her pregnant."

"No," I say immediately, rejecting the thought outright. "No, that's not possible."

"It is," Nate says gently. "He fathered another child. Little bird, she..." His eyes move over my shoulder.

I hear another almost-sob.

She.

Twenty-seven years ago.

My heart pounds faster.

My father had an affair.

An affair that resulted in a child.

A twenty-six year old child.

A twenty-six year old *girl* with hair the same shade as mine, and a face that's almost the exact same shape as Parker's, and big blue eyes, and a great sense of humor, and a terrible tendency to speak in run-on sentences, and a sun-shaped necklace hanging around her neck that looks just like the one Cormack took from me.

I turn slowly to face Gemma. I don't know what look is on my face — I can barely discern the emotions tumbling around inside my chest — but hers is a mask of horrified anticipation.

She's scared. I can see the fear in her eyes.

"You." My voice is emotionless. *"You."*

SHE TAKES a hesitant step toward me; I instantly step back, bumping into Parker in the process. I feel his big hand land firmly on my shoulder, squeezing to show his support.

"Phoebe." Gemma's voice breaks.

"No." I cut her off with a swift shake of my head. "I'm sorry, I can't do this right now."

I turn blindly for the elevator. I feel wetness on my cheeks and realize absently that I've started crying. I'm not sure when — I just know that tears are streaking down my face faster and faster, in time with the breaths pumping too quickly in and out of my lungs.

"Sweet P—" Parker starts.

I freeze as a thought occurs to me, whirling on him. "You knew? You knew about this, and you never told me?" My eyes sweep the room from Parker to Chase to Nate, fury and accusation burning in their depths. "You all knew?"

Chase looks totally uncomfortable. Nate's face is a stone mask, but his eyes are simmering with guilt.

"Not my secret to tell, little bird," he says softly.

Ugh. I hate when he's right.

I whirl back to Parker.

"I wanted to tell you, Sweet P." My brother swallows. "I

didn't know how. And I didn't want to hurt you. If I'd known she was going to insert herself into your life—"

"You're just as bad!" I throw out a hand, gesturing from Gemma to Parker. "Both of you lied. Guess you must be siblings, after all." My throat feels like it's closing up. I head for the elevators. "I have to get out of here. I need air."

"Phee—"

"Phoebe—"

"Sweet P—"

"Little Bird—"

"Just listen—"

"Don't go—"

"I'll come—"

"Please stay—"

So many voices, tugging me so many directions. My feet freeze and I pivot to face the four of them.

"ENOUGH!" I yell at the top of my lungs.

When I open my eyes, they're all staring at me warily.

"Enough," I repeat in a much softer tone, turning to Gemma. I suck in a breath at the look on her face. "How could you not tell me?"

"I didn't know how." Her voice cracks. "I wanted to, so many times, but..."

"So, you decided to lie to me instead?" I ask, voice shaking. "To pretend to be my friend, pretend to *like* me, because... Why? You wanted to see how the other half lived? Wanted to get to know me out of some kind of morbid curiosity?"

"I wasn't pretending," she says, eyes watering. "You're my sister—"

"You're not our sister," Parker says coldly. "We may share blood, but that doesn't make us family."

"Actually, it does," Gemma snaps back at him, regaining a

little of her spirit. "Though if I'd known I was related to such a dick, maybe I wouldn't have been so eager to meet you."

"You have no idea, do you?" he volleys back. "The damage you and your mother did to our lives? Otherwise you'd have left us the hell alone."

Her spine straightens. "You can try to blame me, but it's not my fault Milo had an affair. I'm sorry if I've tarnished your view of your lifelong hero—"

"Is that what you think?" Parker laughs coldly. "That Milo West is a hero? That he's going to be the daddy you never had?"

"Watch it," Chase growls in warning.

Nate steps purposely into the space between them.

Parker holds his hands up in surrender. "I'm just being honest, here. She wants to be part of this family, she should know what she's getting into."

"Parker," I murmur.

He's too pissed to listen. His eyes are locked on Gemma. "I know all about you. I've made it my business to know about you." He swallows hard. "You may not have had a father, but you had a mother. That's more than me or Phoebe ever had."

My heart clenches.

Parker's voice cracks but he keeps going. "Because when dear old dad had an affair with *your* mother... Do you know what happened to *ours*? Do you have any idea?"

I go still.

Nate's suddenly standing in Parker's face. I didn't even see him move — he's just there, out of nowhere. "Let it go. Walk away. You're not doing this here."

Parker glares at his best friend in the world and, for a split second, I actually think he's going to take a swing at him — that's how far gone Parker is, in this moment.

"Get out of my face," my brother says flatly. "This isn't your family. It isn't you fight."

"It is, actually," Nate corrects. "Phoebe is my family. You're my family. Don't tell me this isn't my business."

Their eyes lock and the air between them grows so tense, I clench my hands to keep from stepping between them.

Gemma appears at my side, Chase trailing close behind her. Her face is twisted in pain and regret.

"Phoebe..." Her voice is a whisper. "What happened to your mother?"

I swallow, tears still in my eyes as I stare at her. I sense Nate and Parker fall silent, but I don't shift my eyes off my friend.

Off my *sister*.

That's going to take some getting used to.

I take a deep breath and force out the words. Words I've made a habit of burying deep down inside my soul, because they're too painful to say aloud. I make myself say them now.

"She killed herself."

My words are barely above a whisper, but she hears them. Her whole body flinches back.

"What?" she asks, horrified.

I swallow. "She was always fragile. She had a depressive personality disorder. A lot of times she wouldn't get out of bed, would go days without coming out of her bedroom. She was on medication, but more often than not she couldn't be counted on to take it." My eyes go unfocused as I retreat into memories. "When she found out about the women, the affairs... something just seemed to break inside her. Something that couldn't be fixed. I was young. I didn't know how to make her better. Neither did the doctors or the specialists or any of the psychiatrists my father paraded into our house. For years, we watched helplessly as she retreated into herself more and more each day..."

Parker's eyes are red. Even Nate and Chase, ever stoic, look a bit shaken. Gemma doesn't say anything, but there are silent tears tracking down her face. When she reaches out to take my hand, I don't pull away. I lace my fingers through hers and hold tight.

"We think she went in the middle of the night. Took some sleeping pills, waded into the ocean in her nightgown and..." I trail off. "It was me, who found her the next day. Covered in sand and surf. I remember thinking she was like some kind of mermaid washed ashore."

My eyes cut to Nate. His stare moves over my face, full of strength and support — I absorb it like a sponge for several long seconds before turning to focus on Gemma.

"I didn't know," she whispers brokenly, horror in her clear blue eyes. "I had no idea, Phoebe..."

"I know." I try a smile, but my lips won't cooperate. "None of this is your fault, Gemma."

"But..." She swallows hard, and I know she's overwhelmed. "I understand if you hate me. I understand."

In that moment, I think about Nate. Hear his voice in my head.

Never say it. Even if you don't mean it.

I think about my mother, even at her most fragile, telling me not to be afraid to test my wings no matter what life throws at me.

Fly far, little bird. Jump the nest.

I steady my shoulders and meet Gemma's eyes. "We didn't have a choice about how we got here. Not one of us," I say, squeezing her hand tighter. "But we have a choice now."

She squeezes back.

I take a deep breath. "I loved my mother. It took me a long time to forgive her for leaving us. It took me an even longer time to forgive my father for his part in making her leave. But I did, because when it comes down to it... you either die alone, surrounded by the ghosts of all the people who ever let you down, or you live a life full of flawed people whose imperfections you've made a choice to overlook. I don't know about you but if given the choice, I'll pick the imperfections every time. I choose understanding over resentment, love over hate, forgiveness over loneliness." I look at Parker. "Some of us are still working on the forgiveness part."

His eyes are still red, but his lips tug up in a half smile.

I take a deep breath. "You don't get to pick your family. You don't get to choose the people who work their way into your heart and build a home there." My eyes move to Nate. "And life is too damn short not to spend it with the people who matter. Not to say *I love you* when you still can. Not to hold each other close and admit, out loud, *You matter to me. My life wouldn't be the same without you.*"

Something stirs at the back of Nate's eyes, and I turn away before it makes me break down.

I look at Parker. "I love you. You matter to me. My life wouldn't be the same without you."

"I love you too, Sweet P," he says. His voice is gruffer than usual, and I know he's holding his emotions tightly in check.

I look at Gemma, smiling through my tears. My voice cracks. "I love you. You matter to me. My life wouldn't be the same without you."

Her tears drip faster and she nods, unable to speak. Her eyes return my sentiment, though. Tenfold.

I extend my free hand, the one not twined with Gemma's, and hold it out for my brother to take. After a moment's hesitation, his palm engulfs mine in a warm grip. The three of us stand there for a long time, tethered together by the tips of our fingers as much as we are by our common strands of DNA.

We didn't have a choice about how we got here.

But we have a choice now.

And as I clutch my siblings' hands, I know we've made the right one.

CHAPTER 27

I KNOW WE NAME OUR DOGS...
  BUT DO YOU THINK THEY NAME US, TOO?

Phoebe West, wondering whether Boo refers to her as She-With-Many-Shoes or She-Who-Feeds-Me.

THE LOFT IS quiet when Nate opens the door and ushers me inside. Boo is curled in my arms, sleeping soundly. He barely stirred when we finally left the penthouse and headed back to Knox Investigations. It was all I could do to get him to pee on the patch of grass outside before his puppy eyes drifted closed again. All this moving around has really messed up his beauty-sleep schedule.

I figured Parker would crash at Nate's again but he headed to his boat instead, promising to meet us at the private airfield where we keep the jet at seven sharp. Nate assures me one of his men is keeping close tabs on Parker, in case Mac's boys decide to change things up by kidnapping a different West sibling.

Now I understand the conversation between Nate and my father at the WestTech offices.

Does Mac know about her?

They'd been talking about Gemma.

"So..." I set Boo down on the couch, grab the plush duck toy out of my duffle bag, and set it beside him, grinning as I watch him curl up with it. "That was heavy. New York Cheesecake heavy. Fettuccine Alfredo heavy. Double chocolate milkshake heavy."

Nate looks at me, eyebrows raised. "You hungry?"

"No, I ate, like, four cupcakes." My brow knits. "Why?"

"Your analogies were all food related."

"I couldn't think of other heavy things."

"Seriously?" His lips twitch as he stares at me. "Bowling ball. Elephant. Bag of bricks. Stonehenge. Orca whale." He pauses. "I could go on..."

"That's the wrong kind of heavy, smartass." I roll my eyes and walk toward the bed. "I meant the kind of heavy that sits in the pit of your stomach and makes you feel sort of nauseous."

"Cheesecake makes you nauseous?" he asks, amused. "That's funny. I seem to remember you consuming several pieces at the WestTech Christmas party last year." He grins. "And by *several* I mean *four*."

"You know what's odd?" I ask, spinning to face him with my hands planted on my hips. "You know what I do on Thanksgiving. You know where I take my lunch breaks. You know how I drink my coffee. You know my favorite type of seltzer." I pause. "If I didn't know better, I'd swear you've been keeping close tabs on me for years, Nathaniel."

He crosses his arms over his chest. "And if I have?"

I reach for the zipper on the side of my dress. "I'd be oblig-ated to tell you it's creepy and weird."

His lips tug up on one side. "Really?"

"Yep." I start to slowly work the zipper down my side. His eyes darken. "It's not normal to stalk people. Just for the record."

"Well, add this to your record: the things I feel for you aren't normal, little bird."

My heart leaps in my chest. "Is that so?"

He nods and takes a step toward me as the zipper reaches the end of its tread. "What are you doing?"

"Getting ready for bed," I say innocently.

His eyes find mine. "Phoebe..."

I release the fabric and the dress slides halfway down my body, exposing my black strapless bra. "Yes?"

His stare is hot as it roams my skin. It follows my fingers as I push the dress further down my hips.

"We have to be at the airport in six hours," he reminds me, taking another step closer.

"Plenty of time," I breathe, as the dress pools around my ankles. I step out, so I'm standing in only my Kate Spade pumps and a lace bra and panty set. I see his chest moving up and down as he attempts to get his breathing under control.

I flick the clasp of my bra and it tumbles to the floor.

"Unless..." I trail off, lifting a hand to my mouth and faking a large yawn. "I guess if you're too tired..."

I see a flash of his grin — dark and devilish — in the second before he launches into motion.

WE WRAP around each other like vines, entwining tighter with each passing moment. I kiss him with joy in my heart and realize all the anger I spent years harboring toward him is finally gone.

All the feelings of inadequacy and hopeless unrequited love have fled on the wind. He's forced them out. Chipped away at the walls of the tiny box I'd shoved him into — with dark-eyed looks and teasing comments and passion-fueled fights and breath-stealing kisses — until the tiny cage where I'd locked him away for almost a decade disappeared entirely.

His eyes never leave mine as I pull his shirt over his head, as he kicks off his jeans and stretches out over me, until we're skin on skin with not a single barrier left between us. The veins cord tightly in his arms as he braces his body above mine. I kiss him again as my legs loop around his hips to pull him against me.

"Come closer," I demand, arching up into him.

"Oh, I'll come." He grins against my mouth as his hands slide lower. "But not before you do."

Holy frack.

For what feels like an eternity, his fingers move over my skin – a bow over strings, pulling notes of pleasure from my body until I'm shaking with it. He's the conductor and I'm his private symphony, crying at his command and singing at his touch until the melody of passion he's been playing with his hands builds to a crescendo and I can't take another moment of torture without him inside me.

"Nate," I whisper, a chord of desperation in my tone. "Please."

"Are you sure?" he mutters, control hanging by a thread as he stares down into my eyes. "We don't have to do this, if you aren't ready. If you want to wait..."

"We're naked. There's a condom on your dick. Your hands are on my boobs. I just *licked your abs* with my tongue." I glare at him. "What possibly gave you the impression that I don't want to do this?"

His forehead drops to mine. "I just want you to be sure. This isn't the kind of thing you get to do-over."

"Nate." I kiss him until we're both shaking with need. "You keep saying I've been waiting — don't you know what I've been waiting for?"

He stares at me with a question in his eyes.

"You," I whisper. "I've been waiting for you."

"Phoebe." His voice vibrates with electricity and emotion. "*Phoebe.*"

In the space between two heartbeats, he drives into me and changes my life forever.

NOT LONG AGO, I thought of Nate and me as a natural disaster that would kill us both. Two opposing landmasses whose collision would cause catastrophic damage to both sides if they ever gave way beneath the tension building between them.

I was right; we are an earthquake.

We shift and sigh and shape each other with fingertips and lips — until the ground shakes and boundaries fall, until fault lines are crossed and every bit of terrain is left unrecognizable.

Nate makes love to me and it levels us both to rubble.

But there's beauty in the wreckage. Pleasure in the pain. Because, in the end, his ruins are indiscernible from mine. We're together when the dust settles and the shakes subside, holding each other so close I can't tell my soul from his.

"DO you remember the first day we met?" I ask absently, running my fingers down the length of his bare chest.

He goes still. "Of course I do."

"Do you remember the prayer you came up with to bless the bird funeral?"

A chuckle moves through him. "I think it was *I Believe I Can Fly* by R. Kelly."

"I thought you were *so* cool." I laugh lightly. "So grown up and original. Had I known you were just plagiarizing sub-par R&B songs, I wouldn't have been half as enamored with you."

He tilts my head up so our eyes meet. The soft look in his makes my heart turn over. "You were enamored with me, huh?"

"Yep." I nod. "Thankfully I grew out of *that* nonsense."

He leans in and nips my bottom lip in punishment. "Bullshit."

I laugh and kiss him until my blood is pounding in my veins. My laughter dies as I hold his stare.

"Do you remember what we vowed? After we buried the bird?"

His hands slide up the bare skin of my back. "I said you'd never catch me falling in love," he whispers, voice rough around the edges. "Because I wasn't going to risk dying of a broken heart."

I nod slowly. "And I agreed it wasn't worth the risk." A small grin tugs at my mouth. "Then again, I would've agreed with almost anything you said — you were much older and wiser, with vast life experience and extensive song-lyric knowledge."

"What do you mean *were*?" he jokes. "I'm still older and wiser and my music collection has only expanded, through the years."

I snuggle closer, until my chin rests on his chest, just above his heart. I know if I turn my cheek a few inches, I'll be able to hear it pounding beneath the skin.

"Thing is..." I swallow. "I broke the vow we made that day."

His heart pounds faster — I feel it vibrating through his ribcage. "Did you, little bird?"

"Yeah." I nod miserably, doing my best to fight back the tears building behind my eyes. "I said I wasn't ever going to fall in love, but..." I swallow hard. "I did."

He's silent for the longest five seconds of my lie.

"You want to hear something crazy?" he says finally.

I nod.

"I broke that vow the day we made it." His eyes catch mine, burning brighter than I've ever seen them. "I've been in love with you since you looked up at me with wet eyes and told me a story about birds who mate for life. About love so powerful, you can't live without the other person. Can't move on, can't forget, can't even breathe without them by your side." He shifts to cup my face in his hands. "I spent a long time trying to convince myself you were better off without me. That keeping away from you was the best way to keep you safe. But I can't do it anymore. I won't. See, you and I mated for life about a million years ago, little bird. Without you, there's no music. No love. No life."

A single tear escapes. He brushes it away with the pad of his thumb.

"Are you going to cry?" he asks, echoing his words from long ago, that day we buried a dove beneath my maple tree.

"No," I say in a choked voice, lips trembling with effort.

"Do you love me, little bird?"

"Yes," I croak, barely able to speak.

"Forever?"

"Yes." Another tear escapes. "I've loved you since you hopped that fence into my back yard, and I'll love you until my last breath. Even if you *are* bossy and rude about my footwear choices."

"Good." I feel his grin against my forehead as he presses a kiss there. "Because I have no intentions of ever dying of a broken heart."

WE DON'T SLEEP. I think we both know time is running too short, that our hours together in this bed are numbered and real life is approaching at hyper speed. So we laugh and love and touch and talk until dawn is knocking at the door.

"We have to go." Nate's voice is full of regret as he drops a kiss on the tip of my nose. "It takes thirty minutes to drive to the airfield."

"Do I really have to go?" I ask, though I already know the answer.

"I need you safe, little bird."

I sigh. "But maybe Milo came through. Maybe he somehow worked things out with Mac and..." I trail off, recognizing the naivety of my own words even as they leave my mouth.

"Believe me, if I thought it was safe, I'd keep you here with me." Another kiss lands on my nose. "I don't want you to go. But you and Parker are better off away from here, until things are resolved."

"Come with us," I whisper.

"As soon as we settle things with Mac, I'll be on the first plane." The love shining in his eyes is so bright, it lights up the room. "I promise."

"You make it sound simple. Like everything is easily fixable. But you can't just walk up to the Irish mob and say *Hey, let's let bygones be bygones*." My brow crinkles. "What if you get hurt? What if—"

"Nothing's going to happen to me." His words are adamant as presses a lingering kiss to my mouth. "Now get your ass out of bed, pull on some clothes, and put on a pair of those damn sexy shoes that will no doubt give me a hard-on for the next week." He slides off the bed, bends to scratch Boo behind the ears, and struts into the kitchen, naked as the day he was born.

Holy frack.

"Phoebe!" he calls a moment later, when he catches me staring.

"Yeah?" I gulp.

"My eyes are up here." His voice is thick with amusement. "Now get changed."

I lift my glaring eyes to his and hop out of bed.

"YOU HAVE EVERYTHING?"

I shoot him a look. "If I didn't know better, I'd think you were stalling because you don't want me to leave your lair."

His lips twitch. "We've been over this. It's not a lair."

"Uh huh." I sling the strap of my duffle over one shoulder. Boo's leash is tight in my other hand. "Have demon-dog, will travel."

He takes a step closer, eyes warm on Boo. "I admit, I'll miss the little rascal."

"Just him?"

His eyes flash up to mine. "And you."

"Good answer," I murmur, smiling as I lean into his chest and brush my lips against his.

"Almost forgot," he says, pulling away. He reaches into the pocket of his leather jacket and pulls out a pendant. It's shaped like a sun and looks almost exactly like the one Cormack took from me – the twin of Gemma's – except a fraction larger and silver rather than gold. "This is for you. Happy birthday, Phoebe."

My breath catches in my throat as he moves behind me and slips it around my neck. His body presses into mine as his large fingers fumble with the clasp.

"How did you know?" I ask.

CROSS THE LINE   319

"I know *you*. I know how important that necklace was. So, I had another made specially for you."

"Nate..." My voice cracks. "I don't know what to say."

He pulls my hair up, drops a kiss on the nape of my neck, and squeezes my shoulders. "Don't say anything. Just keep it close to your heart until I see you again. And remember I love you, little bird. Forever."

CHAPTER 28

There are still people out there who use actual *COINS* to pay at the tollbooth.

What is this, the Dark Ages?

Phoebe West, feeling grumpier than usual during Boston rush hour.

"THIS DOESN'T FEEL RIGHT."

The words are hushed as they leave Nate's mouth. We're walking across the tarmac toward the WestTech jet at a private airfield just north of the city. There's a hangar to either side, a small control tower in the distance, and a short runway strip about the length of two football fields stretching in front of us.

Someone's pulled the jet from its hangar onto the tarmac but as we get closer, there's no mechanical hum in the air — the engines are off. The runway lights haven't been illuminated. The hangar doors yawn open in the early morning light. It's completely deserted. Not a single soul in sight.

Our steps slow as the men switch into high-alert mode.

Parker and Theo — a muscular giant with floppy black hair, gorgeous caramel skin, and some seriously beautiful green eyes — met us in the parking lot behind the hangar. Theo is one of Nate's "men" and between him and Alden, the buzz-cut cutie I met two days ago, I'm beginning to wonder if there's some kind of stipulation in the Knox Investigations contract that says you have to be ridiculously good looking as well as badass to work there.

Macho men less than a 9.5 on the hotness Richter scale need not apply.

Theo shot me a dimpled grin when he caught me staring at him, but otherwise hasn't said much of anything since they arrived.

I walk between the three of them like I'm Taylor Swift surrounded by hulking bodyguards, clutching Boo to my chest like a stuffed teddy bear. For once, he doesn't fight my hold. We're almost at the jet when things get tense.

"Where's the crew? The pilot?" Parker's eyes narrow as they sweep the abandoned airstrip. "They should be here, by now."

Theo grunts in agreement.

Great. Another monosyllabic caveman. Just what I need in my life.

Nate stops, listening intently. Something dark flashes in his eyes and then he launches into motion, shoving me to the ground and yelling, "Down!" a second before the first shots ring out.

Shots.

From a gun.

Because someone is shooting at us.

What the hell is going on in my life?!

My duffle goes flying as his body lands on mine, covering me like a human shield. Boo lets out a yap of displeasure as I squish him against my chest, fear pounding through my veins like a drug. We half-run, half-crawl behind the jet for cover, flattening our bodies against the tarmac to stay out of range.

I hear a groan of pain, followed by the thud of a body landing beside me.

"Christ," a familiar voice grits out. "The fuckers *shot* me!"

Parker.

"Parker!" I scream, but the sound is swallowed up by the sharp rapport of a gun firing less than a foot from my ear. Nate's pulled his gun from the back of his jeans and is returning fire beneath the wheels of the jet. I try to turn my head to see if Parker's hurt, but I'm pinned too tight against the earth by the weight of Nate's body. I feel him shift on top of me as he repositions his gun.

"On your left!" His voice is gruff as he fires off another shot. "They're in the hangar!"

I hear the sound of bullets pinging off the jet's metal panels overhead.

"How many?" Theo yells back.

"Four, maybe five."

Theo grunts. "Too many."

There's a brief pause as whoever's shooting at us stops to reload. I don't have time to be relieved, because Nate's mouth is on my ear and he's speaking rapidly.

"You remember what I taught you? How to use that gun?"

"Yes," I squeak, recalling my abysmal target practice.

His hand finds mine and he presses something cold and metallic into my grip. "Take it. It's already loaded. Use it if you need it."

"But what if you need—"

"I have a spare. In a second, Theo and I are going to give you some covering fire. You and Parker are going to run for the car and get the fuck out of here."

"What about you?" My voice shakes with fear.

"I'll be fine. I'm right behind you." He ducks closer when shots ring out again in our direction. "Parker? Still with us?"

"I'm here." He wheezes out the words. Just hearing the pain in my brother's voice makes me cringe.

"You got the car keys?"

"In my back pocket."

"You gonna be able to run?"

There's a pause. "Have you seen this body?" He forces out a pained laugh. "I'm a cheetah. An Olympian. Even with a bullet in my shoulder."

I'd roll my eyes at his ridiculous comments if I weren't so scared.

"On three," Nate orders. I hear the sound of a fresh clip being shoved into his gun.

"Wait!" I hiss.

He pauses.

"I love you," I say, not caring who hears me. "I love you, Nate."

"Love you too, little bird." His voice is thick. "You ready?"

I nod. "Yes."

"One."

I hear the click of the chamber cocking back.

"Two."

I feel shift of his body as it eases off mine.

"Three."

I hear the sound of his gun firing in tandem with Theo's, followed by distant cursing as the men in the hangar duck for cover.

"Go!" Nate hisses between clenched teeth.

And then I'm up, Boo crushed against my chest with one

hand, the gun tight in my other. My ears are still ringing from the gunfire and with each step across the thirty feet of tarmac, I'm expecting a bullet to tear into me. Thankfully, Nate and Theo seem to be holding them off.

For now.

I don't let myself think about what'll happen when they run out of ammo. I don't let myself look back at the man I love, lying on an airstrip in a firefight with hardened criminals.

He'll be okay. He has to be okay.

Parker's right beside me, matching my strides and shielding me as best he can, even though he must be in excruciating pain. I dart a glance at him and see his face is pale, a sheen of sweat coating his forehead, his dark blond locks damp with perspiration.

There's a cramp knifing through my side. I ignore it and push faster, stilettos pounding against the concrete.

"You all right?" I gasp out as we career past our abandoned luggage.

Halfway there.

"Just... dandy..." he wheezes back.

We reach the parking lot and race for the SUV.

"I'm driving," I hiss.

"Shotgun," he jokes through the pain, hitting the unlock button and heading for the passenger side. I hear his door slam shut as I round the back of the car at full speed, mind totally occupied by thoughts of escape. I'm so focused on getting out of here, I nearly smash straight into someone.

No, not *someone.*

Padraic.

AKA Petey.

AKA a one of Mac's boys, intent on revenge.

Crap on asiago focaccia.

I DROP Boo almost as a reflex, both hands lifting to wrap around the gun. I aim it at Petey, wishing my arms weren't shaking so much.

He smiles darkly when he sees the gun bouncing.

"Scared?" He smirks as he takes a step toward me. "You should be. I'm gonna get you."

"And my little dog, too?" I wisecrack while my finger searches for the safety button.

He takes another step. "You aren't gonna shoot me."

"I wouldn't be so sure about that." I find the button at last.

Yes! Victory is mine!

I push it. The magazine falls out the bottom of my gun.

No! Victory is so not mine!

"Frack," I whisper, staring in disbelief at my utterly useless weapon. I hit the wrong damn button. Again.

Petey laughs as he makes a lunge for me. I recoil away, knowing I'm not fast enough. The only thought in my head is that I'm pretty sure I'm done for, when I hear it.

A growl.

My eyes drop just in time to see a white blob of fur launch itself at Petey's outstretched hands.

"What the fu— AHH!" Petey curses as a row of tiny, razor-sharp teeth clamp down on the fleshy part of his palm. "FUCK!"

He whips his injured hand sharply and I see Boo go flying.

"No!" I scream, watching his tiny body bounce off the side of the SUV with a sickening thud. He lets out an unmistakable yelp of pain when he hits the asphalt, before his body goes completely still. "Boo!"

He's not moving.

My adorable demon-dog is not moving.

Something inside me snaps.

I don't think. I hurl myself at Petey, hell-bent on destruction. My fists flail out and I feel vindication pump through me as one collides with his nose. My nails rake down his cheek so hard blood beads in their tracks.

"Fuck!" His hands come up to block my assault. I notice one of them is bleeding.

Good. Boo drew blood, too.

I kick him, one of my stilettos making contact with his most prized possession — the space directly between his legs. He grunts in pain and hunches in on himself involuntarily. He seems stunned I'm fighting back.

I use that to my advantage.

"You hurt my dog, you fucker!" I scream at the top of my lungs, kicking him in the shins, the thighs, anywhere I can reach. Again and again and again, until he falls to the ground, groaning.

"You shot my brother!" I scream, barely recognizing my own voice.

I kick and kick and kick, with a savagery that surprises me.

"And that's for Lila, you sonovabitch!"

He moans and curls tighter into himself.

"Sweet P."

The tension in my brother's tone makes me look up from my assault. Petey is whimpering on the ground like a coward. I feel a strange, detached sense of satisfaction when I see that, along with some serious undercurrents of horror at my own barbarity.

Perfect Phoebe West — socialite and secret sociopath. Who knew?

My eyes swing up toward the sound of Parker's voice and I feel them widen as they take in the sight a dozen feet from me. My throat closes, not letting any air in or out as I stare at my big brother.

He's standing there looking at me, a bright crimson circle staining his t-shirt at the shoulder, with a gun barrel pressed to his temple. My eyes trail from the hand holding the gun, up one muscular arm, and finally, to the face of the man who's been haunting my nightmares.

"CORMACK." The word barely makes it past my lips. "Let him go."

"I don't think so, Phoebe." He smiles — a cold, cruel grimace. "See, I need one of you. Your father isn't being cooperative. I think he needs a bit of incentive."

I hear gunfire in the distance — Nate and Theo are still occupied on the tarmac. I'm on my own.

My razor-sharp stiletto heel is poised over Petey's temple. I know if I stepped down with all my body weight, I could kill him instantly.

I'm not an exceptionally violent person. Never have been.

I don't believe in the death penalty. I cried when hunters killed Cecil the Lion, for god's sake. But in this moment, right here, with my brother's life on the line and my dog lying motionless and the man I love in jeopardy...

I could do it.

I know I could.

"Let go of my brother or I'll kill him." My words are flat, emotionless.

I've been spending too much time around Nate.

Cormack's smile twitches wider. "I like you like this, Phoebe. You're much feistier than I gave you credit for, in the beginning. I used to think you were just a dumb heiress." His eyes narrow. "Now, I think you're a dumb heiress with no sense of self-preservation."

"Let him go," I repeat.

"You wanna kill Petey? Go ahead." Cormack shakes his head, amused. "He's useless, anyway."

Frack.

There goes my only bargaining chip.

Petey grunts and starts to shift. I press my heel down tighter and he goes still.

"This isn't gonna go your way, Phoebe." Cormack stares me down. "It only ends one way." He sidles closer to Parker and I see my brother flinch when the gun digs into his skin. "You've got ten seconds to decide. Do I blow his brains out right here? Or are you going to move that heel?"

Frack. Frack. Frack.

Out of options. Out of time. My eyes cut to Parker for a fraction of a second.

"Phoebe, run!" His voice is pleading. "Don't worry about me, just get the fuck out of here."

"I wouldn't do that, if I were you." Cormack adjusts his grip on the gun, pressing it more firmly against my brother's temple. My heart skips a beat. "He'll be dead before you make it two steps."

"Go, Sweet P." Parker's voice breaks. "Don't give this fucker what he wants."

I ignore him, staring straight at Cormack.

"Take me," I say, voice empty.

"No!" Parker yells instantly. "Fuck no, Phoebe."

I don't look at Parker. I can't. If I look at him right now, I'll fall apart.

"He's injured. He won't be a good hostage if he bleeds out before you get your ransom." I swallow. "Take me instead."

Cormack stares at me. "Maybe I'll take you both. Or maybe I'll put a bullet in your pretty little head instead, and leave you here for your boyfriend to find."

I go completely still.

Cormack's smile widens. "He's been making life difficult for me. Asking lots of questions, digging into my past, talking to the FBI about me. Maybe I should make things difficult for him, too."

My mind reels. "You don't want to do that. My father won't give Mac his cut if you kill either of us."

"Maybe." Cormack shrugs, as though he couldn't care less either way. "Maybe not."

"You'll let my brother and Nate live. If I go with you, you'll let them live." The words are almost steady as they pass my lips. Almost. "I won't fight you."

"No!" Parker yells.

"Deal," Cormack agrees, smiling at me. "Now step away from him and put your hands up."

I look at my brother for a long moment before I comply.

"I love you," I tell him, tears blurring my eyes. "Tell Nate...." I search for the right words as I listen to the guns firing fifty feet away and wonder if he's even still alive. "Tell him..."

Tell him he's the love of my life.

Parker's eyes flash with something I have trouble deciphering.

"Tell him I'm sorry," I finish lamely, trying not to let the tears escape.

"Phoebe, don't do this!" Parker's voice is anguished. "Sweet P!"

I close my eyes, take a deep breath, pull my heel from Petey's temple, and lift my hands into the air.

NO DANK BASEMENTS or rope-burn this time — that's a positive, right?

Not that there are a lot of positives to being kidnapped. By the mob. For the second time in a week. But I'm trying to look on the bright side.

This time, I'm brought straight to the source — the infamous Keegan MacDonough. The big kahuna. The King of Evil himself.

I'd be flattered I merit a meeting with a veritable mob boss if, you know, my heart wasn't racing three times its normal speed, my legs weren't trembling with each step, and my palms weren't coated with a sheen of sweat so slippery I could slick down a stripper pole.

I try to straighten my blouse and brush some of the dirt off my jeans as we move through the abandoned warehouse toward Mac's office, but there's not much of a point. I have a feeling I won't make it out of this meeting alive, anyway.

As a general rule, evil-doers don't bring you to their lairs without a blindfold unless they're going to off you afterward.

At least, not according to the many, many hours of *Nikita* I binge-watched on Netflix last month.

Sigh.

Petey's got a firm grip on my arm as he pulls me down the hall, so tight I'm sure I'll have a cuff of dark bruises around my bicep in an hour or so. He's a wee bit upset about the whole *getting-the-shit-kicked-out-of-him-by-a-girl* thing.

The thought makes me smirk as I replay those last moments in the parking lot.

As soon as my hands hit the air, Petey scrambled to his feet and backhanded me across the face so hard, the world went out of focus for a few seconds. Parker tried to fight to get to me, but Cormack punched him hard in the shoulder where the bullet was lodged, and I watched in horror as my brother crumpled to the ground, incapacitated by the pain.

"Nate!" I screamed at the top of my lungs, earning another slap from Petey. "Help!"

He was too far away. Still holding off the rest of Mac's boys on the airstrip. Every few seconds, the sound of a shot rang out in the distance.

Please don't die.

Cormack grabbed my chin. "Keep fighting, make another goddamned sound, and I'll shoot your brother in the head."

All the fight went out of me. I stood there, staring at Parker's limp body, wondering if I'd ever see him again.

They dragged me off to one of their cars, a nondescript tan sedan stashed out of sight in the bushes behind the hangar, leaving Parker and Boo lying on the cold ground mere inches from each other.

I was too far away to tell if their chests were moving.

I'd lost them all — Parker, Nate, Boo.

As we rode away from the airfield, sounds of gunfire fading into the distance behind us, I thought of Nate, wrapping the memory of his words around me like a blanket.

We're worth everything.

You and I mated for life about a million years ago, little bird.

I love you.

I keep those words close to my heart now, as we come to a stop outside a black door.

"When Mac's through with you, you and me are gonna have a meeting of our own," Petey says, his mouth so close to my ear I can feel his hot breath on my neck.

I try to stay still, to show him he doesn't scare me.

He chuckles darkly, hands slithering down my body as he checks to see if I'm wearing a wire or concealing any weapons. Or maybe he just wants to cop a feel. Who knows.

"Proud little bitch, aren't you?" His hands roam beneath my shirt and I try not to react. "We'll see how proud you are when you're sucking my dick."

I keep my eyes on the door. "Sorry," I murmur, voice sweet. "I was warned never to put small objects in my mouth. Choking hazard, and all."

"Bitch!"

I wince as I see his hand pull back in my peripheral, anticipating the pain of another strike. To my surprise, his fist never connects. From the corner of my eye, I see Cormack's got his hand around Petey's forearm, halting it midair.

"Mac will be pissed if you hit her again," Cormack says, eyes on his partner. "Don't be a fucking idiot."

Petey growls in displeasure, yanks his arm free, and scowls. "Whatever. She's clean. No wires, no cell, nothing."

I bite the inside of my cheek so I don't wilt as relief washes through me.

It's short lived.

The door swings open and I'm shoved into the office of Boston's most notorious crime lord.

CHAPTER 29

I'M PRETTY INTO WATCHING SPORTS.

BY *SPORTS* I OBVIOUSLY MEAN DAVID BECKHAM.

Phoebe West, detailing the best attributes of soccer.

"MISS WEST. PLEASE, SIT."

I'm stunned to find myself face to face with a pleasant looking man in slacks and a button down, his sandy, red-blond hair well groomed and his lithe, athletic stature non-threatening. I'm not sure what I was expecting Keegan MacDonough to look like (maybe someone with massive muscles and a perpetual scowl and possibly even fangs or claws) but it certainly wasn't *this* — an unexceptional middle-aged man I wouldn't glance twice at if I passed him on the street.

His eyes are light blue and hyper-intelligent, tracking my

every move as I step further inside. There's hardly any furniture
— just a heavy-looking metal desk and two steel-backed chairs,
bolted to the ground. The windows are blacked out with dark
spray paint. It looks more like an interrogation room than an
office.

"Sit," he repeats, authority ringing in his tone.

Anyone who underestimates this man based on his appearance is a fool; it's clear from the first two seconds in his presence,
he's not someone to be trifled with.

I sit.

He does the same, settling on the other side of the industrial
desk. His hands steeple in front of him as he stares at me.

"Do you know why you're here?" he asks, after a long silence.

"I'm assuming it's not for a chick-flick marathon with
popcorn and hair-braiding." I'm proud my voice doesn't shake.
"Which is a shame, 'cause I do a mean fish-tail."

He doesn't smile or laugh. His lips don't even twitch.

"Your father broke the terms of our agreement. So long as he
pays me, you won't be harmed."

I swallow. "The way he tells it, you're the one who broke the
terms."

"So you know about our arrangement."

"If by arrangement you mean mistake, then yes. I know about
the mistake my father made, dealing with you."

"A mistake?" His head tilts. "No, I don't think so. Mistakes
imply you don't know what you're getting into. Your father knew
exactly what he was doing, when he decided to negotiate with
me. That's not a mistake. You may blame me for how things
turned out, but he's as much at fault as anyone."

"You're the criminal, here. Don't turn it around on my
father."

"You call me a criminal because I make deals in a seedy bar in
Charlestown; you'd call me something else if I made those same

deals from a corner office downtown. *Entrepreneur.*
Businessman." He leans back in his seat. "Criminal is just an
arbitrary label, Miss West. A state of mind."

"Says the criminal," I mutter.

"Your father is a wealthy man. You think he's gotten that way
by following the law? You think *he's* not a criminal, for the things
he's done?" His eyes narrow to slits. "He's greased the palms of
every zoning official and city surveyor since he started building
his little green-development empire. And before then, a decade
ago, when he laid his submarine communications cable from
Boston to England and made the bulk of his fortune... You think
that project would've passed regulations, if he hadn't bribed
everyone standing in his way? Silenced every environmental
group and opposer with threats and defamation lawsuits?"

My heart is pounding a sharp staccato inside my chest.

For the first time, a hint of a smile crosses Mac's lips. "Bribes
and threats — that's what makes the world go round. Your father
knows that better than anyone."

My mouth presses shut. I don't know what to say — how do I
defend my father when my own faith in him has crumbled like
stale bread? When he's just as untrustworthy as a mafia lord?

"You've been dealing with my father for years. He knows
your secrets. You hurt me, he'll go to the police," I bluff. "He'll
testify against you."

His lips twist in a cold almost-smile. "The police won't move
against me."

"The FBI will," I say, desperate to believe my own words.

"Miss West, your father can't take me down without incrimi-
nating himself as well." He smirks. "I don't see him voluntarily
destroying his own life, throwing away everything — his family,
his company, his fortune — and spending his final days in a
federal prison just to take me down. Do you?"

No. No, I do not.

I don't respond, though I have a feeling my silence is answer enough for him.

"You know it, I know it, Milo knows it. And yet, he won't pay me. So you see my problem." He lays his hands flat on the desk. "He's not an easy man to deal with, your father."

My throat is too dry to respond so I just nod my head, feeling somewhat dazed.

"Any suggestions for me?" he asks, amused.

I cough to clear my throat. "You could let me go."

He laughs, at that. A real, genuine laugh.

"You seem like a nice girl, Miss West." He sits back in his chair. "It's a shame I'll have to kill you, if your father doesn't pay me."

Frack.

"So, that's a no on the hair braiding, then?" I ask.

"If I ever had a daughter, I'd have wanted her to be like you," he says, surprising me. "Brave. Perhaps too reckless, but brave."

"It's not too late." I shrug. "You could do it."

"So I can suffer the same fate I've inflicted on your father?" He shakes his head. "When you have as many enemies as I do, Miss West, you can't have a family. Any child of mine would be a target from the moment it took its first breath."

"I'm sorry," I say, meaning it.

Something like surprise flashes in his light blue eyes. "You really mean that, don't you?"

"I'm not exactly in a position to lie." I shrug. "And yeah. No family, no one to trust... it sounds lonely. I know what that's like, and I'm sorry for anyone who feels that way. Even if they're a mobster crime lord who's killed a zillion people."

"I haven't killed a zillion people." His mouth twitches. "Only a hundred or so. And most of them deserved it."

A chill zips down my spine at his casual tone.

*Great, Phoebe. Just great. Sympathize with the psycho mob
boss who readily admits to murder.*

"Um," I say intelligently. "What about the ones who didn't?"

His eyes get distant. "I try not to think about those."

"Does it work?"

"Most of the time."

I stare at him. "I don't believe you."

His gaze moves to mine. "Smart girl."

CORMACK COMES IN, calls Mac out into the hallway, and for
a while, I'm left in the office alone. I hear the click of the lock turn
over, so I know I can't get out. There's nothing I can use as a
weapon. The desk surface is empty. There's not even a damn
pen. Every drawer is locked tight.

I sigh.

Honestly, being kidnapped is a lot more waiting around than
I'd have imagined before all this mafia drama went down — if
you're not waiting to be killed, you're waiting to be rescued or
waiting to get a chance to go to the bathroom... Always waiting.
This time is even more boring than the last, but at least I'm not
tied to a chair.

It's the little things.

I run my finger along the pointed edges of the sun necklace
Nate gave me as my mind turns over thoughts of him and Parker
and Boo. I pray to god they're all still alive.

If I listen hard, I can almost make out the conversation in the
hallway. I creep to my feet and ease toward the door, pressing my
ear flat against the wood so I can hear better.

Cormack's voice is rising with anger, a stark contrast to the
measured tones of his boss. Straining, I catch fragments every few
seconds.

...West...
...may have flipped on us...
...FBI...
...get you out of here...
...take care of her...
...body at the marsh....

None of that sounds good. In fact, all of that sounds pretty fucking terrible. I can't make out Mac's words, but a few seconds later I hear the sound of footsteps. My ass is barely back in my seat when the door swings open and Cormack steps into the room.

His smile gleams as darkly as the gun in his hand. "Just you and me now, Phoebe."

I gulp.

Somehow, I felt safer with the mob boss.

***

"WHERE ARE YOU TAKING ME?" I ask for the twentieth time.

Cormack doesn't answer as he pushes me through the empty warehouse, using the barrel of his gun like a cattle prod whenever I'm not moving fast enough for his liking.

"Where's Mac?"

"Why? You think he's gonna save you?" Cormack snorts. "He's the one who ordered the hit."

The hit? As in....

Crap on ciabatta loaf.

"You can't kill me." I swallow. "You need me."

"Apparently not anymore." His voice is casual, like we're discussing the weather. "Your father surprised us. Didn't think he had the balls to go to the FBI about Mac, but we just got word he flipped."

CROSS THE LINE 339

Dad went to the FBI?

Cormack's feeling chatty. "He must love you. Thought it'd save you, probably. That the boys in blue would find you in time." He laughs, like he's told a great joke. "Stupid of him, really."

My heart clenches.

We reach the end of one hallway and turn down another. I see a doorway up ahead, light shining in around its edges, illuminating dust motes in the stale air. We're headed outside.

Cormack's still taunting me as his gun barrel presses between my shoulder blades. "Not only will he fail to help you, he'll go to jail for his trouble. The amount of shit Milo West has done — collusion, blackmail, extortion — even a testimony won't get him off scot-free." I can hear the smirk in his voice. "Still, we can get to him. Mac's reach extends far. Even to federal security prisons. Your daddy's days are numbered, whether he walks or does time."

I clench my hands so tight, my fingernails cut into my palms like knives.

"All for nothing, too. They won't be able to make any of the charges against Mac stick. Never do." He chuckles. "Witnesses have a way of... disappearing."

"You don't have to kill me," I say, breathing too hard. "I don't have anything to do with this. My father will go to jail, you just said that. His life is over. So, you already have your revenge. Please... you don't need to hurt me, too."

We reach the door. Cormack steps around me to haul it open with his free hand. He uses his gun to gesture me outside.

I squint against the sudden brightness. It's around noon, judging by the sun's position straight overhead, and after my eyes adjust I see nothing but swamp. Dried mud and tall grass form a bog for at least a mile in every direction. My heels sink in with each step.

I know immediately that we're somewhere far outside the city limits — an old abandoned mill or factory, somewhere long-forgotten by everyone except Mac and his boys. There are no other buildings anywhere in sight. The tan sedan is the only car left parked beside the warehouse.

"Keep walking," Cormack orders, eyes cold. "Toward the marsh."

With his accent it sounds like he's saying *toad tha mash*.

I turn to look at him. "Please don't do this."

He takes a step closer and his voice gets even harsher. "Walk toward the marsh and get on your fucking knees."

I swallow. "No."

He smiles a scary smile. "No?"

"If you want to kill me, you're going to have to do it looking into my eyes, you bastard."

He raises the gun toward my head. "Fine by me."

My eyes press closed when the shot goes off.

CHAPTER 30

CAN you die of a broken heart?

A tear-stained little girl asked that question to a boy on the grass beside her almost twenty years ago.

He didn't know the answer. Neither of us did.

Not then.

But I know now.

Truth is, any number of things in this life can kill you. Turn on the news any day of the week, and you'll see the stories.

A soccer mom totals her minivan on the way to pick up her kids from practice. A renowned physicist has a heart attack in the middle of his Nobel Prize acceptance speech. A child climbs into a van with a stranger and is never seen again.

War, famine, disease, drought.

Electrocution, car accident, fire, drowning.

Cancer, spider bite, shark attack, childbirth.

Our world is a hypochondriac's nightmare and a survivalist's dreamland.

Anything can kill you. Anything.

Even a broken heart.

I always kind of thought I'd go that way. That I'd love Nate so much, it physically killed me.

I sure as hell didn't expect a bullet to the brain in a swampy marsh.

But as I stand here with my eyes closed, waiting to die, I can't help but think it's not how we go that matters. It's not our deaths that define us.

It's how we *live.*

The choices we make. The lives we change. The people we love.

That's the legacy we leave behind, when we blink out of existence. Not how we die, whether it's after a long, brave battle with cancer or a short, unexpected trip over your shoelaces into oncoming traffic.

Life is precious. Days are numbered.

It's not a dress rehearsal.

There are no do-overs or second chances at getting it right.

I wish, more than anything, that I'd lived every single day like I was dying. I wish I hadn't been so afraid of getting hurt or making a fool of myself that I went years without telling Nate how I felt. I wish I could take back every wasted moment I spent without him.

Most of all, though, I wish I'd never told him about those damn turtle doves who mate for life. Because if I die...

It may just kill him, too.

THE BANG IS SO LOUD, it makes my ears ring. I flinch back, waiting for the impact.

It never comes.

I hear a dull thud, the sound of running footsteps. My lashes fly open to see Cormack on the dirt at my feet — a bullet in his head, his green-blue eyes wide and unblinking as they stare up at the sky overhead.

The screech of the warehouse door makes me turn. My eyes are glassy with shock, my heart is lodged firmly in my throat, and I know I'm shaking like a leaf as I take in the sight of the men in black fatigues flooding out of the warehouse like ants at a picnic.

I barely see them — my eyes cut straight through the group to the man in the leather jacket standing ten feet from me, his gun still smoking in his hands. His dark eyes are locked on me, burning bright with love and fear and anger.

"Nate," I choke, taking two steps toward him. My ankles wobble and I think I might fall, but suddenly he's there, wrapping his arms around me so tight I can barely breathe. His mouth presses against my hair. I can hear his heart pounding beneath my cheek.

"I've got you, little bird." His voice is ragged with worry. "You're safe. I've got you."

I try to turn in his arms, but I'm crushed too tight against his chest.

"Let me go," I say.

He goes still. "Why?"

"So I can kiss you, idiot."

His arms loosen, his hands come up to frame my face, and then he's kissing me. I taste anguish and longing and terror on his tongue, love and joy and relief on his lips. I keep kissing him until my hands stop shaking and my knees quit quaking.

"You got kidnapped again," he growls when he pulls away, glaring at me. "You promised never to do that."

"Sorry," I whisper. "They had Parker, and— Oh my god, Parker! Is he—"

"He's fine." Nate's eyes soften and he runs a hand over my hair. "Shot to his shoulder was a through-and-through."

"Thank god," I say, voice breaking. "And Boo?"

Nate's eyes flash with worry. "He's..."

My heart stops. "Dead? He's dead?"

"No." His hands cup my face again. "He's at the vet. They're going to do everything they can for him."

"But... He's alone?"

"Lila and Gemma are with him."

"We have to go," I say immediately, stepping out of his arms. "I need to see him. If he doesn't make it..."

"He knows you love him, Phoebe."

A tear drips down my face. "Swear to god, if my demon-dog doesn't pull through this... I will kill Keegan MacDonough myself."

Nate's lips twitch. "He'll get what's coming to him. Don't worry about that. Your father's testimony against him is all the FBI needed to move in. They'd been waiting for probable cause to search this place." He gestures at the swamp. My eyes follow his hand and I see the SWAT guys moving methodically through the tall grass, scouring the area for something.

"What are they looking for?" I ask quietly.

Nate doesn't answer. When I meet his eyes, I see they're guarded.

"Bodies," I whisper, answering my own question. "They're looking for bodies."

He nods. "A lot of Mac's hits were rumored to take place out here. But it's private land so they needed a warrant. Your dad's information on Mac, on some of their dealings, things he's learned over the years... He gave the FBI exactly what they needed."

I swallow hard so I don't panic. "Is my dad... is he in custody?"

Nate nods again.

"He tried to save me the only way he knew how," I whisper. "He gave his life, his freedom, for mine."

"He's the reason your life was in danger in the first place," Nate rumbles, dislike etched clearly on his features. "I know he's your dad, but I can't forgive him for that. He deserves to go to jail, along with Mac and all his boys."

I sigh and my eyes land on Cormack. Two men in black are zipping him into a body bag.

"Don't look at that, little bird," Nate says, turning my face up to his. "He deserved to die. He would've—"

"I know." I take a breath. "If you'd gotten here one second later..."

"Don't think about it." He pulls me into his chest again, hugging me until my ribs ache. "I got here. That's all that matters."

A thought occurs to me. "How did you even find me? How did you know I was here?"

A chuckle moves through his body. He snags the chain of the sunshine pendant hanging around my neck with one finger, and pulls it up to the light.

"This necklace?" His voice is wry. "I told you I had it made specially, didn't I? After they took you the first time, I decided I wasn't taking any more chances."

When I look up at him, there's a mischievous light in his eyes. "What did you do?"

"Let's just say, it's not made of sterling silver." His lips twitch. "There's a GPS tracker chip embedded in the center."

"You bugged my necklace?" I gasp out, not knowing whether to be offended or flattered. "That's insane."

"Maybe." He shrugs, unapologetic. "But it saved your life."

I can't argue with that. He's right. Still, I wish his macho man antics hadn't been validated.

I narrow my eyes. "You're going to be impossible to live with now, aren't you?"

"No," he lies, grinning at me.

I sigh. "Do I have to debrief with the commando dudes?"

His eyes flash with mirth. "They aren't commandos."

"Whatever." I eye their black-on-black attire and large guns. "If it walks like a duck and quacks like a duck..."

"They're an FBI tactical team."

"Do I have to talk to them, or not?"

"You do."

"Figured you were gonna say that," I mutter.

"It won't be bad. Just a few questions." He drops a kiss on my forehead. "I know one of the lead investigators on Mac's case. Sometimes we help each other out when we're in a bind – off the record, of course. Good guy. Name's Conor Gallagher, he's a special agent who relocated from New York City not too long ago."

"What, are you two drinking buddies?" I ask, noting the familiarity in his tone.

"Poker night once a month." He grins. "Boston. It's a small town."

"Especially for you commando types," I murmur.

"Come on." He wraps one arm around my shoulder and leads me back toward the warehouse. "Let's go talk to him so we can get the hell out of here."

THE DOOR OPENS and all of our heads swivel in sync toward it.

A vet tech walks out with a bouncy golden retriever.

I scowl.

Nate's arm tightens around me.

"I'm sure he's next," Gemma says, squeezing my hand.

"Totally," Lila agrees. "The little fur-ball will be out any minute."

"Want me to go check what's taking so long?" Chase offers, smiling. "Receptionists like me."

Gemma shoots him a look. "Oh, do they now?"

His eyes are warm on her. "Jealous, sunshine?"

"Yep," she admits easily, grinning back at him.

I roll my eyes and snuggle closer to Nate.

"If I'd known I was going to be fifth wheeling, I'd have dragged Parker along," Lila grumbles.

Nate chuckles and I feel it vibrate through me.

I sigh happily. "He's still recovering."

"How's he doing?" Gemma asks hesitantly. We're still testing the waters, when it comes to the sibling stuff. One toe at a time. In the shallow end. Wearing those inflatable arm-floaties.

"He's crashing at my place, sleeping a lot because of the pain meds and watching the entire series of *Sons of Anarchy* on Netflix while yelling at me to bring him a near-constant supply of snacks." I roll my eyes. "He doesn't seem too upset about the bullet wound. In fact, he keeps saying it'll be — and I quote — *total chick bait.*"

Everyone laughs.

"If you don't mind me asking... What's going to happen to the company, now that your father's in federal custody?" Chase asks. I can see the CEO wheels turning in his mind — it's only natural he'd be curious. WestTech and Croft Industries have done business together in the past.

"We're still figuring that out," I say softly, worry churning in my gut. In the two days since the FBI raid, there's been so much going on I haven't had time to think what Milo West's incarceration will do to the family company. "I guess Parker and I will need to have a discussion. Preferably when he's no longer hopped up on percocet."

"If you need anything, don't hesitate to call," Chase offers kindly. I can tell by the look in his eyes it's not some empty offer, either — he means it.

"Thank you."

The door to the back room swings open again.

We all look at the same time... and sigh in unison when we see a chubby corgi waddling out.

"I hate this." I knit my hands together.

A kiss lands on my temple. "Don't worry, little bird. It won't be too much longer."

"So, Knox." The forced nonchalance in Lila's tone makes both of us glance her way. "Now that Mac is behind bars – at least temporarily – and the police are rounding up his boys and Phoebe's officially out of danger... does that mean your men aren't going to be on the clock 24/7 anymore?"

His eyes narrow. "I don't follow."

I elbow him. "She's asking if Theo and Alden and whatever other hotties you've got on payroll are going to have nights off."

He glances at me. "Hotties?"

I nod.

He scoffs and looks back at Lila. "I don't do matchmaking."

"You owe me!" she tells him, pointing a finger at me. "That one never would've gone for you without a push." She pauses. "A push from *me*, in case that wasn't clear."

He looks at me, eyebrows raised.

I shrug. "It's kind of true."

He sighs deeply. "Theo doesn't date. Alden had a girlfriend last time I checked. I really don't know about Lucas or Owen." Nate sounds pained. "I *suppose* I can check with them."

"Ohhh, Lucas and Owen?" I murmur. "I *knew* there were more hotties."

Lila squeals happily. Gemma and I squeal, too. (For moral support.)

Chase and Nate both look at the ceiling, seeking guidance.

The door swings open. I hold my breath as I turn to look, then jump to my feet when I catch sight of the tiny Pomeranian. He's limping, there's a bandage wrapping his bruised ribs, and his pristine fur coat looks a bit worse for wear...

But he's alive.

"Boo!" I yell, running toward him like we're in a slow motion movie reunion. I fully expect him to start running toward me too, leaping into my arms and covering my face in kisses as I hug him tightly...

Instead, he glances dismissively at me for about two seconds, then wanders over to the chubby corgi and sniffs his butt in greeting.

I can hear my friends laughing hysterically in the waiting room behind me.

I glare at them. "He loves me. He just..." I hedge. "Maybe he has amnesia." I look at the vet tech with pleading eyes. "Dogs can have amnesia, right?"

"Uh." She shifts from one foot to another, looking uncomfortable. "Look, I'm just the tech... But I don't think they found any head trauma..."

I sigh.

The goons behind me laugh louder.

Taking the leash from her hand, I crouch down to Boo's level. After a second, he turns his beady eyes toward me.

"Hey, Boo," I whisper.

He cocks his head at the sound of my voice. A few seconds pass before he wanders closer, plants his tiny paws on my knee, and licks my downturned face.

"Aww, you do love me," I say, stroking him gently. "But, for the record, that kiss would've been so much nicer if you'd done it *before* you had your face up in that corgi's butt."

As I lift him into my arms, he licks his tiny tongue up the length of my cheek a second time – ignoring my wishes, per usual.

Clearly, there's been no permanent damage to his personality.

I hug him close as I walk back toward my friends, who are still cackling like hyenas. (Assholes.) Right then, in that moment, with my dog in my arms and a room full of crazy people who love me, I know that somehow everything is going to be all right.

That lonely feeling I carried around for so many years has vanished with the knowledge that I couldn't just disappear one day, winking out of existence without causing so much as a ripple.

Because these people, in this dingy waiting room?

They'd notice.

CHAPTER 31

I DID IT, ONCE. WOKE UP FIVE HOURS LATER COVERED
IN GLITTER AND FULL OF REGRET.

*Phoebe West, describing her one and only experience
using Pinterest.*

"THANK GOD YOU'RE HERE," I mutter, yanking Nate inside
and slamming the front door behind him.

He stands in the entryway, looking at me strangely.

"What?" I ask defensively.

"Your shirt is on backwards and you're wearing *flats*." His
eyes narrow. "I don't know whether to run for my life or take your
temperature."

I smack him on the arm. "You're supposed to be here to help,
not make fun of my fashion choices."

"Give me a kiss hello and maybe I'll help you."

I rise up onto my toes and peck my lips against his. "There."

Something dark flashes in his eyes and before I know it, he's spun me around, backed me up against my front door, and is kissing me with so much heat it's all I can do not to melt into a puddle right there on the floor of my foyer.

Holy frack.

"*That* is a kiss hello," he rumbles against my lips.

"Hello," I breathe, feeling dazed.

He chuckles and pulls back slightly to look at me. "Now, tell me the big emergency."

"He won't leave. He's moving around all my stuff and he spilled nachos on my favorite Anthropologie blanket and he's kidnapped my dog. They haven't left that bedroom in days except to pee and eat. *Days!* The doctor said *take it easy* not *turn into Howard Hughes.*" My voice gets more and more frantic as the words pour out. "You have to help me."

"What do you expect me to do?" Nate's voice is amused.

Amused!

"Make him leave that room," I beg. "Or at least make him shower. I think he's starting to mold."

"Little bird—"

"He's your best friend," I point out.

"Exactly. I'm his friend, not his nursemaid."

I glare at him. "Did I mention he's in the guest room? As in, the bedroom next to mine?"

He stares at me blankly.

"Nathaniel Xavier Knox," I whisper intently, eyes locked on his. "If you ever want to have sex again, you have to get him out of there. We can't do it while we're sharing a wall with my brother."

Comprehension flares in his eyes and before I know it, he's moving. His long legs take the stairs two at a time. I follow, heart pounding in my chest.

"Knox!" Parker says when we open the door. He's lying in bed, arm in a sling, eating a bag of potato chips. Boo is tucked close by his side. "What's going on, man?"

Nate reaches into his back pocket, removes his house keys, and tosses them toward the bed. Parker catches them with his good hand.

"What are these?" he asks, staring at the keys.

"Keys to my loft," Nate says. "You're staying there, till you find a place."

"Sweet, thanks man." Parker's eyes find mine. "You kicking me out, Phoebe?"

"No! Of course not!" I'm suddenly hit with a wave of guilt. "It's just..."

"I'm moving in here," Nate says. "And we need our space."

Parker grimaces and hops out of bed. "Enough said."

Boo looks forlorn at the sudden absence of his snuggling partner.

I try to pick my jaw up off the floor so I can effectively glare at Nate. "I'm sorry, you're doing *what* exactly?"

"Moving in." He says it like it's the simplest thing in the world. "Did you not hear me?"

"I heard you." I stare from Nate to Parker, who's shoving clothes into his duffle one-handed. "But... I..." I swallow. "Moving in. Here. With me."

His eyes crinkle. "That's what moving in means."

"But... it's only been, like... a week... since we started..."

Dating? Screwing? Living a life without the ever-present threat of mobsters?

"AH!" Parker yells. "Do not finish that sentence, for the love of god."

I sigh and shoot a look in Nate's direction. "You can't move in with someone after five minutes of being together. That's crazy."

"Know what's crazy?" he asks, stepping close. "Being in love with someone for more than half your life and *not* waking up to their face every morning."

My mouth goes dry.

Damn, he's good.

"God, you're mushy," Parker says, staring gloatingly at Nate. "Never thought I'd see the day."

Nate cuts a look at his best friend. "Wait till it happens to you. You'll never see it coming."

"Oh, I'll see her coming." Parker's eyebrows waggle.

I make a gagging noise.

"Relax, I'm joking." He slings the duffle strap over his good shoulder, wincing. "I'm not the relationship type. You guys know that."

"Uh huh," Nate says.

"Sure you aren't," I murmur.

Parker rolls his eyes and heads for the doorway. We follow him down the stairs, Boo at our heels.

"I'll miss you, Sweet P. Who am I going to call when I need snack refills?" He makes a sad face. "Your nachos are unbeatable."

I laugh. "Nate has an oven, you know."

"But *my* nachos won't be the same. Yours are prepared with love."

"Fine, fine." I roll my eyes. "I'll come visit."

"Great! Bring that guacamole you made the other day. That shit is amazing."

Nate snorts.

Parker turns to look at his best friend. "And you." He makes a disappointed *tsk* noise. "As soon as this arm is healed, I'm delivering."

"Figured as much," Nate says, grinning.

"Delivering?" I ask.

"I owe him a punch in the face." Parker smiles and ruffles my hair. "For going after my little sister."

"That's ridiculous."

"Those are the terms we set forth at age nine, Sweet P."

"We have to honor the code, little bird."

Parker and Nate are both grinning as they do some kind of weird handshake back-slap thing.

Boys.

"Take care of her," Parker says, his expression sobering. "I mean it."

Nate nods. "I will."

Parker turns to me. "Love you, kid."

I roll my eyes. "For the last time, I'm not a kid. If you're really going to stick around, you have to accept that."

"I told you I'm sticking around and I'm serious. For now. At least until the company is sorted out." He looks at me, lips twisted in a grin. "Guess you're not my baby sister anymore."

"I'll always be your baby sister," I say, eyes watering. "Now go, before I start crying."

"Don't I get a hug goodbye?" he asks, offended.

I wrinkle my nose. "When was the last time you showered?"

He chuckles and sweeps me into a bear hug anyway. Well, *half* a bear hug. But I have a feeling he'll be back to fighting shape in no time.

THE HOUSE FEELS QUIET, with Parker gone.

Nate and I are in the kitchen. He's washing the large stack of dishes that have accumulated over the past few days of catering to Parker's every whim; I'm sitting on the counter with my legs swinging, staring unabashedly at his butt.

What? Don't judge me. It's a good butt.

And it's all mine.

"Did you mean it?" I ask suddenly, making him turn to face me.

"Mean what?"

I tilt my head. "About moving in. Did you mean, like, until Parker gets a place? Or were you talking about something a little more..." I trail off, blushing. "Never mind. It doesn't really matter."

He pulls his hands out of the water and crosses toward me. His fingers are soapy and wet when they slide around my neck.

"I'm moving in." His lips brush my forehead. "I'm moving in, and I'm staying." His mouth hits my temple, where the bruises are finally almost faded away. In another few days, they'll be totally gone. "I want my clothes in your closet next to your unreasonably large shoe collection; my razors in your shower next to that damn body wash of yours that smells so good; my beer in your fridge next to that seltzer you're always sucking down." A kiss lands on the tip of my nose. "I want you. Every day. Every minute. Forever." His lips hover over mine. "I told you before, little bird. The second I met you, I was in it for life. For years, I tried to fight it. Told myself to walk away, that you were better off without me. But the thing is, I can't live without you. Don't want to. Not anymore. Not ever again."

I suck in a breath, fighting tears. "Are you going to kiss me, or are you going to talk me to death?"

He's grinning as his lips land hard on mine.

NEED MORE BOSTON?

**Not ready to leave Boston behind?
There's plenty more love & laughter in your future...**

Don't miss Gemma & Chase's story in **NOT YOU IT'S ME.**
Swoon over Parker & Zoe in **ONE GOOD REASON.**
Laugh along with Luca & Lila in **TAKE YOUR TIME.**
Fall for Shelby & Conor in **SO WRONG IT'S RIGHT.**

All five Boston books are now available in e-book, paperback, and audio! They are all standalone, and can be read in any order.

THE BOSTON LOVE STORIES:
NOT YOU IT'S ME
CROSS THE LINE
ONE GOOD REASON
TAKE YOUR TIME
SO WRONG IT'S RIGHT

Never miss a new release! Make sure you've subscribed to Julie's newsletter: http://eepurl.com/bnWtHH

ACKNOWLEDGMENTS

Thank you.

Two little words.

They seem painfully inadequate to describe the depth of my gratitude to my readers who, against all odds, have stuck with me on this amazing journey. I'm a little bit in love with each and every one of you, and I doubt you'll ever know how much your support means to me.

One of my favorite quotes about writing comes from John Cheever. He said, "I can't write without a reader. It's precisely like a kiss - you can't do it alone."

And he's right.

None of my dreams would be possible without *you*.

From the readers who reach out on Facebook, Twitter, and Instagram, to the amazing ladies in the "Johnson Junkies," to the incredible bloggers and reviewers who leave feedback on *Amazon* and *Goodreads*... every single one of you have changed my life for the better.

To my parents, Dave and Christine, who've been my biggest cheerleaders and supporters from day one... I'll never be able to repay you for the unconditional love you've provided. Thank you for encouraging me to chase my dreams.

To my big brother Zack, who's provided plenty of sibling inspiration for my characters, thank you for being there for me even when you're thousands of miles away.

To my friends, who don't question it when I need to disappear into my writing cave for weeks at a time, and who welcome me back with open arms when I eventually reemerge... thank you for your unfailing support and understanding.

And, lastly, to my dog Scout. You may weigh about seventy-five more pounds than Boo, but you inspired his character all the same. Thanks for being my writing partner, snuggle buddy, and constant source of joy.

PLAYLIST

- **I Found** by Amber Run
- **Not In That Way** by Sam Smith
- **Clean Getaway** by Maria Taylor
- **Beautiful Birds** by Passenger
- **Landfill** by Daughter
- **Shadow Preachers** by Zella Day
- **Like I Can** by Sam Smith
- **Shame On You** by Mariah McManus
- **Ace of Hearts** by Zella Day
- **Take Me to Church** by Hozier
- **The Last Time** by Taylor Swift
- **Latch** (Acoustic) by Sam Smith
- **Compass** by Zella Day
- **Let the Light Back In** by Maggie Eckford
- **This Love** by Taylor Swift

ABOUT THE AUTHOR

JULIE JOHNSON is a twenty-something Boston native suffering from an extreme case of Peter Pan Syndrome. When she's not writing, Julie can most often be found adding stamps to her passport, drinking too much coffee, striving  to conquer her Netflix queue, and Instagramming pictures of her dog. (Follow her: @author_julie)

She published her debut novel LIKE GRAVITY in August 2013, just before her senior year of college, and she's never looked back. Since, she has published more than a dozen other novels, including the bestselling BOSTON LOVE STORY series, THE GIRL DUET, and THE FADED DUET. Her books have appeared on Kindle and iTunes Bestseller lists around the world, as well as in AdWeek, Publishers Weekly, and USA Today.

You can find Julie on Facebook or contact her on her website www.juliejohnsonbooks.com. Sometimes, when she can figure out how Twitter works, she tweets from @AuthorJulie. For major book news and updates, subscribe to Julie's newsletter: http://eepurl.com/bnWtHH

Connect with Julie:
www.juliejohnsonbooks.com
juliejohnsonbooks@gmail.com

ALSO BY JULIE JOHNSON

STANDALONE NOVELS:

LIKE GRAVITY

SAY THE WORD

FAITHLESS

THE BOSTON LOVE STORIES:

NOT YOU IT'S ME

CROSS THE LINE

ONE GOOD REASON

TAKE YOUR TIME

SO WRONG IT'S RIGHT

THE GIRL DUET:

THE MONDAY GIRL

THE SOMEDAY GIRL

THE FADED DUET:

FADED

UNFADED

THE UNCHARTED DUET:

UNCHARTED

UNFINISHED

THE FORBIDDEN ROYALS TRILOGY:

DIRTY HALO

TORRID THRONE

SORDID EMPIRE

THE DON'T DUET:

WE DON'T TALK ANYMORE

WE DON'T LIE ANYMORE